RED STRIKE

CHRIS RYAN

RED STRIKE

CORONET

First published in Great Britain in 2019 by Coronet
An Imprint of Hodder & Stoughton
An Hachette UK company

3

A CIP catalogue record for this title is available from the British Library

ISBN 9781444784145
eBook ISBN 9781444784114
Tradeback ISBN 9781444784138

Typeset in Bembo by Hewer Text UK Ltd, Edinburgh
Printed and bound in Great Britain by Clays Ltd, Elcograf S.p.A.

Hodder & Stoughton policy is to use papers that are natural, renewable
and recyclable products and made from wood grown in sustainable forests.
The logging and manufacturing processes are expected to conform
to the environmental regulations of the country of origin.

Hodder & Stoughton Ltd
Carmelite House
50 Victoria Embankment
London EC4Y 0DZ

www.hodder.co.uk

ONE

Six minutes past two in the afternoon. A quiet Thursday in early March. Detective Sergeant Dave McKinnon was sitting in the sparsely furnished living room, sipping his fourth brew of the day, watching *Judge Rinder* on the crappy TV. Around him sat the three other officers drawn from the South West Region Protected Persons Unit.

The four of them were holed up in a secluded stone-built cottage, deep in the wilds of the Lake District, surrounded by a sprawl of farmland, densely wooded copses and craggy fells. About as far from humanity as it was possible to get in England. The nearest home was a mile away; the closest village was a ten-minute drive on a potholed country road. It was the kind of area that rich southerners paid a small fortune to stay in.

The building had once been a holiday home, owned by a family from Bristol, purchased by the government and transferred to the National Crime Agency. The NCA owned hundreds of similar properties up and down the country, used as safe houses as and when needed. McKinnon himself had stayed in at least thirty of them. They were all of a type: isolated, tidy, in good physical condition with no major maintenance work to be done. The entertainment options were limited, and this place was no different. There was a shelf of paperback thrillers by Alistair MacLean and Jack Higgins, a rack of mid-nineties DVDs and an Internet connection about as reliable as TV guide horoscope.

They were officially in the middle of nowhere.

Which made several kinds of sense, on an operational level. Because of the man they had been ordered to protect.

Nikolai Ivanovich Volkov was a high-value target. Much higher than anyone else McKinnon had dealt with in his career.

Nine weeks had passed since the former double agent had been found slumped outside the public toilets in a park in Swindon, arms jerking wildly, mouth foaming. The story had quickly hit the news. *Ex-Russian spy critically ill after being exposed to deadly nerve agent.* Three other people had been admitted to hospital in the hours after the attack, including the French jogger and off-duty doctor who had first arrived on the scene. Dozens of police and medical staff had been treated for symptoms of infection. Teams of counter-terrorism officers and Porton Down scientists had swarmed over the park, dressed in hazmat suits, gathering evidence. A week later the British Government had gone public, accusing the Kremlin of carrying out the hit.

The story had dominated the news cycle ever since.

Conspiracy theories circulated on Twitter. Russian diplomats were expelled from various European capitals. Sanctions were discussed. Threats made.

There was speculation that the Russians had targeted Volkov in revenge for defecting to the UK, several years before.

But McKinnon didn't give a crap about any of that.

My only job is to protect Volkov until he's sorted out with a new life.

Which would not be for a while yet, McKinnon knew. He'd worked dozens of cases since transferring to Protected Persons: witnesses to revenge killings: foot soldiers who'd turned grass against local crime bosses. Giving someone a new identity – a new life – was a complicated business these days, even in relatively simple cases. There was a whole mountain of paperwork to be completed. Bank accounts had to be set up. Passports arranged. Cover stories established. Social media accounts populated.

For a high-profile case like Volkov, it could take several more weeks until he was ready to be permanently relocated. He would probably have to change his appearance, move abroad. To the US or Canada, perhaps. Some backwater town, far from the big cities. Somewhere he was less likely to be recognised.

Eleven days had passed since they had taken the Russian to the safe house. The last time McKinnon had checked in with regional headquarters he had been told that it might be another two months before anything was sorted.

Which suited McKinnon just fine.

Two teams had been assigned to safeguard Volkov, rotating on a weekly basis. McKinnon and his guys were on their fourth day of their first rotation and nicely settled into their routine. In the mornings they fixed brews, checked the weather, called in to their regional HQ and made supply runs to the village. In the afternoons they chilled. Watching TV, chatting with their families on the secure line. A couple of the guys passed the time catching up on their homework for the courses they were taking in their spare time. At night they rigged the alarms and checked the doors and windows were securely locked. Other than that, there was nothing for them to worry about.

No paperwork. No morning briefings. No one looking over your shoulder.

It doesn't get much easier than this.

Even the guy they were protecting was easy to deal with.

In McKinnon's experience the people going into witness protection were a pain in the arse. Most of them were known to the police already as criminals, or closely associated with them. They tended to be ungrateful towards the officers looking after them, or openly hostile. Many of them believed that going into protective custody was some sort of get-rich-quick scheme. They figured that testifying against their former business partners or bosses entitled them to a shiny new car and house, a six-figure reward. But that wasn't how the service worked. When someone went into witness protection there was no big pot of gold waiting for them on the other side. They were given the same income, the same lifestyle as they'd had before.

Some people just couldn't accept that.

Volkov wasn't one of them. The guy hadn't kicked up a fuss when they'd moved him. All he did was ask a few harmless questions about the guns they were carrying, where they were stored, how many rounds they were permitted to carry. Which was understandable, McKinnon guessed. Volkov was an ex-spy, after all. He probably had a professional curiosity about such things.

The Russian sometimes moaned about the British weather or the side effects from the cocktail of the drugs he had to take. Otherwise he kept to himself. Which was just fine by McKinnon.

More time for the rest of us to chill. Besides, he thought, *there's noth-ing to worry about.*

Their location was a closely guarded secret. Aside from their liaison officer and their CO, only a handful of senior figures in the National Crime Agency and Whitehall knew where Volkov was being held.

We're not in any danger here.

Then he heard the rumble of an approaching motor, and everything changed.

The sound was distant at first. A faint growl, piercing the quiet of the English countryside. Then it swelled to an incessant thrum. Above the roar of the engine McKinnon heard the soft crunch of gravel as the vehicle pulled up in the front driveway.

'Who the fuck is that?' the officer opposite McKinnon asked.

McKinnon glanced at his mucker. Steve Flowers was a shaven-headed Brummie with a thickset physique, halfway between muscular and overweight. He'd transferred to the unit at the same time as McKinnon, and the two of them had instantly hit it off, keeping each other's spirits up during the long periods of down-time while on duty. In front of him on the rustic wooden dining table was a hefty textbook. *Tree Surgery for Beginners.* Homework for a course Flowers had enrolled on at the local adult college. He was six months from early retirement and planned to go into the tree-hacking trade as soon as he left the force. Like the rest of the team, Flowers was dressed in plain civvies, with his standard-issue Glock 17 pistol holstered to his belt.

McKinnon didn't reply. Instead he turned to the computer monitor set up at the opposite end of the dining table. The number of security cameras installed at the safe house had been deliberately kept to a minimum. Too much obvious surveillance and the building would have stood out like a fake tit. A single camera overlooked the front of the property, discreetly installed inside a Yale siren mounted to the exterior brickwork. The camera wirelessly fed a live stream to the computer monitor, allowing the guys to monitor anyone approaching the house.

The image quality was impressive. Especially to an old guy like McKinnon. Back when he'd started out the resolution had been so poor that faces looked like a jumble of Tetris blocks. But the clarity on this camera was striking. As good as anything shot on an iPhone. A single-lane path led from the front drive to the main road, a hundred metres to the east. The path had originally been a dirt track but at some point the previous owners had paved it over. Now it was riddled with cracks and potholes.

McKinnon could see the two dark-green Land Rover Discovery SUVs belonging to the team, parked up to the left of the driveway, ten metres away from the entrance to the house. At the edge of the driveway, twenty metres away from the house, a commercial delivery van had parked up.

The van was a Mercedes-Benz Sprinter. McKinnon could tell from the three-pointed metal star fixed to the grille. A distinctive purple corporate logo was splashed down the side of the van, with the name of the company below. McKinnon recognised the name as one of the big delivery firms. His kids were forever ordering crap online. He'd seen such vans pull up outside his house more than once.

He looked on as the driver debussed from the front cab. A stocky guy in knee-length cargo shorts and an ill-fitting polo T-shirt with the company logo embroidered on the breast pocket, like the crest on a football kit. The driver hooked round to the back of the van and returned a few moments later carrying a parcel the approximate size of a shoebox. Then he beat a path towards the front door.

Flowers frowned at the screen. 'What the fuck is he doing? We ain't expecting anything.'

'Must be for you,' another officer said. 'It's that sex doll you ordered.'

Flowers glared at the guy who'd spoken. A slender, slightly built bloke, youthful looking, with short neat hair. Joe Bentley was the youngest member of the team, recently transferred from the Met's counter-terrorism unit. He had a lot of enthusiasm for the job, but in McKinnon's opinion he treated the witnesses with far too much respect. Sympathising with them, rather than putting them in their place. As if they were decent upstanding members of society, not criminal scum.

'Piss off, you cocky bastard,' Flowers said. 'I get plenty of action as it is.'

'Reading books about trees?' Bentley laughed. 'Bound to impress the ladies, that.'

'At least this is practical stuff, son. Hands on. Not that a city tosser like you would know the first thing about nature.'

'Says the bloke who lives in a third-floor flat in Salisbury town centre.'

'Twat.'

The doorbell chimed.

The officers looked round at one another. All of them waiting for someone else to volunteer to answer the door.

Finally, the fourth officer spoke up. 'Someone should get that, like.'

McKinnon glanced at the guy. Pete Jagielka was tall and lanky, with deep-set eyes and a thick Scouse accent. He was also a lazy bastard. Jagielka didn't lift a finger unless it was absolutely necessary, never volunteering to make a brew or cook dinner for the rest of the team. Instead he spent long hours slouched in front of the TV, reading the red tops or playing games on his phone. McKinnon strongly suspected that Jagielka had transferred to the PPU because he thought it was a doss.

'Fuck it, then. I'll get it,' McKinnon said.

'Is there problem?' Volkov asked, glancing away from the TV.

McKinnon looked at the guy. The Russian was about eighty pounds lighter than the snaps that had done the rounds on BBC News. Gone were the round cheeks and the drinker's nose. Now his sixty-something face was drawn and horribly pockmarked, his skin jaundice-yellow. There was a V-shaped scar an inch below his Adam's apple that McKinnon assumed was from some kind of invasive surgery. He wore a Charles Tyrwhitt green-and-white striped shirt and a pair of beige cotton chinos, both of which looked about three sizes too big. Volkov had been permitted to return to his house after leaving hospital to pack a few personal items but none of his existing clothes fitted his gaunt frame. The Russian had cut an extra notch on his belt just to stop his trousers from falling down.

'Nothing for you to worry about,' McKinnon snapped, already irritated at having to deal with this unwanted intrusion.

'Who is it?' asked Volkov.

'Nobody. Just some driver. Stay put and keep away from the front door.'

He turned and ducked out of the living room, marching down the hallway towards the front door. He breezed past the dining room and the solid wooden gun cabinet with their long weapons locked inside: four Sig Sauer MCX carbines with sixteen-inch barrels, chambered for the 5.56 x 45mm NATO round. Twelve twenty-round clips were secured in a separate compartment, with their Kevlar bulletproof vests stored in a smaller cabinet to the left. Strictly speaking the team should have kept the longs less than an arm's length away at all times. But it was less hassle to keep them locked up and really, who was going to know any different?

To the left of the hallway was the kitchen. Next to the kitchen was a small study that had been converted into a strong room. Every safe house had one: reinforced door, constructed from high-grade steel and designed to blend in with the rest of the house. Concrete-lined walls gridded with steel rods, strong enough to withstand small-arms fire or intense heat from an explosion. Medical supplies, secure phone line. The room was about as secure as a vault at a national bank.

McKinnon stopped just before he reached the end of the hallway, remembering the Glock 17 holstered to his waist. He untucked his plaid shirt from his jeans, making sure the material concealed the pistol. Then he opened the front door.

The delivery driver stood in the doorway. Parcel in his right hand, a portable GPS device in his left. Behind him was the gravel driveway and the potholed track leading towards the main road. In the distance stood the jagged peaks of several hills, wreathed in thin clouds, their gentle slopes covered with scrub and stunted trees. There were no cars on the road. No sounds of distant traffic or human noise. That was one of the reasons why McKinnon's team had been ordered to bring the Russian to this particular house.

No fucker could approach this place without being spotted or heard.

The driver smiled apologetically.

'Delivery, boss,' he said, tapping the parcel he was holding. 'Package for Mr Castman.'

McKinnon did not consider himself a racist. But one look at the guy in front of him and the tiny voice inside his head screamed *Eastern European*. He had a weathered face, wrinkled and worn down to the nub from a lifetime of hard labour. The guy could have been anywhere from twenty-five to fifty. His bushy eyebrows were a couple of arches above his tiny black eyes.

McKinnon stared at him. The driver saw the blank look on McKinnon's face and tried again.

'Hawkshead Lodge? Mr Roger Castman? You expect delivery, yes?'

McKinnon shook his head. 'Wrong address, mate. This is Lakesmoor Cottage.'

'Lakesmoor?' The driver glanced around the front drive. A tiny groove formed above his brow. 'But my GPS says this is the place.'

'There's no Roger Castman here,' McKinnon said. 'I'm telling you, you've got the wrong place.'

The driver muttered something under his breath. He glanced down at his handheld device like it had insulted his mother. Then he looked up again.

'Sorry, boss. This stupid GPS. Sending me all over the shop.'

'No worries, mate.'

'You know where I can find this Hawkshead Lodge, perhaps?'

'Can't help you. We're not from around here. We're just renting the place for the summer.' McKinnon indicated the main road a hundred and fifty metres away. 'Your best bet is to continue north on that road. There's a B&B about four miles further along. Loudwater Inn. Someone there should be able to give you directions.'

'Four miles to the north, Loudwater Inn. Got it.' The driver nodded, smiled again. 'Thank you, boss. Sorry. Bloody GPS. You know how it is.'

McKinnon smiled and shrugged as if to say, *What can you do?*

The driver turned away and hurried back to the delivery van, a man in a hurry, behind schedule, with packages to deliver and orders to fulfil. McKinnon watched him climb behind the wheel, dumping the parcel on the passenger seat. He cranked the ignition and three-point-turned in the driveway before steering back down the potholed track. He hit the main road, turned left and motored north.

McKinnon continued watching the van until it was lost from

sight. Then he shut the front door and headed back down the hallway. Past the locked gun cupboard and the kitchen and the strong room. He reached the living room in another six strides.

Jagielka had turned his attention back to *Judge Rinder*. Flowers had his head down in his textbook, boning up on his tree surgery knowledge. Bentley was checking something on his phone. Fantasy football league stats, probably. Volkov sat bolt upright, looking keenly at the officers.

On the TV, the judge was banging his gavel to bring order to the studio courtroom.

'What did he want?' Flowers asked, looking up from his book.

'Wrong address,' McKinnon said.

'Where he was looking for?'

'Hawkshead Lodge.'

Bentley looked over, creasing his brow. 'That's fucking miles from here.'

'I know.'

'How did he end up this far out?'

McKinnon shrugged. 'Reckoned his GPS was on the blink.'

'And it sent him all the way over here?'

'That's what he said.'

'We should call it in,' Bentley said after a beat. 'Report it to the liaison.'

McKinnon clenched his jaws. Standard operating procedure was to call in to the regional HQ and report any unusual activity. Which was a royal pain in the arse, he knew. He was staring down the barrel of an afternoon of actual work.

'Fine,' McKinnon muttered. 'I'll do it.'

He dug out his force-issue phone from the side pocket of his combats. A Samsung Galaxy Note with custom-built software, apps and push-to-talk buttons that functioned like the outdated police radios. He swiped to unlock, tapped the phone icon and scrolled down through his call history until he found the number he was looking for. He stepped out into the hallway, moving away from the noise of the TV.

Then he dialled.

Three rings later, the person on the other end of the line picked up. A familiar female voice said, 'Detective Sergeant Stanley.'

'It's me,' McKinnon said. 'Listen, we've just had a strange one here, Liz.'

'Strange how?'

McKinnon verbally walked the liaison officer through his encounter with the delivery van, repeating the name and address the driver had given him. As he spoke he heard the tap-tap of fingers dancing on a mechanical keyboard, the delicate click of a mouse.

'That does sound a little weird,' Stanley admitted. And then: 'Did you catch the reg plate?'

'One step ahead of you,' McKinnon said.

There was more frantic tapping on the end of the line as he read out the registration plate he'd committed to memory.

When he'd finished Stanley said, 'We'll run the plate and check out the address for Mr Castman. I'll need to update our friends at the NCA as well. Let them know what's happened.'

'How long will that take?'

'Ten minutes. Maybe less. Leave it with me.'

'You're a star, Liz.'

'Tell me something I don't know.'

Stanley hung up. McKinnon returned to the living room and glanced round. Flowers was trying to refocus on his textbook. Bentley and Jagielka were looking at one another, both of them thinking the same thing.

It might be nothing.

But then again, it might be something.

'What did they say?' Bentley asked.

'They're looking into it,' McKinnon said.

From the corner of his eye he saw Volkov staring intently at his cheap plastic watch. The Russian looked agitated. Which made sense, McKinnon thought. The Kremlin had already tried to assassinate him once. The president didn't seem like the forgiving type. They would surely try to knock him on the head again. It was just a question of when.

Nine minutes past two in the afternoon.

Nineteen minutes until the ambush.

The delivery driver tooled north for exactly three minutes, until he was well out of sight of the safe house. He drove past a scene lifted right out of a country life magazine. There were rolling green fields dotted with sheep and cattle, hedgerows, ancient stone walls. He felt like he was in a Thomas Hardy novel.

He encountered no other cars on the road, but he drove cautiously anyway. Keeping the Sprinter to a steady forty miles per hour, obeying all the rules of the road.

Half a mile further on, he took a left turn. He drove on for another three hundred metres, past piles of felled timber and an abandoned barn, until he found it: a rutted track leading off the road into a small copse of birch, mountain ash and fern. A rusted field gate sealed the entrance with a sign staked into the ground next to it that read WARNING! PRIVATE PROPERTY.

The driver pulled over, easing the Sprinter to a halt on the patch of loose gravel in front of the field gate. He killed the engine and looked around. No one in sight. Just as the driver had been told. The RV was well away from the nearest village, several miles from the main tourist hotspots. The manager of the woodland, the only person who might typically be seen in the area, was on his annual holiday in the Scottish Highlands.

The driver dug out his ghost phone. Which was really just a fancy description for an old Android device with an end-to-end encrypted messaging app loaded on to it. The app generated disposable mobile numbers, rerouting incoming and outgoing calls to the fake number via a secure server in Estonia. As soon as you were done with the fake number, you simply wiped it from the phone and manually created a new number. Quicker and more convenient than carrying around a burner phone and a case of disposable SIM cards, the driver thought.

He opened the messaging app. Started a new conversation with the other disposable number stored on his device.

He wrote, *At the RV.*

Hit send.

Twelve seconds passed. Then came a one-word reply.

Report.

The driver thought for a beat. Then he wrote, *A plain-clothed police officer answered the door. It's definitely the place.*

Another pause. *Did they take the bait?*

Yes, the driver wrote. *They were immediately suspicious.*

The officer is probably on the phone to his people right now, the driver thought with a smile. Checking the registration plate and delivery address, like the good British copper he was.

Twenty seconds. Then another reply.

Wait there. Be ready to move. We'll let you know when it's done.

Exactly six minutes later, McKinnon's phone buzzed.

It was Stanley.

McKinnon answered and stepped back into the hallway. 'What's the craic?'

Stanley paused a beat.

Then she said, 'We have a problem.'

'What problem?' McKinnon asked.

Stanley took a deep breath. 'Actually, there's two. The first problem is that we've checked the Land Registry records and electoral roll and there is no Roger Castman at Hawkshead Lodge. Never has been, in fact.'

'And the second?'

'The vehicle reg you gave us doesn't match the make of the van. That reg belongs to a 2013 Ford Focus reported as stolen from a shopping centre car park in Stoke-on-Trent, two weeks ago.'

Shit, McKinnon thought. *Someone switched the plates on the van.*

But if the guy wasn't a delivery driver, and the van was running with stolen reg plates, then who was he?

'Deputy Chief Constable has just finished briefing the NCA,' Stanley continued. 'Be advised that your location has been compromised. I repeat, you've been compromised. You need to get out of that house, Dave. Right now.'

TWO

McKinnon gripped the phone hard. His mind raced ahead of him as he listened to DS Stanley on the other end of the line.

That delivery driver was here to recce the safe house, now McKinnon realised. He was getting a mark-one eyeball on this place. Which could mean only one of two things.

One, the guy was working for a criminal gang, looking for potential holiday homes to rob.

Or he was looking for Volkov.

Which meant the driver was going from place to place, probably within a confined area, assessing the security arrangements at each house, looking for any sign of the Russian or his British protectors. And then reporting back to the people above him.

Either way, the safe house had been blown.

We need to get out of here.

'Dave?' asked Stanley. 'Are you still there?'

McKinnon quickly recovered his composure and said, 'What's the plan?'

'Leave the safe house immediately and head straight to Leeds Central station on Park Street. Report to DCI O'Keefe when you get there. She's in the loop. You'll wait at Leeds until we can arrange a new location.'

'How long will that take?'

'Not long,' Stanley said. 'DCC is liaising with the NCA as we speak. She reckons we should have something for you very shortly. Matter of hours. We'll be in touch. Just get out of there as fast as you can.'

'Roger that,' McKinnon said. 'I'll check in with you from the road.'

He cut the call and stepped back into the living room. The other officers were staring at him with grave expressions.

'Well?' Bentley asked.

McKinnon relayed his conversation with Stanley, keeping his voice low so the Russian wouldn't overhear. The other three officers listened in silence. When he'd finished, Flowers screwed up his face. 'I thought no bastard knew about this place.'

'They don't,' McKinnon replied.

'Then how did they find us?'

'No fucking clue, mate.'

Volkov looked questioningly at McKinnon and the others, alarm flickering in his dull grey eyes. 'What is it? What's going on?'

'We're moving. Get your stuff packed.'

The Russian's eyes widened. His eyebrows hitched up a full inch. 'Why?'

'No reason,' McKinnon bullshitted. 'Just something that didn't check out with the driver. A precautionary measure, that's all.'

'My enemies . . . they have found me?'

McKinnon clenched his jaws. *That's all we need right now*, he thought to himself. *The Russian freaking out.*

'We don't know that for sure. It might have been someone else trying their luck, for all we know. But it's better we don't take any chances.'

That seemed to settle Volkov's nerves. He nodded slowly. 'When do we leave?'

'Now. Pack everything. We leave in five.'

Volkov rose from the sofa, took a step towards the hallway and winced, putting a hand to the side of his stomach. For a moment he looked as if he might collapse.

'You all right, fella?' Bentley asked, his voice full of concern.

'He's fine,' McKinnon cut in. 'Leave him.'

Bentley shot McKinnon a look. He turned back to the Russian as the latter regained his balance, breathing heavily.

'It's nothing,' Volkov replied weakly. 'Just the sickness. Comes and goes. I go to the bathroom, okay?'

McKinnon sighed. They had been warned about this. One of the doctors treating Volkov had addressed the officers at the mission briefing. The basic takeaway was that no one could be sure of the long-term effects resulting from exposure to an experimental nerve agent. There were no case studies they could refer to, no articles on the subject. But the doctor felt it reasonable to assume that Volkov would have respiratory difficulties, impaired physical movement and short-term memory loss. In addition to violent bouts of sickness and diarrhoea.

'I need the bathroom,' Volkov repeated. 'Please.'

'Come on, Dave,' Bentley said. 'Look at the poor fucker. We can't stick him in the wagon looking like this.'

That much was true, McKinnon conceded. He had a sudden vision of the Russian shitting his pants in the back of the Land Rover, filthy brown streaks all over the place. Better to get it out of his system now.

'Fine. But make it quick. We can't stick around here for long. Five minutes, then we're out of here.'

Volkov nodded. 'Five minutes, okay.'

He shuffled off towards the downstairs toilet, clutching his guts and grimacing in pain.

At the same time Jagielka and Flowers hurried upstairs to their bedrooms to pack their holdalls. McKinnon turned to follow them and then nodded at Bentley.

'Grab the longs,' he said, indicating the gun cabinet. 'Put them in the lock box in the rear of the Discovery. Load up the vests as well.'

Bentley made a face. 'Shouldn't we be wearing them, sarge?'

'What for?'

'Protection.'

McKinnon shook his head. 'It's a waste of time. We'll be out of here before any fucker can show up. Trust me.'

Bentley opened his mouth to protest but McKinnon set off up the stairs before the younger officer could argue further. McKinnon was feeling confident. Bullish, even. Despite the setback, he felt sure that his team had the tactical edge over whoever had been doing the recce on the safe house. McKinnon and his guys had been alert. They had seen through the set-up with the fake delivery van. Whereas the enemy had no reason to think that their plan had been rumbled. No reason at all.

We've got time on our side.

The enemy would be cautious, McKinnon reckoned. They

would wait for the delivery driver to report back from his recce. There would be a big meeting. Strategies would be discussed. Pros and cons weighed up. It would be a while before they were ready to attack. Whoever *they* were, McKinnon thought to himself. By the time they were ready, the PPU team would be on their way to Leeds.

Right now, we're winning.

Twenty-one minutes past two in the afternoon.

Seven minutes before the ambush.

The police van was parked three miles to the south, in a small gravel lay-by at the side of a narrow country road. The man behind the wheel was called Pavel Vasin, but everyone knew him as the Afghan. On account of his combat experience in the last days of the Soviet–Afghanistan War, almost thirty years earlier. Thirty years, but Vasin still remembered the conflict as if it had happened yesterday. He recalled the bodies of Soviet soldiers slumped by the side of the road, their hands, ears and noses cut off and their genitalia stuffed into their mouths. The men who had been skinned alive and strung up from trees to roast beneath the blazing sun. Some of those who had served in the war had come back broken men, but not Vasin. Afghanistan had made him stronger. He had spent every day of his life since then in the service of Mother Russia, determined to make sure that his country never again suffered such a humiliating defeat.

Which is why Vasin found himself in a van in a remote corner of the Lake District, disguised as a British police officer.

The van was a Volkswagen Crafter. An ex-force wagon, bought for nine grand at a public auction in Wolverhampton and paid for in cash. For a heavy-duty vehicle with ninety thousand miles on the clock it was in surprisingly good condition. The result of being operated by a professional, Vasin guessed, rather than a regular motorist. It ran smoothly, handled every manoeuvre Vasin threw at it and the cooling system was more efficient than anything he'd seen in a civilian motor.

His police uniform had been just as easy to source. Vasin wore a pair of black 5.11 Stryke trousers and a matching short-sleeved shirt with a black police duty vest worn over the top. The trousers and shirt had been purchased online from a generic security shop. The vest, handcuffs and Sepura radio kit were dummy versions bought from a company that specialised in film, stage and TV props. Vasin's uniform lacked the correct badge, but from a distance he would pass as an officer from the local constabulary.

The fake delivery van had been phase one of the operation.

Vasin and his men were the second phase.

There were four guys crammed into the main passenger cabin behind Vasin, two in the first row of seats and two in the middle row. There was no need for them to wear police uniforms. They were dressed in black work overalls and undershirts, and each operator also wore a clear plastic face mask and a pair of Kevlar slash-resistant gloves. They all carried Hungarian-variant AK-47 assault rifles, along with two spare twenty-round clips apiece of 7.62 x 39mm brass. The same basic weapon system Vasin had used in Afghanistan, with a few minor modifications.

The Russians had steered into the lay-by twelve minutes earlier, right around the time that the delivery van had pulled up outside the safe house. From their location they could reach the front of the stronghold in less than five minutes.

Everything depended on the timing, Vasin knew.

Once they received the signal, the team was on the clock. They would have to bomb out of the lay-by and race down the country road as fast as possible.

The detailed information they had received from their source had confirmed their initial suspicions. A frontal assault on the house was out of the question. The defenders would see them coming long before they could breach the main entry points. Things would get noisy. The authorities would be alerted. The target might get slotted in the crossfire. Similar incidents had occurred in the past. And Vasin's orders had been clear.

No police casualties. No fuck-ups.

So they had decided on an alternative strategy. Luring the officers out into the open. Then hitting them hard.

'Still nothing?' one of the guys in the middle row asked.

Vasin turned to face him. A burly former Spetsnaz operator,

arm muscles bulging beneath his dark overalls. One of the new generation. Gymmed-up and brash, full of unearned confidence. They had no idea what men like Vasin had gone through. No idea at all.

The Afghan glanced down at his phone, shook his head. 'No word.'

'Taking too fucking long.'

'Patience, Alexei. It won't be long now. Or maybe you want to sit this one out? Cool off in the cage, eh?'

Vasin pointed with his head at the steel cage built into a separate compartment aft of the passenger cabin. The cell had, surprisingly, been left intact when the van had been put up for auction. A dispenser for hand sanitiser was fitted to the panel to the left of the cage, another relic of the van's former life. British criminals had low standards of personal hygiene, clearly.

The younger guy went quiet.

'That's what I thought,' Vasin said.

Sometimes it was good to assert your authority over the younger operators. Remind them of who you were.

Ninety seconds later, his phone trilled.

New message.

He tapped on it. The message was from another randomly generated number. Not the delivery driver, but the other contact Vasin had been in touch with. He read the message once, then tapped delete.

He tucked his phone away. Kickstarted the engine.

'Time to roll,' he said.

McKinnon lugged his black nylon holdall downstairs and dumped it beside the front door. Jagielka was on luggage duty, cramming everything into the boots of the two Land Rovers. Bentley was loading the last of the carbines into the steel lock box mounted under the rear seats of one of the wagons. Flowers was doing a final check of the downstairs rooms, looking for any equipment the guys might have forgotten to pack in their hurry to bug out of the safe house. Phone chargers, laptops, textbooks.

McKinnon stood in the hallway, checked his watch. Twenty-six minutes past two. A grand total of five minutes, from getting off the blower with Stanley to being ready to roll.

We've still got time on our side, he thought. Whatever the enemy was planning, he figured they would need longer than five minutes before they were ready to attack the safe house.

As long as we leave quickly, we'll be fine.

Bentley marched back over to the house, waiting to see if there was any more kit to be loaded into the SUVs. Jagielka flipped the rear seats down over the lock box and followed closely behind. A moment later Flowers emerged from the living room and paced over to his muckers.

'House is clear, mate,' he said. 'That's everything, by the looks of it.'

McKinnon furrowed his brow. 'Where's the Russian?'

'Thought he was in one of the wagons?' Flowers said, fixing his gaze on Jagielka.

The Scouse held up his hands. 'Don't look at me, fella. I ain't seen him.'

'Then where the fuck is he?'

Jagielka shrugged. McKinnon said nothing. His eyes wandered over to the downstairs toilet. The door was still closed, he noticed. He brushed past Flowers, approached the door and tested the antique brass handle.

Locked.

McKinnon thumped his fist on the solid oak panel. 'You still in there, fella?'

There was a beat of silence. Then a weak voice came from the other side. 'Give me a minute, okay?'

Before McKinnon could reply he heard an explosive burst of retching and heaving from inside the toilet. He pictured the Russian former spy hunched over the bowl, emptying the dregs of his stomach.

'Fuck's sake,' Flowers muttered. 'We haven't got time for this shite.'

'He can't help it,' Bentley put in. 'The guy's sick, mate.'

'He'll be even sicker if he doesn't get a bloody move on.'

'We're supposed to be protecting the guy, for Christ's sake.'

Flowers laughed. 'All that diversity training has gone to your head, fella. We're the ones calling the shots here. Not him. I ain't sitting around here waiting for some bastard to show up because he's got a dose of the shits.'

McKinnon banged on the door again. Twice, to emphasise his frustration. The frame trembled with the impact.

'Hurry it up,' he said, louder. 'We need to leave. Now.'

More retching noises echoed from inside the toilet. Flowers fumed through his nostrils, cursing under his breath. McKinnon glanced impatiently at his watch. Twenty seconds passed. Then thirty.

A whole minute later, the toilet flushed.

There was a metallic click as the locking bolt retracted. Then the door cracked open and Volkov shuffled out, looking exhausted. His forehead was beaded with sweat.

'Thank fuck for that,' Flowers muttered.

'Sorry,' Volkov groaned. 'I can't help it. When it's bad like that . . .'

McKinnon bit back on his rage and resisted the temptation to lay into the Russian. They had already pissed away valuable minutes. There was no point wasting more time by tearing strips off the guy.

If we leave now, we'll still have the upper hand.

'Forget it. Let's get moving.' He turned to Flowers. 'You and Pete take the lead Discovery. We'll follow you in the other wagon.'

'My bag,' Volkov rasped. 'I left it upstairs. In my wardrobe.'

'I'll get it,' Jagielka said.

'Hurry up,' McKinnon cut in. 'We've wasted enough time as it is.'

Jagielka doubled backed down the hallway and hurried upstairs to grab the Russian's go-bag.

The other four guys turned and made for the front door. Flowers led the way, with McKinnon close behind. Then Bentley, with Volkov pulling up the rear. Bentley was paying close attention to the Russian, making sure he was okay. McKinnon could hear the guy's voice at his six o'clock.

'It's all right, pal. There's water and blankets in the wagon. Just a little further now. You can do it.'

Christ, thought McKinnon. *With that kind of attitude, the kid really isn't going to last long.*

He reached the entrance in four quick strides. Then he stepped outside.

The front drive was a patchwork of mud and loose gravel. To the left of the farmhouse, ten metres away, stood the two Land Rovers. They were parked up beside a heap of stones, rocks and firewood. To the right of the drive was a small barn that had been converted into a garage with a separate studio and games room built into it. McKinnon and the rest of the guys had used the fitness equipment in the games room from time to time, whenever they grew bored of sitting around the house.

Directly in front of the gravel drive stood the track that led directly towards the main country road. The road ran north to south past the safe house. North led deeper into the valley, with its peaks and streams and woodland. South led past the lake, towards the quaint villages and towns hugging the southern fringe of the park. It had rained heavily for most of the morning and the distinct tang of rain on tarmac hung thick in the air. Puddles filled in the potholes along the narrow track. Raindrops hung like diamonds from the leaves of the surrounding ferns.

McKinnon led Bentley and Volkov over to the rearmost Land Rover Discovery, ten metres away at his ten o'clock. Meanwhile Flowers headed for the other Land Rover, parked at an angle eight metres further forward.

Before leaving, McKinnon had plotted out the route to Leeds Central. The station was a hundred and fifty miles away from the safe house. A two-and-a-half-hour drive. They would reach the police station at around five o'clock.

He mentally ran through the next several hours in his head. RV with DCI O'Keefe. Get the Russian some medical attention. Then a long stretch of waiting until someone at the NCA fixed them up with an alternative safe house. He figured that they wouldn't want a high-value target like Volkov sitting around in a police station for longer than necessary. A maximum of twenty-four hours, say. A day from now they would be in a new pad, putting their feet up. McKinnon and Jagielka could go back to bingeing on daytime TV. Flowers could catch up on his tree surgery homework. And Bentley could get back to doing whatever he liked best. Acting like Volkov's best friend, probably.

He looked ahead. Flowers had already reached the other Discovery, eight metres away. The guy circled round to the driver's side, digging the keys out of his pocket, wrenching the door open.

McKinnon stopped beside the rearmost Discovery, glancing over his shoulder. Bentley was four metres behind him, an arm around Volkov's shoulder, patiently helping him along.

A moment later they reached the side of the wagon. Bentley opened the rear passenger door, waiting for Volkov to clamber inside. The Russian was bent forward beside the wagon, hands planted on his knees, gasping for breath, like a runner at the end of a marathon. At the same time Jagielka came hurrying forward from the direction of the safe house, clutching the Russian's bag. McKinnon grabbed the bag, dumped it in the back seat, nodded at Jagielka.

'Get forward. I'll the set main alarm. As soon as the house is locked we'll piss off out of here.'

'About bloody time,' Jagielka grumbled.

He turned and paced over to the lead Discovery, moving round to the front passenger side. McKinnon spun round to face Bentley, cocked his head at the Russian.

'What's wrong with him now?' he asked.

Volkov was bent forward at the waist, groaning. Palm of his right hand pressed against the side of the wagon.

'Nothing, sarge,' said Bentley. 'Just catching his breath. He'll be all right. Won't you, mate?'

'Yes, fine,' Volkov managed. 'Just weak.'

'Wait here,' McKinnon said, addressing Bentley. 'I'll sort the alarm. He'd better be ready to go then. We ain't fucking about here any longer.'

He turned to set off in the direction of the safe house. Took a step forwards and then stopped. Because at that moment he heard Jagielka calling out to him.

He looked round and saw Jagielka standing beside the other Land Rover Discovery, arm thrust out as he pointed towards the main road. McKinnon looked in the direction the Scouse had indicated, squinting in the pale afternoon light.

Then he saw it.

A police van, three hundred metres due south.

Speeding towards them.

THREE

The police van motored down the country road at a decent clip. McKinnon watched it draw steadily closer to the safe house. A white Volkswagen Crafter, emergency lights fixed to the roof, POLICE stencilled across the front panelling in stark blue lettering. Neon yellow and blue stripes running down the side.

Eight metres ahead of McKinnon, Flowers debussed from behind the wheel of the lead Discovery. He stood beside Jagielka, watching the Crafter as it motored along the winding stretch of asphalt leading towards the safe house. The police van was two hundred metres away from the safe house now and closing fast.

McKinnon took a couple of steps forward, Bentley moving alongside him, his smooth face creased into a frown. 'Local plod?'

McKinnon shrugged. 'Who else?'

'What are they doing here? We didn't send for them.' Bentley tipped his head at the officer. 'Did we?'

'Wasn't us, mate.'

'Then who called 'em?'

McKinnon thought for a moment. 'Must have been someone at Regional HQ. Or some desk jockey over at the NCA.'

'Whoever told them, they got here fucking quick.'

'They'll have come up from Penrith,' McKinnon replied, thinking rapidly. 'That's the nearest station.'

'But why? This case has got nothing to do with them.'

'That's not how they'll see it.'

McKinnon had worked his way up from the lowest ranks of a provincial police force to organised crime. He knew the mindset. The new arrivals would want to take charge of the scene. Question

McKinnon and the other officers. Put out a description of the delivery van and driver, on the off chance that the guy was still in the area. Make themselves look important. The Lake District wasn't exactly a crime hotspot. The local police would have the occasional theft of farm equipment to deal with, a few armed robberies, but not much else. This was probably the most exciting call the constabulary had received all year.

No wonder they're in such a rush to get here, he thought. *They don't want to miss out on the drama. They probably raced out of the station as soon as they had received the call.*

Bentley grunted. 'This is the last thing we need,' he said. 'We'll be lucky to make it to Leeds by nightfall at this rate.'

McKinnon nodded, sharing his frustration.

We should have been on the road by now, he thought. Instead they would have to waste more time dealing with the local coppers.

The Crafter slowed to a crawl and turned off the main road. McKinnon watched it arrow down the path leading towards the front drive. The wagon was a hundred metres away from the safe house now. Flowers and Jagielka edged forward, drawing to a halt ten metres ahead of the lead SUV, forming a welcoming party. Bentley and McKinnon were standing fifteen metres further back, cautiously eyeing the police van. McKinnon glanced back and saw Volkov standing beside the rear Discovery, four metres away. The Russian had made a miraculous recovery. Two minutes ago he'd looked desperately sick. Now he stood ramrod straight, eyes locked on the police van.

McKinnon looked back towards the driveway. At a distance of fifty metres he could just about make out the van driver. A burly policeman in his late forties or early fifties, wearing a standard-issue duty vest over his short-sleeved shirt.

Jagielka waved at the driver, signalling for him to stop. The Crafter skidded to a halt twenty metres from the officer, at the point where the gravel driveway met the edge of the track.

'Why would they send up a van?' Bentley wondered aloud. 'They should have just sent up one of their patrol cars, surely?'

McKinnon sighed and shook his head. He didn't want to think about it. He just wanted to get this out of the way and get on the road. 'Come on,' he said. 'We'd better go and greet them.'

He stepped forward with Bentley at his side, the two of them edging away from the rear Discovery. Jagielka and Flowers were fifteen metres ahead of them, ten metres ahead of the lead Discovery, trudging towards the police van.

The side door on the Crafter sucked open.

A split second later, McKinnon saw the first figure charging out through the opening.

Not a cop.

A gunman.

And in that instant, he realised they had sleepwalked into an ambush.

The first gunman out of the Crafter was huge. The biggest guy McKinnon had ever seen. Like the Incredible Hulk bulking up for a weightlifting competition. His shoulders were like a couple of bowling balls on a rack. His legs were as wide as bookcases and he wore a transparent plastic face mask, obscuring his features. The guy was holding an assault rifle in a two-handed grip, McKinnon noticed, an AK-47 assault rifle. An instantly familiar firearm. The gun looked like a child's toy in his huge hands.

Three more gunmen quickly piled out of the main passenger cabin in quick succession. All dressed in the same kit as Mr Hulk, only several sizes smaller.

All of them wielding AK-47s.

Several things happened very fast.

Mr Hulk dropped down to the ground and immediately swivelled towards the nearest two targets, Flowers and Jagielka. The second gunman was coming up fast behind his mucker: a thickset, squat guy with his sleeves rolled up to the elbows, revealing a tattoo of a spider spinning a web on his left forearm. The two gunmen moved with urgency and controlled aggression, their rifles already raised, Spider shouting at the officers in heavily-accented English.

'Hands up! Don't fucking move!'

Jagielka and Flowers stood frozen in shock at the sight of the gunmen swarming towards them. Neither of them reached for their holstered Glock 17s. Time and physics were against them.

They would have to go through a whole range of movements in order to bring their weapons to bear: lever their firing hands down to their grips, pull their guns out. Bring the Glocks up to shoulder height. Aim. Fire. Two or three seconds, from start to finish. Whereas the gunmen already had their rifles aimed at the officers' centre masses.

'Hands in the air!' Spider shouted. 'NOW!'

Flowers and Jagielka hesitated for a beat, assessing the situation. But the facts were staring them right in the face. They were outnumbered. No point trying to fight back. The oldest rule of the jungle. Don't pick a fight with someone bigger than you. They reached a mutual, unspoken decision and threw up their hands in surrender.

Spider shouted something at Jagielka. The Scouse didn't respond. Spider took a step towards the officer and swept his AK-47 round, slamming the wooden stock into the latter's midriff. The officer folded at the waist, gasping for air. In the same instant Mr Hulk struck Flowers clean on the jaw. The force of the blow stunned Flowers, his head snapping back, legs buckling before he fell away and crashed to the dirt. In the next moment Spider grabbed hold of Jagielka and threw him to the ground beside Flowers. The two gunmen yelling at the stupefied Brits, rifles trained on their backs.

The next two gunmen swept forwards.

Heading straight for McKinnon and Bentley.

They were forty metres away. The nearest guy was tall and wiry, built like a greyhound, with a pair of battered white trainers and a gold necklace dangling from his neck.

The fourth gunman was a step behind Greyhound. He was heavyset and bronze-skinned, with peroxide-blond hair moulded into a flat top. He looked like a Soviet villain in an eighties action film.

Both Greyhound and Flat Top had already lined their weapons up with their targets. Shouting at McKinnon and Bentley to surrender.

McKinnon froze. Bentley stood at his side, feet rooted to the spot, a look of fear etched across his youthful face.

McKinnon was thinking clearly, in spite of the AK-47 pointing directly at his chest. At a range of thirty-something metres, the two gunmen could hardly miss their targets. If we disobey or resist, he thought, they'll kill us. And McKinnon had no intention of becoming a martyr. He was a police officer, on a public servant salary, with a family to think about. They didn't pay him enough to risk his life in a firefight. Not by a long fucking measure. He made no attempt to go for his gun.

Neither did Bentley.

We're done for, McKinnon thought.

But there was still time for the Russian to escape.

He glanced quickly over his shoulder. Volkov was next to the rear Discovery, six metres away. With the front door to the safe house a further ten metres to the west. The door was still ajar, McKinnon noticed. He had been about to set the alarm when the gunmen had rocked up.

Volkov was sixteen metres from the front door. Which meant he had a fifty-metre head start on the two nearest gunmen. If he made a run for it, the Russian could reach the house before Greyhound or Flat Top could close on him. Seal himself inside the strong room and wait for reinforcements to show up. The gunmen wouldn't risk sticking around here for very long, McKinnon presumed. They were in the middle of the British countryside, dangerously exposed. If Volkov made it to the strong room, he would safe. The gunmen would have no choice but to abandon their plan.

A long shot.

But better than nothing. Better than allowing a key witness, to be captured, or worse.

'Run!' McKinnon shouted. 'Inside the house! Get to the strong room!'

The Russian didn't move.

He just stood there, staring dumbly at McKinnon, eyes blinking rapidly.

McKinnon figured the guy was suffering from sensory overload. He'd seen it before, when civilians were confronted by sudden acts of violence or life-threatening situations. Everything shut down. Too much information to process. Better to stand still than run into potential danger.

Only Volkov wasn't a civvy. He had more than twenty years of experience in Russian foreign intelligence.

McKinnon tried again. 'Run! For fuck's sake, go!'

The Russian still didn't move.

McKinnon had just enough time to wonder why Volkov didn't try to escape. The guy was forty metres away from men who had been sent to kill or capture him. Probably the same men who had poisoned him two months ago. His worst enemies. All he had to do was turn and dart inside the safe house, and he might survive.

So why isn't he legging it?

Then McKinnon was out of time.

He heard Flat Top roaring at him in broken English. He spun round and saw the gunman a few metres away, screaming at him at the top of his voice. Black hole of his AK-47 muzzle trained on McKinnon's chest, his index finger taut on the trigger.

'Hands in the fucking air, bitch!' he shouted. 'Do it!'

McKinnon raised his hands. Slowly. He didn't want to make any rapid movements and give the guy a reason to plug him. Bentley held up his hands too. McKinnon saw him out of the tail of his eye. The kid was bricking it. Hands quivering, the colour dropping from his face.

'On your knees!' Flat Top ordered them.

McKinnon did as he was told. He dropped to his knees, keeping his hands raised, his heart pounding inside his chest.

Bentley did the same.

Flat Top turned and barked an order at Greyhound. The latter peeled away and swept past McKinnon and Bentley, moving swiftly towards the rear Discovery. Towards Volkov.

McKinnon glanced behind him. He could just about see Volkov, standing next to the wagon. The guy hadn't moved. Hadn't shifted an inch. Like he was in some sort of trance.

Greyhound approached the former spy, AK-47 sights lined up with the latter's face. He shouted at Volkov in a strange foreign tongue that McKinnon assumed was Russian. A threat of some kind, probably. Greyhound was offering Volkov a choice. The same one the officers had been given. Surrender or die.

Volkov didn't move.

Greyhound repeated his threat. Louder this time. There was a long pause. Then Volkov's arms went vertical.

Greyhound kept his weapon raised. For a moment McKinnon thought the guy was going to execute Volkov. A quick three-round burst to the chest, problem solved. But then Greyhound took a step closer and grabbed hold of the Russian by the bicep, dragging him forwards and shouting at him, gesturing frantically with his rifle at the police van.

McKinnon couldn't understand a word that Greyhound was saying. But his hand actions and tone of voice were easy enough to interpret. *Get over to the van.*

The gunmen aren't here to kill the Russian, he realised.

They've been sent to snatch him.

Volkov got the message. He broke out of his stupor and stumbled on ahead of Greyhound, hands above his head, whimpering incoherently as he staggered towards the Crafter. Greyhound stalked behind him, occasionally prodding Volkov in the back with the tip of the rifle barrel.

Flat Top kept his rifle fixed on Bentley and McKinnon. Muzzle flitting between the two officers, ready to drop either of them if they tried to fight back. He called out at the two other gunmen, thirty metres away. Mr Hulk and Spider. They were busy restraining Flowers and Jagielka. The two officers were lying flat on their chests, their hands bunched behind their backs. Mr Hulk had his knee planted on Jagielka's spine, pinning him down while he tied the guy's wrists together with a pair of white plasticuffs. Spider was doing the same to Flowers.

As soon as they had secured the two men Mr Hulk sprang to his feet and hurried over to Flat Top, leaving Spider to pad down Flowers and Jagielka, seizing their tactical radios and mobile phones. The guy took each handset, flipped out the SIM cards and then stamped on the devices as if he was crushing bugs.

Flat Top said something to Mr Hulk. The latter fished out two more pairs of plasticuffs from his pockets, manoeuvred so that he was directly behind McKinnon.

'On the ground,' he ordered. 'On your front. Both of you.'

McKinnon obeyed, lowering himself until he was flat against the damp, cold gravel. His heart was beating steadily faster now.

He tried to reason with himself. There was no point in the gunmen killing McKinnon and his fellow officers. Executing the police would be counter-productive. It would elevate a kidnapping into a multiple homicide. These guys wouldn't want that kind of heat on them, especially if they were planning on bugging out of the country.

But that didn't make his situation any less terrifying.

McKinnon felt a pair of gloved paws clamp around his forearms as Mr Hulk braced his hands behind his back. He felt the plastic loops slide up past his knuckles until they were cinched tight.

Mr Hulk stood up. He left McKinnon lying face down on the ground and shifted across to his right, dropping down beside Bentley, plasticuffing him as well. Once he had finished he said something to Flat Top. The latter lowered his weapon and knelt down next to McKinnon, frisking him. He retrieved the Galaxy and his police radio, along with his wallet and the keys to the Discovery. Flat Top gathered up the items, tossed the wallet and keys aside and handed the phone and radio to Mr Hulk. The huge gunman had retrieved Bentley's own comms units. He took all four handsets and went through the same ritual as Spider had done, prising out the SIM cards from the phones, then stamping on the devices until they were shattered beyond repair.

Now we've got no way of contacting HQ, McKinnon realised.

No way of sending for help.

Which was actually good news, in a weird way. McKinnon considered it unlikely that the gunmen would go to the trouble of trashing their comms kit if they were planning on slotting them.

They're trying to give themselves enough time to get clear before we can call for help.

Thirty metres away, Greyhound manhandled Volkov towards the rear of the Crafter. The Russian was begging with his captors, pleading loudly with Greyhound, tears glistening on his cheeks. The gunman ignored his desperate pleas as he unlocked the door leading to the tiny metal cage built into a separate compartment at the back of the Crafter. He stepped back, grabbed hold of

Volkov by his shoulder and shoved him head first into the cell. The Russian was still begging for mercy as Greyhound slammed the outer door shut, locking him inside. He thumped his fist twice on the door and whistled.

A moment later, the Crafter engine roared into life.

McKinnon looked on helplessly.

We had one job to do. Protect Volkov.

And we fucked it up.

Greyhound cupped a hand and shouted at the other three gunmen, waving them over. Mr Hulk and Flat Top sprang into action. They snatched up their assault rifles and raced back across the driveway to the waiting van, clambering inside the main passenger cabin. Greyhound swung round from the rear of the Crafter and followed them.

Spider was the last of the four to return to the van. He was halfway to the Crafter when he stopped in his tracks, as if remembering something. He did an about-turn and raced over to the Land Rover Discovery parked next to Flowers and Jagielka. Hiked up his trouser leg, unsheathed a black boot knife strapped around his ankle and slashed the front and rear tyres, plunging the nine-inch blade deep into the tread line. He repeated the trick for the second Discovery a few metres away from McKinnon and Bentley. Both SUVs had run-flats but driving on slashed tyres would slow them down, giving the gunmen more time to escape before the alarm was raised.

The ambush had been cleverly worked, McKinnon knew. The gunmen were professionals. They had correctly foreseen that the police officers would call in to HQ and report the strange encounter with the delivery driver. They had even known that the team would be compelled to abandon the safe house as soon as they had been alerted to the security breach.

All they had to do was wait for their targets to emerge through the front door and launch their assault.

But that led to more worrying questions.

As in: *How did these guys know where to find us?*

And how did they know exactly when to attack?

The second question troubled McKinnon the most. If the gunmen had rocked up sixty seconds later, they would have been too late. Volkov and the team would have been on the road down to Leeds. Instead, they had arrived just in time.

Spider sheathed his boot knife, snatched up his assault rifle and scurried back across the driveway towards the police van. Hopped inside the main cabin, wrenched the sliding side door shut.

A moment later the driver gunned the engine. The Crafter growled, throwing up a tyre spray of loose gravel, stones and mud as it backed out of the driveway and steered down the path. Ten seconds later, the Crafter hit the main road.

Twenty seconds after that, the van disappeared from view.

Volkov was gone.

FOUR

Four minutes later, Vasin hung a left off the main road, arrowed down the narrow lane and pulled up in front of the field gate behind the delivery van. The track leading into the wooded area was empty and so were the surrounding fields. It reminded Vasin of the penal colony he had once spent time in, deep in the forests of the Urals, barren and grey and windswept.

He tore the keys out of the ignition, flipped open his side door and hopped out of the wagon.

'Everybody out,' he ordered. 'Into the Sprinter. Make sure you leave nothing behind.'

The four guys wrenched the side door open and jumped down, boots pounding on the gravel. The Sprinter driver swung out of the front cab, paced round to the side of the vehicle and pulled back the sliding door on its metal tracks. Then the guys piled into the Sprinter cabin.

Two banks of folding seats had been installed in the panel van by the team's specialist mechanic. Four seats for Vasin's guys, plus another for Volkov. A tight squeeze, for a two-hundred-mile journey. But better than risking it in the Crafter. Thirty minutes from now, every cop in the country would be on the lookout for that van.

While the others bundled inside the Sprinter, sliding their weapons beneath the seats, Vasin hooked around to the back of the Crafter. He dug out the set of spare keys from the side pocket on his 5.11s, popped open the rear doors and located the lock on the outside of the cell door, an inch or so below the handle. Vasin shoved the key into the lock and gave it a clockwise twist. There was the grinding and clanking of bolts shifting, a distinct click as the lock released. He grabbed the metal door handle, heavily scuffed and scratched from years of overuse. Levered the handle. Wrenched the cell door open.

Nikolai Volkov was sitting on a metal bench inside the tiny cell, hands dangling between his legs. Vasin grinned. 'You can come out now, Nikolai Ivanovich. There's no one watching you.'

Volkov paused for a beat and peered outside, as if suspecting a trap. Then he rose from the bench and climbed out of the cage with as much dignity as he could muster. Which wasn't much.

The former double agent was much smaller than Vasin had pictured in his head. And physically weaker, too. His shoulders were slouched. He moved with considerable pain and difficulty. But some of the old steel was there in his grey-blue eyes, Vasin noted. They were intense and alert, taking in every detail. Possible escape routes, allies, potential threats. They were the eyes of a man used to calculating his every move, watching his back, with an allegiance to nobody but himself. Vasin could hear the warnings of his superiors ringing in his ears.

Don't trust him. Watch him carefully. He betrayed us once. He might do so again, if it's in his interests.

Volkov straightened up and said, 'You took your time. You were nearly too late.'

'We came as soon as we could. What else were we supposed to do?'

'That wasn't part of the plan. You were supposed to get there as soon as I sent the message.'

Vasin felt his temper rising. 'Put in a complaint with our boss. I'm sure he'll be sympathetic. Now get in the fucking van.'

Vasin waved a hand at the Sprinter. Volkov stood his ground, a flicker of defiance in his eyes.

'My daughter. When do I get to speak to Nadezhda?'

'Soon. Once we're out of the country.'

'I want to speak to her now. Let her know I'm safe.'

Vasin shook his head. 'There's no time for that. We've got to get on the road.'

'We had a deal,' Volkov said. 'My cooperation, in exchange for seeing my daughter. I want to hear her voice.'

'And you will,' Vasin said. 'You'll talk to her very soon, my friend. But right now, we have to get the fuck out of here.'

Volkov pursed his lips. He stared levelly at Vasin, as if trying to decide whether it was worth pursuing the argument any further. Decided against it, nodded and followed Vasin towards the panel van parked just ahead of the Crafter.

The delivery driver was kneeling beside the Sprinter's rear bumper, peeling off the stolen reg plate. He had already ripped off the plate for the front end of the vehicle. Most manufacturers fitted licence plates with tape these days. Vasin didn't know why. Budgetary reasons, perhaps. Maybe double-sided tape was cheaper and more convenient than drilling holes in the car. Marginal savings.

The driver tore off three strips of double-sided tape from a roll and applied them to the plate frame, forming a wide 'H'. He peeled off the top layer from the tape strips. Then he took the original rear plate and pressed it against the frame, rubbing the surface with the bottom of his bunched-up fist to stick it down.

Vasin stopped beside the Sprinter and turned to Volkov, indicating one of the empty seats. 'Get in.'

Volkov looked at him. 'Where are we going?'

'South of here. Two hundred miles. There's another car waiting for us. We'll switch motors and head straight for the airport.'

'And then I'll see my daughter?'

There was a pathetic look of optimism in Volkov's eyes that Vasin found mildly amusing. 'Yes. Then you'll see your daughter. Now get in the fucking van.'

The former agent clambered inside the Sprinter, squeezing himself into one of the empty seats. Vasin tugged the sliding door shut.

Almost ready to roll.

Vasin signalled to the driver. 'Ready?'

'Yes, boss.'

Vasin tipped his head at the van. 'Get the fire started. Then we're leaving.'

'Yes, boss.'

The driver shot to his feet. He scooped up the stolen reg plates and dumped them inside the front of the Crafter. Paced back over to the panel van and peeled off the large magnetic sticker from the side, the one with the forged company logo printed on it. He carried the sticker over to the Crafter and chucked it inside the front cab too. With the original plates on display and the logo on the side removed, the Sprinter would pass for just another white van clogging up Britain's streets.

The rest of the team waited inside the Sprinter, guarding Volkov while the driver took out three items from the back of the van. A worn car tyre, a twenty-litre jerry can filled with petrol and a plastic bag with a change of clothes. He handed the bag to Vasin, lugged the tyre over to the police van, placed it on the floor of the main cabin and doused it in petrol. Vasin stripped out of his duty vest and uniform and changed into the clothes provided in the bag: an oversized plaid shirt, T-shirt and acid-washed jeans. He tossed the police kit into the van, stepped back and nodded at the driver.

'Burn it,' he said.

The driver dug out a lighter from his shorts pocket, thumbed the spark wheel and applied the naked flame to the doused car tyre. The fire quickly took hold. Nothing burned as effectively as petrol-soaked rubber. Thick black smoke and flames engulfed the main cabin of the police van, licking at the seats and carpet, spouting out of the opening, eddying into the grey sky. The smell of burning plastic and rubber hung in the air as the driver and Vasin hurried back over to the Sprinter and jumped inside.

They weren't worried about the flames attracting local attention. They were miles from the nearest house, even further from the closest village. By the time a passing motorist or walker spotted the blazing van and called the emergency services, Vasin and his men would be far away. Besides, it was more important that they destroyed any potential DNA evidence. They would leave nothing for the police except a blackened metal shell. There would be no prints, no forensic evidence.

Nothing to tie Vasin and his men to the attack.

The next part of the plan was easy. Head south for two hundred miles, to a multi-storey car park on the outskirts of Coventry.

Change vehicles again, switching to a rented Vauxhall Insignia. There was a go-bag stowed inside the boot of the Insignia, with everything the team would need for the final leg of their escape from the UK. Seven Hungarian passports, three thousand pounds in cash and a similar amount in local currency. Plus seven one-way tickets for a Turkish Airlines flight to Istanbul, with an onward connection to their final destination. One ticket for each guy on the team, plus Volkov.

The tickets had been booked a fortnight ago, from an anonymous office in Dubai, using a secure VPN service. No way of tracing anything back to the Russians.

He watched the police van burn for a moment. A beautiful sight. Then he turned to the driver.

'Okay,' he said. 'Let's go.'

As they pulled away, Volkov watched the glow of the flames through the van's rear window. For a few minutes they travelled along at motorway speeds, putting some serious distance between themselves and the crime scene. Engine growling, the cabin lurching this way and that as it rolled over the deep potholes in the road, rattling the guys buckled up inside. After three or four miles he heard the crunching of gears, the engine-roar dialling down to a low thrum as the van settled into a gentle cruise, rumbling through the countryside at around forty miles per hour.

For the first time in many weeks, Volkov breathed a sigh of relief.

The past few days had been some of the most stressful of his life.

Volkov hadn't wanted to go into witness protection. He didn't believe the bullshit explanation the detectives in charge of his case had given him. *This is for your own safety, Nikolai.* The British police were polite and approachable, which was probably a good thing when it came to arresting drunks on a Saturday night in a market town. But they didn't understand his world. They couldn't protect him from his enemies.

Nobody could.

That had been the message behind the poisoning, Volkov knew.

The assassination attempt had failed, but the message from his enemies was clear.

We can get you anytime. Anywhere.

Nowhere is safe.

Volkov had lived a lonely existence in Britain. He had no friends to speak of. His old comrades in the Foreign Intelligence Service, the SVR, had abandoned him after he had been accused of selling state secrets to MI6. Volkov had fled before the authorities could arrest him, defecting to the UK. But that was where his luck ran out. His wife had refused to join him in England and divorced him a year later. Six months after that, his son had been killed in a motorcycle accident in Minsk. The only person he had left was his beloved daughter, Nadezhda.

She was beautiful. Playful. Radiant. She had her father's intelligence, her mother's toughness and a sense of humour neither of them possessed. And Volkov had not seen her since he'd fled Russia seven years earlier.

They had spoken almost daily before the nerve agent attack, but the police had refused Volkov's requests to call her while he was in hospital. No outside contact, they had said.

For your own safety.

They assured him Nadezhda wasn't at risk.

Volkov knew better. He knew he had to find some way of warning her. So he had smuggled a burner phone into the safe house.

Which had been easy enough to do. The police had allowed him to return home after his discharge from hospital to fetch some personal items. Clothes, toiletries, books. They couldn't let him go to the safe house wearing a hospital gown.

He had a go-bag packed in his wardrobe, ready to use in case he had to leave Swindon at short notice. An old habit, from his days as a spy. The police had searched the go-bag thoroughly before returning it to him. They had found the burner phone and the fake passport, the bundles of sterling and euros stashed inside his vintage leather wash bag.

But they hadn't found the additional burner phone, secreted in a hidden compartment sewn into the bottom of the wash bag.

Volkov had memorised Nadezhda's mobile number. During

the first few days in the safe house he had sent her a stream of text messages. He would sneak into the downstairs bathroom, take out his phone from the secret wash-bag compartment, power it up and check in with her. Telling her not to worry, that he was okay, he couldn't say where he was, but that he hoped to make a full recovery and speak to her again soon.

He also told her to leave St Petersburg, where she had been studying acting, immediately. Get out to the countryside, he wrote. Preferably somewhere remote, where the authorities can't find you. Don't panic.

Everything will be okay. Papa will fix this.

She hadn't replied.

Volkov had started to get anxious. He feared the worst.

On the fifth day, a new message came through.

Actually, there were two separate messages. Both sent from Nadezhda's phone. But not from her. The messages were from the people who had tried to kill him.

The first message had said, *We have your daughter. She is safe and well. If you want to see her again, do exactly as we say.*

The message didn't say what would happen if Volkov refused. But it didn't need to.

The second message had been much longer than the first. Practically an essay. It had contained a detailed list of instructions for Volkov to follow. Obligations that he would be required to fulfil. They were non-negotiable, the messenger had warned. If he wanted to be reunited with Nadezhda, he would have to carry out the instructions to the letter. Any deviation from the plan would have fatal consequences.

The messenger added that, should Volkov agree to the terms, all would be forgiven. Life could begin anew. He could go home. There would be a new job waiting for him, an unelected position in the administration. Volkov would become an unofficial spokesman for the Kremlin on issues of national security. There would be regular paid appearances on TV and the radio. Who knows? In time he might even be selected to run for mayor someplace. Rostov, perhaps. Or Nizhny Novgorod.

The choice facing Volkov had been simple.

Work with his enemies, or turn his back finally and irreversibly on the motherland and suffer.

The death of his only child, versus potentially thousands of lives lost.

Personal sacrifice or global disaster.

An impossible call to make.

They gave him twelve hours to decide.

Volkov didn't give a damn about himself. He was sixty-three, with more miles on the clock than he had road left ahead. But Nadezhda was everything to him.

Besides, he reasoned, his life in the UK hadn't turned out as he had hoped. When he had first cut a deal with the British authorities they had painted him a picture of a golden future in exile. A glamorous apartment in Chelsea, a six-figure job at a Marylebone think tank, the works.

They had lied.

The home turned out to be a modest terraced house in an anonymous cul-de-sac in Swindon. The highly paid job never materialised. His only source of income was the occasional fee he received from MI6 for the intelligence reports he produced. Volkov made it his business to keep in touch with a loose network of exiled former agents and Kremlin officials, embittered oligarchs and investigative journalists. People opposed to the regime, those who had a personal axe to grind. Each report earned him a few grand, barely enough to pay the bills. He tried applying for a few positions but his English was poor and his computer skills non-existent. There wasn't a huge demand for sixty-something former Russian agents.

His only regular contact was with his local newsagent and his handler at Six. He had no future. Nothing to live for, except his daily phone call to Nadezhda.

Volkov could have refused the Kremlin's offer. He could have stayed put in the safe house, biding his time, waiting for the police to move him to some other town, in some other remote part of the country or overseas.

But he would never be able to relax. He would have to spend the rest of his life looking over his shoulder, wondering whether this was the day they would finally catch up with him.

And he was tired of hiding.

Twelve hours after receiving the message, Volkov had agreed to their terms.

We'll send a team to get you, the messenger had replied. *Keep Thursday afternoon free.*

Today.

They had triangulated the location of the safe house using Volkov's phone. Questioned him about the officers on the Protected Persons Unit. Numbers, firepower, rounds per weapon. It had been unbelievably easy for Volkov to provide them with such information. The police, bored and with nothing else to do, had readily answered his questions.

There had been one final task for Volkov to carry out that morning. A small but vital part of the plan.

He had been told to send a message to a disposable number as soon as the police were ready to leave. That would be the signal for the ambush team to approach in the Crafter.

You'll have to find a way to delay your minders, the messenger had informed him. *Give the team enough time to drive up and rescue you.*

So Volkov had hit on the idea of feigning sickness. He'd locked himself in the bathroom, made a few retching noises and pained groans. The officers had believed him, of course. They knew how ill he was. How painful his recovery had been.

It was simply a question of waiting in the bathroom until he received the final message from the team. The one telling him that they were sixty seconds away.

Then he'd flushed the toilet and followed the officers outside.

They had staged the whole attack as a kidnapping. For security purposes, the messenger had explained. It would be preferable if the British believed that Volkov had been taken against his will. Otherwise they might get suspicious. Figure out that he'd been in on the plan all along.

Now he was on his way to see his daughter.

Before the poisoning, Volkov had learned something huge. Bigger than anything he'd uncovered during his days working in foreign intelligence. Something catastrophic, with the power to bring down both the Russian and American presidents.

He had been on the cusp of sharing that int with his handler when the poisoning had happened. But now Volkov was glad he hadn't spilled his guts. Because for the first time in many years, he could look forward again.

At last, after all these years, he would be reunited with Nadezhda.

But first, Volkov had a job to do.

One last task, in the service of Mother Russia.

FIVE

John Bald, the one-time hero of the Regiment, was poring over a stack of paperwork when the squat Mexican stuck his head through the office door.

'Two men for you, Mister John.'

Bald looked up from the sheaf of papers on the desk and frowned. In front of him was the itinerary for the motorbike tour he would be leading the following day. A nine-day guided trip from Playa del Carmen to Zipolite on the Pacific coast, via the jungle of Palenque. One of the most popular deals offered by his company, Mayan Motorbike Tours. It was Bald's usual custom to run a last-minute check before each ride. Travel arrangements, restaurants, lodgings. Making sure everything was in order. He liked to be prepared.

'Who are they?' asked Bald.

Hector Gallardo, the twenty-year-old kid from Tulum and the sole employee of Mayan Motorbike Tours, shifted uneasily on his feet.

'They didn't say, Mister John. Just asked to speak with the boss.'

Bald peered out through the office window at the main garage. Amid the clutter of motorcycles and spare parts he could see a couple of pale guys in loose-fitting T-shirts and baggy jeans, hands stuffed inside their front pockets. Two of the customers booked in for tomorrow's tour, perhaps. Or tourists looking for a cheap self-hire motorbike for a few days.

Bald gritted his teeth and sighed. 'I'll be right out.'

'*Sí*, Mister. I go tell them.'

Hector turned and hurried out of the office, grinning like the village idiot.

Bald had inherited the kid when he'd bought out the company

a few months back. He had initially been prepared to let Hector go. The kid was clumsy, getting the orders wrong at lunch, making a fucking mess or forgetting basic stuff. His grasp of English was piss poor, and he had a special knack for getting on Bald's nerves with his gormless smile and happy-go-lucky demeanour.

But after his first week of running the business, Bald had changed his mind. Hector was a grinning fool, but he had a natural talent for fixing up bikes and was a proper wizard when it came to using a torque wrench. Plus, he came cheap. The kid was a mechanic, tour guide, cleaner and general Man Friday, and all for less than the minimum wage back in the UK.

The developing world. Bald appreciated it.

He slid out from behind his desk, sweat pasting his polo shirt to his back. Ten o'clock in the morning, early March, and the temperature was already nudging past the thirty-degree mark. The prehistoric PC on his clutter-free desk was whirring noisily, the fan overhead spinning slowly, blowing down stale fan-diced air on Bald.

Life in Playa del Carmen had its drawbacks, he thought. The local women weren't much to look at and the food got boring after a while, endless variations of maize and meat and guacamole. But he had no complaints about the weather.

It's a fuck of a lot warmer than back home in Dundee.

Bald had bought the garage six months ago from a retired German plastic surgeon called Wolfgang Wolf. The German had lost his life savings after investing heavily in a luxury development in Cancun that had gone south. Bald had heard about the guy's financial worries over a conversation with a local moneylender and had made Wolf a lowball offer for the place, knowing that the guy needed the cash to pay off his debts. He'd acquired the garage and its inventory for a pittance.

It was the one bit of good fortune he'd had in the past year.

Nine months earlier, things had been looking up for Bald. He had a million in Swiss-stamped gold bullion, getaway funds he'd stolen from the brother of the Russian president during an MI6 op. He had a stunning Thai fiancée half his age.

Then his Thai bride-to-be had shafted him.

Told him she knew a guy who would buy the stolen bullion

45

from Bald. A dealer based in Manila. Straight-shooting guy, she had said. He'll give you a good price, no questions asked. Trust me.

The meeting had turned out to be a set-up.

The Filipino dealer had robbed Bald. Kamlai, his Thai princess, had been in on the whole thing. She'd done a runner with the dealer, left Bald in a crappy hotel room with his fake passport and the few gold bars he'd kept secret from her. Converted into hard cash, there was barely enough left over for Bald to start over and fly out to Mexico's Mayan Riviera. He had no good reason for being there, other than the fact that it was hot, cheap, and very fucking far away from his troubles. He spent a month getting pissed, lying low and considering his options. Waiting for an opportunity.

Then he'd heard the German surgeon's sob story and he'd sunk the last of his capital into the garage. Now Bald spent his days in the workshop and his evenings sipping Modelo Negros down by the beach.

It wasn't the millionaire lifestyle Bald had planned for himself.

But, hey, it was better than nothing.

For the first time in his life, Bald was close to settling for what he had. No more big plans. No more dreams of easy money. Time to face the truth: he was nearing fifty, his glory days in the Regiment were a long way behind him, his prospects of future employment extremely limited. Maybe it was time to admit defeat. Accept that this was the best that the son of a Dundee council estate could hope for. There were plenty of others who made do with less, whose lives were shittier.

Maybe, he thought, it was time to stop fighting the world.

He stepped out of the back office and into the main garage.

There was the smell of motor oil and lubricants in the air, Mexican folk music playing on the local radio station. The garage was split roughly down the middle. At the rear was the company office and the adjacent workshop where the various checks and repairs were carried out. Hector was in the workshop area, draining the engine oil from a Honda Shadow that had just made the journey to Chichén Itza and back. Several forty-five-gallon drums were lined up against the back wall, some filled to the brim with used motor oil. Once a week a guy came by in a truck and took the drums over to a processing facility in Valladolid, where it was recycled before being sold on as re-refined oil.

Bald, doing his bit for the environment.

The front of the garage was the showroom. Sales counter to the left, with stacks of sun-faded colour leaflets detailing the various tours Bald offered. To the right of the counter stood the rows of motorbikes: BMW F700s, Harley-Davidson Softails, Ducati Monsters. A handful of scooters for the older clients who just wanted a convenient way of getting around town. There were racks of bike leathers, shelves piled high with spare parts, helmets and tyres. The walls were lined with memorabilia left behind by the previous owner: faded photographs of tour groups, vintage US licence plates. A classic Triumph X-75 Hurricane – Bald's pride and joy – hung from a pair of metal chains looped around the ceiling crossbeams.

There was no front door. The garage opened out directly on to the cracked pavement. A steel roller shutter came down at night to protect the place. Outside, a street dog lay sprawled beneath the unrelenting sun. There was a nail salon opposite and a convenience store a few doors further along. It wasn't the glitzy end of town. Few tourists wandered this far away from the main thoroughfares along the seafront.

This place looks exactly like what it is, thought Bald. A business that had seen better days, half-forgotten, struggling to make ends meet. Surviving, but only just.

Story of my life.

He tried to ignore the anger simmering in his veins and put on his winning smile. Approached the two customers.

They were standing just inside the entrance. Both in their late thirties or early forties. Not in the prime of their lives. They had the kind of bulky, heavyset physiques of former professional footballers who had let themselves go in retirement. The taller guy was pale, with long black hair flowing down past his shoulders and a scruffy goatee. A dog tag necklace hung from around his neck. Some sort of fashion accessory, Bald presumed. He didn't know. He wasn't big on European fashion.

The smaller guy gave away about six inches in height to Dog Tag. He wasn't much taller than Hector, five-six or seven, heavy in the arms and neck. He had a round freckled face, with narrow eyes like a pair of stab wounds in a torso and a neatly shaven jaw. He wore a stained graphic T-shirt with the Harley-Davidson logo splashed across the front. Together they looked like the tribute act for a late-nineties thrash metal group.

'Help you lads?' asked Bald.

Dog Tag and Harley both turned to greet the ex-Blade. Dog Tag looked him up and down, visually screening him. The guy had a tear-shaped scar beneath his left eye, Bald noted.

'You're the owner? John Bald?' Dog Tag asked. His Eastern European accent was as thick as cement.

'Aye. That's me, lads.'

Bald hadn't bothered to change his name when he'd quit Britain. He considered it unlikely that Six would be actively looking for him on the other side of the world. And besides, living under an assumed name in the era of social media and data harvesting was fraught with complications. Easier to just go with the flow.

Dog Tag pointed to himself.

'I'm Kristians. This is my brother, Ritvars. We're booked on the tour. To Palenque. The email said to report here when we arrived in town.'

Bald nodded. Although he rented out a few motorbikes, most of his business came from selling tour packages through the company website. Bald led the groups personally as the road captain, charging a hefty fee for the privilege of guiding the tourists through the Mexican countryside, taking care of all the hotel bookings and logistics. A chase vehicle, driven by Hector, carried any luggage the customers might have with them.

'You're the Latvians, right? The Pahars brothers?'

Dog Tag nodded.

'First time you fellas have been riding in these parts?'

'First time in Mexico, full stop.'

Bald was looking at Dog Tag, but in the periphery of his vision he noticed the other guy sweeping his eyes round the garage.

'It's just you here?' asked Harley.

'Me and the kid, aye. Just the two of us.'

'What about the others? We're not the only ones on the tour, no?'

'Not here yet. You lads are the first to check in.'

The Latvian nodded slowly, as if this was somehow vital information. He glanced sidelong at Dog Tag. Said something in his native tongue. The two of them were having some kind of debate. Haggling over what bikes they wanted to take on the ride, maybe. Or perhaps they were debating whether to abandon this rundown joint altogether and try their luck elsewhere.

Dog Tag slid his gaze back to Bald and smiled. He seemed the friendlier of the two. 'What do you need?'

'All your documents,' Bald said. 'Passports, licences. Credit cards and payment, cash only.'

Dog Tag and Harley exchanged a knowing look. The latter glanced over his shoulder at the street outside. Still empty, except for the street dog and the rubbish drifting like tumbleweed across the pavement.

'No problem,' Dog Tag said.

He reached for something in his rear jeans pocket.

Just then Bald heard a voice from further down the street.

Dog Tag paused. So did his brother. They simultaneously turned towards the street, Bald looking in the same direction as two guys swept into view.

They were decked out in matching dark jeans, Salomon Gore-Tex trail boots and plain dark T-shirts. Both of them were carrying brown leather holdalls, talking in low voices as they marched purposefully towards the shop entrance. One of the guys looked a bulked-up gap-year traveller. He had cold blue eyes, long dark hair, unkempt beard and a deep suntan. Not the reddened sunburn from a few days roasting on a lounger, but the kind of all-over brown acquired from months of working outdoors. He looked sinewy and lithe, like a triathlete. Bald guessed that his body fat was somewhere in the low single digits.

The other guy was the bigger of the two. A serious-looking black guy in his thirties, also thickly bearded, with a freshly shaven head. He had the broad build of a middleweight boxer, six-foot-plus of explosive power and fast-twitch muscle fibre. He said something to his mucker in a distinctive North London accent, aggressive and flat.

The blue-eyed guy stepped into the garage with his mate, scanning the building, examining every nook and cranny, as if he was looking for a security camera.

Bald watched them carefully. Blue Eyes glanced quickly at the Latvians before he settled his gaze on Jock.

'Is this the place for the bike tours, mate?'

'That's right,' Bald said, shifting his attention to the new customers. 'You lads are booked in for the Zipolite trip?'

Blue Eyes nodded and thrust out a hand. 'Phil Lyden. And this is Jordan Rowe,' he added, gesturing to the middleweight boxer standing next to him.

Bald glanced at Rowe, taking him in properly for the first time. His muscles were huge. His shoulders were the size of rock formations. His hands were calloused, Bald noted, and there were tiny pinkish scars on his cheeks and above his eyebrows. He looked like someone who had been in a lot of scraps in his time and had an unbeaten record. Maybe he was in the fight game, thought Bald. A fighter in the amateur ranks. Or perhaps he was a mixed-martial-arts teacher.

Lyden and Rowe. Bald recalled the names from the online booking. Sounded like a high-end cosmetics firm, the kind that supplied complimentary bars of soap to Park Lane hotels.

'Got some luggage for the trip,' Lyden said, patting the holdalls. 'Thought we'd drop the bags off before we check into the hotel, like. Save us some time.'

Dog Tag and Harley had been watching the exchange in silence, glaring openly at the two Brits as if they were a bad smell that had just wafted in from the streets. Which was weird, Bald thought to himself. They didn't appear to know one another. So why were they acting as though the Brits had pissed them off?

'Be with you in a minute,' Bald said. He nodded at the Latvians. 'Just let me get these lads sorted first.'

Lyden set down his holdall and held up his hands. 'Don't mind us, mate. Take your time.'

Bald looked back towards the two Latvians. 'You got them documents? Won't take more than a couple of minutes.'

Dog Tag glared at the Brits for a moment longer before he

reached into his jeans pocket and pulled out a burgundy-red passport with the Latvian coat of arms emblazoned on the front. Dug out his faded leather wallet, plucked out his licence and credit card. Took out a roll of bills from his other pocket, counted out two thousand dollars in US sterling, handed everything over to Bald. Harley did the same.

Bald gave the passports and licences a cursory glance. He ducked back into his office, made copies of the passports and licences, retrieved a sheath of carbon-copy documents from a tray on his desk. Gave the Latvians a pen and asked them to fill out the forms, returned their passports, swiped through the credit cards for the damage deposits. Took the four thousand dollars in cash and paced over to the back office. A small grey safe had been fitted to the rear wall, next to the metal filing cabinet. Bald punched in the eight-digit code and pressed the Unlock button. A green light above the keypad lit up. He flipped the safe open, stashed the money inside, next to several bundles of petty cash, the company books and the sets of keys for each motorbike. Then he shut the safe again, locked it and returned to the front of the garage.

The two Brits were inspecting the bikes, pointing out various features. The Latvians lingered beside the sales counter, keeping their distance. Dog Tag stared at them with narrowed eyes. Harley was still giving the Brits the screw-face.

Bald handed the Latvians back their passports, cards and licences. Gave them a receipt for the damage deposit and a carbon copy for each of the forms they'd signed.

'That's you lads processed,' he said. 'See you tomorrow. Nine o'clock sharp. Don't be late, or we'll set off without you. No ifs or fucking buts. Got it?'

'Nine o'clock,' Dog Tag replied. 'Okay.'

The brothers snatched their documents and paperwork, stuffed them in their jeans pockets and turned to leave. Harley shot a final fuck-you look at the two Brits and muttered something to Dog Tag. The latter grunted.

Then they left.

Lyden watched them slide out of view, Rowe by his side, his huge arms crossed in front of his chest. The bulging veins on his forearms were as thick as tautened ropes.

'Where did they say they were from?' Lyden asked, turning to Bald.

'Latvia,' Bald said. 'Riga. Why?'

'No reason.' Lyden shrugged. 'I bet you get all sorts in here, don't you?'

'It's an interesting crowd.'

'Been doing this for a while, have you?'

'Something like that, aye.'

Bald didn't want to get drawn into a question-and-answer session about his dodgy past. He changed the subject. 'Where did you lads say you're from?'

'We didn't,' said Lyden. 'I'm from Stretford. Jordan here is a Tottenham lad, born and bred.'

Rowe nodded but said nothing. Bald formed the distinct impression that the guy wasn't one for small talk.

'Been travelling for a while?' he asked.

'What makes you think that?'

'The long hair.' Bald shrugged. 'The beards. You look like you've been getting some good rays.'

Lyden shook his head. 'We landed in Cancun a couple of days ago. Came straight from Nigeria. Me and Jordan work on one of the offshore rigs down that way.'

Which explained the guy's deep suntan, Bald thought.

They chatted some more while Bald checked their documents and took their luggage. The Brits were friendly enough, he decided. But something wasn't right about them. Something about the way they carried themselves. The way they oozed confidence and were totally aware of their environment, absorbing every small detail. It almost reminded him of the lads in the Regiment.

Bald shook his head. No. These lads aren't SAS. Lyden's long hair, their unkempt beards: that wasn't part of the Regiment look. The guys at Hereford took pride in their appearance. No self-respecting Blade would go around looking like a scruffy fucker.

Your mind is playing tricks on, Bald thought. *They're oil-rig workers. Nothing more.*

Later that afternoon, Bald was getting ready to close up. The day had passed quickly. In addition to the Brits and the Latvians, Bald had to process the other customers booked in for the tour the following day. A middle-aged German couple from Dresden, a Canadian dentist who'd turned up dressed like he was auditioning for *Easy Rider*, and an obese retired cop from Montrose, Georgia with a MAKE AMERICA GREAT AGAIN T-shirt, on honeymoon with his equally overweight wife. There had been luggage to load on to the chase vehicle, checks to carry out on the bikes, hotel reservations to double-check. At five o'clock sharp Bald had pulled down the roller shutters and called it a day.

He was ready for a beer. Or ten.

He had his evening all planned out: a few hours at one of the bars along the beachfront, sipping ice-cold Modelo Negros and watching Sky Sports. Then a nightcap with the American woman he was currently shagging. Terra, a twice-divorced Californian from Long Beach. Bald had met her a few months back at some local dive bar. Stupid fucking name, but great in the sack. She was forty-four but with the body of someone twenty years younger, toned and slender, with curves in all the right places and tight everywhere else. The benefits of clean living and Californian sun and spin classes. Terra had a cracking daughter as well, an undergraduate at Stanford who was visiting her mother for the spring break.

Bald's dirty mind visualised various pleasing scenarios. He was sure he could work something out.

Maybe life wasn't so bad after all.

He powered down the piece-of-shit PC, switched off the overhead fan and stepped out of the back office. Hector was over by the workshop, sweeping the floor, still grinning. As if working a broom was one of life's great pleasures.

'Almost done, Mister John.'

'That's enough for one day,' Bald said, itching to get down to the beachfront. 'Finish up, mate.'

'One minute.'

The kid usually left just before Bald, returning home to the gang-infested slum where he lived with his extended family of uncles and cousins. Getting him to leave on time was always a test of Bald's patience.

'Leave it,' he said. 'Now.'

'Okay, okay.'

Hector reluctantly set aside the broom, like it was a punishment. He flashed his gap-toothed grin at Bald. All that sugary crap the kid drank. 'You need me to do anything else? Clean the bikes, maybe?'

'Not tonight, fella. I'm on the clock.'

Hector grinned. 'You go to the bar tonight? Drinks with the *chicas*, maybe?'

'More than drinks, I hope. A lot more.'

'You a dirty man, Mister John.'

'Go home, kid.'

The kid took the hint. He wiped his hands on a dirty rag and made for the entrance. Ducked through the small door built into the shuttered front. The door slammed shut as Hector set off down the street at a gentle trot.

Finally, thought Bald. A few more tasks and he could get stuck into half a dozen pints and Terra, in that order.

He emptied the cash register, turned off the garage radio and packed away the tools left on the workbench countertop. He was halfway through the job when the shutter door opened again with a loud grating rasp.

Hector, he figured.

Kid was always forgetting something. His phone, maybe. Or his keys.

He looked over. Saw two burly figures stepping through the door.

It wasn't Hector.

The Latvians.

SIX

The Latvian brothers were both decked out in the same gear they had been wearing earlier that day. Bald's first thought was that they had returned to drop off some extra luggage ahead of the trip. A bag they had forgotten about, discovered only when they had returned to their hotel room after a day of sightseeing and drinking. Then he saw that neither of them was holding a suitcase or holdall.

Dog Tag was first through the door. He breezed past the sales counter, slanting his gaze across the interior, as if searching for something. Or someone. His mean eyes settled on Bald. Harley, his overweight mate, closed the shutter door behind him and moved alongside his brother.

Second thought: maybe they didn't understand the instructions he'd given them. Some of the customers Bald dealt with had a fairly limited grasp of English.

Idiots probably think we're leaving tonight.

'You're too early,' Bald said, trying not to sound too irritated. 'We don't leave until tomorrow morning, lads.'

Dog Tag didn't reply.

Neither did Harley.

Bald stepped forwards from the workbench, struggling to mask his irritation. All he wanted to do was get down to the bar and get some beers in him and relax. These two idiots were beginning to piss him off.

'You hear me, fellas? I said—'

The first punch caught Bald by surprise. He wasn't expecting a physical confrontation. His posture was all kinds of wrong. He was standing square-on to Dog Tag, hands by his sides, presenting a whole shopping list of targets to his opponent. Kidney, abdomen, throat, jaw, groin.

Dog Tag didn't go for any of those. He went off-piste, aiming for the solar plexus. The bread basket.

The Latvian was fast. He didn't so much move as *blur*. Dog Tag shifted his weight to the right, bent at the knees and then pushed up off his feet, rotating his hips as he drove his balled fist up into Bald's stomach at an angle. Minimum back lift, all the kinetic energy from the punch generated by the explosive twist of his hips. An expert uppercut, delivered to the spot just below the sternum. No time to block the attack. Bald felt the bony ridge of the guy's knuckles slam into his midriff, driving the air from his lungs. Nausea surged up into his throat. A billion nerve endings flared up and he folded slightly at the waist, gasping for oxygen.

'Where's the fucking money?' Dog Tag demanded.

Bald couldn't speak. Couldn't breathe or think. The pain shooting through him was excruciating. Dog Tag unloaded another dig, aiming a few inches lower. A solid gut punch.

Another wave of pain exploded inside his stomach.

Harley stood a step behind Dog Tag, blocking the only exit from the garage, letting his mucker take the lead. The guy had whipped out a pistol from the waistband of his jeans. A small semi-automatic Makarov. Bald was vaguely aware of it as Dog Tag loomed over him.

'Where is it?'

Bald still didn't reply. He was too busy trying to breathe, sucking in shallow draws of air, his pain sensors screaming inside him. Dog Tag took a step back and recovered his right arm. Ready to unleash another blow, Bald saw. The Latvian was already thinking about his next move. He had it all planned out in his head. A neat combo. A couple of disabling punches, followed by a knockout blow. The big-budget sequel to the original indie hit.

He wasn't worried about a counter-punch. The blows to the torso had stunned Bald, taking his arms out of the equation.

But not his head.

Bald was still bent slightly forward at the waist, head lowered. Which meant he was within easy striking range of his opponent. But which also gave him the perfect opportunity for a head-butt. Bald rode the next surge of pain and nausea and stepped into Dog Tag, surprising the Latvian with a quick upward jerk of his head.

There was a dull crack as the hard shell of Bald's forehead slammed against the guy's nose, shattering the bones, doing all kinds of damage to the cartilage. Dog Tag let out a nasal grunt of pain as he staggered backwards, blinking rapidly, blood streaming out of his flared nostrils. Before he could recover Bald shoved him backwards and sent the guy crashing into Harley. The latter lost his balance and fell backwards, the Makarov tumbling from his grip, taking him out of the fight. Not for long, Bald knew. No more than a second or two. But long enough to give Bald a chance to take care of Dog Tag and level the odds. Following the oldest rule of fighting.

Deal with the threat right in front of you first.

In the next half-second Dog Tag launched himself at Bald again, throwing a wild right hook at his opponent's face. He wasn't thinking clearly now. Anger was taking over, telling him to drop Bald, and fast. *Teach him a lesson.* Dog Tag cocked his right arm back as he wound up for the punch, generating as much force as possible. Bald saw the blow coming. It was so telegraphed the guy might as well have live-streamed it on Facebook.

Bald had stayed clear of trouble since he'd rocked up in Mexico. But he still knew how to handle himself in a scrap. He'd spent the best part of thirty years fighting and killing for his country. He didn't try to evade the punch. In his experience, defensive action was a waste of time. It didn't bring you any closer to winning the fight. It was better to counter the attack, rather than evade it.

Meet the threat head-on.

He stepped into the Latvian, left foot forward, bending his left arm at an angle. Turning his elbow into a lethal weapon. Bald parried the incoming punch with his raised right forearm and swung out with his left elbow, clubbing Dog Tag on the jaw. The Latvian grunted and jerked backwards, his arms going slack, his face registering shock and pain. He stayed vertical for a moment longer before he fell away to the side, crashing into a rack of BMWs in a loud clatter of metal, tyres and moving parts.

Round one to Bald.

He looked round for a weapon. Spied a torque wrench lying on the sales counter. Bald grabbed it and spun back round to face Harley. Ready to deal with the second threat.

Then he froze.

Harley had recovered his weapon. He stood two metres away, holding the Makarov in a two-handed grip. Business end of the weapon trained on Bald's centre mass.

'Drop the tool,' he said.

Bald released the wrench. It clanged as it hit the floor, the sound echoing around the garage.

Harley kept the Makarov fixed on the ex-SAS man as he muttered something to his mucker. Dog Tag scraped himself off the floor and stood upright, grimacing in pain. He looked like he'd walked into a lamp post. Gouts of blood, gristle and snot bubbled beneath his nostrils. His lower lip was badly cut. He shook his head clear and dug out a pistol stuffed down the back of his jeans. Another Makarov. The guy glowered at Bald, spat out blood on the newly swept garage floor.

He said, 'You're gonna pay for that, bitch.'

Bald kept his mouth shut. Hands by his sides as he warily eyed his attackers, trying to figure a way out of his situation.

Harley said, 'The money. Where is it?'

'Don't know what you're talking about.'

That drew an amused smile from Harley. 'Yeah. Yeah, you fucking do. The money you stole from our boss. A million, in gold bars.'

Several pennies dropped simultaneously inside Bald's head. He understood at once who these guys were, and why they had ambushed him in his garage. They're not Latvians, he realised. They're Russians.

Here to collect what I stole from them.

'We know you took it,' Harley went on, moving a step closer to Bald. 'We spoke to your friend in Manila. Ramos, the black-market dealer.'

'Don't know him,' Bald said.

'Suit yourself.' Harley shrugged. 'But Ramos told us an interesting story. Said you showed up at his office a few months ago, looking to sell some gold bullion. Told us he bought a few bars from you. We're here to collect the rest.'

'I don't have it. It was stolen from me.'

'Bullshit.'

'It's the truth.' Bald took a step back, retreating deeper into the garage. 'My fiancée, she cleaned me out. Took off with most of it and left me with fuck all.'

Dog Tag spat on the ground and bared his blood-stained teeth at Bald. 'You want to play games, fuck face? We can play it that way. Make you scream like a little bitch.'

'Spare us the hard luck story,' Harley said. 'Where is it?'

'I'm telling you, I haven't got it.' Bald gestured to his surroundings. 'Christ, if I had taken all the gold and legged it, do you really think I'd be living in this dump?'

'You think we're idiots? Think you can trick our boss, eh? We know your game, bitch. You hid the cash some place. Gonna wait until no one is looking for it.'

'I was robbed,' Bald said. 'These four walls are all I've got.'

'Bastard's lying,' Dog Tag cut in. 'I can see it, Sergei. He's hidden the gold somewhere.'

'Take a look for yourselves. Search the place. You'll find nothing.'

Harley shook his head. 'We're not going to do that,' he said.

He took another step forward, sidestepping the toppled motorbikes. Stopped a metre away from Bald, the Makarov barrel pointed directly at Bald's eyes. Dog Tag at his three o'clock, shoulder muscles heaving up and down with exertion and rage, pistol at his side.

Harley smirked.

He said, 'This is what's going to happen. I'm going to count to three. Before I'm done, you're going to tell me where the gold is. Otherwise, you get to fucking die.'

'This is a mistake,' Bald said. 'I don't have it.'

'One.'

Harley didn't get to two.

Because in the next half-second the shutter door flew open.

SEVEN

Bald saw them first. He glanced past Dog Tag's shoulder and glimpsed a pair of young familiar figures sweeping through the garage doorway. A slender guy with a deep suntan, followed by a muscle-bound freak with a goatee. Lyden and Rowe, in that order.

The Brits.

Lyden was a half-metre ahead of Rowe. The guy was gripping what Bald's professional eye instantly identified as an FN Five-Seven semi-automatic pistol. A large handgun, with a wide grip, chambered for FN Herstal's very own 5.7 x 28mm round. A small but fast bullet, with a lot of stopping power. Originally designed for submachine guns, not pistols. There was a suppressor screwed to the barrel.

Rowe was carrying the same suppressed weapon. He was arcing the Five-Seven up towards eye level, going through the same process as Lyden as he surged into the garage.

Lyden already had his Five-Seven fully drawn. Arms extended, eyes level with the sights as he zeroed on the nearest target.

Dog Tag.

The Russian was still turning towards the door when Lyden depressed the trigger.

A single round exploded out of the Five-Seven's snout. It didn't sound like a gunshot, the suppressor blunting the sound of the discharge, softened the bark to a dull, whip-like crack. The round struck Dog Tag behind the ear and punched through his skull in an explosive spray of blood and shattered bone. His head snapped round to the other side, as if someone had just given him the world's biggest bitch slap. Then his legs gave way and he slam-dropped head first to the concrete. He was dead before he'd even kissed the ground.

Harley instantly spun away from Bald. His Makarov was already raised and ready to fire, which gave him an advantage over his dead friend. But that merely gave him another problem to deal with: which target to go for? Both Lyden and Rowe were fully inside the garage now, spreading out either side of the doorway, both arcing their Five-Sevens towards the one remaining Russian. Harley found himself at the sharp end of a classic two-on-one dilemma. Kill one guy, the other will drop you.

He was still making his mind up when Rowe fired twice.

Bald hit the deck. He didn't want to get accidentally nailed by one of the rounds passing through the Russian. Two sharp pops echoed through the garage as the rounds smacked into the Latvian's chest, gave him a pair of wound channels as wide as the Eurostar. He spasmed and flopped to the ground, landing face down a couple of metres from Bald, the stink of his blood mixing with the acrid odour of spent gunpowder.

For a moment, the garage was silent.

Bald picked himself up. Rowe stepped towards the shutter door while Lyden stepped around the pair of slotted Russians, lowering his Five-Seven as he approached Bald.

'What the fuck's going on?' Bald growled. 'Who are you?'

Lyden made a face. 'Is that how you greet another Blade, Jock? Jesus. Next time we won't bother.'

He knows my nickname, thought Bald. *Only the guys at Hereford know me as Jock.*

Rowe shut the front door behind him. Bald shifted his gaze back to Lyden, gears turning inside his head. Recalling how the two Brits had expertly scanned the garage for cameras when they had first showed up that morning. Their hyper-awareness.

He said, 'You're with the Regiment?'

Lyden nodded. 'We just got back from a rotation in Afghan,' he said. 'I'm from B Squadron. Jordan here is from D Squadron.'

Bald nodded slowly. Now he understood why the two guys looked so scruffy. The lads would have grown their beards long before heading out to Afghanistan, to gain respect when meeting with tribal leaders.

'What the fuck are you doing here?' Bald demanded.

'We're with the Wing,' said Lyden. 'Six sent us.'

Bald stared at them, letting it all sink in. The Wing was Regiment shorthand for the Revolutionary Warfare Wing: the elite group within 22 SAS that provided support for MI6 operations. A dozen or so guys, trained in everything from electronic warfare to counter-surveillance tactics. Unlike the CIA, Six had no paramilitary wing of its own, so it relied on SAS men to provide the muscle and firepower for operations in the field.

Bald knew all this because he had been part of the Wing once himself. He knew how it worked.

'How did you find me?'

'Come on, mate,' Lyden said. 'This is Six we're talking about. Did you really think you could hide from them lot?'

Bald didn't need to answer that question. He knew the answer. MI6 had long arms. They had probably known his whereabouts all along.

He shrugged. 'I thought those twats might have lost interest in us by now.'

'You should be glad they didn't, otherwise these two would have sent you over to the dark side. The only reason you're still alive is because of us, Grandad.'

He waved a hand at the dead Russians. Bald fixed his gaze on Lyden, rage sweeping through his veins. The guy was arrogant, cocky, full of himself and his own abilities.

Everything Bald had been, fifteen years earlier.

'That's why they sent you here? To nail these bastards?'

Lyden nodded and said, 'We had a tip-off from one of our sources inside the Russian security services. They told us the FSB had found out where you were living and was sending out a team to neutralise you. Two guys on fake passports. President ordered the hit himself, apparently. You've made some serious enemies, mate.'

'I've made worse.'

'So we've heard,' said Rowe.

Bald smiled. 'They still talk about us at Hereford, then?'

Rowe gave a derisive snort. 'Yeah. You could say that.'

He looked at Bald with a very different expression from Lyden. Less friendly. Not hostile. More like professional suspicion. The way a police officer might assess a fellow dirty cop.

Lyden pistol-pointed at the dead Russians and said, 'As soon as Six found out about the hit, they flew us out here to shadow the team. We made these two jokers as soon as they arrived at the airport. Been following them around ever since. When we saw them approach the shop this evening, we knew they were going to do you.'

So that's why Dog Tag and his mate had looked so pissed off earlier that day, Bald realised. They had been planning to put a fucking hole in my head, right there and then. Only these two gym freaks had rocked up and had forced the Russians to delay their plan by a few hours.

'You should have told me,' he said. 'Given us a warning. I could have skipped town and saved you the hassle.'

Lyden shook his head. 'If we had tipped you off, the Russians would have found out. They would've realised very quickly that they had a leak at their end. It would have compromised the source. Six was reluctant to put their asset in any danger.'

'So they almost let these pricks slot me instead?'

'I'm sure you've been in tighter spots.' Lyden grinned. 'Maybe you can tell us a few stories on the flight home.'

Bald narrowed his eyes. 'What the fuck are you talking about?'

'We've got orders to bring you back to London,' Rowe said tonelessly. 'There's a private charter jet waiting for us at Tulum. You're flying back with us. Tonight.'

'No fucking way.'

'We're not asking nicely. That's an order.'

'I couldn't give a toss. Go back and tell your bosses thanks for sending the Hitler Youth and Mike Tyson to my rescue, but I'm done working with those back-stabbing twats.'

Rowe smiled thinly. 'That's not how it works. They're done with you when they say they're done.'

Bald said, 'The last time I dealt with Six, I told them one more job and I was out. They gave me their word.'

'The situation has changed,' Lyden said.

'See this?' Bald pointed to his face. 'This is me giving a shit.'

'At least hear them out, mate.'

'Forget it. Whatever crap they want to rope me into, they can get some other mug to do it. There must be a few lads left at Hereford they haven't screwed over yet.'

'They specifically requested you,' said Rowe.

'Why? What's the op? Pretend I care.'

'We're not allowed to say,' Lyden cut in. 'You know that, mate. Even if we knew what this was about, we couldn't tell you.'

'I'll need more than that, if you want me to drop everything and get on a fucking plane.'

'Look, all we can tell you is that we've been told to bring you back to the UK for an immediate briefing. That's it. If you want to know more, you'll have to come back with us.'

'And if I refuse?'

Rowe shrugged his shoulders. They were huge. The size of wrecking balls. 'That would be unwise.'

'What are you, my careers adviser?'

A sudden dull pressure flared up between Bald's temples, as if someone was pressing their thumbs against the sides of his skull. The migraines had started to come back recently. Bald had been clear of them for a few months after touching down in Mexico, and for a while he'd dared to believe that he was rid of them for good. But in the last few weeks the pressure had started to build up again, a dull throb that reverberated through his head. They hadn't yet transformed into the crippling pains that Bald had experienced in the past.

But it was just a matter of time.

He said, 'I'm not going anywhere. End of.'

'We can't force you to leave,' said Rowe. 'But if you won't get on that plane, we can't guarantee your safety.'

'I'm a big boy. I can look after myself.'

'Like you took care of those two?'

Rowe nodded at the two dead Russians. Blood was leaking out of their exit wounds, red-pooling across the garage floor.

Bald didn't reply.

'You're looking at this the wrong way,' Rowe added. 'This is an opportunity. A second chance. It's not as if you're really crushing it out here, is it?'

Bald still didn't reply. He stared hard at Rowe, imaging various creative ways of rearranging his face.

Lyden said, 'Our source in Russian intelligence said the men sent to slot you were hired toughs. Gangsters, paid upfront in cash. Moscow will be expecting to hear back from them, once they've done the job. And when they don't . . .'

He shrugged. Left the threat hanging in the air.

'You know what the Russians will do,' Rowe said. 'They'll send another team after you. The second team will be better than the first. Professional killers, not gangsters. And the next time, Six won't be able to save you.'

Bald clenched his jaws. Bastards were right. Now that the Russians knew where he was living, they'd keep coming after him until they had put him in the ground. He could relocate again, perhaps. Sell the business, pack his stuff and move to somewhere more remote. Guatemala, maybe. Or Nicaragua. But how long before the Russians caught up with him again?

He knew the answer.

Not very long.

Either you do as Six says and go back home, the voice inside Bald's head told him. Or you take your chances alone. But with the Russians on your case, you won't survive for long. Christ, you'd be lucky to make it to the end of the year without getting dropped.

Wankers at Vauxhall have got me by the balls.

Again.

At the very least he could hear them out. See what they had to say for themselves. If he didn't like the offer on the table, Bald reasoned, he could still walk away. He had no ties to six anymore. And a small part of him was curious to find out more about the briefing. Whatever MI6 had in mind, it had been important enough to send two of its best operators halfway round the world to save his life. Bald had made plenty of enemies during the years he'd worked with Six. He knew their mentality. They wouldn't have lifted a finger to help him unless they had a bloody good reason.

So what do they want with me now?

He cleared his throat. Looked Lyden hard in the eye. 'If I come back,' he said, 'it's only temporary. A one-off.'

Lyden said, 'That's not up to us, mate. You'll have to talk to our boss. Argue your case.'

'I did that last time. Look where it got me.'

'It's a different crowd now. New broom and all that. The new faces might be more sympathetic.'

'I'll need a better guarantee than that.'

'Tough shit,' Rowe said through gritted teeth. 'That's the only one you're going to get.'

Bald shot a look at the guy. There was no point wasting his breath with these two, clearly. They didn't have the authority to cut him a deal. He'd have to take his chances with the higher-ups.

They made a deal with you once before, the voice inside his head told him. Maybe this is a chance to cut a new one. On better terms than before. Maybe even make some money out of it. His retirement fund was empty after that Thai bitch had ripped him off. Could do with being topped up.

'Fuck it,' he said. 'When do we leave?'

'As soon as we're finished here,' Lyden replied. 'We're parked up the street. We'll drive straight to Tulum and take the charter jet. It's all rigged up and ready to fly.'

'What about these two?' Bald waved a hand at the corpses. 'They're a problem. Can't just leave them here.'

Lyden grunted in agreement and said, 'You know this area better than us. Is there somewhere we can dump them? Somewhere they won't be found for a while?'

Bald's eyes wandered over to the back of the garage. To the workshop. He looked past the partly dismantled motorbikes and the tools scattered across the floor, towards the forty-five-gallon drums lined up against the far wall.

'I've got an idea,' he said.

It took all three of them to dispose of the Russians. Dog Tag and Harley were big guys, two hundred pounds apiece of dead muscle and fat. Getting them to fit inside the drums required some creative thinking. First Rowe padded them down, removing their wallets, passports and burner phones. Anything that might identify the bodies. Then Bald and Lyden hauled the bodies over to the workshop, while Rowe manoeuvred the drums into place. The three of them worked fast, in spite of the clammy heat inside the garage. They had a two-hour window before rigor mortis began to set in. They crammed Harley into the first drum in the foetal position, then switched their attention to Dog Tag. The bigger of the two Russians. Getting him into the second drum was hot work. They had to contort his limbs at wildly unnatural angles before they finally got him to fit. They sealed the drums with the clip-top lids and lugged them over to the back of the garage, left them amid the heaps of rusted metal, worn tyres and discarded plastic containers.

Then they turned their attention to the garage. Mopped the blood-pooled floor, wiped down the counter surfaces, getting rid of every last drop of blood and brain matter. Rowe gathered up the bloodied rags and the spent brass, the Russians' IDs and wallets, guns and phones. He broke apart the phones and crushed the SIM cards under the heel of his Timberland boot. Emptied rounds from the guns, stashed everything in a black plastic bag sealed with a cable tie and carried it outside. Dumped it in a storm drain a hundred metres up the street.

At the same time Bald headed up the stairs leading to his modest apartment, built directly above the garage. He ducked into the bedroom and retrieved the black holdall from above the rickety wardrobe: the go-bag Bald always kept packed in case he needed to make a quick getaway. Stowed in the bag were vital supplies, changes of clothes, trainers, wash bag and his passport, along with three thousand dollars in US currency. All that Bald had managed to save during his time in Mexico.

He checked the contents, zipped up the holdall and lugged it back downstairs to the garage. He detoured into his office, sprang open the wall safe and pocketed the two thousand dollars in cash the Russians had paid for their bike tour. Spoils of war.

They took the Russians' luggage from the chase vehicle parked outside the garage, wheeled it up the street and dumped it in an unlit alley north of the storm drain. Returned to the garage, checked over everything one last time. Every trace of the Russians had been removed. If anyone came around asking questions, it would look as if two Latvian males had booked in for a bike tour and simply never showed up.

Bald had one final task to do. One loose end to tie up. He sent a text message to a local number stored on his Alcatel mobile. Twenty seconds later, he got a response. Bald wiped his phone clean with a hard reset, flushed the SIM card down the garage toilet, crushed the device underfoot and tossed the screen-cracked casing in the bin.

Two minutes later, the three Brits left the garage.

It was past six o'clock in the evening when they finally stepped outside. Despite the late hour, the heat was still oppressive. Bald felt the hot breath of Caribbean wind against his cheek, wafting in from the coast, rustling the fronds of the distant palm trees.

He locked the garage up, then followed Lyden and Rowe west for thirty metres until they reached a silver Dodge Journey parked on the side of the road. Lyden took the wheel, Rowe riding shotgun. Bald clambered into the rear seats, wedged his go-bag in the footwell.

They didn't head straight for Tulum airfield. Bald had the loose end to tie up first. Lyden steered the Dodge through the backstreets for several minutes, following Bald's directions, until they reached the address he had given them. A crumbling two-storey house on the outskirts of Playa del Carmen. Metal bars on the windows and doors, gang tags graffiti sprayed on the walls of the neighbouring properties. Weeds poking through the cracks in the pavement. The area of the city that didn't show up in the tour guides.

Hector was standing outside the front door, just as Bald had instructed in his text message. Lyden parked across the street and waited in the Dodge with Rowe while Bald debussed and crossed the road. No reason for the two Blades to accompany him. He wasn't going to make a run for it.

Hector looked at Bald like an obedient dog seeing its owner arrive home. He glanced quizzically at the Dodge before looking back at the Scot. 'Mister John? Is everything okay?'

A note of panic in the kid's voice. Bald flicked him a reassuring smile. 'Everything's fine, mate. Something has come up, that's all. I've got to disappear for a while.'

Hector frowned. 'You're leaving?'

'Aye. I'm gonna need you to take over the business, Hector. Think you can handle it?'

'Me?' Hector's jaw sagged so far it practically thudded against the ground. He stared at Bald in disbelief. 'For real, boss?'

'Some fucker's got to take over,' Bald said. 'Might as well be you, kid.'

'For how long?'

'For good. I won't be coming back.'

Bald fished the master keys out of his pocket and chucked them at Hector. The kid looked at them as if he'd just been given the keys to the Playboy Mansion.

'I'm giving you a head start in life,' said Bald. 'Don't piss it away.'

'*Sí, sí*. I won't, Mister John. Don't you worry. I take good care of everything.'

'Good man.' Bald paused. 'One more thing.'

'*Sí*, Mister John?'

'There's a couple of oil drums at the back of the garage. Them green ones. Whatever you do, don't lift the lids off or let anyone else look inside them. Understood?'

'Why? What's inside?'

'Nothing for you to worry about. Just keep them sealed and find a way to get rid of them. Somewhere no one will find 'em.'

Hector thought for a beat. 'My uncle, Miguel. He owns a pickup truck. I can call him. Take the drums over to the landfill site.'

'Do that,' said Bald. 'Just remember, if anyone takes a peek inside them drums, your business is shafted.'

The kid nodded dutifully. As Bald had known he would. Hector was pathetically loyal. Bald could rely on him to make sure those drums were quietly disposed of.

Hector started to thank him again but Bald was already turning away and pacing back across the road to the Dodge.

He took one last look at the city he'd called home for the past several months. Knew he wouldn't be here again for a long time. Maybe ever. And maybe that wasn't such a bad thing, Bald thought to himself.

The old Jock Bald would have seen the two Russians coming from a mile off. He would have seen straight through their bullshit story and slotted them before they had the opportunity to isolate him.

Instead, Bald had allowed himself to grow soft in his enforced retirement. He'd lost his edge. Slacked off on his training so he could spend more time on the drink, getting his end away with attractive divorcees. He'd started to let himself go.

You got sloppy, the voice in his head warned him. *Almost got yourself killed. Needed a couple of young Blades to bail you out.*

Bald vowed not to make the same mistake again.

He climbed back inside the Dodge.

Two hours later, they were airborne.

EIGHT

The private jet was a Gulfstream 650, one of the newer models. It was quiet and powerful and climbed effortlessly into the air as they headed east out of Tulum. Lyden explained that the aircraft was owned by a recently knighted British businessman who'd made his fortune in chemicals. The businessman was a patriot, Lyden said, and MI6 regularly chartered his private jet via a series of front companies registered in the British Virgin Islands. The Gulfstream was used for renditions mostly, lifting high-value targets from overseas, extracting agents from the field.

Lyden was the talkier of the two. Rowe didn't say a word to Bald the whole flight. He sank into one of the armchairs in the aft cabin, folded his huge arms across his front and looked straight ahead, like he was in a staring competition with the seat opposite. Bald pressed Lyden for more information about the mission but the guy wouldn't say anything except that they were flying in to Gloucestershire Airport in Staverton. A car would be waiting there to ferry Bald to the Regiment's training ground at Pontrilas.

Which got Bald wondering.

Most of the ops he'd worked with Six, the meeting was usually held in a suite at a mid-range London hotel. MI6 agents weren't in the habit of holding briefings in the less glamorous surroundings of the SAS training camp.

Unless they didn't want him to be seen in Hereford. *Maybe that's why they've arranged to meet at Pontrilas*, thought Bald. *So I won't run into any of the lads from 22 SAS. If I'm bottled up in a briefing room at Pontrilas, no other fucker is going to know I'm there.*

He questioned Lyden again, but the guy wouldn't tell him anything more. Bald gave up. Instead he sat back and enjoyed the ride. The interior of the Gulfstream was luxurious, with beige leather seats and soft lighting and polished walnut surfaces. There was a coffee pod machine in the galley and a fridge stocked full of bottles of sparkling water and cans of Diet Coke. On the downside, there was no curvy stewardess for Bald to work his magic on. No booze, either. But it was a step up from the economy-class ticket Six usually laid on for him. Now they were giving him the five-star treatment.

Whatever they've got planned, it's important enough to lay on a private jet.

He passed the time sipping black coffee and watching the news on the 42-inch flat-screen TV. There were about a billion channels to choose from, streamed live through the jet's built-in broadband. Sky News was running a piece about the upcoming G7 summit in Loch Lomond, Scotland. The report said there was a major security operation planned. The American president wasn't a welcome guest in Bald's homeland, apparently. People were marching in the streets, loudly protesting against his imminent arrival.

The president himself didn't seem too bothered. He was planning to spend more time on his nearby golf course than meeting with the other world leaders, the report suggested.

Bald slept through the rest of the flight, and when he looked out of the window again he saw that they were closer to the ground as they made their final approach to Gloucestershire Airport. He saw ploughed fields to the north and south, Cheltenham to the east, Gloucester to the west, the airfield nestled between the towns, like an 'X' scrawled on a treasure map.

They landed at a few minutes past noon, taxied along the main runway and parked on the apron. The engine drone cut out. A minute later the flight steward opened the hatch and Bald followed Lyden and Rowe down the lowered steps.

Lyden led him into the terminal building and said, 'Your driver's waiting outside.'

'You're not coming with us?'

'Got another job to do, mate.' He grinned. 'Not like the old days in the Regiment, when you lot pissed around on training exercises in the desert, roaming around on Pinkies. We're bang it on these days. On the clock twenty-four-seven.'

Bald fought a compulsive urge to wipe the smile off the guy's face. But there was a truth to Lyden's goading, he knew. The Regiment was a different beast now. The new generation of Blades were constantly out doing ops, flying in, getting briefed, slotting targets, clearing the lines. In Iraq, the lads had been doing multiple hits in a single evening, hitting one target, heading on to the next one, barely pausing to catch their breath. A lot had changed since the days Bald had called Hereford home.

He said, 'What's the craic once I get to the camp?'

'The sergeant major will meet you there. He's expecting you. You'll wait with him until the guys from London come up with the ops officer. The other bloke will be waiting at the camp too.'

'What other bloke?'

'The second guy on the team,' Lyden said, without explaining further.

'Who is he?'

'They didn't say. One of the fellas from L Det, I think. Another dinosaur. That's all I know.'

Bald nodded. L Detachment was the reserve unit attached to the Regiment. Veterans, mostly. Guys who had done their time in the SAS and were settled into a part-time role, using their skills whenever they were called upon.

Whoever this other guy is, thought Bald, *he's probably around the same age as me. Someone I would have known during my time at Hereford.*

Lyden said, 'Bet you can't wait to get back to the camp, eh? Mind you, the place has changed a bit since you were last there.' He flashed a pearly white grin. 'When was that again, Jock? Before the war, was it?'

'Piss off.'

'Cheer up. An old fella like you, you should be on cloud nine that Six is still interested in your services.'

'Yeah,' Bald deadpanned. 'Thrilled.'

'What's the deal between you and Six, anyway?'

Bald thought for a beat. 'Let's just say that we haven't always seen eye-to-eye.'

'What's that supposed to mean?'

'The guys at Vauxhall still live in the Dark Ages,' Bald said. 'They think it's about Queen and country, all of that shite. They'll do anything to defend the realm. Even if it means shafting one of their own.'

Lyden shrugged. 'They don't seem that bad to me.'

'Trust me, mate. I've been in this game longer than you. I've seen how them lot work. They're your best friends, right up until the moment everything goes sideways. Then they'll drop you faster than a hot brick.'

'That was then. Things are different now,' Lyden said. 'Times have changed. It's not like the old days any more.'

Bald laughed. 'I may be over the hill but I'm not a fucking idiot. Believe me, nothing ever changes with those twats.'

A battered dark-blue Ford Mondeo was waiting for Bald outside the terminal building. The polar opposite of the Gulfstream, in terms of luxury. He took the front passenger seat and nodded a greeting at the driver: a plain-clothed guy with a slight paunch, greasy crew cut and a humourless expression. The guy didn't introduce himself. Didn't volunteer any information, didn't ask Bald where he was going or why. Bald guessed he was with the MoD police, the blokes in charge of security at Pontrilas.

They drove north for several miles, then headed west towards the Welsh border. Thick clouds the colour of asphalt hung low in the sky, threatening rain. England in March. Grey and gloomy and cold. Mexico, with its sun-kissed beaches, was already beginning to feel like a distant dream.

Twenty minutes later Bald arrived at the training camp.

There were two entrances to the Pontrilas Army Training Area. A country road ran through the middle of the camp, a mile or so north-east of the nearest village, with entrances on opposite sides of the road. Both sides of the camp were protected by an eight-foot-high wire fence topped with razor wire, with a high hedgerow designed to stop outsiders from peeking in.

On the right side of the road was the entrance to the training facility, a wide grassy expanse circling around the base of a densely wooded mound known as Gilbert's Hill Wood. The base had been an ammo dump during the Second World War. Munitions produced at a nearby factory had been housed in reinforced concrete storage bunkers surrounded by high earth embankments, to protect them from aerial bombardment. After the war the surviving bunkers had been converted into stores or briefing rooms. The rest of the training area was a scattershot of ranges where the guys could practise everything from 360-degree shooting to pulling off J-turns and emptying rounds out of a car window. There was even a concrete mock-up of a commercial airliner to rehearse plane hijacking scenarios.

Left of the road was the gated entrance to the main camp, a maze of one- and two-storey buildings: lecture rooms, administration offices, accommodation blocks. Inside the camp the guys learned everything from Jap-slapping on the martial arts courses to interrogation techniques. A pair of rising arm barriers guarded the entrance and exit points, flanked by a cluster of security cameras mounted on tall poles. Armed MoD police and guard dogs patrolled the grounds of the camp. It looked like the world's most heavily guarded industrial estate.

Bald had spent thousands of hours at Pontrilas, practising drills, fine-tuning his skill sets. Turning himself into one of the hardest bastards ever to pass through Hereford.

In his day, he had been a legend in the Regiment. Respected by half the lads, feared by the rest.

But then Bald had gone over to the wild side. The last time he'd walked out of the gates at Pontrilas, he'd imagined himself getting filthy rich. Running his own private military outfit, counting his millions, with his own personal harem.

Somewhere along the way, the plan had gone wrong.

Now I'm coming back without a pot to piss in.

The driver turned left. Heading into the camp, not the training area.

He eased the Mondeo to a halt in front of the barrier. Left the engine running idle while Bald jumped out and made his way over to the guardhouse. A stern-faced duty officer looked up at him.

'Yes?'

'Jock Bald. I'm expected.'

'One moment.'

The duty officer consulted a clipboard. He scrawled through a name, then picked up the secure line and made a call. Letting the camp commandant know he'd arrived, presumably. Then the officer hung up, nodded at Bald.

'In you go,' the officer said. 'Head for the admin building. The sergeant major will meet you there.'

'Roger that.'

Bald hurried back to the Mondeo as the barrier arm lifted. The driver arrowed the Mondeo through the entrance and into the main camp. He made a couple of quick turns and then nudged the motor into a free parking slot in front of a drab concrete building. Bald debussed and nodded again at the driver. A deep and meaningful conversation. The driver pulled away, headed back towards the camp entrance.

A moment later, a figure emerged from the building opposite and marched purposefully over. Hard-looking with a weathered face, decked out in Crye Precision field shirt, boots and trousers. A familiar figure.

The guy was much older than Bald remembered. Late thirties, with a bony, angular face, wrinkled brow and piercing blue eyes.

Steve Vickers smiled and thrust out a hand. 'Jock Bald, Jesus. You're back. Never thought I'd see the day.'

'Me neither.' Bald pumped the guy's hand, noting the gleam of admiration in Vickers's eyes. *At least someone round here still respects me*, he thought to himself.

'Doing well for yourself, Steve,' he added.

Vickers grinned. 'What can I say? I learned from the best. You're a bloody legend round these parts, mate. To some of us, anyway.'

The last time Bald had seen Vickers, the guy had been a fresh-faced Tom who had just passed Selection a few months earlier. Now he was the sergeant major of the training facility for the SAS.

Everyone's on the upward slope, the voice inside Bald's head told him.

Everyone except you.

'When they told us you were coming up I couldn't believe it,' Vickers banged on. 'Christ, there were rumours floating around that you'd been fucking killed.'

'Fake news,' said Bald. 'Everywhere these days.'

'Well, it's good to have you back. Whatever them lot from London want, they couldn't have picked a better man for the job.'

'We'll see about that.'

Vickers looked at him curiously but didn't press Bald for more information. Regiment etiquette. You didn't put another Blade on the spot by greasing them for int on a future op. Vickers was no doubt wondering why Bald had been recalled to Pontrilas at short notice, what the mission was about. But he'd keep any questions he had to himself.

Instead he smiled warmly and said, 'Can I get you anything? I can have the slop jockeys over at the cookhouse rustle something up, if you're hungry?'

'I'm fine.'

'You sure, mate? It's no hassle.'

'Maybe later,' said Bald. 'When's this briefing happening?'

'Two o'clock. I just got off the phone from the ops officer at Hereford. He's on his way over now with the guys from London. Should be here in twenty minutes or so. You can wait in the brew house until then.'

Bald nodded. 'Lead the way, mate.'

They marched towards the building entrance, Vickers fussing over Bald, acting as if the latter was still his old boss, making sure he was looked after.

'I've sorted you out with a room,' he said. 'You're on the second floor of the surveillance block, up the corridor from the briefing room. I've blocked the floor off, so none of the other lads will bother you. It's not exactly the Hilton, but at least you'll have some privacy.'

Bald thought about his grotty digs in Playa del Carmen. He remembered the bare plastered walls, the cockroaches the size of beer bottles. 'It'll be fine, I'm sure.'

'Always happy to help a Regiment legend.' Vickers's face puckered. 'How long has it been since you were last here, Jock? Eight, nine years?'

'Something like that,' Bald muttered. 'What's changed?'

'Not much, actually. There's a new gym. Some new cardio equipment and the like. A new three-sixty shooting range. The rest is pretty much the same as it was in your day. Those two pubs in the village are still open, if you fancy a pint.'

'I might need more than one, after the day I've had.'

Vickers grinned. 'Still on the drink then?'

'I'm Scottish,' said Bald. 'It's in the blood.'

Vickers smiled again and said, 'Before I forget. There's a Scaley coming up for the briefing well.'

'The lads from 264 Signals?' Bald stopped in his tracks and frowned. 'What the fuck do I need to see one of them for?'

'Orders from the head shed. They want the Scaley to bring you up to speed on the latest surveillance and tracking kit. Encryption systems, all of that. One of 'em will be briefing you as soon as you've finished your meeting with the London lot.'

An op involving an over-the-hill ex-Blade and a bloke from L Det, thought Bald. With an emphasis on surveillance. He wondered briefly what the hell Six wanted him for. Then he decided that he really didn't give a toss.

'You'll be wanting some time down on the ranges, I imagine,' Vickers added.

Bald nodded and said, 'An hour or two, aye. Shake off the cobwebs before I get back into the field.'

He knew he was rusty. Every ex-Regiment man sensed that moment when he'd lost his fighting sharpness and Bald hadn't fired a weapon in months. He was like a boxer who'd been out of training for the better part of a year. Mexico had been a warning shot. *Whatever the mission is, I'll need to be sharp as fuck.*

'No problem,' said Vickers. 'Just give us a shout when you're ready and I'll get it sorted with the range wardens. Whatever you want to practise with, longs or pistols. Same goes for the driving range.'

They swept into the building and strode down a dull, draughty corridor until they reached the brew house. Which was basically just a canteen, a quiet place for the guys at the camp to have breakfast or catch a brew between training courses or briefings.

Even after so many years away, the smells and sounds of the place were instantly familiar to Bald.

The closest thing to home he'd ever known.

'Wait in here,' Vickers said. 'I'll come fetch you as soon as the ops officer gets in. Anything else you need in the meantime, just give us a shout. I'll be in my office next door.'

Bald nodded but said nothing. The guy's slavish admiration was beginning to grate. Really, he just wanted Vickers to piss off so he could enjoy a brew in peace. *A few minutes to myself, until those wankers from Six try to get inside my head.* Instead Vickers took a slip of paper from his trouser pocket and handed it to Bald.

'My mobile number,' he said. 'You need anything while you're here, you give me a call and I'll get it sorted. Don't waste your time dealing with any of the other camp muppets.'

Bald folded the paper, pocketed it. 'I'll do that. Thanks, Steve.'

'Any time, fella,' said Vickers. 'Anything for a legend.'

He turned and strode briskly down the corridor. Bald watched him leave for a beat. Then he stepped into the brew house.

There were a few lads sitting at the tables inside, chatting or watching the TV while they sipped mugs of tea and coffee and helped themselves to snacks. None of them looked up or even acknowledged Bald as he stepped inside. The lads would naturally assume he was there for one of the intelligence courses, checked in under an assumed name and with strict orders not to talk to anybody inside the camp. They all knew the deal. They'd leave him well alone.

Which was just the way Bald liked it.

He took another step inside. And froze.

His eyes locked on a figure sitting at the nearest table.

Staring right at him.

The other bloke will be waiting at the camp, Lyden had said. *The second guy on the team.*

He was older than Bald by several years. Early or mid-fifties, with hunched shoulders and shabby dark hair shot through with streaks of grey. He wore a pair of faded jeans, muddied trainers and a flannel shirt, and he was nursing a steaming hot mug in his right hand.

His left hand was flat on the table beside him, Bald noticed. A pair of gnarled stubs where the guy's index and middle fingers had once been.

No, Bald thought. *No fucking way. I know who that is.*

Bald found himself staring at a face he hadn't seen in nine months.

'Hello, Jock,' John Porter said.

NINE

Bald didn't reply. Not at first. He just stood rooted to the spot in the brew house doorway, staring at his old mucker. John Porter, the alcoholic Blade had known for more than twenty years, first in the Regiment and then later on when they had worked for the various private military contractors that carried out MI6's dirty work. The last time they had worked together, Bald had faked his own death. He'd left Porter and his former life behind, determined to start over. Put his past behind him, once and for all.

Bald had never thought he'd see Porter again.

Now I'm standing right in front of him.

He clamped his eyes shut for a long beat. He could feel the migraine coming on again, the pressure steadily building between his temples, tightening like a vice grip around his skull. He popped his eyes open again and made his way over to the table.

'The fuck are you doing here?' he demanded.

'I could ask you the same question,' Porter replied. 'Seeing as you were supposed to have died in Russia.'

He didn't look surprised to see Bald. But he didn't look pleased either. In fact, he looked at Bald with an accusing glare. Judging him. Like the relative of a murder victim, coming face to face with the killer.

Bald didn't care. He had spent his whole life not giving a shit. He wasn't about to change this late in the game. He pulled up a pew opposite Porter, grinned and said, 'Did you have a funeral for me?'

'Fuck off, Jock. You had everyone thinking that you died back there. Me included.'

'What can I say? I'm a genuine Houdini.'

'Lying bastard, more like. When the ops officer called us up and told us you were being ferried over for the briefing, I thought he was taking the piss. Then they told us you'd survived the blast. I couldn't believe it.'

'Were all the lads grieving for me?'

Porter stared hard at him. 'You're not exactly Hereford's favourite son.'

'True.'

Bald cast his mind back to the mission, nine months ago.

Porter and Bald had been working as MI6 assets, sent to Russia to retrieve a rogue British ex-spy. They had ended up foiling a plot by the president's brother to detonate a nuke, but only just. With minutes to spare, Bald had taken the bomb out on a boat to the middle of an isolated lake. His actions had saved thousands of lives and a potential nuclear catastrophe. But when the investigators had picked through the wreckage of the countryside, they had found no sign of Bald. Six assumed that he had been killed in the resulting blast.

At least, that was what Bald had allowed everyone to believe.

'How did you do it?' Porter demanded.

'Lady luck,' said Bald.

Porter was shaking his head furiously. 'Christ, I saw the explosion myself. There's no way anyone should have survived that.'

'I got lucky, mate. That's it.'

'How?'

'I ran the boat back to the jetty after I dumped the nuke over the side. Took one of the vehicles the president's brother had left in his garage. Found the keys to it in the pocket of one of his dead bodyguards. Managed to get myself out of the blast radius, but it was fucking close. I came within a cunt hair of being incinerated.'

'You should have met up with us afterwards, at the RV.' Porter shook his head again, as if he was trying to rustle loose change out of it. 'Like we planned. You could have told Six you were finished with them.'

'Wake up, mate. This is MI6 we're talking about here. Do you really think they would have listened?'

Porter ignored the question. 'So you just decided to go off the grid instead?'

'I had the bullion I'd nicked from the president's brother. Had myself a golden opportunity to start over again, with no bastard from Vauxhall knocking on my door. What would you have done?'

Porter hesitated while he considered. He could see the logic of his mucker's argument, the appeal of jacking it in and starting over. Bald wasn't capable of settling down to a nice, quiet life. He wanted a personal harem, money, status. What he felt the world owed him, after everything he'd sacrificed in the Regiment.

And yet here he was. Back to square one.

'If that was your grand plan,' Porter said, 'why the fuck are you back here?'

Bald briefly told him his hard-luck story about the gold bullion and the Thai fiancée and the Filipino black-market dealer who'd shafted him. He told Porter about the ramshackle motorcycle business he'd been running in Mexico. How the two guys from the Wing had tracked him down and made him an offer he couldn't refuse.

He left out the part about the two Russians who came within a few seconds of plugging him. Not his finest moment. Porter listened in silence, swigging his brew and staring into empty space, lost in thought. When Bald had finished Porter looked over at him and said, 'You should have found some way to tell us you were alive.'

'Couldn't risk it. The moment I reached out to you, I would have had half the blokes from Six kicking down my door.'

Not that it made much difference, Bald thought. *Bastards found me anyway.*

'You had us thinking you'd died a hero,' Porter said. 'You had us thinking that you'd martyred yourself, for fuck's sake.'

'Jesus, if you're that pissed off, I'll buy you a pint. Make it up to you.'

Porter made a face. 'Just the one? I know times are hard, but that's tight even for a sweaty sock like you.'

'Southern pooftah.'

Porter smiled weakly at his old mucker. During their time in the Regiment together they had shared an unshakeable bond, forged in the blood and sweat of a desperate firefight in Sierra Leone. A bond that he thought could never be broken. But it had definitely weakened. There was a distance between them now. Porter could sense a gap opening up between them. He was wary of Bald. The guy had faked his own death, turned his back on his oldest friend. Something that Porter would never do.

He'd endured more than his fair share of problems over the years. There had been the bungled hostage-rescue op in Beirut, a clusterfuck that had led to the death of three Blades, the loss of two of Porter's fingers and ultimately his career in the Regiment. The long years as an outcast, sleeping rough in Pimlico, getting out of his skin on own-brand vodka, living off scraps. He had gone through some dark shit in his life, but he'd never lost his sense of loyalty to the SAS. To his friends.

That's what makes me different from Jock, Porter thought. He's only concerned with himself, loyal to no one but himself. A guy like that is capable of anything.

Bald said, 'I hear you're working with L Det these days.'

Porter nodded and polished off the dregs of his tepid brew. 'The head shed offered us the gig after the Russia op, doing jobs here and there. The rest of the time they've got us doing contract work for various news agencies. Looking after the camera teams, keeping Hereford in the loop.'

Porter didn't say any more. He didn't need to. Bald knew the score. Porter would be working for the likes of CNN and ITN, presenting himself as an independent contractor with a background in SF. Officially he would be providing security arrangements for the news teams, accompanying them whenever they were filming in hostile environments like Syria and Iraq, making sure the crews stayed safe. Unofficially, Porter would pass over any valuable int to the Regiment, keeping them informed of potential terrorist targets, border crossings, land routes, the location of rebel strongholds, favoured meeting points. Anything Hereford might find useful.

'Pays well, does it?' asked Bald.

'Not bad,' Porter replied evasively. 'Between the security work and the L Det retainer, I'm doing all right.'

Which Bald considered an understatement. The security work alone would pay a decent whack. Throw in the salary Porter was on with L Det and the bastard was probably raking it in.

'Good for you,' he muttered. 'Whereabouts are you living now?'

'Just a place in town,' Porter said vaguely. He wasn't sure why, but he didn't want Bald knowing his exact address. 'Put the deposit down last month, in fact. It's not exactly Buckingham Palace and the place needs a bit of maintenance, but it's a decent pad.'

Bald stared at Porter for a moment. *This guy is small-time,* he thought. *A Regiment fuck-up. Kicked out of Hereford and blackballed by the head shed, and yet he's managed to land on his feet.*

'Not bad for a lifelong drunk,' he muttered.

Porter shrugged.

'Speaking of which.' Bald tipped his head at his mucker's mug. 'Is there a slug of whisky in there?'

Porter shook his head slowly. 'I haven't had a drink in months.'

'Bollocks.'

'It's true,' Porter insisted. 'I kicked the bottle after the shit that went down in Russia.'

Bald regarded his friend suspiciously. 'The last time I saw you, you couldn't go a day without a drop of the hard stuff. Now you're telling us you're clean?'

'That was then. I'm a changed man. Got Sandy to thank for it, as it happens.'

'Your daughter?' Bald raised an eyebrow. 'How's that?'

'She found out I was on the drink again. She moved in with us, right after Charlie was born. Her kid. My grandson. I told her she could stay with us for a while, help her get back on her feet, like. I tried to hide the drinking from her, but she knew all my old tricks. One day she caught me in the garage, necking a bottle of vodka from my secret stash. That was it, Sandy said. She'd lost me once to the drink and wouldn't let her kid go through the same experience. Told me that she'd rather Charlie grew up without a grandad than some sad old alcoholic. That was the reality check I needed, mate. I gave up the booze on the spot.'

'You've not touched a drop? Not even a crafty pint?'

Porter shook his head proudly. 'Not saying that it's been easy. Christ knows, there are days when I feel like slipping. But you know what they say. One day at a time.'

Bald looked at Porter in disbelief. But even as he searched the guy's face he could see that his mucker was telling the truth. He didn't look like a heavy drinker. His face looked leaner and less puffy than Bald remembered. His hands weren't trembling. His eyes were no longer bloodshot.

Fuck me, he thought. *Porter really has cleaned up his act.*

The guy has got a house, a secure job, a family.

And I've got nothing.

Bald had always taken pride in his survival instincts. His ability to adapt. Other guys had left the Regiment as broken men, struggling with their demons. But not Bald. He'd always managed to get by, relying on his natural cunning.

Now I'm the one in the gutter, he thought. *Even this sad fucker is doing better than me.*

He could feel his rage increasing by the minute.

'What about this op?' he asked, changing the subject. 'Any idea what this is about?'

'Your guess is as good as mine,' Porter said. 'They haven't told us anything except to be here for this briefing. You know how secretive them lot are at Vauxhall.'

'Yeah, well. Whatever it is, there'd better be something in it for us. I'm not working for those tossers for free.'

'What makes you think Six would give you anything?'

'They went to a lot of trouble to bring me here,' Bald replied. 'Which means whatever they've got lined up for us, it must be urgent. That gives me leverage over them.'

'If you say so, mate.'

Bald shot a look at Porter. 'What are you saying?'

'You trusted Six once before and look where it got you. Why do you think it would be any different this time? Especially after what you've done.'

'I'm a free agent,' Bald said. 'No ties, mate. I don't work for Six any more. They can't make me do a fucking thing. If I don't like what they're offering, I'll walk away.'

He got up and fixed himself a brew. Coffee, black, no sugar. They passed the time with small talk. Hereford gossip. What the other old faces from the Regiment were up to, guys who had gone on to work in the Circuit or were running their own companies, others who had retired to Vietnam or the Philippines. Porter was friendly enough, but Bald sensed a distance opening up between them. Porter had his guard up. *He doesn't trust me*, Bald thought.

Twelve minutes later, Vickers swept inside the meeting room and marched over to their table. 'They're ready for now you, lads,' he announced. 'Follow me.'

Bald set down his mug. Porter necked the dregs of his tea and stood up. They followed the sergeant major out of the brew house and across the training camp, passing several low-level buildings until they reached a plain two-storey structure set back from the main gate. Bald recognised it as the surveillance block.

From the outside it looked like a dull office, but a lot of dark shit went on inside those four walls, Bald knew. A lot of secret meetings and shady ops. The kind no one ever discussed outside of Hereford.

Vickers ushered the two of them through the entrance. They quick-walked down a long corridor and climbed one flight of stairs, before Vickers stopped outside a solid-looking door. He knocked twice, levered the handle and stepped aside, gesturing for the others to enter.

Porter trudged into the room first. Bald lingered in the doorway, feeling like he was on the edge of a precipice. About to leap off and plunge into the unknown.

Then he stepped inside.

TEN

He entered a windowless, sparsely furnished briefing room. Bald had spent time in hundreds of such rooms over the past twenty years. Fluorescent panel lights, dull-coloured walls, industrial carpet. There was a whiteboard at one end of the room, a flat-screen TV fixed to the far wall with a laptop rigged up to it. A large table dominated the space in the middle, with a couple of secure landline phones.

Two figures sat on the chairs at the far end of the table. A man and a woman.

Bald recognised the man immediately. David Moorcroft, their former handler at MI6. The last time Bald had seen Moorcroft he'd been a senior intelligence officer with the General Support Branch: the secretive department at Vauxhall that carried out black ops, using current and former Regiment men to provide the muscle in the field.

Moorcroft wore his age badly. The lines on his face were deeper, the crow's feet more pronounced now. His white hair was thin and wiry, like steel wool. He looked every one of his sixty-plus years. But there was a determined glint in his eye that Bald hadn't seen before. He had the look of a man who had just been given the all-clear after a cancer scare. The veteran spy was still immaculately dressed in his Savile Row sharkskin suit, grey silk tie and brilliant white pocket square. A pair of bright yellow socks, decorated with Martini glasses, were visible beneath the hemline of his trousers, the one nod to his unconventional personality.

Bald hadn't seen the woman before. She was younger than Moorcroft – much younger. Late thirties, he reckoned. She had a no-nonsense manner about her. She was dressed in a black trouser suit and light-blue shirt, with a tan-leather cross-body bag resting on the floor beside her chair. Her hair was cut short, her face slender and angular, her green eyes fixed on her phone. She was puffing on some kind of long pen-shaped device that Bald guessed was an electronic cigarette. Her right foot tapped impatiently up and down on the rough carpet, he noticed. She had a busy, restless energy about her. The kind of person who checked their emails every five minutes on holiday. Someone who never switched off. Who probably didn't know how to.

At the sight of the two Blades trooping into the room Moorcroft rose from his chair. The woman stayed seated, continuing to tap away on her phone, hurriedly typing a message. Moorcroft smiled wanly at Bald and Porter and gestured to the empty chairs.

'Guys, thank you for joining us. Sit down, please.'

They took up a couple of seats at the table. Moorcroft locked eyes with Bald. The smile on his face crumbled.

'Jock. I must say it's a privilege to see you here today,' he said, his voice dripping with condescension. 'I've always wondered what a ghost must look like.'

Bald stared back at the veteran spy, controlling his anger.

'You very nearly had us fooled back there,' Moorcroft added. 'There were plenty of us over at Vauxhall mourning the death of one of Scotland's finest sons. Didn't take us long to figure out what had happened to you, of course. A polite suggestion. Next time, try hiding somewhere rather more remote than the Mexican coast.'

'What are you doing here?' Bald growled. 'Last time we met, you said you were up for retirement.'

'Postponed, old fruit.' Moorcroft attempted to resurrect the smile. It was a half-hearted effort. 'The demands of the service.'

'Meaning what?'

'We've had a change of direction after this Swindon business. Downing Street has finally woken up to the threat from the East. Old Russia hands like me are suddenly back in fashion. Our funding has been increased. Specifically, the Moscow desk. The powers that be have asked me to stay on for a while. I agreed, for my sins. I'm afraid the dream of retiring to the Cotswolds has been put on hold for the time being. My wife didn't take the news too well, as you might imagine.'

'Tragic.'

Despite his attempt to look disappointed, there was a smugness in Moorcroft's voice. Nine months ago the guy had been on the way out, part of the old guard being cast aside in favour of a younger, hungrier generation of spies. Now Moorcroft found himself front and centre of the action again. Which was right where the guy wanted to be, Bald thought. Moorcroft was a lifelong spy, the type who died on the job. The retirement cottage in the Cotswolds wouldn't hold the same thrill, however hard his wife tried to argue otherwise.

'Of course,' he said, looking hard at Bald, 'national duty is a concept quite alien to you.'

Bald stared at the spy with flat eyes. 'Did you invite us here just to tell us about the sad state of your marriage, or are you going to tell us what the fuck is going on?'

'In due course.' Moorcroft sat down and gestured to the woman at his left. 'First, allow me to introduce my colleague, Madeleine Strickland. Madeleine is working with me at General Support. She'll be your point of contact during this operation.'

Strickland finished tapping on her phone, thumbed it to sleep and slipped it into the front pocket of her leather bag. Bald realised he was looking at Moorcroft's new number two. Strickland smiled politely at him. Not cold, but not exactly friendly either.

'No need to introduce yourselves,' Strickland announced, raising a hand. 'I've read your files. Both of you.'

She spoke with a broad Scottish accent, although it wasn't as strong or as rough around the edges as Bald's Dundee brogue. Clearly Strickland had worked hard to tone it down for the benefit of her well-spoken English colleagues.

'Let me guess,' Bald said. 'Glasgow?'

Strickland smiled. 'Maryhill,' she said.

'Rangers or Celtic?'

'Neither,' Strickland replied. 'Partick Thistle.'

She smiled again. A proud Scotswoman. Probably a good drinker, too. Bald liked her already. 'What did you make of our files?' he asked with a grin.

Strickland shifted on her chair. 'There were some interesting notes. Particularly in your case.'

Porter said, 'What happened to Tannon?'

Bald glanced quickly at his mucker as he recalled their last mission together. Back then, Dominique Tannon had been their contact at the GSU. The brightest prospect in the department at the time. Porter and Tannon had been close, Bald knew; closer than Porter had ever let on. Bald had suspected there had been something between them, although Porter had always rigorously denied it.

'She didn't work out for us,' Moorcroft replied brusquely. 'You'll be dealing with Maddy from now on. Unless that's a problem?'

As he spoke Bald noticed the smug expression on Moorcroft's face. The veteran agent had been on the cusp of losing his job to Tannon, Bald recalled. Now she was out of the picture, and he wondered how sorry Moorcroft was to see her go. He also wondered how much Moorcroft might have had to do with it.

He might play the role of the good old Etonian, thought Bald, *but Moorcroft is as crafty as any of those bastards at Six. No wonder the bloke has got some of his old spirit back.*

Moorcroft crossed his legs. 'Now that we've all been introduced, guys . . .'

He nodded at Strickland and gave her a paternal smile, giving her the floor. All eyes turned towards the younger agent.

Strickland cleared her throat, her foot still tapping rapidly against the worn carpet. 'Tell me,' she began. 'How much do you know about Derek Lansbury?'

Porter and Bald looked briefly at one another. 'The politician?' Bald asked with raised eyebrows. 'The one who's always on TV smoking fags and sipping pints of bitter?'

'Yes. Him.'

'Not much,' Bald said. 'Just the bare bones. He was one of them blokes campaigning against the EU a couple of years back. Good mates with the Yank president. On Twitter a lot.'

Moorcroft smiled thinly. 'Once again, Jock, your breadth and depth of knowledge continues to astound.'

'I'm a soldier. I don't really give a shit about politics. That's best left to you and the other greasy-pole monkeys in Whitehall.'

Strickland said, 'Derek Lansbury isn't just a politician. He's much bigger than that. He's the leading voice of populism in the

West today. Perhaps the most influential voice on the right-wing in a generation.'

'Not bad for a chap who once ended up in detention for calling his geography teacher a nig-nog,' Moorcroft added.

'You know the bloke?' asked Porter.

'Vaguely. He was in the year above me at Charterhouse. Derek was a bloody nuisance even then, as I recall. Not exactly what you'd call a star pupil. He was always protesting about something or other, handing out Young Tory leaflets at lunch. A good fly-half, mind you. And a fine public speaker. He became school prefect after promising everyone free sweets at the tuck shop. Chap has come a long way since then.'

'Clearly.'

Strickland said, 'After Charterhouse, Lansbury read PPE at Brasenose College and then took a job at the *Daily Telegraph*, reporting on the weekly goings-on at Brussels. He left three years later to become a speech-writer for the eccentric anti-federalist, Michael Sidebottom. Lansbury adopted many of Sidebottom's core ideas and principles, subsequently took over the party and rebranded it as the British Independence Movement.' She hesitated. 'I'm going to go out on a limb here and assume you've both heard of it.'

'Aye, we have,' Bald said. 'That's the one with the logo of a ship with a Union Jack flag flying from it.'

Strickland said, 'Lansbury has spent the last twenty years of his life waging a one-man war against the European Union, railing against the Establishment and denouncing Brussels on his weekly podcast and YouTube channel.'

'No one else took Derek seriously, of course,' Moorcroft added. 'From what we can gather, he was something of an embarrassment to his political colleagues. One of those fringe politicians, pandering to the worst instincts of the electorate. This was before the referendum.'

'Which is when everything changed for Lansbury,' Strickland said. 'Overnight he went from being a virtual unknown to one of the most recognisable figures in politics, rubbing shoulders with the American president and posing for selfies with Eastern European strongmen.'

'And cashing in on it, I bet,' Bald grumbled.

Strickland nodded. 'Since the referendum, Lansbury has been quick to position himself as the de facto head of the populists, campaigning on behalf of his chums, lighting up Twitter with inflammatory statements. He's even got himself a gig on American radio, hosting his own talk show. Quite an achievement for a man who almost got himself expelled from school. Whatever you think of his political views.'

Porter said, 'What has any of this got to do with us?'

Strickland didn't reply. She looked towards Moorcroft, as if seeking permission. He nodded.

'We have reason to believe that Derek Lansbury is working for the Kremlin,' Strickland said. 'And you're going to help us bring him down.'

ELEVEN

No one said anything for a cold, long beat. Bald looked from Strickland to Moorcroft, waiting for one of them to continue. Strickland looked towards the old Etonian, deferring to her superior. Moorcroft uncrossed his legs and said, 'We've long known that Lansbury has Russian sympathies, of course. It's no great secret that many of Europe's populists and strongmen admire the Russian president and his particular way of doing business.'

Porter rubbed his stubbled jaw, deep in thought. 'I thought all them Tory types hated the Russians?'

'That was true in the bad old days of the Soviet Union. Thatcher, Reagan and all that. But times have changed, old bean. Dramatically so. The populists and Moscow suddenly find themselves on the same side of the political fence, so to speak. Both of them despise the liberal consensus of the West. Both want to see the break-up of the various major post-war institutions, for different reasons. And they have both been extremely successful at challenging the status quo, portraying themselves as defenders of a white cultural tradition raging against a morally corrupt liberal elite.'

'Lansbury has been more successful than most,' Strickland added. 'He's not exactly shy about his pro-Russia stance, either. He's a frequent contributor to Russian state television, peddles the Moscow party line on his YouTube show and through social media.'

Moorcroft cleared his throat. 'Obviously, there have been rumours floating around about Lansbury's involvement with the Russians. Unfounded speculation, mostly. Idle tittle-tattle. Worthy of the gossip columns, but nothing that ever pointed to a definitive link between Lansbury and Moscow. But then our source at the FSB reached out to us.'

Bald nodded. The FSB. Russia's Federal Security Service and the successor to the old KGB. 'You've got a source inside the Kremlin?'

'Indeed.' Moorcroft smiled thinly at Bald. 'The same source that told us about the threat to your life, Jock.'

Porter flashed a quizzical glance at his mucker. Bald blanked him and stared straight ahead, arms folded, as Moorcroft went on.

'Our source had heard a rumour that someone at the FSB was running Lansbury as an asset. Nothing they could substantiate, unfortunately. But our source is dependable. We took it seriously enough to start running surveillance on Lansbury.'

'What did you find?'

'At first, not much. Lansbury is a shrewd operator, despite his bumbling Lord-of-the-Manor shtick. We uncovered some mildly embarrassing personal revelations, porn habits, some quasi-illegal tax stuff. A few boozy lunches with some unscrupulous individuals. But nothing scandalous. Nothing to tie him directly to the Kremlin. Until three weeks ago.'

Bald said, 'What happened three weeks ago?'

Strickland said, 'We had one of our assets watching Lansbury on his annual holiday in the Maldives. Two days later, our asset reported seeing a high-ranking FSB agent on the same island, at the exact same resort.'

'Sounds like too much of a coincidence, that,' Porter said.

'That's our assessment, too. People don't randomly bump into one another in exclusive five-star resorts in the Indian Ocean. Especially not agents on FSB salaries.'

Moorcroft cleared his throat and said, 'Our assets have reported Lansbury meeting with two other known FSB agents in the past two weeks. That makes three meetings with Russian officials, in less than a month.'

'Why is Lansbury meeting with the Russian security services?' Porter wondered aloud.

'We're not sure. Our agents couldn't get close enough to hear what they were discussing, unfortunately. But we think it might have something to do with Lansbury arriving in Budapest.'

That drew a puzzled look from Porter. 'What's he doing there?'

'Officially, Lansbury is in Hungary to support the re-election campaign of his good friend, Prime Minister Márton Fodor.' Moorcroft shot a quick look at Strickland before he went on. 'But unofficially, we think he's there to broker some sort of meeting.'

'Who with?'

'Fellow populists,' Moorcroft said. 'Fascists. Far-right extremists. Anyone who's anyone on the emerging right wing in Europe. Every major figure and leader of a populist or nationalist group is going to be at this meeting.'

'Which is about all we know,' Strickland interjected. 'Lansbury and the other attendees are keeping it very secretive. No press, no publicity. Nothing on social media. We don't know why they're meeting in Budapest. We don't even know where the meeting is being held. This thing is so clandestine it makes the Bilderberg conferences look like an office Christmas party.'

Bald frowned heavily. 'If this shindig is a big secret, how come you lot have heard about it?'

'Lansbury has been travelling extensively around Europe for the past two weeks, meeting with various populist allies and strongmen. We've got assets in those other countries, watching them for us. Looking to see if there's some sort of connection between his meetings, or a pattern to his movements.'

'What did you find?'

'Something really weird. Every single person Lansbury has met with has cancelled their appointments and told their staff that they are taking an unplanned holiday, for the same three-day period. All of them are heading to Budapest. All of them are due to arrive the day after tomorrow. We think they're assembling for the meeting.'

'Who else is going to be at this thing?' asked Porter.

'All the major players on the far right, as far as we can tell. Roberto Zanetti, the Italian Minister for European Affairs. Henri Marveaux, from the French People's Front. Fodor, the Hungarian strongman. German neo-Nazis. Polster, the Austrian Vice-Chancellor. Not to mention the usual suspects from Eastern Europe and Greece,' Strickland added. 'This thing is like the far right's version of the G7.'

Moorcroft said, 'Populists have these get-togethers all the time, but they don't hold them with anything like this degree of secrecy.

Usually you can't keep those fellows away from promoting their every waking movement on social media.'

'And we have no fucking clue what's happening at this thing?' asked Bald.

'Not really,' Strickland conceded. 'Our best guess is that Lansbury is trying to fix a deal with the other populists.'

'What kind of deal?'

'We're not sure. They might be planning on forming a new underground alliance. Or maybe they're plotting campaign tactics. But whatever Lansbury is up to, we think he must be doing it on behalf of the Russians. That would explain the pattern. First the meetings with the FSB agents. Then the big conference with the far-right groups.'

Porter nodded slowly. 'It points to something. I just can't see what.'

'Might be a honey-trap situation,' said Bald. 'Maybe Lansbury is luring his mates out to this meeting so his Kremlin friends can bring the stinkers in. Get them populists caught shagging some Russian redhead and use it to blackmail them.'

Moorcroft cocked an eye at Bald. 'Is that a theory of yours, or a private fantasy?'

'Just saying. It's a possibility. You've got a bunch of horny old farts having some private get-together, and Lansbury's dodgy Russian connections. The Russians can't resist a bit of bribery and blackmail, can they?'

Strickland said, 'We've thought about that. But it's unlikely. The truth is, these individuals are already on the same side as the Russians. Their election campaigns have been financed by Russian money. They've had troll factories in St Petersburg working on their behalf, spreading fake news. They're in Russia's pocket, whether they publicly admit it or not.'

Moorcroft nodded at Strickland and sat forward, folding his hands in front of him.

'What Maddy is saying is that right now, we simply can't be sure what Lansbury is up to in Budapest. It might be something big. But it might also be nothing at all.'

'But you don't think it's nothing,' Porter countered. 'Otherwise you wouldn't have called us here.'

Moorcroft nodded again. 'Lansbury is a potential Russian agent, running around Europe, setting up clandestine meetings. Whatever it is he's planning, we think it must be big. We need to get eyes on him, guys. Which is where you two come in.'

He paused for a beat. Looked Bald and Porter hard in the eye.

'You're going to get on Derek Lansbury's bodyguard team. You'll earn his trust and accompany him to this meeting, and wherever else he goes for the next several months. Then you're going to gather enough evidence to put him away for the rest of his life.'

The room was silent for several moments. Porter and Bald stared at the two spies, frowning heavily, heads tilted, like a couple of posers at a gallery, interpreting a piece of postmodernist art.

'This is a long-term assignment,' Moorcroft explained. 'We expect you'll be working close-protection for Lansbury for the foreseeable future. We'll need evidence of his collusion with Russia, the names of people he's dealt with, conversations he's had, payments made. The works.'

'Let me get this straight. You want us to get on Lansbury's team, so we can gather all this stuff for you and your Vauxhall pals?' Bald asked.

'Precisely.'

'Why not just lift the fucker? Put him in a cell in Vauxhall, slap some plastic cable ties around his bollocks and get him to spill his guts?'

'Won't work,' Strickland said. 'For two reasons. One, Lansbury would simply deny everything. All we have right now is some second-hand intelligence from a foreign asset, and three suspected meetings with Russian FSB agents. Neither of which would stand up in a criminal prosecution. If we snatch Lansbury now, we'd spook him. Put him on high alert. All we'd be doing is sending him deeper underground.'

'What's the second reason?'

'Arresting Lansbury would flag up to the Russians that we're on to their man. Whatever he's planning, the FSB would presumably abort the mission and cover their tracks. It's self-defeating.'

'Not to mention politically toxic,' Moorcroft put in. 'The moment we place Lansbury under formal arrest, the conspiracy theorists are going to go into overdrive. Lansbury's supporters in the US and Europe will come to his defence, accusing us of a witch-hunt. Which is why we have to build the case against him first. If we're going to bring him down, this thing has to be absolutely rock solid. We don't want to arrest him just because he's confessed to murder, so to speak. We want to catch him on the doorstep of his intended victim, with a gun in his hand.'

The veteran spy leaned back in his chair, folded his hands behind his head, a fiery glint in his eye. 'Rather a good plan, don't you think?'

'Aye,' Bald replied. 'With one great big fucking hole in it.'

'What's that?'

'I'm guessing that a man who gets as many death threats as Lansbury already has his own close-protection team.'

Strickland nodded. 'Ex-Special Branch. Two of them.'

'And they've probably been doing it for a while.'

'Two years, to be precise.'

'So why would Lansbury suddenly ditch his trusted BG team and go with a couple of randoms?'

'We've thought about that.' Moorcroft smiled broadly. His eyes were twinkling with excitement, Bald noticed. The guy was in his fucking element.

Moorcroft looked across the room at the clock mounted on the far wall, eyes narrowed calculatingly. He said, 'Eight hours from now, Derek Lansbury's bodyguards are going to have an unfortunate accident. One that will keep them out of action for several weeks. Which means that there will be a couple of short-term openings on Lansbury's team. Derek will be desperate to replace them, especially if he's busy organising a secret meeting with his populist chums.'

Bald said, 'What kind of accident?'

'That's none of your business, old bean. All you need to know is, Lansbury's current team is going to be out of the picture. It's taken care of.'

Porter shook his head, puzzled by something. 'That doesn't solve the problem, though.'

Moorcroft's bushy eyebrows came together. 'How do you mean?'

'Once Lansbury's bodyguards have been knocked on the head, how are you gonna make sure he chooses us? I'm guessing loads of other lads will be putting themselves forward for the gig.'

'We've already thought of that,' Strickland said. 'Lansbury has a close friend in the House of Lords. Lord McGinn. Former army officer, Chief of the General Staff under the last PM and a long-time ally of Lansbury. He's going to call Derek after the attacks on his bodyguards have gone public and recommend you two for the position.'

'He's agreed to help?'

'He doesn't have a choice.' Moorcroft smiled. 'McGinn is already in our pocket. If he fails to cooperate, we'll release the pictures we have of him at a brothel in Leeds, dressed head-to-toe in BDSM gear. Pictures his wife and sixteen-year-old daughter would love to see, I'm sure.'

Bald puffed out his cheeks. 'Fuck me, is there anyone you lot don't have dirt on?'

Moorcroft merely shrugged.

'What if Lansbury ignores his mate's advice?' asked Porter.

'He won't,' Strickland replied confidently. 'He and McGinn are tight. McGinn has been active on the anti-EU scene for several years. They're both members of the Oriental Club, both big rugby fans. Lansbury will trust whatever he says.'

'Anyway,' Moorcroft added, 'there won't be any time for Lansbury to consider other applicants. He's going to need some-one in place as soon as possible, especially if he's up to no good in Budapest.'

Porter said, 'Let's assume this all goes as planned.'

'That's a big fucking if,' Bald muttered.

Strickland shot a glance at him before Porter continued. 'What happens once we land the job?'

Moorcroft said, 'As soon as you've been hired, you'll get on the next flight to Budapest and rendezvous with Lansbury at the Royal Duna Hotel. Maddy will give you the details, won't you, dear?'

He glanced at Strickland and smiled condescendingly. Moorcroft was throwing his weight around, letting everyone in the room know who was calling the shots. Strickland quickly masked her irritation and looked towards Bald and Porter.

'We'll need you to plant listening devices in each and every room Lansbury is staying in,' she said. 'Wherever he goes, you need to bug it. He travels frequently, so there's going to be a lot of planting and hiding of devices. We understand that his existing BG team conducts regular sweeps of his rooms, especially before meetings, so we'll equip you with fake bug detection kits to get around that.'

Which made sense, Bald thought. Bodyguard teams for high-value targets regularly swept down rooms for bugs. Part of the job description. Bald and Porter would be expected to check every room Lansbury slept in or conducted business in.

'What if he meets with someone who insists on doing their own sweep of the room?' asked Porter.

'In that case, we'll warn you in advance and turn off the devices remotely. We can do that from Vauxhall, with the flick of a switch. If the devices are turned off, they won't show up on any electronic sweep.'

Moorcroft noted the uneasy look on the faces of Bald and Porter and smiled reassuringly.

'The surveillance guys will brief you immediately after this meeting. They've got some fascinating technology that will make this all very easy to do. Far beyond my understanding, I'm afraid.'

'No surprises there,' Bald replied drily. 'This stuff wasn't around in the 1800s.'

Porter ignored his mucker and said, 'How long will me and Jock be doing this job for?'

'As long as it takes,' Strickland responded. 'But we expect your assignment to last for six months. Minimum. We'll need that long to gather enough evidence to build a watertight case against Lansbury.'

'His bodyguards won't take that long to recover from whatever injuries they have,' Bald pointed out. 'What happens if he wants to hire them again?'

'You'll have to win him over. Earn his trust. Get him on your side so he forgets about the other two bodyguards.'

'Lansbury is a populist,' Moorcroft emphasised. 'They're a thin-skinned bunch. The best way to gain their confidence is often to indulge in a spot of old-fashioned arse-kissing. Make yourself the flavour of the month.'

Bald stared at Moorcroft, lips curled up in disgust. 'You want us to blow smoke up the arse of some right-wing nutjob?'

'We're not asking you to have an intellectual conversation with the man, for Chrissakes. You just need to give him a few compliments, so he takes a shine to you. Tell him how much you enjoyed his views on the burqa, that kind of thing.'

'Bloody hell. This just gets better and better.'

Porter was grinning. 'Cheer up, Jock. You're passing yourself off as a racist, far-right bigot. Shouldn't be too hard for you.'

'Fucking do one.'

Strickland looked at them both for a moment. 'It's important to earn Lansbury's trust. We're going to need you both on this thing for the long term. The more data you can harvest, the better our chances of bringing him to justice.'

'What about backup?' Porter asked.

'We'll provide you with as much support as possible, within limits. That means utilising local assets, as and when we need them: additional surveillance teams, drivers, making supply runs. Whatever you need, we'll be able to engage local assets to help out. At the same time, we'll check in regularly with our sources. If there is a genuine threat to Lansbury, you'll be the first to know about it.'

'We'd fucking better,' Bald muttered. 'Because if someone does take a pop at that twat, I ain't taking a bullet for him.'

'It won't come to that.'

'What if we need to make a fast exit?' asked Porter.

'You'll be given instructions for a ratline run,' Strickland said. 'Our assets have got ways of smuggling you across the border while avoiding manned checkpoints. If for some reason you can't make it out of the country by land, we'll have a Dauphin helicopter on standby across the border in Austria, at a military base a few miles outside of Graz. The Dauphin can be anywhere inside Hungary within the hour.'

Bald grunted. 'That's supposed to make us feel better?'

'Cheer up, guys.' Moorcroft flashed them a matey smile. 'This is a straightforward gig. Low-risk, minimal chances of contact. Most of the time you'll be standing about looking hard or escorting the principal around town. Even you two should be able to handle that particular challenge.'

Porter cocked his head at Moorcroft. 'Why us?'

'Because you two fit the bill. You're ex-Regiment men, guns for hire, looking for steady work and available immediately. And you won't arouse any suspicion with the target. If we had gone with a pair of full-time SAS men, it would look strange to Lansbury. He might wonder why they had forfeited a generous pension to join his bodyguard detail.'

'And it's easier for you to wipe your hands clean if me and Porter here get rumbled,' Bald growled.

'Why you're here is none of your business,' Moorcroft snapped. 'We called you both here to discuss the operation. That's what you're here for: to provide the muscle. Now you'll do the job as directed or we'll find someone else who will. Is that clear?'

'Aye,' Bald muttered. 'We get it.'

'Good.'

Moorcroft fixed his gaze on Bald for a moment, as if emphasising his point. Then he relaxed his expression and eased back in his chair, smoothing out a crease on his trouser leg. 'Right, I think we've covered the basics. Maddy will run through the specifics with you. Unless you have any questions?'

'I have one,' Bald said.

A thin smile spread across Moorcroft's lips. 'Yes, Jock?'

'What's in it for me?'

The veteran spy laughed cruelly. 'We just saved your life, old bean. That's all the reward you're going to get. Unless you'd prefer us to stick you on the next flight to Moscow?'

Bald snorted and shook his head. 'I'm in a different situation from Porter. You've got no authority over me. If I'm gonna do this, I want something in return.'

Moorcroft did a double take. 'You must be joking. Who the hell do you think you are, making demands of the British Government?'

'I'm a bloke you need, with fuck-all to lose.'

'You should be doing this out of duty, for Christ's sake.'

'Yeah. Tried that once. Didn't work for me.'

Moorcroft screwed up his face and regarded Bald as if the latter was something he'd trodden on in the street. Strickland sat upright, brushed a stray strand of hair behind her ear and smiled sympathetically at Bald. He had the sense that Strickland was on his side, in a way that Moorcroft was not and never had been. Maybe it was a Scottish thing, Bald thought. Or maybe the relationship between Strickland and her boss was more complicated than he had assumed.

'We can't offer you money,' she said. 'It's simply not in our gift . . . not after everything you've done. But perhaps we can offer you something else. A job with L Detachment, perhaps?'

'Work for the Regiment again? You must be fucking joking.'

'Why not? You're clearly good at what you do. A man in your position, you should be desperate to get back into the service.'

Bald shook his head. 'I've done my time. That's all behind me now. Anyway, we had an agreement after the last job. You lot agreed to leave me the fuck alone.'

'That was before you decided to cut and run with a million in stolen gold.' Moorcroft smiled wickedly. 'Besides, if we *had* honoured that agreement, you'd be dead by now. All things considered, we did you a favour.'

'I'll send you a thank-you card in the post.'

'This deal is better than nothing,' Strickland said. 'You can see that, right?'

'I want a better one,' said Bald. 'I need something steady in my life, but I ain't going back into the Regiment.'

'What, then?' Moorcroft threw up his hands.

'I know you've got your fingers in all them big oil companies. I want a job in security with one of 'em, I don't give a toss which one. Something that pays well, with a tidy pension and full insurance. Some management position in health and safety, preferably.'

Moorcroft cocked his head at Bald, drummed his fingers on the table. He glanced over at Strickland, as if seeking her approval. She nodded at him. He turned back to Bald, stopped piano-playing the table and sighed.

'Very well. I'm sure we can come to an arrangement.'

'Glad to hear it,' Bald said.

'On one condition.'

'Aye?'

Moorcroft leaned forward. 'You do this job properly. You make sure that we get everything we need on Lansbury to bring him down. If there's insufficient evidence at the end of your operation, then the deal is off. Think you can manage that?'

'I'll do my best.'

Moorcroft stared at Bald for a moment. Gave him a look so cold you could have played ice hockey on it.

'You need to do better than that,' he added. 'Because if you fuck this one up, I'll make sure that you pay for the crimes you've committed over the years. Every single one of them. I'll bury you, if it's the last thing I do before I leave Six.'

TWELVE

Moorcroft left the briefing room a short while later. He explained that Strickland would be staying on at Pontrilas for the next twenty-four hours, to oversee the operation to install Bald and Porter on the bodyguard team. The three of them would remain in the camp, monitoring the situation with Lansbury's body-guards, reacting to events on the ground as they happened. The look on Strickland's face suggested she wasn't happy about stay-ing on. Perhaps she resented having to carry out a task that would normally be left to a junior liaison officer, thought Bald. She probably felt she had more important things to do than sit around in a cramped room with a pair of veteran operators.

Thirty seconds after Moorcroft had departed, the guy from 264 Signals showed up. Strickland made her excuses and left the room to get settled into her accommodation, leaving Bald and Porter to be briefed by the Scaley. A neatly presented guy with short dark hair and a finely-stubbled jaw who introduced himself as Sergeant Corey Hogan. He didn't look much like a computer whizz, but Bald knew the type. Scaleys were all the same, in his opinion: tech fanatics who spent most of their lives in front of computer screens, geeks trapped in the bodies of soldiers.

Bald and Porter looked on as Sergeant Hogan laid out a series of items on the table in front of them. An iPad Mini and a pair of iPhones, several wiretap devices and a bug sweeper. Plus a shiny black clip-like device the size of a thumb drive.

Porter puffed out his cheeks. 'That's a lot of bloody kit to run through.'

Hogan grinned and said, 'This is all new equipment, lads. Cutting-edge stuff. You're lucky to have the chance to use it in the field.'

The Scaley had a dull, monotone voice that belonged in a secondary-school physics laboratory.

Fuck me, Bald thought. *Half an hour with this bloke is going to put us both to sleep.*

'Yeah,' he grumbled. 'Can't wait.'

Hogan pointed to the thumb drive first. He took one look at the two grizzled men in front of him and said, 'I'm assuming neither of you lads has seen one of these before?'

'Don't get cheeky with us, mate,' said Bald. 'Just tell us how the fucking gizmo works.' He smiled but there was an edge to his voice.

Hogan nodded quickly. 'Right you are, lads.' He snatched up the tracker and pressed his thumb and forefinger together, working the clip. 'This is a wireless tracker,' he continued. 'It transmits a GPS signal whenever it's switched on. Clip it to a shirt or belt, and it'll track the target's movements wherever they go.'

Porter nodded. 'Same as them Fitbits everyone wears these days.'

'Kind of. Except this device has a microphone hidden inside it, for picking up chatter. This is how we'll keep track of the target whenever he's in private meetings or locations outside of his hotel. Attach it to the side of the belt, if you can. You'll get better audio quality that way.'

A frown line formed above Bald's brow. 'We're supposed to get him to just wear this thing? Won't he get suspicious?'

'He shouldn't do. Plenty of bodyguard teams use similar devices these days, as a way of keeping track of the principal at all times. Using them is totally legit. You can ask the target to wear it without raising any red flags. This one even comes with an SOS button they can press, in case of emergencies.'

Bald nodded at the tracker, said, 'How are we supposed to track the target, once we've fitted this thing to him?'

Hogan set down the tracker and reached for the iPad Mini. He entered the passcode, swiped across the screen and tapped on an orb-shaped grey icon, opening an app. Bald leaned over for a closer look. The app interface was broadly similar to Google Maps, with a blinking blue dot fixed over their current location. At the bottom of the screen were three smaller icons. Hogan pointed to the one on the left.

'This button here initiates the two-way recording feature,' he said. 'Press it once and it'll start broadcasting live audio back to a secure room in Vauxhall. Press it again to stop broadcasting.'

'I get the idea,' Porter said, nodding keenly. 'This is just like them rebro kits we used back in Northern Ireland.'

Hogan suppressed a laugh. Barely. 'Yeah, sort of. The concept is kind of similar.'

Bald said, 'Those other icons. What do they do?'

'This one allows you to geofence the tracker,' Hogan said, indicating the middle icon. 'Which basically means you can mark out a specific area on a map, and if the tracker strays outside that zone an alarm goes off. Useful if you want to make sure your mark doesn't leave the area around a hotel, for example.'

'And the other icon?'

'Location history. Tap on that and it'll bring up everywhere the tracker has been within a certain period.'

'Could be useful,' Porter mused.

'Unless the principal decides to ditch it,' Bald pointed out. 'If he knows we've stuck this thing on him, what's to stop him from taking it off whenever he feels like it?'

'Nothing,' Hogan admitted. 'Best practice is to plant a secondary device on the target whenever possible. That way you lull them into thinking that by removing the first device, they're clean.'

'Which means finding a way of planting something on them, without them knowing about it.'

Hogan pointed to a series of tiny metal devices, each one no bigger than a two-pence coin. 'These beauties look like commercially-sold GPS trackers. They're the same design and size, but instead of transmitting a signal they have a tiny built-in microphone. You can place them virtually anywhere. They come with a reusable sticky back that'll stick to anything. Once you're done, just wash it off with cold water and it'll be as good as new. Although the sound quality isn't as good as the bigger devices, obviously.'

'How do we deactivate them?' Porter asked, inspecting one of the coin mics up close.

'You send a text,' said Hogan. Seeing the blank looks on their faces, he went on, 'The coin mics are operated remotely. Each of these devices has a SIM card inside it. Simply enter the correct six-digit code on your phone and send it to the number stored on your device for the coin mic. Depending on which code you enter, you can activate the mic or shut it off, or adjust the volume. I'll go through the relevant codes with you both once we've run through all the kit.'

Bald said, 'If these mics are operated from our phones, does that mean we need a good signal to work them?'

Hogan nodded keenly, swept an arm in a broad arc across the kit on the table. 'All these devices transmit through the GSM network. Signal range is important.'

'What happens if he goes somewhere the signal is shite?'

'Then you won't be able to operate the devices remotely,' said Hogan. 'But if you're in a built-up area then you shouldn't have any problems.'

He set down the coin-sized listening device and picked up a white plug with a USB charging cable sticking out of it.

'This is a modified phone charger,' Hogan carried on. 'Our guys have planted a bug inside the charging house. We're very proud of this. Some of our best work.'

Porter picked up the adapter and stared at it. 'How does it work?'

'Replace this with Lansbury's regular adapter, and when he plugs his handset in, we'll have instant access to any information stored on his phone. We'll be able to open files, access the camera, his iCloud passwords. Everything. And it'll pick up and transmit chatter within a five-metre radius. We'll also be giving you a couple of matching adapters for his iPad and laptop as well. They work on the same principle. Plug them in, turn them on and they'll pick up anything being said in close proximity, as well as giving us a backdoor into the devices.'

'Do these things only work when the gadgets are recharging?'

Hogan shook his head. 'Once the target plugs the phone in, that gives us a backdoor into all their accounts. Unless they subsequently change their passwords, we'll be able to access all their accounts remotely from Vauxhall, whenever we want.'

'Fuck me.' Bald sighed and shook his head. 'It's a long way from wearing a mike and stuffing it under your shirt, like.'

Hogan laughed. 'Wait 'til you see what we've got next. You'll like this.'

He set down the bugged adapters and picked up a solid bronze coin, roughly the size of a poker chip. Bald leaned in for a closer look.

There was an engraving of the Regiment's famous downward-pointing blade, wreathed in flames, with the motto beneath it. The words 22 SPECIAL AIR SERVICE had been etched around the rim in silver lettering. A small blue gemstone had been set into the coin above the sword, with a pair of sniper crosshairs carved into it. Bald had seen the lads from Delta Force carrying something similar in the past, but with an image related to their own specific unit. Challenge coins, carried by anyone who had served in the same outfit. Some Yank tradition going back to the First World War. A soldier would draw his coin in a bar, and the person being challenged had to produce their own coin or buy the next round.

'This is an SAS challenge coin,' Hogan said. 'You've heard of them?'

'I thought only the Yanks went in for that crap,' Bald replied.

Porter chuckled and said, 'You've been out of the loop for too long, Jock. All the lads have got them now. It's becoming something of a tradition.'

'Christ. Give me strength.'

Hogan tapped the gemstone fixed above the Regiment insignia. 'There's a tiny microphone fitted here, and a GPS tracker. It can be activated or turned off remotely, using the same text-message procedure as the sticky mics. Battery life lasts for thirty hours on continuous use. If it runs out of juice, you can replace it with any standard watch battery.'

'What good is a fucking challenge coin going to do us?' asked Bald.

'It's the perfect excuse for either of you, if you need to carry a microphone into a secure location. Anyone asks you to empty your pockets or pats you down, you can just claim to be carrying the coin as a former member of 22 SAS. No one will suspect that it's a bug.'

'What's the range on them things?'

'The bug will transmit across a range of twenty-five metres on high frequency,' Hogan replied in his boring matter-of-fact voice. 'If it's a building with walls of eighteen inches or more, the range drops down to twelve metres. Try not to put it next to a radio or TV, anything that emits an audio source, as it'll drown out the reception.'

'We might not know this shit,' Bald said, shooting Hogan a look, 'but we're not complete fucking idiots.'

Porter said, 'What if me and Jock aren't able to listen in to what's being said? We've got jobs to do to maintain our cover. We can't spend all day sitting on our arses, listening to the chatter.'

Hogan smiled to himself and shook his head. 'You'll be taking portable hard drives with you.' He gestured to a couple of passport-sized devices protected by rugged cases. 'Any bugs you plant in the principal's room will automatically transmit audio data to these encrypted drives. Once a month, you'll deliver the drives to a contact at the British Embassy. They'll send everything digitally back to Vauxhall to be de-encrypted and processed.'

Porter looked sceptically at the hard drives. 'Those things are capable of storing a month of audio?'

Which prompted a chuckle from Hogan. 'These drives have a storage capacity of two terabytes. One terabyte can store up to seventeen thousand hours of audio, so I think you'll be okay.'

He set down the SAS challenge coin, reached for one of the two iPhones laid out on the table.

Bald said, 'If you're planning on explaining to us what one of them is, you're gonna regret it.'

'These aren't regular phones,' Hogan replied. 'You'll be using these to stay in contact with your handler at Vauxhall. These are false-screen phones.'

'What's one of them?' Porter asked.

Hogan said, 'False screen phones look and function exactly the same as any regular smartphone. You can send WhatsApp messages from them, play games, take pictures and so on. But there's a difference. Here.'

He unlocked the phone. Pointed to an icon.

'This is a fake Flashlight app. Open up the app and it'll bring up another screen asking for your passcode. Punch in the code, seven-four-eight-two. Then you'll get another screen. Like this.'

Hogan walked them through it. The display went black for a second, then woke up again. Bald found himself looking at a sparsely populated Home screen. Plain wallpaper, no downloaded apps.

Hogan said, 'Once you get this screen, you'll know that the phone is encrypted. You can send and receive messages and make calls to your handler without anyone listening in. Once you've ended the call, go back to the flashlight app, enter the code again, and the phone will return to its normal state.'

'And there's no way of anyone finding out what we've been doing on the encrypted side?' asked Bald.

'Not unless they know how to access the keypad, and the code that goes with it. Otherwise, the only dodgy thing they're going to find is your browsing history.'

'As long as they don't find anything else.'

'They won't. Trust me.'

Porter said, 'What if Six needs to reach us, when the phone isn't encrypted?'

'They'll only contact you if it's an emergency,' Hogan said. 'If your handler thinks you're at risk, one of you will receive a call from a number in Hereford, telling you that your Uncle Jim has died unexpectedly. If you receive that message, you know that your cover has been blown and you'll have to extract immediately.'

'Let's hope it doesn't come to that,' Bald muttered.

Porter grinned. 'We're running a routine close protection job, Jock. Not hunting down targets in some Syrian shithole. What kind of trouble do you think we'll run into?'

'No clue. But it always seems to find us. That's for fucking sure.'

THIRTEEN

Hogan spent another thirty minutes running through the rest of the surveillance equipment: matchbox-sized bugs they would be expected to plant in Lansbury's hotel room, a room-sweeping device that had been modified not to pick up any bugs that Bald and Porter had planted. Bugs that had been fitted inside light bulbs. Hogan ran through the operation of the false-screen iPhones and the iPad rebroadcasting system a few times, making sure that Bald and Porter had committed everything to memory. Bald got a kick out of watching Porter struggle to get to grips with the various bits of kit. *The guy's really starting to show his age*, thought Bald. Hogan told them he would be on hand at the camp for the rest of the evening, if the guys had any further questions. He wrapped up the briefing and stepped out of the room. A few minutes later, Strickland returned.

Four o'clock in the afternoon.

Two hours since the original briefing.

Six hours until the hit on Lansbury's BG team.

'How did it go with Hogan?' Strickland asked them between long puffs on her e-cigarette. Bald caught a whiff of the vapour. It smelled vaguely of peppermint.

'Cracking,' Porter said. 'If this op goes sideways, there'll always be a job for us at PC World.'

He smiled at Strickland. Bald just stood there, rolling his eyes at Porter's lame joke. *I don't know what's sadder*, he thought to himself. *The fact that this sober prick thinks he's funny, or that he thinks he's got a chance with our handler.*

'What's the plan now?' Bald asked.

'We wait,' Strickland replied. 'Now that you've been fully briefed, there's nothing else to do until our friends take out the bodyguards.'

'When's that happening?'

'Tonight. Five hours from now, we think. Once Lansbury's bodyguards are out of the picture, we'll be in a holding pattern until the word filters out through the news channels about the incident. Then Lord McGinn will make the call to Lansbury, recommending you for the job.'

Porter shot the agent a questioning look. 'How are you lot gonna make sure that story hits the airwaves in time?'

'There's a journalist at the *Mail Online*. She's working for us. She's in Budapest right now, covering Fodor's re-election campaign. She's going to be nearby when the attack takes place. Then she'll write up a small story and reach out to Lansbury for comment. Once the story is posted, we'll reassemble here and wait for the call to come through from Lansbury's office.'

'That could take fucking ages,' Bald growled.

'We don't think so. Lansbury is deeply paranoid, like many of his populist friends. He's going to be alone, in a foreign country, without protection and with a big meeting coming up. He won't be dragging his feet about getting in some replacements.'

'How long until we hear back?' asked Porter.

'We're hoping to get you out there within twenty-four hours of the hit. Ideally, you'll be on a flight to Budapest tomorrow afternoon.'

'Assuming he takes the bait,' Bald muttered.

'He will. Trust me. It's under control.'

'No offence, but I've heard that before.'

Strickland stared at Bald for a beat. 'For an ex-SAS man, you don't seem to have much faith in your employer.'

'Force of habit. I've worked with you fuckers enough times in the past and had my fingers burned. Why should I trust a word you say? In fact, I'm starting to wonder why I bothered coming back.'

Strickland stared at Bald. 'Is that a threat?'

'Just giving it to you straight,' Bald countered, staring right back at the MI6 agent. 'Which is more than Six has done for me in the past. I'm fucking done listening to the same old promises.'

'You can't walk away.'

'Watch me. Besides,' Bald added, 'this op has got clusterfuck written all over it. I'm not risking my neck just to put some right-wing dickhead behind bars.'

'But what about the job we promised? The corporate gig?'

'I'll take my chances on Civvy Street.' Bald held up his hands. 'No offence, lass. You seem solid enough, like. But as long as Ayatollah Moorcroft is running the show, it's a hard no from me.'

He turned to leave.

Strickland said, 'Walk away now, and you'll regret it.'

'Nah,' Bald replied. 'Don't think I will.'

'Moorcroft won't be around for long,' Strickland called after him. 'He's on the way out.'

Bald stopped. Turned back round to face Strickland and looked searchingly at her. 'What do you mean?'

'The old regime is being shown the door. The old guard is stepping aside. Including Moorcroft. I'm his replacement.'

That drew a confused look from Porter. 'I thought you were Moorcroft's number two?'

'That's what David likes to think.'

Bald frowned at her. 'Why didn't you tell us about this in the briefing?'

'We haven't made it official yet,' Strickland explained in her soft Glaswegian accent. 'The directors agreed that it would be advisable for me to shadow David until my appointment is formally announced. Let me see how things work, get a feel for the place. David likes to act as if he's still in charge, and I suppose technically he is. But he's on borrowed time. You'll be reporting to me directly soon enough.'

'Doesn't change anything,' Bald said.

'Actually, it does. Right now, I'm the only friend you've got. David wasn't keen about bringing you back into the fold. And he's not the only one. There were plenty of colleagues warning me not to touch you. They said you were damaged goods.'

'Why bring us back, then?'

'Because I worked with Tannon, a long time ago. She said you were reliable despite your faults. You're not worried about rules and regulations. You get the job done.'

Bald stared at Strickland, as if seeing her for the first time. She obviously didn't fit the white-male-privilege profile of many of her Vauxhall colleagues. A Glasgow-born woman, trying to make it in a world dominated by the old boys' network at Vauxhall. No wonder she looked restless, Bald thought. She would have had to fight tooth and nail to get ahead at Six. There would have been endless late nights, weekends at the office, supreme dedication. Against his better judgement, Bald found himself admiring her.

'Whatever bad blood there is between you and David doesn't concern me,' Strickland continued. 'All I care about is bringing down Lansbury. If I lose, the likes of David will close ranks. They'll use my failure as an excuse to undermine me. I'll spend the rest of my career fighting a rear-guard action. But if we get a big win, you two have got a friend for life. Help me, and I'll do what I can for you. No lies, no bullshit.'

Bald spread his hands. 'That's all I'm asking for.'

'Good.' Strickland smiled at him. 'David might argue other-wise, but I think there's still a place for men like you at Vauxhall, you know. Believe it or not, there aren't many of you left.'

'I'm not that old. Porter's older than me. He's so ancient he can remember the Big Bang.'

Strickland kept on smiling at Bald. 'Are we good?'

Bald nodded. 'You think you can get us on Lansbury's team?'

'We'll take care of that,' she said. 'Don't worry. Just focus on getting on his good side once you've got the job. The more he takes a shine to you two, the more likely it is he'll hire you for the long term. And the better our chances of obtaining the evidence we'll need to put him away for the rest of his life.'

Porter said, 'You really think that Lansbury is a traitor to his country?'

'One hundred per cent. We're as certain as we can be. Our source inside the FSB is bulletproof, but we still really need that smoking gun. You two are our best hope of getting it.'

'Don't worry. We'll get the fucker.'

Strickland's phone buzzed. She dug it out, frowned at the screen. 'I need to take this. I'll see you later. I suggest you go over your preparations this evening. And catch some sleep while you can.'

'When are we expecting the call?'

'Sometime after midnight. The duty sergeant will be

monitoring the phones. He'll notify us as soon as the bodyguard hit has been confirmed.'

She promptly turned on her heel and stepped out of the room, phone glued to her ear. Bald watched her disappear from view and nudged Porter, grinning at him.

'At least they left us with the Doris instead of that bus-pass wanker Moorcroft. I know who I'd rather be cooped up with in that briefing room tomorrow.'

'Fancy your chances, do you?' Porter sniffed.

'Not my type, mate. I get plenty of action as it is. Should have seen some of the talent I was ploughing in Mexico.'

Bald glanced at his G-Shock watch. 'I'm gonna get a lift down to Hereford, pick up a couple of suits for this job, then head down the range for a bit. Join us for a pint after at the Red Lion?'

Porter hesitated, then shook his head. 'You go on ahead. I'm bushed. They've set us up with a room here. Think I'll just hit the cookhouse, then get my head down for a stretch.'

'Come on, mate. Have a beer. Just the one.'

'We're on duty, Jock.'

'Two-pint rule,' said Bald.

They had both done time in the SP Team at Hereford, the Regiment's counter-terrorism unit. Back then the standby team had been allowed to have two pints while on rotation: enough to deal with the boredom while remaining ready to deploy at short notice.

'I don't think it works like that now,' Porter replied quietly.

'It does in Jock Bald Land.' Bald gave him a dirty grin. 'Who knows, we might even find a couple of Hereford groupies down there. Come on. Just one drink.'

'I can't, Jock. I told you already, I'm done with all that. I don't touch that stuff anymore.'

Bald stepped back, sneering with contempt. 'Bloody hell, at least when you were a pisshead you were fun to be around. Now look at you. Can't even let your hair down with a couple of drinks. Pathetic.'

'Says the bloke who hasn't got two pennies to rub together.'

'I'd rather be poor than a sad old tosser. You're supposed to be a Blade, for fuck's sake.'

'I still am,' Porter growled. 'I've still got what it takes.'

'Could have fooled me, mate. The Porter I used to know was a hard bastard. Couldn't handle his drink, maybe, but he was one of the toughest lads in Hereford. This?' Bald gestured at Porter, his face screwed up in contempt. 'This is just fucking lame.'

Porter glowered at Bald and stepped towards him, his hands balled into white-knuckled fists.

'Listen, I'm off the shit and that's the end of it, all right? So don't try and tempt us off the wagon. I'm doing well for myself these days . . . no thanks to you.'

Bald stood glaring at him for a long moment. Then his expression crumbled, and he roared with laughter. Porter felt anger rising like bile in his throat. 'What's so fucking funny?'

'I'm taking the piss, you daft bastard,' Bald said. He continued laughing heartily as he shook his head. 'Fuck me, do you really think I'd try and tempt you back on the drink? After everything you've been through?'

Porter's expression darkened. 'You were joking?'

'Of course I bloody was, mate.' Bald punched his mucker playfully on the shoulder. 'Christ, the number of times I've helped you kick the booze in the past, why would I want you to drink again? Only a twisted bastard would do something like that.'

Porter felt his cheeks burning with rage as he stared daggers at Bald. 'Then why did you say all that stuff about having a cheeky pint?'

'I was testing you, you idiot. Seeing if you really meant what you said about getting clean. You've told us that enough times in the past and slipped off the wagon again, I wanted to see if it was more of the same old bullshit.'

Porter felt his blood boiling, resisted an urge to lamp Bald in the face. Jock knew how to push his buttons, that was for sure. He let the anger pass and took a step back from his mucker, still glowering at him.

'You're a bastard, Jock.'

'Maybe. But it was worth it for the look on your ugly mug. Fucking priceless, that.'

Porter shook his head. 'I meant what I said before. I'm not

drinking any more, and that's final. Just worry about keeping your own hands clean from now on.'

Bald inclined his head at Porter, crinkling his brow. 'You trying to suggest something?'

'I wasn't born yesterday. Everyone in Hereford knows you're a dodgy fucker. Always on the take, always looking for a way to line your own pockets.'

'No idea what you're talking about,' Bald said.

'Yeah, you do. Just like you know about them rumours floating around Hereford about you getting involved in cocaine smuggling, nicking diamonds. That business with the gold. It's like an addiction for you, Jock.'

'You can't prove any of that stuff.'

'Maybe not,' Porter conceded. 'But if you try any of that shite again, you're gonna put us both in trouble.'

Bald stepped into Porter's face. 'What I get up to doesn't concern you.'

'Yes. Yes, it does. If you get caught with your fingers in the till, we'll both take the blame. I worked hard to rebuild my career. My reputation. After all the shit I've been through, I'm not gonna let you screw us just because you saw a chance to make some dirty money.'

'Is that a threat?'

'No, mate. Just a friendly word of advice.' Porter stared hard at his mucker, a warning look in his pale eyes. 'Keep your nose clean on this one. I'm serious. Because if you try and pull any shit, me and you are gonna have a fucking problem.'

FOURTEEN

Five hours later, Derek Lansbury's two bodyguards walked out of the five-star Royal Duna Hotel and stepped into the gloom of the late evening in Budapest.

Gary Steer and Mick Hutton had spent another long day guarding their client. The man they had been hired to protect had kept up a punishing schedule since arriving in Hungary earlier that week. Practically non-stop. The guy was a proper Duracell bunny. There had been working breakfasts and lunches, endless meetings with businessmen and government officials, handshakes with fringe figures on the far right, photo ops and TV interviews, and appearances at campaign rallies with the head of state.

At seven minutes past ten, Lansbury had finally called it a night. While he was tucked up in bed, firing out late-night tweets, Hutton and Steer had a few hours to themselves. A chance to grab some fresh air, stretch their legs and enjoy a late-night supper at their usual spot. Grouse about how much they hated guarding Lansbury. All the crap they habitually took from him.

Steer was the younger of the two bodyguards. He'd spent twelve years with Special Branch before he'd decided to go private, working close-protection jobs. At first sight he didn't look much like a bodyguard. He was lean and wiry, rather than bulky. Steer kept himself in good nick, unlike some of the lads who'd quit the force. An early morning jog through the streets, followed by a high-intensity weight circuit in the hotel gym. Crunches, kettle bell swings, pull-ups. Then a protein shake for breakfast. At the age of forty-three he wasn't a Greek god anymore, but he wasn't far off. He was dressed in a sharp black suit, had the same short-back-and-sides haircut as in his days on the force and he wore a Rolex Submariner watch.

The Rolex was a gift to himself, after landing the contract to guard Lansbury. He could afford it now, after all. He was making good money. Better than anything he'd earned on the force.

The other guy, Hutton, was six years older than Steer and about fifty pounds heavier. He had the filled-out look of an athlete gone to seed. He was all-over big, an immense slab of a man, with shoulders as wide as football pitches and hands the size of shovels. His arms hung by his sides like meat from a pair of hooks. With his wrinkled face and comb-over he looked like a middle-aged accountant who had been lifting weights at the gym.

The pair of them got on well enough, although they could sometimes get on each other's nerves. Steer felt that Hutton could be a huffy fucker at times, moody and lazy. Hutton was often irritated by the way Steer conducted himself, acting as if he was the next James Bond. But the two of them were professional enough not to let their differences get in the way of doing their job.

Besides, they took plenty of shit from their principal, who they both agreed was an arrogant, slimy prick. They were also fairly sure he was shagging a local mistress, with his occasional unscheduled disappearances across town. Meetings he was adamant Hutton and Steer could not attend. Now they were both looking forward to a few hours away from his company.

They breezed past the valets and porters loitering outside the hotel and hung a left down the wide main thoroughfare. The Royal Duna was situated in the political and financial heart of Budapest, amid a sprawl of Gothic Revival buildings, casinos and government offices. The local equivalent of Westminster, thought Steer. They were half a mile from the Hungarian Parliament and two hundred metres due east of the River Danube. The view was impressive, even at night. Lights twinkled on the stone-built suspension bridge linking the metropolitan east with the more genteel western side of the city. On the far side of the river, maybe half a mile away, Steer could make out the brightly lit dome of Buda Castle. Like something out of a medieval fairy tale.

They continued down the thoroughfare for forty metres and took another left, turning up a dimly lit side street. Standard operating procedure dictated that the bodyguards shouldn't venture more than a hundred metres from the hotel in any direction. The place they frequented was technically too far away, a New York-themed steakhouse situated two hundred metres east of the Royal Duna Hotel. But the food portions were generous, and it was cheaper than the over-priced sushi bars and brasseries lining the riverfront, with a good selection of beers on tap. Plus, it was still comfortably within walking distance of the hotel. They felt it was an acceptable compromise.

As they strolled down the side street, Steer consulted his Rolex. No particular reason. He just liked to admire it from time to time. He felt the Rolex was significant somehow. A vindication of his career choice. A physical reminder of why he was out here, putting up with the long periods of boredom and the snide remarks from the principal.

They were halfway down the street when Steer saw the guy.

A shadowed figure, shuffling out of the doorway of a rundown housing block, ten metres ahead of them.

The figure limped towards the two bodyguards. In the faint glow of the street lamps Steer saw that he was black, with dirty matted facial hair, dressed in a tattered pair of jeans, scuffed trainers and a zipped-up hoodie. An unusual sight in Budapest. The city wasn't a beacon of multiculturalism. Almost every face Steer had seen was white, with the exception of a few dark-featured Roma gypsies working on building sites or sweeping the streets.

The guy looked filthy. Steer caught a strong whiff of eau de piss coming off of him. He was waving at Steer and Hutton with his left hand.

'Hey, bro!' he called out in some sort of accent that Steer guessed was West African.

The bodyguards kept moving. The guy stepped in front of them five metres ahead, moving to intercept them. Blocking their path. Hand outstretched. Another beggar, thought Steer. The streets of Budapest were crawling with them these days, especially around the wealthier parts of town.

'Brother. Hey, man! Talking to you ...'

The guy was two metres away now. At this distance Steer noticed a large wet patch down the front of the man's jeans. The stench of urine hung thick in the air, Steer wrinkling his nose in disgust as he shaped to brush past the homeless guy.

'Bro—'

'Fuck off,' Hutton spat.

But the homeless guy blocked their path. He had a mildly threatening posture. His eyes were wild and his dirt-smeared face was nicked with tiny scars from street fights. The guy was on something. That much was obvious. A crack addict, presumably. Steer had seen plenty of them during his days serving as a bobby on the beat.

The homeless guy's right hand was stuffed inside his hoodie pocket, Steer noticed.

'Give us your fucking wallets,' the guy rasped. He jerked his head at Steer's Rolex Submariner. 'Dat watch too.'

Neither bodyguard moved.

Steer's professional eye instantly assessed the situation. They were in an isolated spot, fifty metres down a poorly lit side street. No witnesses. No passers-by. No one to run for help. All the action was going on in the main streets at either end. In the distance, he could hear the faint drone of passing traffic, the occasional distant shout or peal of laughter. The homeless guy had picked a good spot for a mugging.

'You deaf?' he growled. 'I said gimme dem things, bro.'

Steer cold-stared at him, body tensed. 'No.'

'Fuck off,' Hutton repeated. 'Black bastard.'

The bum hesitated. For a split-second Steer thought the homeless guy might walk away. He'd made a mistake, targeting a pair of well-built bodyguards instead of some fat Yank tourist. Overconfidence perhaps. Or pure greed. Or maybe it was just the deluded thinking of a long-term junkie. Perhaps he'd see sense, turn away and crawl back into his hole.

Then the homeless guy pulled the knife out of his pocket.

He moved fast. Faster than any addict Steer had ever seen. Steer caught a flash of steel as the guy stepped towards Hutton, gripping a folding lock knife. One of the traditional models, with a walnut handle and a stainless-steel blade. Four inches. Long enough to do some serious internal damage, in the right hands.

Hutton had no time to block the first stab. The homeless guy was too close. He was practically in the bodyguard's face. And he was much faster than his opponent.

The beggar stepped into stabbing range, dropped his right shoulder and gut-punched Hutton before the bodyguard could react, banging him in the vitals. Hutton jack-knifed, his mouth forming a wide 'O' of shock and pain as the blade sank deep into his guts. He staggered backwards, clutching his perforated stomach, blood seeping between his fingers.

The mugger wrenched the blade free. Spun round to face his second victim.

No point trying to cut and run, Steer told himself. He was in a knife fight, whether he accepted it or not. And his opponent was surprisingly fast. The addict would surely catch Steer and cut him down before he could leg it to the main thoroughfare.

I'm not going to abandon my mate.

He dropped into a slight crouch, waited for the addict to take a swing at him. In the next instant the mugger lunged forward and stabbed low, intending to give Steer a gut wound to match the one he'd just dished out to Hutton.

Same tactic. Different result.

Steer was younger than Hutton. And sharper. The early morning training and the strict diet gave him an advantage that the older bodyguard simply didn't have. He read his attacker's move and deflected the attack with a downward sweep of his left forearm, driving the knife away from his torso. Then he bent his right arm and swung out with his elbow, cracking the addict on the side of his skull. The first rule of defending yourself in a knife fight: find a way to get rid of the weapon. Stun the attacker, disorientate them. Do whatever it takes to take the knife out of the equation.

The mugger stumbled backwards a couple of steps, momentarily stunned. His grip unclenched. The knife fell from his loosened grip and clattered to the ground with a brittle clang.

I've disarmed the fucker, thought Steer. *Now the fight's on.*

Except that it wasn't.

Steer made the oldest mistake in the fighting manual. He got cocky. He stepped towards the mugger, still mentally celebrating the success of his last attack, thinking he'd done all the hard work.

124

He didn't have any grand strategy. Just a sense that he had levelled the playing field and that all he needed to do now was finish the job.

He charged forward, aiming to deliver a heavy right hook. The knockout blow. But the mugger surprised him by recovering from the previous blow to the temple and adopted a boxing stance. Fists raised in front of him, muscles tensed, eyes laser-focused, left leg slightly ahead of his right. Transforming himself from a limping mess into something much more agile and deadly.

Steer saw the change in his body shape. He knew something was wrong. But it was too late to adapt his game plan. He was already mid-swing, driving his fist round towards the mugger's face.

His punch never made contact.

The mugger struck out with the speed and coordination of a professional fighter. He dropped low and slipped outside the punch, deftly evading the blow, and in the same motion he sprang forward. Launched a vicious left uppercut at Steer, slammed the hard ridge of his knuckles into the latter's ribcage. The kind of move that required lightning-fast reflexes, speedy footwork and years of practice.

Not the kind of move you learned on the streets, shaking down tourists.

Pain exploded through Steer's torso. He heard something crack, like a branch snapping underfoot. He tried to step out of range and defend himself, but the mugger was on him in a flash, unleash-ing a menacing flurry of body blows, jabbing him in the sternum and ribs. The punches kept coming. Unrelenting. Like a boxer doing some heavy bag work. Steer couldn't get a shot in, couldn't block the attacks or fight back. He wasn't thinking about winning the fight now. He was just trying to survive from one second to the next.

Another punch crashed into his upper left side. The liver shot. His neck muscles clenched, like a fist clamping around his throat. The pain was suffocating, intense. Worse than anything Steer had ever known. He lost his balance and bent forward, arms lowered, arms shielding his torso from further punishment.

Leaving his head exposed.

The mugger accepted the invitation. Steer was coughing and spluttering, gasping for air. He saw the mugger twisting at the waist, arcing his fist round, shaping to throw a right hook.

The blow was devastating. Steer saw white briefly. He staggered backwards, dazed and stunned, electric pain flaring up behind his eyeballs.

A single clear thought cut through the fog thickening inside his skull.

This bloke isn't a homeless drug addict.

No one on the streets fights like this.

So who the fuck is he?

The mugger was suddenly in Steer's face again. He drew his elbow back and shot his right arm up at an angle, aiming at Steer's skull.

The bodyguard saw the punch coming. But it didn't matter. Steer couldn't have avoided it even if he had wanted to. He was too numb and out of breath and confused to react. The last thought he had was to wonder who the hell had attacked them.

The mugger's palm shot up, slamming into the underside of Steer's chin, sent his jaw crashing into the roof of his skull. His world shuddered and jarred.

Then everything went black.

Jordan Rowe stepped back as the second bodyguard dropped to the ground. Rowe made sure the guy was out for the count, then turned away to check on the other victim. The older bodyguard was lying on the ground, writhing in agony, blood pumping steadily out of the deep wound to his stomach as he made a lame attempt to reach for the knife that Rowe had dropped. Rowe hurried over to the bodyguard, dropped to a knee beside him. Lifted the man's right arm by the wrist and then slammed it down over his right leg, breaking his bones. The bodyguard screamed. His busted right arm flopped uselessly to the ground. He wouldn't be practising his golf swing for a while.

Rowe snatched up the folding lock knife. Rushed back over to the unconscious bodyguard and stabbed him repeatedly, giving him a series of puncture wounds to his thighs. Rowe didn't want to kill the guys. His orders were to incapacitate them for a few weeks. Make the thing look like a mugging gone badly wrong.

He hadn't expected the second guy to fight back. The plan had been to cut down the older bodyguard first. Take him out of the picture, get the second guy to surrender. Seize their valuables, bang the second bodyguard with a couple of rapid stabs and leg it.

Then the guy had unexpectedly fought back, and the plan had very nearly gone to shit.

Rowe padded down the comatose bodyguard. Fished out his wallet and phone, unhooked the Rolex from around his wrist. He did the same with the older guy, ignoring the man as he hissed and moaned with pain. Both of their wallets were stuffed full of fifty-pound notes.

He was rising to his feet when he heard voices. More than one of them. English native speakers. Not locals. Rowe spun round and faced the western end of the side street, fifty metres away.

A pair of middle-aged guys stood at the edge of the side street, dressed in wool coats and neatly pressed trousers. Tourists out for a late evening stroll along the Danube, perhaps. Or returning to their hotel from some swish nearby restaurant. One of them stopped and called out to Rowe. He pointed the SAS man out to his friend.

They shouted for help.

Rowe took one last look at the bodyguards and broke into a run, sprinting towards the eastern end of the side street, sixty metres ahead. Heading in the opposite direction to the tourists.

'Stop!' someone called out at his back. 'You!'

He heard more voices now. Rowe risked a glance over his shoulder. Saw a couple of Hungarian police officers sweeping into view around the corner.

He sprinted on, chopping his stride, running for all he was worth. In another thirty metres he emerged from the side street and hooked a right on Nádor Street. He saw the rental van twenty metres away, an unmarked white Opel Vivaro parked in a loading bay at the side of the road. The engine was already running. Rowe ran over to the van, reached the passenger side door in half a dozen strides. Wrenched it open and dived inside.

Phil Lyden was behind the wheel.

He didn't need to ask Rowe how the hit had gone down. Until roughly twenty seconds ago, Lyden had been lurking in shadows at the far end of the side street, observing the fight. If Rowe had been in serious difficulty, Lyden would have rushed over to lend a hand to his mucker.

'Go, go!' Rowe gasped as he slammed the door shut.

Lyden took off the handbrake, pulled out of the loading bay and accelerated south for a hundred metres. They hit a set of lights, slung a hard left at the junction and made a few quick turns and bulleted east on Rákóczi Street, Lyden shifting through the gears.

When they were clear of the scene Lyden checked the rear-view mirror and breathed a sigh of relief. 'Fuck, that was close.'

'I had it under control,' Rowe muttered.

Lyden glanced sidelong at his mucker. 'Did you have to give that fella a broken arm as well?'

'He called us a black bastard.'

Lyden looked ahead, nodded. 'Fair enough.'

They drove on for another three minutes. Lyden drove one-handed, extended his other hand towards Rowe. 'Give us the phones.'

Rowe handed over the top-end smartphones he'd snatched from the two bodyguards. Lyden caught sight of the Rolexes and cash-stuffed wallets and whistled. 'Fuck me, we're in the wrong job here.'

Rowe merely shrugged.

Lyden buzzed down his window. Air rushed through the gap as he tossed out the handsets into the chilly blackness of the night. Getting rid of the phones was a security precaution, in case anyone tried to track the GPS signals from the devices. The rest of the loot would be quietly disposed of later, thrown into storm drains or dumped in public bins. The guys didn't want to hang on to the valuables for longer than necessary, in case they were stopped by the local plod for whatever reason.

Stealing the bodyguards' valuables would give the investigators a clear motive for the attack, Lyden knew. They'd treat it as a simple robbery. The bodyguards were walking down the side street at night? Carrying all this stuff? Of course they would have been targeted!

They raced on. Past the synagogue and the train station and the national football stadium, until they joined the motorway funnelling traffic south towards the airport.

Lyden and Rowe were booked into a three-star airport hotel. They left the rental van in the long-stay car park and checked into their room under their real names. Cleaned themselves up, changed into fresh sets of clothes. Chucked their old threads in a dumpster at the back of the hotel.

They would spend the night at the hotel. Catch the 06.15 flight to Vienna the following morning. From there they would head back to a friendly military base outside of Graz.

Lyden sent a message on his encrypted phone to a UK mobile number: *It's done. The door is open.*

FIFTEEN

Exactly two hours after the attack had taken place, Phoebe Gallent, junior crime correspondent for the *Daily Mail*, finished writing up her copy for her next story. The article ran to two hundred and fifty words, plus six slightly blurry photographs of the crime scene she'd managed to capture on her phone. It wasn't her best work, but it didn't need to be. That wasn't what her handler had asked for.

Three days earlier, Gallent's editor had invited her to a secret meeting at the Landmark Hotel. There she had been introduced to a woman called Madeleine, who explained that she was from the Secret Intelligence Service. She said that Gallent had been recommended by her editor as someone who was discreet and trustworthy. And, most importantly, she was on good terms with Derek Lansbury.

Over coffee, Madeleine had explained what she needed. She emphasised that if Gallent wasn't comfortable with their request, she could walk away at any time. There was no obligation. But Gallent was an ambitious young hack. With rent to pay on a room in a shared house in Hackney Wick, crushing student loan repayments and the endless fear of redundancy that came with working for a newspaper in the age of Instagram. She sensed that if she passed up an offer to work with SIS then she would be closing the door on the opportunity of a lifetime. She agreed, right there and then.

Madeleine had left the details to Gallent. All she had been told was that there would be an incident involving Lansbury's bodyguards in Budapest, and Gallent would need to be on the ground to cover it.

The issue was time-sensitive, Madeleine had stressed. The

sooner she could get the story out the better. Within reason, of course. Gallent felt that three hours after the event was about right. Long enough for a junior reporter to get to the scene of the crime, interview witnesses, get a statement from the police, make a few calls and type up a first draft. Any sooner and it might arouse suspicion.

Madeleine had said that would be fine.

They had decided it was best if Gallent was close to the attack when it happened. If anyone asked, Gallent could claim to have been drinking in a nearby bar when she had been alerted to a cry for help. It was plausible. The incident was taking place in the city centre, yards away from the throng of tourist-friendly restaurants and watering holes along the riverfront. The kind of place a young, single journalist might find herself at the end of a long day.

At six minutes past midnight, Gallent saved the first draft of her article. She celebrated by pouring herself a glass from the bottle of cheap wine she'd smuggled back into her hotel room from a nearby convenience store. She took a long sip, picked up her phone and called Lansbury on his private number.

He answered on the fourth ring. Gallent apologised for the late hour of the call and wondered if he had heard the news that his bodyguards had been attacked in the street outside his hotel two hours ago. She asked if he was okay. Would he care to comment?

She decided she couldn't print his response.

An hour later, she emailed the article to her editor.

At seven o'clock in the morning, local time, the story went live.

By eight o'clock, all the other major news outlets were running the same story.

Eight o'clock in the morning in Budapest was seven o'clock in the morning in Wroxham, Norfolk.

Lord Alan McGinn, former Chief of the General Staff, was sitting at the desk in his private study, listening to the morning news on Radio 4. His office displayed the fruits of a lifetime spent in the service of Queen and country. The walls were lined with pictures of McGinn pressing the flesh with various dignitaries and prime ministers, shots of him visiting the troops in Pristina and Basra. Pride of place was given to a framed photograph of

McGinn receiving his knighthood from the Queen. On the desk was a pile of signed hardcovers of his bestselling autobiography, *Leading from the Front*, with a foreword by Prince Charles.

Above all, McGinn had a reputation as a man of immaculate morals. Deeply religious and devoted to his country, always putting the national interest above personal ambition. It was a reputation that McGinn had come dangerously close to losing recently. Until someone from MI6 had approached him and quietly suggested that they might be able to make the pictures of him in a gimp suit disappear.

McGinn sipped his Earl Grey tea and listened to the headlines.

The main story was an update on the security preparations ahead of the G7 summit in Loch Lomond. The security operation was costing millions, apparently. Protestors were gathering in London ahead of a mass demonstration.

There was a piece about anti-Semitism in the Labour Party.

Another story about Brexit.

Forest fires in Canada.

Climate change, trouble in the markets.

McGinn sipped his tea.

The seventh headline was the one he had been told to wait for.

A terse six-sentence report of a violent attack on the body-guards working for Derek Lansbury. The attack had taken place in the streets of Budapest the previous evening. A suspected mugging, according to early reports. Both men had been taken to hospital with serious injuries. There was no indication that the mugger knew the identity of the men in question or had been targeting Lansbury himself. Hungarian police said that their investigation was ongoing. Mr Lansbury was in the country to offer political support to his friend, the Hungarian strongman Márton Fodor.

McGinn finished his tea.

Three minutes later, he picked up the phone.

Scrolled down to a number in his Contacts list, hit Dial.

There was an international ringtone. Four long beeps, and then a voice answered on the other end. 'Alan, old chap,' said the voice. 'I was wondering when you might call.'

'Derek, my God.' McGinn hoped his voice sounded anxious without over-egging it. 'How are you? I literally just heard the news on the radio.'

Lansbury grunted. 'Bloody shaken up, as you can imagine. It's not every day that your security detail gets knifed in the streets. Can you imagine what would have happened if I'd been there at the time?'

'Thank God you weren't.' McGinn swallowed. 'Have they caught the culprit, by any chance?'

'Not yet. The prime minister called earlier to personally assure me they're on the case. They think the attacker was a migrant from Djibouti or somesuch.' Lansbury snorted derisively. 'And they wonder why people like me enjoy such widespread support. I give it two days until the *Guardian* runs an article sympathising with the bastard.'

'And your bodyguards?' McGinn enquired. 'How are they?'

'Incapacitated. They'll be out of action for months, I'm told.'

'My God.'

'I know, it's a bloody shambles. Makes me look like a flaming idiot too, hiring a pair of halfwits who don't know how to defend themselves.'

'That's why I'm calling, actually.'

'Oh?'

McGinn paused. He took a deep breath, then dived in. 'I know this is all rather sudden, but if you're in need of replacements, I've got just the chaps. Two fellows who would do a very good job.'

There was an unsettling pause, followed by a deep sigh. 'Look, I appreciate the gesture but I've got several of the big agencies on the case. They're going to take care of it.'

'Yes, of course. But I've used these two personally in the past, on overseas operations,' McGinn said. 'They come highly recommended.'

'Who are they?'

'Ex-SAS men. They're infinitely better qualified than those two you've been using. Put it this way, they wouldn't be getting mugged in the streets.'

'I see.' McGinn could hear what sounded like fingers

drumming on a table on the other end. 'And these two ex-SAS men … are they available now?'

'I believe so. They're up in Hereford at the moment, I'm told. Just come off a big job.'

There was another voice in the background, young and female, vying for Lansbury's attention. The line went quiet for a moment and then Lansbury came back on, sounding harried.

'Look, I'm afraid I'm rather busy here. I'm about to do an interview live with Fox News. Can't this wait until later?'

'Not really. These men I mentioned, Derek, they're highly capable and—'

'Are you taking a cut for these chaps or something? You're giving me the hard sell here.'

Lansbury's tone was matey, good-humoured, but McGinn detected an undercurrent of irritation. He changed tack.

'I don't give a damn about these chaps, Derek, I'm concerned about you. Believe me, you can't skimp on this stuff. It only takes one madman with a weapon and a determination to make a name for himself. If you're out there alone, without protection … well, who knows what might happen?'

'Yes, yes, I know that.'

Lansbury went quiet again. More background chatter. McGinn felt his shoulders deflate. For a moment he worried that he'd lost the argument. Then Lansbury came back on the line and said, 'Tell you what. Why don't you send the contact details for your men through to Freya? She'll give them a call, size them up. If they're as good as you say they are, we'll work something out.'

'Yes. Yes, of course. I'll do that right away.'

'Good man. Oh, and let's catch up when I'm back. Drinks at the Club.' More voices in the background. Lansbury raised his own. 'I've got complimentary tickets to the South Africa test at Twickenham next month. Bring Catherine and Bertie along, why don't you. Should be a cracker.'

McGinn found himself nodding enthusiastically. 'I'd love that, very much.'

There was a beat of silence. 'Thanks for looking out for me, chum. I do appreciate it, you know.'

'Anytime, old chap.'

McGinn set down the receiver. Relief flushed through his system.

It was done.

He turned to the man in the off-the-rack suit, standing in the doorway. The agent Vauxhall had sent.

'Was that good enough?' he asked.

'Yes,' the man from Vauxhall replied. 'That'll do just fine.'

Two hundred miles away, Bald, Porter and Strickland were back in the same briefing room as before.

They had regrouped in the room shortly before six o'clock that morning. Bald and Porter had been awoken by the duty sergeant a few hours earlier, letting them know that the hit on Lansbury's BG team had gone down as planned. The second knock had come at around five-thirty. The same duty sergeant, telling them that Vauxhall had received confirmation that the *Mail Online* story was about to be posted. Bald and Porter had quickly washed and dressed, packed their kit into their holdalls and grabbed breakfast in the camp cookhouse, forcing down mouthfuls of grease and carbs before they joined Strickland in the briefing room.

Strickland looked like she had been up for most of the night. Which probably wasn't far from the truth, thought Bald. She was dressed in the same dark trouser suit and shirt as the previous day, and her face looked drawn and tired. She was talking in urgent machine-gun bursts on her phone, taking long draws on her e-cigarette and helping herself to constant refills from a pot of coffee. Her foot was doing the tapping-against-the-floor thing, Bald noted. Her anxiety was understandable. They were dealing with a fluid situation. There were a lot of pieces on the board. A lot of factors to consider. She was having to respond to events as they happened.

Bald and Porter had a series of maps of Budapest spread out in front of them on the conference table. They were orientating themselves with the city, marking out key locations, identifying routes to and from the Royal Duna Hotel. Lansbury's favourite haunts. Places he had been known to go to for supper or for business meetings. Nearby public transport links. Tourist spots. Along with the physical maps, they had Google Maps blown on up the screens of a pair of thirteen-inch laptops. One window showed the Royal Duna on Street View. Another displayed a satellite view of a nearby Japanese restaurant Lansbury frequented. Regiment SOP before deploying to an unfamiliar environment: get your bearings, so you don't have to waste valuable time on the ground orientating yourself. When they landed in Budapest, Bald and Porter wanted to be able to hit the ground running.

Their bags were packed – clothes, wash bags. Bald had picked up a pair of suits from a chain store in Hereford. Black trousers, sports jackets, plus two plain white shirts and black ties and a pair of polished black lace-ups. All the kit they had been handed by the Scaley had been divided between their holdalls: clip-on GPS trackers, small sticky mics, modified phone and laptop adapters. Plus the SAS challenge coins and the passport-sized 2TB hard drives. They had their passports, a few hundred quid in pounds and the equivalent sum in Hungarian forints. Everything was set and ready to go.

All we need now is the call.

Strickland got off her phone. She took another long puff on her e-cig. Poured herself her fourth cup of coffee of the morning and said, 'That was our asset in Wroxham, at Lord McGinn's house.'

Porter looked up from the map, rubbing the bridge of his nose. 'And?'

'He says McGinn made the call to Lansbury a few minutes ago. Lansbury sounded a bit shaken up by the whole thing, but he's confident that his PA is going to call.'

'Did he say when?'

'No, but the fact that Lansbury is unsettled is good news for us. The more panicked he is about this attack, the more likely he is to want to get a new bodyguard detail in place soon.'

'Unless he decides to go with someone else,' Bald said.

'That won't happen,' Strickland replied firmly. 'We've been through this already. McGinn assured us that he has Lansbury's complete trust.'

'He would say that, wouldn't he? You've got him by the balls. He'd say anything to get out of a tight spot, just like the rest of them posh arseholes in the House of Lords.'

'McGinn will persuade Lansbury to hire you two. I'd bet my life on it.'

'You'd better be right,' said Bald. 'Because if he doesn't convince Lansbury we're the ones for the job, then this mission is fucked before it's even got off the ground.'

Strickland looked away, chewing anxiously on her bottom lip. The young woman from Maryhill, Glasgow, taking on the old boys' network, needing a big win. She turned back towards Bald and said, 'Give it three hours. We'll hear from Lansbury's office by then. I'm sure of it.'

Which turned out to be wide of the mark, but not by much. At twelve minutes past ten, the false-screen phone Bald had been given vibrated with an incoming call. There was a long mobile number on top of the screen that Bald didn't recognise, prefixed by a country code. *+36.* The dialling code for Hungary.

'This is it,' Strickland said, nerves creeping into her soft Scottish voice. 'Remember what we discussed. Stick to the script. Don't sound too enthusiastic and try to act surprised at getting the call.'

'I know what I'm doing,' Bald said brashly. 'I used to do this kind of thing for a living.'

He tapped the green icon on the lower-right corner of the screen. *Accept.* Put the call on speakerphone, so Porter and Strickland could listen in.

'Hello?' Bald said.

'Am I speaking with John Bald?'

The voice belonged to a woman. Young and professional, with a cut-glass accent so sharp it could have chopped fruit.

'Aye,' said Bald. 'That's me, lass. The one and only.'

The signal kept jumping around. Four bars, then three. Then two. Then back to four again. There was some kind of intermittent droning noise in the background, horns beeping. Traffic. He figured the PA was in a car. With Lansbury, perhaps. Being chauffeured to some meeting, maybe.

The woman said, 'My name is Freya Jansen. I work in the office of Derek Lansbury. I was given your details by a close friend of Mr Lansbury. Do you have a moment, by any chance?'

Jansen did most of the talking. She was curt and to the point. Mr Lansbury's security detail had fallen victim to an unfortunate street mugging the previous evening, she said. Perhaps Mr Bald had seen the item on the news? To cut a long story short, there was an immediate opening on his BG team. Two bodyguards, for an initial four-week period, possibly lasting for up to six months. The pay was £500 a day, non-negotiable. Mr Bald would receive a float for expenses and full medical insurance. They would need him to fly out at once, if he was interested. The same day, preferably.

'Mr Lansbury is a very busy man, and at considerable risk due to his outspoken stance on a number of issues,' Jansen said, as if she was reading from a script. Or perhaps her boss was listening in. 'I'm sure you can appreciate our need for a prompt response.'

'You're in luck,' Bald said. 'I just got off a big job, love. But I'll have to check with my partner first, see if he's free as well.'

'That would be …' Jansen paused. Bald heard the rustling of papers. 'Mr John Porter, correct?'

'Aye, that's him. Give us your details and I'll get back to you.'

'You can reach me on this number. But I would appreciate a prompt response. Mr Lansbury doesn't like to be kept waiting, you know.'

Bald said that he understood and would reply within the next fifteen minutes. He hung up. Looked over at Porter, grinning from ear to ear. 'Well, Mr Porter? Are you available?'

Porter laughed easily. The tension between them began to evaporate. Even Strickland relaxed, half-smiling, her foot no longer tapping anxiously.

Bald waited exactly nine minutes. Then he called Jansen back, gave her the good news. She perked up immediately. She took their passport details and said she would book them both on the 20.45 British Airways flight to Budapest, leaving from Heathrow that evening. Their tickets would be waiting for collection at the information desk. Time was of the essence, Jansen said. They needed Bald and Porter out in Hungary at once.

'I'll send you a message to confirm you're booked on the flight,' Jansen went on. 'Once you arrive in Budapest there will be a car waiting to take you to the hotel. We're checked in at the Royal Duna Hotel. I'll text you the details before you're due to take off.'

'Got it,' Bald said. 'Can't wait.'

Jansen said a few more words about how grateful Mr Lansbury was for their services, and how much he was looking forward to working with them. Which Bald was fairly sure was complete bullshit. He said a few similarly meaningless words in return.

Then he killed the call.

Porter turned to him, grinning. 'Easiest job interview I've ever had, that.'

'The Jock Bald charm, mate. Never fails.' He nodded at Strickland. 'Looks like you were right. Whatever your man said to Lansbury, it did the trick.'

Strickland ditched the smile. 'Don't get ahead of yourselves. That was the easy part. This is when the hard work really begins.'

SIXTEEN

They bugged out of Pontrilas twenty-three minutes later. Bald and Porter changed into their suits and ran through a series of last-minute checks on their surveillance equipment. At the same time, Strickland made a series of calls. First she rang through to the duty sergeant to arrange for a car to pick them up. Then she called Moorcroft to update him on the situation. A necessary measure, she explained to Bald and Porter. Although Strickland would be their daily point of contact during the op, it was important to keep Moorcroft in the loop. It would hurt his dignity if she tried to assert control while he was still in the job. She wished Bald and Porter good luck, said that she was rooting for them, and that if they needed anything then they should call her. Strickland was tough and straight talking and completely without front. Everything that Moorcroft wasn't, in fact. Bald found himself liking her more by the minute. And she was a Glasgow lass. You couldn't ask for a better handler.

Eleven minutes later, Vickers rang up to the briefing room and announced that their driver was waiting for them. Bald and Porter grabbed their kit, nodded at Strickland and left the surveillance block.

The car was a Vauxhall Insignia. A dated model, the silver bodywork worn and dented in places and lined with scratches. One of the range cars, Bald presumed. Vehicles that had been blown on previous ops and were given a new lease of life on the advanced driving ranges at Pontrilas.

They drove from the training camp up to Hereford train station. Bald and Porter paid cash for a pair of one-way tickets to London Paddington. Which cost them roughly the same as a discount flight to the Canary Islands. They took the next direct train and arrived in central London three and a half hours later, in the thick of rush hour. They threaded their way through a swarm of fast-moving commuters, rode the Heathrow Express and debussed at the stop for Terminals 1, 2 and 3. Then they collected their tickets from the BA desk, deposited their luggage in the hold and headed straight for Departures.

As part of their cover, they kept all their receipts. Bald and Porter were posing as independent contractors, Strickland had reminded them: they would be expected to claim back any monies they had spent on train fares and food while travelling to the job.

They had an hour to kill before their gate was announced, so they took a table at an airside pub, a garishly lit sports-themed bar with football and rugby memorabilia lining the walls. A handful of business types sat at the tables, sipping pints of lager, checking their phones or watching the news on the massive TV fixed to the back wall.

Bald ordered a cheeseburger and side of thick-cut fries, along with a Diet Coke. Porter went for the battered cod, chips and mushy peas, plus a glass of tap water. Bald watched his mucker carefully.

'You sure you don't fancy a pint with that, mate? Slug of vodka, maybe?'

Porter shook his head. 'No, Jock. I told you, I'm off that shit for good.'

'How long has it been, now?'

'Two hundred and seventy-three days,' Porter replied without a moment's hesitation. Pride in his voice. 'I haven't touched a drop for nine months.'

Bald took a hit of his Diet Coke. 'Just as long as it stays that way.'

'What are you saying, mate?'

'Nothing. But we both know what happens when you're stressed. Your first instinct is reach for the top shelf.'

'It won't happen again.'

'Good. Because I'm not picking up the slack for you again. Or have you forgotten what happened last time?'

Porter's face hardened. 'Course I fucking haven't.'

He looked away, casting his mind back to the Russia op. Back then, Porter had slipped. He'd given in to the dark voice in the back of his head, the one telling him to have a drink. He'd been pissed during a firefight. Almost got himself killed.

Porter had struggled with the demon drink for as long as he could remember. After the hostage-rescue mission in Beirut went wrong, he had hit the bottle big time. Ever since, it had been a constant battle between the two voices inside his head. One telling him to stay strong, not to go down that road again, to stay sober. The other whispering in his ear at his weakest moments, when he was angry or depressed or bored, urging him to have a drink. Just the one. A livener. Something to take the edge off. But Porter knew he couldn't go there.

I can never have just the one drink. Jock might be a bastard, but he's right.

For me, it's all or nothing. Sobriety, or oblivion.

Porter had chosen the former. But he had to be constantly vigilant, alert to temptation. He was careful never to be around alcohol, or big drinkers. And now he was about to go on an op with one of the biggest boozers in the history of the Regiment. But he was determined not to fail.

I won't let myself down, Porter swore to himself. *Not this time. I'm not going to give that Scottish wanker the satisfaction of proving me wrong.*

'This isn't going to be a stressful op anyway,' he said. 'You heard what Six told us. Straightforward job, low risk, every spare local asset ready to support us. And if it goes south, we've got that heli in Graz on standby.'

'True, but we're gonna be spending the next few months on dull-as-fuck BG duty. Plenty of idle time on our hands. All it takes is one moment of weakness.'

'It won't happen,' Porter repeated angrily. 'It took me years to put my life back on track. I'm not gonna piss it away now.'

Bald studied his mucker closely, then changed the subject. 'Let's just hope Lansbury has a loose tongue. The sooner Vauxhall can pin something on him, the less time we'll have to bodyguard the twat. I don't know about you, but I don't plan on spending the next six months working a protection job.'

Porter shrugged. 'If that's what it takes.'

'You're really up for this?'

'The bastard is a traitor. He's corrupt.'

'So are most of them tossers in parliament. Bunch of hand-job merchants.'

'Lansbury is different. He's on another level. He's selling us out to the Russians, for fuck's sake.'

'So what? Half those MPs are probably on the take in one form or another.'

Porter narrowed his eyes. 'Don't you want to nab the fucker?'

Bald said, 'If Lansbury has committed a crime then he deserves to go down for a long stretch in Wormwood Scrubs, picking up soap from the shower floor. But don't fool yourself into thinking he's the only one up to no good. They're all the same, mate.'

'Most MPs aren't working for the Russians. They're not committing treason.'

'If he's guilty. We don't know that.'

'Six wouldn't send us out there unless they were sure. The fucker's guilty. I'm sure of it. And he's gonna pay.'

Bald tilted his head to the side. 'Why do you give a toss whether Lansbury is dodgy or not? He means fuck-all to you.'

Porter stared at his mucker with a bemused expression. 'The guy is a fucking liar, Jock. He's up there on stage at rallies, telling everyone that he supports our military, and all the while he's doing shady backroom deals with the Russians. The bastard is pulling the wool over everyone's eyes.'

'That's just politics, mate. What else do you expect?'

'It's not right.' Porter looked down at his food, his hands trembling. 'I've had enough of those tossers in Westminster hood-winking us. They're all at it. They go on TV, tell everyone how proud they are of our lads and what they're doing, and then they go behind our backs and vote for big cuts to the armed forces, putting our lads' lives in danger. They sell everyone this big idea of a modern streamlined army, and it's just a bollocks excuse for disbanding all the regiments and laying off some poor sods. They give the generals a cosy retirement job in procurement, selling duff kit to the MoD, while they let ex-squaddies sleep rough on the streets. It's a bag of bollocks, Jock, all of it.'

'Christ, if you feel that strongly about it, why don't you get off your soap box and become an MP?'

'Fuck off, mate. You might be all right with Lansbury taking backhanders from Moscow while he poses next to veterans, but I'm not.'

'Guess I'm just a realist,' said Bald.

'No, you're a cynic. Only interested in lining your own pockets. Bet you don't even have a problem with what Lansbury is doing.'

Bald shook his head forcefully. 'That's bollocks. I'm just as determined to nail this bastard as you are. Don't pretend any different, just because you've got a bee in your bonnet about some dodgy politicians.'

Porter gave a dry laugh. 'Do me a favour. The only reason you're desperate to put Lansbury behind bars is so you can land that corporate gig.'

'Someone's got to look out for number one. Might as well be me.'

Bald polished off his last morsel of burger meat, washed it down with a slug of Diet Coke.

'Besides,' he went on. 'If our cover gets blown, those muppets at Vauxhall aren't going to be doing us any favours.'

Porter stopped picking at his chips, looked up at Bald. An expression of unease played out on his face. 'What the fuck are you talking about?'

Bald tapped the side of his head. 'Think about it, mate. Why did they recruit us for the job in the first place?'

'Because we're expendable.'

'Partly that, aye. But we're also legally convenient. We're not serving SAS officers. If this thing goes Pete Tong, they can claim that we're civilian contractors, with no connection to the security services. That takes MI6 out of the loop.'

'I'm in L Det,' Porter said. 'I'm still registered.'

'Part-time, TA, weekend warrior. Six would just say that you did your ninety days and then fucked off. They had no idea what you were up to on your time off.'

'You think they're setting us up?'

'I think they're covering their tracks. Watching their own backs, in case this whole thing turns into a clusterfuck. I know I'd be doing the same, if I was in Moorcroft's position.'

Porter stared at his half-eaten plate of food, his appetite vanishing. Bald was right, he realised. If it came out that the British Army had been spying on a sitting British MEP, there would be a legal and political shitstorm. Questions would be asked in parliament. The higher-ups would want to know who else was involved, who had authorised the operation. Heads would roll. Six would find itself at the centre of a scandal that would cause major embarrassment, domestically and abroad. By co-opting Bald and Porter, MI6 could keep themselves at a discreet distance from the mission. Argue that the two men assigned to guard Derek Lansbury were independent contractors, acting on their own instruction. Bald and Porter would be thrown to the wolves. And Moorcroft would enjoy his Cotswold retirement in peace.

Things are changing, Strickland had said. *We mean it this time.*

That was a lie, thought Porter. Not a deliberate one. She seemed fundamentally a good person. But he knew how Vauxhall worked. The faces might change, but the mentality always stayed the same.

'So that's it? We're on our own?'

Bald considered, then shook his head. 'I think Strickland meant it when she said she'd have our backs. She's not one for bullshit. She'll give us the heads-up if there's an attack planned on Lansbury.'

'But she's not the one calling the shots,' Porter said. 'Moorcroft is. For now.'

'Exactly. If someone gets word of what we're up to, then Strickland can't save us. The people above her will take the decision to pull the plug. And you and me will be fucked.'

Porter left the rest of his food. He could feel his stress levels rising again. The voice was whispering in his ear. Goading him.

You're gonna be on edge for months, guarding a guy you hate, hoping that no one compromises the operation. We both know you can't get through that without a drink.

Just the one. A double-measure of vodka. For old times' sake.

Porter drew in a deep breath, closed his eyes and did what he always did when he craved booze. He took the voice and put it in a box and shoved it to the back of his mind, where it couldn't torment him.

Forty minutes later, their flight was announced.

Ten hours after they had received the call at Pontrilas, Bald and Porter were in the air.

SEVENTEEN

They slept through most of the flight and landed at Ferenc Liszt Airport at twenty-eight minutes past midnight. The terminal was practically deserted. Bald and Porter waved their passports at the border guard, grabbed their luggage from the carousel and strolled through a set of sliding doors leading into the arrivals hall. A loose throng of tourists, taxi drivers and relatives stood around the waiting area. Border guards patrolled the hall, dressed in dark-blue uniforms and garrison caps, armed with black truncheons and Heckler & Koch USP pistols. Bald ran his eyes across the cluster of faces in front of him, searching for the guy they had been told to look for.

Freya Jansen had sent a message to Bald's phone shortly before their flight had taken off, written in the same blunt tone as her phone manner. Instructions for when they touched down in Hungary.

Driver will meet you at Arrivals. He will be holding a placard with your name on it. Car is a silver-grey Mercedes S-Class, licence plate HVZ-619. Driver's name is Tibor. I will be waiting for you at the hotel. I will be wearing dark trousers & shirt & green coat. Any problems, call me. F.

It took Bald about five seconds to identify their driver. A fifty-something man in grey slacks, white shirt and jacket, with a buzz cut and green eyes that were too close together. Bald pointed him out to Porter and the pair of them trooped over and briefly introduced themselves. The driver gave no indication that he spoke English. He simply turned and led them out of the terminal building, down a flight of steps towards the short-stay car park. At one o'clock in the morning the temperature was in the low single digits. A chill breeze hushed across the car park, cold blasts of it running through Bald's hair as he approached the car.

147

The Blades folded themselves into the back of the Mercedes and settled in for the ride. The car was spacious and quiet and smelled of fresh leather. They drove north for twenty minutes, past a poorly lit landscape of office blocks, warehouses and abandoned factories. After eight miles they swept past the national football stadium and then the city opened up in front of them, like something out of a pop-up children's book. They rolled down grey tree-lined streets flanked by scenes of faded grandeur and Soviet brutalism. Crumbling apartment blocks stood shoulder-to-shoulder with imposing Communist towers and corporate glass-and-steel structures. The whole story of the twentieth century, right there.

The driver arrowed north for another mile and made a left. Rolled past a long stretch of worn-down hotels kebab shops and discount supermarkets, and then they hit the inner sanctum. The business district. As if the city's grim past had been acid-washed and replaced with something shinier and more gentrified.

The cheap takeaways gave way to swish Italian restaurants. The supermarkets became designer fashion stores. The apartment blocks transformed into boutique hotels. They could have been in New York or Paris. Traffic was heavier here, even in the dead hours. Yellow taxis hogged the sides of the road. A surprisingly large number of people were out, given the lateness of the hour. Stag groups, couples taking a stroll along the Danube, punters emerging from the casino or heading out to one of the nearby strip clubs.

They turned right after the casino, the driver easing off the accelerator as they neared a grandiose five-storey hotel on their right. The Royal Duna Hotel. Bald recognised it from the maps he had studied back at Pontrilas. Even from the back seat of the S-Class, the building looked impressive. Like the official residence of some minor European royalty.

They debussed from the S-Class, unloaded their luggage from the boot and entered a marble-floored lobby with high ceilings and decorated with mosaics and modernist artwork. Soothing classical music pumped out of unseen speakers.

They made a beeline for the far end of the lobby. A smartly

dressed woman worked the night shift, standing behind a walnut reception desk as wide as a train carriage. There was a seating area to the left of the reception, an arrangement of designer lounge chairs and sofas circled around dark-wood coffee tables. A petite woman with a bob-cut of platinum blonde hair sat at the rearmost table, eyes fixed on her phone screen. She was dressed in plain grey trousers and a black satin shirt, with a bright green wool coat draped across her lap. The only person in the lobby other than the staff. At the sound of Bald and Porter's approaching footsteps the woman looked up, killed the screen on her phone and stood to greet them.

Bald said, 'Freya Jansen, right?'

The woman nodded. Her eyes darted quickly from Bald to Porter, as if trying to decide which one was which. They settled on Bald.

'You must be Jock,' she said. She sounded even more polished in person than on the phone.

'That's me, aye.' Bald had included a brief description of himself and Porter when replying to Jansen's text message. 'This is my partner, John Porter.'

'Pleasure,' Porter said, thrusting out a hand.

Jansen didn't shake it. Her eyes had dropped to Porter's disfigured left hand. A look of disapproval crossed her face. 'Your CV didn't say anything about a disability.'

'It's not a disability,' Porter replied through gritted teeth. 'Just an old injury I picked up on the job.'

'I don't care how it happened, you should have told me. Derek doesn't appreciate surprises, you know.'

'It won't affect my performance, if that's what you're worried about.'

'I sincerely hope not.' She took a deep breath and sighed irritably. 'Well, at least you both made it. Thank God. Derek will be relieved. He's been terribly upset by this whole business.'

Bald looked Freya Jansen casually up and down. She had a small round mouth that drooped at the edges, skin the colour of milk and slanted eyebrows that looked painted on. Not unattractive, thought Bald. A little flat-chested for his tastes. But he could work with that. Her eyes kept wandering off as she spoke,

149

glancing impatiently around the room. She gave the impression of having a million other places she would rather be.

'Where's the great man now?' he asked.

'Asleep. I thought it best not to disturb him, after what happened yesterday. I'll formally introduce you in the morning. He'll be up bright and early. Big day ahead, what with the conference.'

'Conference?' Bald repeated.

'More of a private gathering, actually. Derek and his political allies. They're meeting tomorrow night.'

'Here? In Budapest?'

Jansen shook her head. 'At a private residence outside the city. Derek is overseeing the proceedings personally, as a matter of fact. He'll be spending tomorrow making sure everything is in order. Dealing with any last-minute hiccups, sorting out the travel arrangements, that kind of thing. Going to be a bit of a manic day.'

Bald exchanged a knowing glance with Porter. 'Looks like we got here just in time, then.'

'That depends. If you were hoping for a nice slow start to get yourselves bedded in, I'm afraid you're out of luck.'

Porter said, 'How long is this conference going on for?'

'Just tomorrow evening, as far as I know. Derek will be staying here for a few days afterwards while he assists Mr Fodor in his re-election campaign. Then it's a week in DC and three days in London. Then on to Brussels.'

'Busy man,' Bald said. Because he felt like he had to say something.

'That's Derek for you. Likes to stay on his feet, does everything at a hundred miles an hour. He's got extraordinary stamina for a man of his age. You'll learn that yourselves, soon enough.'

There was a light of enthusiasm in her eyes when she talked about her boss. Bald wondered if there was something else going on there.

'We'll have to go over his schedule,' he said. 'Me and Jock will need to know every relevant detail. Where he's going, what the plans are, who he's meeting with and when.'

Jansen narrowed her eyes suspiciously. 'What do you need all that information for?'

'The more we know, the better prepared we are to keep him safe.'

'We'll discuss all of this tomorrow, when you meet Derek. He can decide what you need to know, and what you don't.'

'What's the score in terms of transport?' asked Porter.

'We have the hotel chauffeur. He drives Derek around.' She peered at him. 'Is that a problem?'

'We'll need a hire car to follow him with. One of us will ride with the principal, the other lad will stay close behind in case of trouble. Basic SOP, that.'

'SOP?'

'Standard operating procedure.'

'I see. Leave it with me. I'll take care of it.' She glanced down at her watch. 'First, let's get you checked in. You'll be staying in the same room that Gary and Mick used.'

'Who?'

'The previous security detail. They were booked into a room a few doors down from Derek. Twin room. I assume that's acceptable.'

'Where will you be?'

'In the adjoining room to Derek. He works very long hours, as you might imagine. He's very much in demand these days. Keeping up with his schedule is a full-time job.'

'I bet it is.'

Bald looked at Jansen closely. Her cheeks were slightly flushed, her hair was ruffled. He got the impression that she was doing more with Lansbury than merely going over his itinerary and making him coffee. A lot more.

They walked with Jansen over to the reception, waited while she barked orders at the woman behind the desk. The receptionist tapped away at her computer terminal. A moment later a dwarf-like bellboy sprang out of some unseen nook, took Bald and Porter's holdalls, dumped them on a metal luggage cart and wheeled the cart into a service lift. An impressive feat, for a guy who stood at around four and a half feet. Jansen took a pair of key cards from the receptionist and led Bald and Porter over to the lift. They rode the next one up to the third floor and paced down the corridor until they stopped outside the door to Room 319.

Jansen swiped open the door, handed over the key cards to Bald and Porter. A moment later the dwarf bellboy wheeled into view, pushing along the luggage trolley. About three times as tall as the guy himself. He unpacked their holdalls from the cart, lugged them inside the hotel room, placed them on the floor next to the twin beds. Bald gave the guy a five-hundred-forint tip. About £1.50 in UK sterling. The dwarf's face lit up. He pocketed the note, bowed and paced back down the corridor. Jansen stepped outside the room and pointed to another door, fifteen metres further down the corridor.

'That's Derek's room,' she said. 'I'll be in the next room along.'

'It's just the two of you here?' asked Porter.

'Yes, why?'

'No reason. Just assumed he'd have a bigger team with him. What with the gathering and everything.'

'Normally, yes. But tomorrow's event is a very private affair. Derek doesn't want word of it getting out. His parliamentary aides don't even know about it.'

'What's with all the secrecy?'

'Derek and his friends are worried about protests,' Jansen said. 'They want a low-key meeting. Minimal disruption. The last thing they need is the usual rabble of anarchists, socialists and militants causing a fuss outside the venue. Understandably so.'

'This conference. Big deal, is it?' asked Bald.

Jansen stared at him. 'You ask a lot of questions for a bodyguard.'

'Just curious.'

'Well, don't be. You're hired muscle, not political consultants. All you need to do is look hard and keep your mouths shut.'

She smiled politely, but there was a coldness to her voice. A young PA in the orbit of power, over-protective of their principal and suspicious of anyone trying to muscle in on their territory. Porter knew the type well. They took shit from their bosses and unloaded it on to the poor sod on the next rung down. Which just so happens to be us, he thought.

He spread his hands. 'We're not looking for conflict here. We're just trying to build up a picture of the principal's security arrangements. The more we're in the loop, the safer he is.'

Jansen stood up straight. 'I wouldn't worry yourselves too much about the conference. Should be a straightforward engagement, and I'll be on the phone if there are any problems.'

'You're not going with him?'

'Me? No.' Jansen sniffed. 'Derek will be attending alone. I'm to stay here and hold the fort until he returns.'

Porter detected a clear note of disappointment in her voice. And maybe bitterness too.

'You'll be expected to keep this information to yourself, of course,' she added. 'There's a confidentiality clause in the contracts you'll sign, non-negotiable. Breach it and you'll be removed from the team immediately.'

'Don't worry, love. You can trust us.'

'I sincerely hope so.' Jansen glanced at her watch again. 'Right, I'm off. If you have any problems, message me. Otherwise I'll see you in the lobby tomorrow morning. Seven o'clock. You'll begin your duties and meet Derek then.'

Jansen turned on her heels and started to beat a path up the corridor towards her room. She stopped, half-turned and looked back at the two ex-Blades. 'Oh, one more thing.'

'What's that?' asked Bald.

'Your CV. It says you left the SAS in 2011, but there's no record of you working in the private sector until 2013. What were you doing for those two years?'

Bad shit, thought Bald.

Drug-trafficking. Gunrunning. Killing.

Working for some very bad people.

He glimpsed Porter staring at him out of the tail of his eye. The migraine sparked up between his temples again. 'I took some time off. Did a bit of travelling and the like. Thought I'd see the world.'

'I see.'

The look on her face implied she didn't. Jansen watched him for a moment longer. Then she turned and headed off towards her room.

Bald watched her for a beat. He didn't like her attitude, but he still wouldn't have minded a crack at that arse.

He followed Porter into their twin room. Entered a space the approximate size of a Kensington flat, decorated in shades of cream and ivory, furnished with a polished black desk, built-in wardrobes and two single beds. One of the smaller rooms in the hotel, probably, but still a step up from the dumps Bald was used to staying in. The bathroom was constructed from dark marble and stocked with complimentary grooming products from brands Bald had never heard of. A pair of French windows on the far wall overlooked the Danube. There was a Nespresso machine and a minibar filled with miniature bottles of Bombay Sapphire, Courvoisier and Johnnie Walker Black Label. All of his favourites. Bald nodded approvingly.

'Now this is more like it. Say what you like about our man Lansbury, but the bloke has got good taste. If this is how he likes to travel, I could get used to this.'

'Makes you wonder, though,' said Porter.

'What's that?'

'Lansbury is on an MEP salary, and yet he's set himself up here. Plus our own wages and expenses, and his staff. Must be costing him a small fortune.'

'He's got that weekly talk show on American radio. Maybe they're paying him a tidy packet.'

'Or he's getting paid by someone else.'

'The Russians, you mean?'

'Who else?'

Bald considered. 'Could be. But if this is what working for the Kremlin does for your bank balance, I can see the appeal.'

'He's selling us out, mate. The bloke's a fucking criminal.'

'And a rich one.'

Porter sniffed. 'That doesn't make it all right.'

'No, but you've got to hand it to the man. If he's committing treason, he's making a success out of it.'

There was a trace of admiration in his voice. Porter looked at Bald and once again wondered about his mucker's loyalties. *Can I really trust Jock? Will he have my back, if it comes down to it?*

Bald disappeared into the bathroom to get cleaned up. Porter dug out his iPhone and went through the sequence he'd memorised to bring up the encrypted screen. It took him a few attempts to get it right. He typed a new message to the one number stored in the address book. The message read, *We're in. All good so far. Meeting BROKEN RECORD tomorrow.*

He hit send. There was a thirty-second delay, and then Strickland replied. *Any news on BROKEN RECORD's plans?*

Gathering taking place tomorrow evening, Porter wrote. *Somewhere outside city. Very private, according to PA.*

Porter waited, and then Strickland wrote back, *Good work. Any idea what BROKEN RECORD is doing there?*

Not yet, Porter typed. *Will find out more tomorrow.*

There was another delay before Strickland wrote back again. *Okay. Watch yourselves.*

Porter wrote back, *Will do.* Then he put the phone to sleep.

He grabbed a bottle of sparkling water and fired up the TV. Toasted himself. Another day of sobriety.

Porter sipped his expensive water and soaked up the news. CNN was running a story about the US president's latest rant. He was standing in front of a podium at a rally somewhere in the Midwest. Behind him stood a heaving crowd of supporters, hollering and cheering his every word. They were overwhelmingly white, Porter noted. And old. Many of them wore baseball caps with slogans about making America great again. Others held up placards with slogans like *Drain The Swamp!* The president was angrily denouncing NATO, railing against Germany and other allies he accused of not pulling their weight. The rally seemed like a big event, thought Porter. Large crowd, blanket media coverage. The kind of event where Lansbury would have appeared on stage to introduce the president. Or perhaps he'd be in a TV studio somewhere, defending his close friend.

So why is he out here in Eastern Europe, meeting with a bunch of fringe populists and fascists?

Lansbury is a Russian agent. Whatever it is he's planning it must be big. But what is it? Porter asked himself.

He couldn't think clearly. He was tired from the day's travelling and the long hours spent in the briefing room at Pontrilas. At some point Porter finally closed his eyes and sank into a shallow and restless sleep.

EIGHTEEN

Bald and Porter rose at six o'clock. They took turns to shower and shave and dressed in their matching dark suits. Porter took one of the clip-shaped GPS trackers from his holdall, remembered what Hogan had told them about best practice and planting a second bug on the target, and grabbed one of the smaller coin-sized listening devices. He made sure the rest of the equipment was hidden from view at the bottom of the holdall, zipped it shut and secured it with a standard travel padlock. Then he followed Bald out of the room and down the stairs to the lobby.

The meeting with Lansbury had been set for seven o'clock, Jansen had said. Which gave them half an hour to grab breakfast. They made their way over to the brasserie, gave their room number to a waitress wearing a frozen smile and helped themselves to platefuls of scrambled eggs, bacon and tomato, wholegrain toast and bowls of fruit, washed down with orange juice and a pot of coffee. At five minutes to seven they headed back out to the lobby and sat down at one of the spare tables while they waited for Lansbury and his PA.

A minute later, Bald's phone buzzed with a new message from Jansen.

Running late. L will be down shortly. F

'Fucking typical,' Bald snarled after he read the message out to Porter. 'We're here bang on time, and the principal is pissing about.'

'Did she say how long they would be?' asked Porter.

Bald shook his head. 'They'll keep us waiting for ages yet, mark my words. Always the bloody same with these people.'

They weren't tense or anxious about being introduced to Lansbury. Both Bald and Porter had worked as bodyguards for several high-profile figures in the past. But they also knew that close-protection jobs were often frustrating. Hours spent sitting around, twiddling your thumbs while you waited for the principal to emerge. This is the first morning on the job, thought Bald, and Lansbury is already getting on our nerves.

Thirty minutes passed. There was still no sign of Lansbury. Bald checked his phone again. Nothing from Jansen. An hour passed. The lobby began to fill up. The early morning checkouts. People with bills to settle and flights to catch. Businessmen heading off to meetings, tourists hoping to steal a march on the big tour groups. Bellboys scurried back and forth with luggage, eager for a tip. A steady stream of guests flowed through the lobby. Bald heard a mix of accents and languages. Mandarin and French and German, the occasional American.

A second hour passed. Bald checked his phone again. Messaged Jansen. *Are you on your way down?* A minute later she wrote back: *Sorry. Held up. Down soon.*

'Bastard is taking his merry fucking time,' Bald mumbled.

Porter laughed cynically. 'I'd get used to it if I were you, mate. You know what these politicians are like. They don't see us as bodyguards. We're just staff members to them. Next thing you know, he'll be asking us to carry his luggage.'

That drew a derisive snort from Bald. 'If that happens, he's getting a fucking slap.'

'We don't have a choice. This is how it's going to be from now on. No point getting worked up over it.'

'Yeah, well. Strickland had best keep her word about that job in corporate. I'm not putting up with this shite for the next six months unless there's a pot of gold at the end of it.'

At nine-thirty the doors on the nearest lift sucked open and Jansen emerged, dressed in a tight bodycon dress and beige heels, with the same striking green coat over the top. She was followed by a short, stumpy man in his late fifties, with ruffled grey hair and the ruddy complexion of a heavy drinker, dressed in a waxed farmer's jacket and mustard-coloured trousers. Bald recognised his face from a hundred different TV interviews and press clippings.

Derek Lansbury.

Jansen led her boss across the lobby, pointing out Bald and Porter. The Blades rose from their seats to greet their principal: the man they would be guarding for the next six months. The famous populist moved in short, urgent strides, his arms swinging heavily from side to side, as if he was on a military march. With his waxed jacket, corduroy trousers and crumpled blue shirt, he was dressed like a gentleman farmer from the shires, popping out for a pint in the lounge bar.

Lansbury stopped in front of Bald and Porter and rested his jacket over the back of the nearest armchair. He ran a hand through his hair and looked the two bodyguards slowly up and down as Jansen introduced them. He reminded Bald of a general inspecting his troops on the parade ground.

'Freya tells me you two are the new Mick and Gary,' Lansbury said.

A statement, not a question. He had a plummy English accent, hoarsened by years of heavy smoking and drinking. Up close the guy looked smaller than he did on TV, thought Bald. Five-five or six, perhaps. He reeked of tobacco and cheap cologne. His forehead glistened. Bald could almost see the alcohol oozing out of his pores. His eyes were small and lizard-like, darting left and right, not missing a single thing.

'Yes, sir,' Porter replied. 'That's us.'

'Good to have you aboard. Let's hope you do a damn sight better than those last two fellows. I assume you heard what happened?'

'Only what's been in the news, sir.'

'I still can't understand it. Two highly trained professionals, thirty years of experience between them, roughed up and hospitalised by a damn mugger.'

Bald said, 'We'll protect you, sir. Don't worry about that. Some bastard migrant takes a pop at you with a knife, he's the one ending up in A&E. Not us.'

'I should bloody well hope so.'

Bald nodded and cleared his throat. 'I just wanted to say, sir, it's a great honour and privilege to be working for you. For both of us. Me and John are big fans of yours.'

'That's good to know. One needs all the friends one can get in this line of work.'

'You've got two supporters right here, sir. Ignore them bleeding heart liberals on the BBC. You've done more for our country than any one of those self-serving twats in Westminster.'

'That's very kind of you.' Lansbury visibly relaxed. His lips parted into a slight smile. 'Freya tells me you're SAS.'

'Former,' Bald corrected. 'John and I both retired from the Regiment a few years ago.'

'And you have the scars to prove your service, I see.' Lansbury pointed to Porter's disfigured hand. 'How did you do that, might I ask?'

'It's a long story, sir.'

Lansbury's eyes glowed with curiosity. 'You will have to tell it to me one day. I do *love* a good war story.'

'It'd be my pleasure, sir,' Porter replied tersely.

There was a smugness about Lansbury that grated with him. The guy carried himself in the same way as the Ruperts that Porter had known at Hereford. Aloof, ignorant and possessing an impermeable self-confidence that verged on arrogance. The kind you get from growing up with a silver spoon stuck up your arse, thought Porter.

'I knew a chap in the SAS, actually,' said Lansbury.

'Oh, yes?' asked Bald.

Lansbury nodded keenly. 'A fellow by the name of Richard Thacker. Friend of mine from my days at Charterhouse. Went to Sandhurst. Perhaps you know him?'

'I know the one,' said Bald. 'Lieutenant Colonel Thacker. He was the commander of 22 SAS back in my day. Excellent officer, sir. All the lads at Hereford loved him.'

Porter looked askance at Bald, eyes wide as saucers. Lansbury's smile broadened. 'Richard will be pleased to hear that. He runs a business now, teaching SAS leadership skills to executive types in the City. Doing rather well for himself, I gather.'

'Good on him, sir.'

Lansbury nodded stiffly and said, 'Listen, chaps, I've got a busy day ahead of me.' He waved a hand at Jansen. 'Freya will talk you through my schedule and arrangements. It's all rather self-explanatory, I think you'll find.'

'Just one thing,' Porter said. 'We'll need you to wear this from now on.'

He reached into his inside jacket pocket, pulled out one of the clip-like GPS trackers the Scaley had given him back at Pontrilas. Lansbury frowned at it.

'What the devil is that?'

'This is a wireless tracker. You clip it to the side of your belt. If you're in trouble, just push this SOS button and it'll send an alarm to our phones.'

'The last two blockheads didn't ask me to wear any such thing.'

Bald said, 'With all due respect, sir, your last team ended up getting beaten up by a homeless thief. Might be worth listening to us instead.'

Lansbury exhaled irritably. 'Is this really necessary?'

'It's for your own personal safety, sir.'

'Fine. Christ. If it'll stop you two badgering me. Although I must say, I really don't see the point.'

He snatched up the tracking clip, unbuttoned his jacket and attached it to the left side of his black leather belt. Secured it to the belt strap and spread out his hands. 'There? Satisfied?'

'Very good, sir,' Bald replied flatly.

Jansen coughed. 'We should wrap this up, sir. Your driver will be outside any moment.'

Bald and Porter traded confused expressions. Bald said, 'What's going on?'

'Mr Lansbury has a ten o'clock appointment across the city,' Jansen answered for her boss.

'Who with?'

'None of your damn business,' Lansbury snapped, his irritation growing more pronounced with every passing moment. 'I'm meeting an old friend, that's all. Nothing for you two to worry about.'

'We'll be coming with you, though?'

'Absolutely not. There's no need.'

Porter shook his head firmly. 'That's not a good idea, sir. Wherever it is you're going, we need to be there with you. Sweep the place, check the layers of security.'

'Not going to happen. This is a private meeting. You're not coming anywhere near it.'

'At least let us accompany you in the car.'

'No. I promised my friend I would come alone. The last thing I want to do is turn up with you two hulking idiots in tow. She'd never forgive me. It would be a betrayal of her trust.'

'I'm with Porter,' Bald said. 'This is a bad idea. We can't protect you if we're not there.'

'And I'm telling you there's no need.'

'Sir, we have to insist.'

'Insist all you want. You'll do as I bloody well say. Or have you forgotten who's paying your salaries?'

Bald masked his anger, kept his voice diplomatic. 'We're not trying to be difficult. But if you go to this meeting without us and something happens, me and Porter will take the blame.'

'And I'm telling you, nothing is going to happen. It's a short hop across the river, for God's sake. Not a bloody trek into the Afghan mountains.'

'Sir, with all due respect, I really think we should go with you.'

'I don't care what you think!' Lansbury suddenly exploded. 'I'm going to this thing alone and that's the end of it. If you're not happy with that arrangement then you can pack your bags and take the next flight home, quite frankly.'

Lansbury glared at them, fuming through his nostrils, bristling with indignation.

Bald held up his hands in a gesture of apology. He could see that this was a battle they weren't going to win. If they tried to push it any harder, they'd find themselves off the team and the mission would be over before it had even begun. And I can kiss goodbye to that corporate job, Bald reminded himself.

'I'm sorry, sir,' he said, glancing quickly at Porter. 'We're just trying to do our jobs. Our only concern is for your safety.'

Lansbury took in a deep breath, calming himself down. 'Look, I'm grateful for your concern. Really. Very professional and all that. But I'm already wearing this tracker of yours. That's enough, surely? If I run into trouble I'll press the button and you'll soon know about it. Otherwise you can assume that everything is fine. Okay?'

'Aye. That'll do just fine, sir.'

'Can you tell us how long you'll be, at least?' asked Porter.

'I've set aside three hours for this thing. Should be back here by one o'clock latest. So there's your answer.'

'What's the deal after your meeting has finished?'

'Talk to Freya,' Lansbury replied impatiently. 'I dare say she knows my diary better than I do.'

They looked towards Jansen. She consulted the calendar app on her phone, reading out from it.

'Mr Lansbury has a brief phone interview at one-fifteen with the *Telegraph*. He'll take that in his room. Then lunch at the Manhattan Bar and Grill across the street. Then back here to make final preparations for this evening's conference. Mr Lansbury will leave here at four o'clock on the dot. Which reminds me. I spoke with the concierge first thing this morning. He's sorted you out with a hire car. Speak to him. He's got the keys.'

Just then Jansen's phone trilled. She swiped to answer, listened for a few seconds and then placed a manicured hand on Lansbury's shoulder. 'Your driver is waiting outside, sir.'

'Tell him I'll be out in a minute.'

Jansen relayed the message, quit the call. She ran through a quick checklist with Lansbury, making sure he had his wallet and phone, fussing over him. She didn't behave like any PA that Bald had ever seen. She was relaxed around her boss. Informal, easy going. Definitely something more going on between them, he decided.

Lansbury clapped his hands together and stood up ramrod straight. 'Right, a quick nip to the loo then I'm off.' He stared at Bald and Porter. 'Unless you two are planning on following me into the toilets while I take a piss as well?'

'No, sir,' Bald replied. 'That won't be necessary.'

Lansbury harrumphed loudly and marched off towards the restrooms at the other end of the lobby. Jansen put her phone away, turned to address Bald and Porter.

Said, 'You'll have to keep yourselves busy until Derek returns from his meeting. Explore the city, or whatever it is you people do in your free time.'

'What about you?' asked Bald.

'I'll be upstairs, dealing with the daily torrent of emails and media requests. The work never stops.'

'I can imagine, lass,' Bald said.

Jansen gave him a funny look.

Porter said, 'We'll need the number for the restaurant you're planning to eat at. Give us a chance to phone ahead and get them to reserve the tables, make sure it's secure.'

'I'll send you the details. Anything else you need, I'll be in my room.'

She spun away and marched back off towards the bank of lifts. Bald waited until she had disappeared from view and turned to Porter. 'Quick. Give us one of those coin bugs.'

'What for?'

Bald jerked a thumb in the direction of the toilets. 'This muppet knows he's wearing a tracking device. What if he ditches it? We need a second bug on him as a backup.'

'You think he's lying to us?'

'I think he's desperate for us not to get eyes on this fucking thing. Which means we need to know what he's up to.'

Porter dipped a hand into his jacket pocket and dug out the coin-sized mic. Bald snatched it up, reached over for the waxed jacket Lansbury had draped over the armchair. Porter kept an eye on the restroom door while Bald peeled off the back covering from the mic, lifted up the corduroy collar on the jacket and stuck the device to the underside. He pressed down on the bug with his thumb until it was stuck in place. Smoothed down the collar again, folded the coat over the back of the armchair and sat down.

A few moments later, Lansbury swept back into view. He quick-walked over, snatched up his farmer's coat and nodded at Bald and Porter. 'I'll see you two fellows in a while, then.'

'Yes, sir. Enjoy your meeting.'

'Oh, I will.'

Lansbury grinned. He threw on his coat and beat a quick path towards the hotel entrance, humming a tune to himself. Through the glass Bald could see a Mercedes-Benz S-Class parked up in front of the main doors. A driver stepped out of the vehicle, circled round and opened the rear passenger door for Lansbury. The same chauffeur who'd picked up Bald and Porter at the airport the previous night. Lansbury slid into the back seat, and then the driver closed the rear door and climbed back behind the wheel. The S-Class moved forward about an inch. There was a line of taxis ahead of them, blocking the exit while they disgorged passengers or loaded suitcases. Nine-thirty in the morning. Prime checkout time. Everyone was in a big hurry.

The chauffeur blasted his horn. Bald turned to Porter and said, 'Get the car keys from the concierge. We need to follow him.'

Porter hesitated. 'We should call it in to Strickland first. Check with her.'

'There's no time. We've got to leave now.'

'What if he spots us?'

'He won't. The prick hasn't set eyes on the rental car yet. He won't have any way of knowing it's us.'

Porter looked uneasy. 'Our orders are to bodyguard Lansbury, not tail him around town. If we call Strickland she might be able to get another team in place. Let them take care of it.'

'Unless he ditches the tracker first. Then we're shafted.'

'What about his room? That needs to be bugged too.'

'We'll do that later,' Bald said. 'Right now, we need to know who this twat is meeting and why.'

Porter shifted uneasily, pursed his lips. 'I don't know, Jock.'

'Come on, mate,' Bald urged. 'Stop being a fucking lackey for Moorcroft and the rest of them suits.'

Porter lingered for a moment longer. Torn between the logic of Bald's argument and their orders from Vauxhall. Then he sighed and stood up. 'Fine,' he said. 'Let's do it.'

NINETEEN

They grabbed the keys from the concierge and hastened down to the underground car park. There was no paperwork to sign. Jansen had taken care of everything. The concierge gave them a Volvo key fob encased in tan leather, roughly the size of a clamshell phone, and directed them to an XC90 SUV parked at the back of the basement parking area. They found the wagon amid a row of Maseratis, Lamborghinis and Tesla Roadsters. Bald took the wheel while Porter tapped open the GPS tracking app on the iPad. There was no ignition key. Bald simply depressed the brake and twisted the engine dial clockwise, towards the START position. The Volvo hummed into life. Thirty seconds later they rolled up the concrete parking ramp and pulled out into traffic in front of the Royal Duna.

The S-Class didn't have much of a head start. Two minutes, by Porter's reckoning. Which worked out to seven hundred metres, give or take. He was tracking the flashing red dot on the iPad screen, watching it crawl forward, giving Bald updates. Progress was slow, clearly. They were in the middle of the sightseeing district, the roads choked with open-top tour buses and delivery vans and taxis and mopeds. Wherever Lansbury was going, he wouldn't be getting there in a hurry.

For the first five hundred metres the distance between the S-Class and the Volvo stayed roughly the same. Most of the inner-city roads operated on a one-way system, meaning there were no obvious shortcuts Bald and Porter could use to close the gap. And all the roads were equally congested. This quarter of the city was one giant traffic jam. They looped counter-clockwise round the square in front of the Royal Duna and headed east, following the same route as the S-Class. Taking them away from the Chain

Bridge, towards the city centre. Chinese tour groups hogged the pavements, posing in front of selfie-sticks and pulling their wind-breakers tight across their fronts. Budapest was still in the grip of winter. The Danube was granite-grey and choppy. Bare trees lined the pavements like matchsticks. Clouds the colour of gravel pressed low in the sky, threatening to spill more heavy rain over the windswept residents.

Porter traced the flashing red dot on the map. It was still on the move. Which meant that Lansbury hadn't yet ditched his tracker.

Twenty seconds later the signal stopped.

They inched along Jozsef Attila for another four hundred metres until they came to a standstill. Then Porter saw it. 'Look,' he said, pointing at the windscreen. 'There!'

Bald craned his neck, peering through the gaps in the crowds of pedestrians. Then he caught sight of it too, a hundred metres ahead. The S-Class had pulled over at the side of the road, next to one of the state-licensed tobacco shops with the familiar 'T' logo hanging from the window.

As Bald and Porter looked on Lansbury emerged from the shop clutching a pack of cigarettes, hands peeling off the cello-phane wrapper like skin from a fruit. He stopped a couple of metres from the S-Class, glanced around. Reached down to his belt. Unhooked something, chucked it into the nearest bin along with the cigarette pack wrapper and foil. Then he clambered back into the waiting vehicle.

'He's thrown away the tracker,' Porter confirmed as the S-Class pulled out into traffic again, a hundred metres ahead of the Volvo. The GPS signal remained stationary, hovering over the location of the bin.

'Bastard is definitely up to something,' Bald muttered.

'The question is, what?'

Bald didn't reply. He kept his eyes on the road as they contin-ued tailing the S-Class at a safe distance, staying at least eighty metres behind. There was little danger of Lansbury spotting them, Bald reassured himself. The guy would be comfortable now that he'd lost the tracking device, thinking that he was safe. He wouldn't be looking for a tail. The Volvo was a brand-new rental, so it wouldn't look familiar to him. And he certainly wouldn't

166

imagine that his brand-new bodyguards would be shadowing him.

Wherever he's going, he doesn't want us to know about it.

They hung a right at the main square at Deák Ferenc, staying five or six cars behind the S-Class at all times. Shuttled south along the bustling main thoroughfare, passing rickety trams and coffee chains and market stalls selling local delicacies and bottles of fruit brandy. They passed brown-brick tenements and futuristic corporate offices, eyesore concrete apartments. There were synagogues and ruin bars, 1920s-style cafes and tanning salons with names like Sexy Brown Solarium. There were no distinct neighbourhoods, as far as Bald could tell. Everything was just kind of mashed together.

Bald glanced around, searching for the waves of migrants the Hungarian prime minister had been banging on about, but he couldn't see any. Maybe he wasn't looking hard enough. Or maybe they were going in the wrong direction.

At his side, Porter reached for his false-screen iPhone, punched in the sequence to unlock the encrypted screen and sent a brief message to Strickland's number. *Heading to a meeting across town. We're following BROKEN RECORD.*

There was the usual thirty-second delay before Strickland wrote back. *Your orders were to stay with BROKEN RECORD. We did not authorise a pursuit.*

No choice, Porter replied. *BROKEN RECORD wanted to go alone. Dumped his GPS tracker.*

There was an uncomfortably long pause before Strickland finally responded with a terse message. *Acknowledged. Have you got audio?*

Already taken care of, Porter typed with his one good hand. *Planted a listening device on him. Will let you know when BROKEN RECORD arrives at RV.*

Strickland wrote, *Stay put when you get there. No further action. Understood?*

Porter replied, put his phone on the dash and looked over at Bald. 'What was all that shit about Thacker back there, telling Lansbury he was some great fucking officer? We both know that bloke was a wanker. Everyone hated his guts.'

'I had to say something complimentary,' Bald said. 'A bloke like Lansbury, half of his mates are probably former Ruperts. Let's just hope the fucker bought it.'

Porter said, 'You had me fooled, Jock. He was lapping it up.'

Bald tightened his grip on the steering wheel and shook his head. 'I can't believe we're having to blow smoke up this twat's arse.'

'As long as it helps to bring him down, who gives a toss?'

They rode south for another quarter of a mile, following the S-Class as it veered west instead of south, heading back in the direction of the Danube. They rolled past some kind of huge indoor market and hit a cantilevered bridge, flanked by statues of falcons resting atop a pair of golden globes. The S-Class took the bridge west across the river, away from the hustle and dirt and noise of the eastern side of the city, towards the tranquil streets, leafy hillsides and ancient citadels of the old town.

They came off the bridge and hung a quick left, tailing the S-Class past the Gellert spa, taking them away from the major tourist attractions further to the north. Porter stared at the iPad, frowning heavily at the map.

'Where the fuck is this bloke going?' he wondered aloud.

'No idea,' Bald replied, glancing over at the screen fixed to the dash. 'But it can't be far from here, if he's gonna make that meeting for ten o'clock.'

They stuck close to the S-Class, heading south for another mile, through what Bald felt must be a university district. The roads were narrower and lined with a mixture of old and new apartment blocks. There were hipster cafes and bookshops, bars that probably sold craft beer. Not Bald's kind of scene. Not his scene at all. He couldn't understand the whole craft beer thing. In his mind, taste was for poofs. Consumption was key. Specifically, quantity and speed. How much you could drink, and how fast. The more you drank, the more of a man you were. Which was what happened when you grew up in Dundee in the seventies, Bald supposed.

After half a mile the S-Class turned right and carried on through a residential suburb, the streets lined with depressing apartment blocks and antiquated public buildings. Home to the lower-paid government employees and city workers, Bald guessed. Not dilapidated, but not great either. The streets were grimier, the shops more worn. Gentrification was happening, but piecemeal. The skyline to the south was dominated by a huge housing estate; concrete blocks stretching out towards the horizon like giant gravestones. A powerful reminder of the city's bleak Soviet past.

The S-Class rolled past an Orthodox church and made the next left, arrowing down a leafy side street for a hundred metres before it came to a halt outside a mid-range hotel.

From the outside, the place looked several star-ratings below the Royal Duna. An eight-storey concrete-panelled block, grey and squat, with small dark windows and a smog-stained facade. At some point it had probably looked cutting-edge, but now it just looked sad and dated. A cheap option for out-of-towners and businessmen who needed a place to stay, but didn't want to pay top whack for somewhere in the city centre. The hotel faced directly out on to the street, towards a small park on the other side of the road. There was a garden terrace to the right of the entrance, Bald noted. Hotel restaurant to the left, looking out over the car park, an ocean of blacktop half-filled with rentals. Bald spotted the name of the hotel spelled out in capital letters atop the roof: HOTEL FLAMINGO.

'Pull over here,' Porter said.

Bald nosed the XC90 into a free parking spot forty metres due north of the hotel, on the opposite side of the road. Gate at their nine o'clock, leading into the park. Low-level apartments at their three o'clock. The Hotel Flamingo was at their one o'clock, forty metres downstream. Lansbury had debussed from the S-Class. He gave the chauffeur the thumbs-up and set off towards the entrance at a quick trot. Behind him the S-Class peeled away, continuing further south of the hotel.

Five seconds later, Lansbury disappeared inside.

Bald frowned. 'Who the fuck is he meeting in this shithole?'

'Could be a mistress,' Porter suggested.

'You reckon?'

'He told us he was meeting a woman.'

She'd never forgive me, Lansbury had said to them back at the Royal Duna. *It would be a betrayal of her trust.*

'If that's true, our man is a randy fucker. He's slinging one up his PA, and then nobbing some other bird on the side as well.'

Porter looked over at Bald, eyebrow arched. 'You think he's shagging Jansen?'

'Definitely. The way her eyes light up when she talks about him, I'd bet my life on it.'

'Maybe he's on Viagra.'

'Aye.' Bald chewed on a thought like it was gum. 'But if he is meeting his bit on the side, he's going to a lot of effort to stop anyone finding out about it.'

'He's a populist, Jock. They're all big on family image. Traditional values, all that bollocks. It wouldn't look good if it leaked out to the press that he was shagging around.'

'Could be,' Bald mused. 'But if he was getting his end away, you think he'd choose a better spot for it than this dump.'

'Maybe that's part of it. He's less likely to be spotted out here than at one of the big hotels.'

'Only one way to find out.' Bald turned to his mucker. 'Get that audio up and running.'

TWENTY

Porter took out his iPhone and sent a text message to the SIM card stored inside the listening device. The text message simply read, *181215*. The code activated the coin-sized bug hidden beneath Lansbury's jacket collar, waking it up from standby mode and switching on the microphone. They couldn't follow Lansbury inside. Too much chance of being spotted by the principal. Which would lead to all sorts of awkward questions. And there was no clear advantage to trailing him on foot. They couldn't exactly follow him into the hotel room. Not unless they were planning to dress up as lampshades. Easier to stay in the car and listen in from a safe distance.

Once the listening device was activated Porter tapped the two-way recording icon on the bottom-left of the iPad screen, transmitting the signal back to a bunker room somewhere in Vauxhall. The two-way icon changed colour, indicating that the recording mode was turned on. The signal strength indicator at the top right of the display showed two bars. Which was okay, but not great, thought Porter, recalling what Hogan had told them back at the briefing, about needing good network coverage in order to remotely operate the listening devices.

He sent a brief message to Strickland's phone. *BROKEN RECORD at Hotel Flamingo. Inside building. No visual but audio up and running.*

We're listening, Strickland replied.

Porter turned his attention to the microphone. For several moments they heard nothing except the rustle of Lansbury's coat, the muffled sound of his breathing. The audio quality wasn't great. A tiny microphone, secreted under a collar, in a dodgy reception area, wasn't going to give them crystal-clear audio. But it was better than nothing. Porter sent another coded message to the bug, increasing the volume on the device. The sounds amplified. They heard the cheery ping of a lift, followed by the metallic scrape and judder of doors sliding open. Then the dull patter of footsteps.

The footsteps abruptly stopped. There was the rap of knuckles on wood, followed by a voice from inside the room that was too far away for the microphone to clearly pick up. Then the diplomatic click of a lock, the groan of a door being opened. More footsteps.

A gravelly male voice said, 'Derek. You're late.'

'I got held up,' Lansbury replied tartly. 'Had to brief my new bodyguards.'

'Ah yes,' a third male voice said. It was soft and nasal. 'We heard about your unfortunate incident the other day.'

Porter counted three voices in total. Lansbury, plus the two unknowns. The guy with the gravelly voice and the nasal one. Both were thickly accented and harsh. Eastern European, he guessed. There was an air of easy informality between the three of them. They sounded chummy, familiar.

Not strangers meeting for the first time.

Not a mistress, either.

So who the fuck is Lansbury meeting?

They listened in silence as the conversation continued. The three men sitting down, the two foreigners offering Lansbury refreshments. *Tea or coffee, Derek? Something to eat?* Lansbury declined. Every so often the chatter became distorted as the network signal weakened. But they heard enough to get the gist of the meeting.

Nasal Voice said, 'We don't want to waste time, so let's get right to it.'

'As you wish,' Lansbury said.

'Our boss has concerns about tonight's arrangements.'

'He shouldn't have,' Lansbury retorted. 'Everything's been taken care of, I can assure you. The last of the guests arrived this morning. Everything is set. Tell your boss that.'

'And how confident are you that everyone will agree to the terms we propose?'

'Some of them may take issue with it. At least to begin with.'

'Such as who?'

'Zanetti can be a stubborn bugger, if the mood takes him. And the Dutch are notoriously flimflam. Big on talk, reluctant to commit to hard action, in my experience. But we'll get there in the end, I'm sure.'

Gravel Voice said, 'Our boss doesn't share your optimism.'

'He bloody well should do. I've been busting a gut over this thing, trying to get it over the line.'

'The issue isn't your commitment. No one doubts that, Derek. But we're concerned that some of your colleagues may prove more resistant to our proposal than you think.'

'Based on what?' Lansbury demanded.

'We've had reports from our assets in the field,' the guy with the nasal voice explained. 'They've been monitoring the other guests, intercepting their communications. Some of them have privately expressed views that suggest they are not as loyal to Mother Russia as we had hoped. The feeling inside the agency is that they will be difficult to persuade. Even for a man of your considerable powers.'

'You're bribing them, for Christ's sake. Isn't that enough?'

'We thought so. Now, we're not so sure. We're asking them to swallow a big pill, politically speaking. If even one person votes against it, others might cave in. We can't let that happen, for obvious reasons.'

'It won't.'

Gravel Voice said, 'You'd fucking better be right.'

'Is this why you called me here? To berate me? I thought I was going to meet our guest speaker.'

'You are,' Nasal Voice said. 'This guy is going to help you get the deal over the line. We think he might help persuade some of your more reluctant comrades.'

'I don't see how he can do a better job than me.'

'This Russian isn't just anybody, Derek. He's high-profile. Very famous. All your friends will have heard of him. And he's got an interesting story to tell.'

'Who?'

'Someone you'll know, when you see him.'

'Where is he now?'

'Not here. We've been keeping his whereabouts a closely guarded secret. For obvious reasons.'

'I assume his attendance is non-negotiable.'

'This request comes straight from the boss. He trusts you'll agree to it.'

'And if I refuse?'

'Then our boss would be pissed off. You don't want to do that. Not a man you want to upset, you understand?'

'I'll need to see him at once, then,' Lansbury said sharply. 'Run through the agenda with him, what he needs to say. All of that.'

Nasal Voice said, 'We'll take you right there. First, we need to make sure you're clean. Are you wearing anything?'

'Not now, no. My bodyguards made me wear one of those damn trackers, but I got rid of it.'

'Where?'

'In a bin. On the other side of town.'

'That might look suspicious. Losing your tracker like that.'

'If you've ever seen me on TV you'll know that I'm rather a clumsy fellow. If those two idiots ask, I'll just say I dropped it when I popped out for a pack of fags.'

'Fags?'

'Cigarettes.'

'And they didn't make you wear anything else?'

'Not that I'm aware of, no.' Lansbury sighed audibly. 'Now can we please get going, gents? I've got a very busy day ahead of me. Time is of the essence here.'

There was a pause in the chat as Nasal Voice barked at the other guy in a tongue that sounded familiar to Bald. Russian, he thought. It sounded as if Nasal Voice was the one calling the shots. Gravel Voice was the muscle, he guessed.

'Andrei will sweep you first,' Nasal Voice said. 'Make sure you're clean.'

'What the hell for? I just told you I'm not wearing anything.'

'Precautions, Derek. As you say in England. Better to be safe than sorry.'

Bald turned to Porter and said, 'They're gonna find the mic. Turn that fucking thing off.'

Porter reached for his iPhone, punched in the six-digit code to deactivate the coin bug. Hit Send. A red exclamation mark flashed up next to the SMS. *Message failed to send*. Porter looked up at the signal-bar indicator at the top of the screen. *No service*.

Shit.

'Well?' Bald asked. 'Is it off?'

Porter shook his head, impotently tapping icons on the screen. 'I can't, mate. There's no signal ...'

'Fuck's sake,' Bald hissed between clenched teeth. 'Useless. Give it here.'

He snatched the handset from Porter, frowning at the screen. He saw the *No Service* alert on the top left-hand corner and held up the phone, pointing it in various directions to try and get the ghost of a signal. Nothing. He tried sending the message again anyway. Got the same red exclamation mark. *Message failed to send*.

Then they were too late.

A loud repetitive beeping noise came down the microphone, like a metal detector hovering over a Viking hoard. In his mind, Bald pictured Gravel Voice standing over Lansbury, sweeping him from head to toe with a handheld radio-frequency detector. They've found the bug, he realised.

There was a pregnant pause followed by a loud rummaging noise. Gravel Voice lifting up the collar and ripping off the bug, Bald assumed.

Nasal Voice said, 'What the fuck is this?'

'I-I don't know. I swear to God.'

Lansbury's voice sounded small and weak.

'Don't fuck with me, Derek. You think we don't know what this is? This is a micro-GPS tracker. It transmits your location on a continuous signal. You told us you were clean. Who the fuck are you working for?'

'Nobody! Christ, I swear!'

'Then why the fuck are you wearing a tracker?'

'I don't know. Someone else must have put it there.'

'Like who?'

'How the hell should I know?'

'I knew we couldn't trust this piece of shit,' Gravel Voice rasped.

'No, you can! Jesus, I'm on your side here! Everything I've done for you lot, I'd never betray you.'

More silence. Nasal Voice said, 'Then it's obvious. Someone is watching you, Derek.'

Bald heard an absurd laugh from Lansbury. 'Impossible.'

'There's no other explanation. Either you hid this fucking thing, or someone else did.'

'I had no idea this thing was on me. You have to believe me.'

Gravel Voice said, 'He's lying, boss—'

'I'm not! I swear on my kids.'

The two foreigners lapsed into a long silence again.

'You'd better not be fucking lying to us,' Nasal Voice said at last.

'I'm not,' Lansbury insisted.

'Good. Because if you are, we'll find out about it. You know that, right? This is what we do for a living. The boss will strap you to a stretcher and cremate you alive. You'll scream like a fucking baby. We'll film the whole thing, send copies to your ex-wife and kids. That's what happens when you fuck with us.'

'Y-yes,' Lansbury replied nervously, his voice cracking. 'I understand.' He hesitated, then went on. 'Perhaps, in light of this, it would be wise to delay things, Victor. Just for a few days, until I find whoever is responsible.'

Victor, aka Nasal Voice, remained quiet for a beat. Then he said, 'We can't. The wheels are already turning. There's a very specific timetable. The boss wants everyone to stick to it. Anyone who fails . . .'

His voice trailed off.

'But if someone is listening—'

'Big deal. Maybe someone followed you here. So what? These things don't have audio. They don't know what we're discussing. If they knew everything by now, they'd have you in handcuffs. You're still a free man. Which means they don't know shit.'

'But they're on to us.'

'Twenty-four hours from now, that won't matter. We stick to the plan. Unless you want to explain to the boss how you fucked up, and his project is in ruins?'

Lansbury didn't reply.

'I thought so,' said Nasal Voice. 'Now, let's get a move on. We've kept our friend waiting for long enough. And from now on, make sure you check your fucking clothes for trackers.'

'Yes,' Lansbury replied. 'Yes, of course.'

There was a brief exchange in Russian between Nasal Voice and his mate. Bald couldn't understand a word of it. But from the tone he guessed Nasal Voice was issuing a series of orders to Gravel Voice. Then he heard a fumbling sound, followed by a sudden electronic squawk, like a burst of radio static.

Then the bug went silent.

Lansbury emerged from the hotel exactly two minutes later. He was sandwiched between a pair of medium-built guys, dark-haired and mean-faced. Both were decked out in black trousers, Gore-Tex boots and North Face puffer jackets. The guy on the left had a black goatee and a Boston Red Sox baseball cap. His mate was a couple of inches shorter, with high cheekbones and a thin nose, wearing a grey beanie hat, hands stuffed into his jacket pockets.

'Get a shot of them, quick,' Bald said.

Porter snatched up his iPhone, tapped on the camera app and pinched the screen, zooming in on the three figures as they strutted over to the car park. He took three close-ups of Lansbury and his two mates before they turned away and stopped beside a dark-blue BMW 5 Series. Beanie Hat yanked open the rear door and gestured for Lansbury to get in. Red Sox took the wheel. Beanie Hat manoeuvred round to the front passenger door and paused for a moment as he scanned the area around the hotel. A casual sweep of the road, searching for anything suspicious. He seemed to stare at the XC90 for a beat before he climbed into the BMW.

A few moments later the BMW pulled out of the car park and headed south, in the opposite direction of the XC90. Porter dialled Strickland's number on his iPhone. She picked up on the second ring

'Talk to me. What's going on?'

'They're on the move,' Porter said. 'BROKEN RECORD and the two blokes he was talking to. They just left the hotel.'

'On foot?'

'Vehicle. They're driving a BMW 5 Series, dark blue with

177

tinted windows, licence plate VSZ-184. Heading south on Demeter Street.'

'Don't follow them,' Strickland ordered. 'Withdraw from your position. We've got guys waiting nearby who can pick them up. Local assets. A surveillance team.'

Porter thought back to the initial briefing. The Hungary-based assets Strickland had mentioned before. *Additional surveillance teams, drivers. Whatever you need.*

'Why not us?' he demanded angrily. 'We're right here, ma'am.'

'No. It's too risky. You might blow your cover. Leave it to our local guys. They know their way around the city. They'll pick up the scent.'

Porter didn't like handing over to another team, but he could see the logic behind Strickland's decision. They were dealing with a pair of potential foreign agents, trained in counter-surveillance measures, already jumpy from the discovery of the listening bug. They would be keeping a close eye on the road behind them, looking ten cars back, noting anyone who took the same turn-offs as them. And Bald and Porter were driving a vehicle that directly linked them to Lansbury. If Red Sox and Beanie Hat made the Volvo, the mission would be fatally compromised.

Strickland said, 'Did you get a look at the people BROKEN RECORD was talking to?'

'We did better than that,' Porter said. 'We took pictures.'

'Send them through. Soon as you can.'

'Who are they?'

'The photos will tell us. But the smart money is that they're with Russian intelligence. We'll ask GCHQ to run a voice recognition check too. See if that throws anything up.'

Porter looked ahead. The BMW had already disappeared from view. *Where the fuck are they taking Lansbury?*

Strickland said, 'Right now, you need to get back to the hotel. Bug the room, while BROKEN RECORD is out of play. We'll keep you posted on his whereabouts.'

'Roger that.'

Porter hung up. He sent the snaps he'd taken to Strickland's number, de-encrypted the iPhone. No need to wipe the messages or phone log. Every scrap of activity was automatically deleted when the phone returned to its false-screen mode. He tucked the handset into his jacket pocket and relayed his chat with Bald. Porter glanced at the Hotel Flamingo in the rear-view mirror as Bald K-turned in the street and pointed the Volvo north, taking them back in the direction of the Royal Duna.

'Let's hope Lansbury doesn't get suspicious about us,' he muttered.

Bald said, 'He won't. We're on his good side, mate. Flavour of the fucking month, just like Moorcroft said. He won't suspect a thing.'

'But he knows someone is watching him. The fucker is paranoid enough as it is. He's going to be looking at everyone with a new pair of eyes after this, Jock.'

'If he does, we'll just deny it. Blame it on the old BG team.'

'He won't buy that.'

'Doesn't matter. All we need to do is keep up with the arse-kissing contest. As long as we stay in his good books, he won't turn on us.'

'And if you're wrong?'

'I'm not. Never am.'

Porter glanced at his mucker. Bald seemed totally calm and sure of himself despite the fact that they had come close to being rumbled. Every guy in the Regiment was a risk-taker but Bald was something else, thought Porter. The bloke was fucking hard-core. He was capable of doing things no one else in Hereford would even think about.

Jock doesn't think the rules apply to him. Which is what makes him such an effective operator.

But it also makes him a dangerous partner.

Porter turned his attention to the map on the tablet screen, swiping left and right, assessing the surrounding area. Hungary was a fairly compact country. Bigger than Slovakia, smaller than Austria. Wherever the two Russians were taking Lansbury, he figured it couldn't be any more than an hour away from their current location. Lansbury had said he would be back at the hotel at one o'clock for his phone interview with the *Telegraph*. Which put the meeting as far as Györ to the west, Kecskemét to the south or the Great Plains to the east. North was the ancient capital at Esztergom and the Slovakian border.

A lot of possibilities. None of them glaringly obvious.

He put the iPad to sleep, looked over at Bald. 'Who do you think this Russian is? The one they're taking him to meet.'

Bald shrugged. 'Could be Garry fucking Kasparov, for all we know.'

Porter thought for a moment. 'It's got to be someone those populists have heard of. Someone recognisable.'

'Probably some right-wing blogger or commentator,' Bald mused. 'One of those conspiracy theorists with their own YouTube news channel. The ones who reckon 9/11 was an inside job, all that bollocks.'

Porter gave him a sceptical look. 'You think so?'

'Why not? Some of those YouTube guys are legends on the far right. The populists love all that shite.'

'But why would the Russians go to all this fuss, just to protect some random conspiracy theorist? It doesn't make sense.'

'Either way,' said Bald, 'we'll find out soon enough.'

Porter nodded and stared out of the window, his mind racing ahead of him.

A high-profile Russian, he thought. Someone with a story to tell. *One that will persuade even the most difficult of your friends*, Nasal Voice had said.

Who could that be?

And what was the proposal they had been talking about?

The boss asked us to find a way of guaranteeing support for his project.

We're asking your colleagues to swallow a big pill, politically speaking.

What the fuck did that mean?

I don't know what Lansbury is planning tonight, Porter thought. But it's definitely something big.

We've got Lansbury meeting with a gang of top populists and fascists.

We've got him attending a secret RV with two guys who are potentially Russian agents.

And now we know he's going to another meeting with a mystery guest speaker.

Someone who Nasal Voice and his mate, and whoever they were working for, believed could sway the populists into agreeing whatever was being proposed at the conference later.

'We're getting close,' Porter said.

'We've got a bunch of random stuff,' Bald countered. 'No smoking gun.'

Porter looked away, his jaw muscles tightening with frustration. Jock's right, he thought. They had pieces, but the bigger picture eluded them.

The drive back to the Royal Duna took them thirty minutes. They retraced their steps through the city, plodding along at twenty miles per hour. The tree-lined streets around Buda, the bridge across the Danube. Then the dirt and crowds and noise of the thoroughfares on the Pest side of the river. By the time they had nudged the XC90 back into the car park beneath the hotel the clock on the dash read 10.49 hours.

Just under an hour since Lansbury had arrived at the Hotel Flamingo. A little over two hours until he was due to give his interview on the phone.

Plenty of time to sneak into his room and set up the bugs, thought Porter.

He said, 'How are we gonna get into Lansbury's room?'

Bald thought for a beat. 'Jansen can get us a key from reception. We'll tell her we need to conduct a routine sweep of his room.'

'Someone will have to keep her busy,' Porter replied. 'Make sure she stays well away from his room while we plant everything.'

'I'll take care of her. Use some of the old Bald magic. I'll take her down to the bar and tell her I need to run through the security arrangements for tonight. Should give you time to get it all sorted.'

'Why don't I take Jansen down instead?'

'No offence, mate, but you're not her type.'

'What type is that?'

'Hard Scottish bastards.' Bald grinned slyly. 'Posh birds love a bit of northern rough.'

'You're a wanker, Jock.'

'Aye. But I'm a wanker who gets his end away.'

They rode the lift to the third floor, passed a cleaning trolley and stopped outside the door to their room. Porter swiped his key card against the electronic lock. There was a beeping noise as the red light above the card reader blinked green. Porter cranked the handle and stepped inside the room, eager to plant the bugs before Lansbury returned to the hotel.

He took another step inside. Stopped dead.

Bald stopped too.

A platinum-blonde figure in a bright green coat was standing over Porter's bed.

Rooting through his nylon holdall.

Jansen.

TWENTY-ONE

Jansen stood very still. Her eyes narrowed to razor slits as she looked from Bald to Porter and back again. Red-painted finger-nails rested on the seam of the unzipped holdall. Several items of Porter's clothing were spread across the duvet. Spare work shirts and socks, a pair of gym shorts and trainers, a charger for his iPad and his engraved Ted Baker wash bag. The one his daughter Sandy had given him for his fiftieth birthday.

Next to the personal items were several black matchbox-sized devices.

The portable listening devices Porter had stashed at the bottom of his holdall. They were all there, he saw, laid out separately from the rest of his gear, along with a couple of the coin-sized bugs, a laptop adapter and phone charger. One of the hard drives for storing all the audio content. The two Regiment challenge coins.

Everything Hogan had given them back at Pontrilas two days ago.

Porter's eyes drifted across to the luggage padlock. It was still attached to the zipper at one end of the opening. For a moment he wondered how Jansen had managed to prise open his holdall without removing the padlock. Then he saw the ballpoint pen, lying next to the listening devices. Jansen would have used the tip of the pen to perforate the meshed teeth, bypassing the padlock. Once she had finished searching through his stuff, all she would need to do is pull the zipper back across the seam and the teeth would clamp shut again. No evidence of entry. Basic knowledge for anyone in Porter's line of work. But not something that a PA would necessarily know about.

So how did she know how to break into my holdall?

Porter slanted his gaze across the room to the other bed. Bald's holdall had also been tampered with, his personal shit hurriedly dumped in a pile, the listening bugs laid out separately.

Bald broke the silence. 'What the fuck are you doing?'

Jansen paused, narrowed eyes fixed on Porter. 'Nothing,' she replied hesitantly.

'Doesn't look like nothing,' Bald growled. 'Looks like you're sneaking around our fucking room.'

'The draft of one of Mr Lansbury's speeches is missing,' she replied hesitantly. 'I was searching for it.'

'In our fucking luggage?'

Jansen said nothing.

Her face said everything.

Porter took another step into the room, blocking her exit. In the corridor outside, he could hear voices. More than one of them. Foreign. Hungarian, probably. The maids. Chatting to one another, trading gossip like cleaning staff the world over. Bald quietly closed the door and stepped forward, drawing alongside his mucker.

'How'd you get in here?'

'I had a spare key card,' Jansen said. 'Gary gave it to me, in case of emergencies.'

'And, what, you just decided to sneak in here behind our backs?'

Jansen said nothing. Bald said, 'Why don't you tell us what's really going on?'

The assistant's eyes darted nervously between Bald and Porter. 'I don't know what you're talking about.'

'Yeah, you do,' Bald said. 'You didn't sneak in here to look for some missing papers, did you?'

Jansen stiffened. 'I'm not the one in trouble. You are.'

'How's that?'

Jansen waved a hand at the kit spread out across Porter's bed. 'I wasn't born yesterday. These are GSM listening devices. The ones you hide bugs inside. You're spying on Derek.'

Porter stood very still. Another question scraped like a fingernail down the nape of his neck. *How does Jansen know what all this high-tech equipment is?*

'This stuff?' Bald laughed. 'This is routine. We carry it everywhere.'

'Nonsense. Gary and Mick didn't have anything like this.'

'How would you know?' Bald took another step towards Jansen, his expression tightening. 'Or did you break and enter their room behind their backs as well?'

Jansen didn't respond. The silence hung heavy in the air.

'All this stuff is legit,' Bald added.

'You're lying,' Jansen said. She tried to strike a pose of defiance, but her voice was hollow and uncertain.

Bald said, 'It's the truth. Just let me explain.'

Jansen hesitated again. Her eyes darted anxiously between Bald and Porter. Outside in the hallway, Porter could hear the voices of the cleaning staff getting louder. Drawing nearer to the room. They had stopped outside the room directly opposite, Porter realised. A sudden shout or cry from Jansen would alert them. In less than a minute, hotel security would be kicking down the door.

And then me and Jock will be well and truly fucked.

Bald took a step forward, edging ahead of Porter.

'Call your boss if you don't believe us. Tell him about the bugs. No skin off our noses. While you're at it, perhaps you can explain to him what you're doing in our room. I'm sure he'd be thrilled to hear that.'

Jansen said nothing. Her face was stitched with anxiety. She backed away from Bald, eyes flitting across the room, as if she was searching for an escape route.

'Go on,' said Bald. 'Call him.'

'Stay back. I'm warning you.'

Bald took another step towards her. Jansen retreated from the bed, backing up towards the French windows on the far side of the room. Bald was ahead of Porter now, with Jansen three or four steps away from him. In the corridor, Porter could make out the distinct voices of the two cleaning maids. They sounded so close they could almost have been in the same room. Bald slowly reached a hand into his jacket pocket, dug out his iPhone. Thumb-unlocked the Home screen and extended his arm towards the PA.

'Here. Use my phone. Call your boss. Or better yet, call the head of the security company me and Porter work for. Ask them about any of the stuff in our bags. They'll tell you.'

'One more step,' Jansen said, 'and I'll scream for help, I swear to God.'

'We're on the same side here,' Bald said in a soothing voice as he edged closer. 'We're just trying to help you understand.'

'Stay away!'

She opened her mouth to scream.

The words never left her throat.

Bald stepped towards her in a flash of movement, hip-twisted his torso, stamped his left heel on the ground and drove forward with his left arm, striking Jansen on the sternum. Not the hardest blow Bald had ever landed. Not by a long shot. He went with the heel of his palm rather than a clenched fist, minimising the impact. He didn't want to cause any long-term damage. He just wanted to knock the wind out of her. Jansen gasped as a wave of pain spread through her stomach, driving the air from her lungs. Bald grabbed a fistful of her hair and planted her face down against one of the plump pillows, muffling her cries. He kept her head pressed down as he looked over at Porter.

'Give us a fucking hand, mate. Get them plasticuffs and gaffer tape.'

Porter hastened over to his bed, fished out a pair of plasti-cuffs and a roll of double-sided tape from the bottom of the half-emptied holdall. Essential travel gear for any self-respect-ing Blade. He took the plasticuffs and manoeuvred around to the back of Jansen. By now she had recovered from the initial shock of the blow and she was thrashing wildly beneath Bald's firm grip, struggling in vain to break free. Porter pressed a knee against her legs, forced her arms behind her back and slapped the plasticuffs around her wrists, cinching the wire tight. Not sufficient to cut off the blood supply, but tight enough to be uncomfortable. Jansen continued to rock franti-cally from side to side, kicking out and screaming hysterically into the pillow as Porter tore off a six-inch strip from the roll of double-sided tape. Bald gave her another quick dig to the kidneys, stunning her for long enough for Porter to slap the tape across her mouth.

'Search her pockets,' said Bald. 'Hurry.'

Porter rummaged through her coat. He found her iPhone and

an Orla Kiely print wallet and a second mobile he assumed was a burner. A crappy no-name Asian brand Porter had never heard of. He set both phones and the wallet down on the side table and helped Bald manhandle Jansen towards the bathroom. Tears streamed down her reddened cheeks as the PA whimpered into the gaffer tape, begging with her captors. Her eyes were mascara-smudged and wide with fear. The confidence of a few moments ago replaced by sheer terror.

Porter wrenched open the bathroom door and flipped the spotlights on. Then Bald threw Jansen inside. She let out a muffled yelp of pain as she stumbled and flopped helplessly to the marble floor, collapsing beside the toilet. Bald stepped out of the bathroom, locked the door from the outside and joined Porter at the other end of the room. The pair of them held a conference in front of the French windows, out of earshot of the bathroom. They switched on the TV and upped the volume. Partly to mask the faint cries coming from the bathroom. But also to make sure that Jansen didn't overhear them.

'What do you think?' asked Porter.

Bald counted off on his fingers. 'One, she broke into our room. Two, she knows how to break into someone's luggage without leaving a trace. Three, she knows what a GSM bug looks like. Only a professional would recognise that stuff.'

'Don't forget the burner.'

Bald rubbed a hand across his bristled jaw and thought it through. 'She's bullshitting. That's for sure. Her story doesn't add up. Got more holes in it than a pub dart board.'

'You think she's working for someone?'

'If she is, she's not a professional. An asset, maybe. Or an inform-ant. But a real pro wouldn't have freaked out. She panicked as soon as we turned the tables on her.'

'Could be a sleeper,' Porter suggested. 'Someone might have told her to search through our stuff. That might explain why she knows about the bugs.'

'Maybe she's working for Six.'

'Jansen?' Porter pulled a face. 'Vauxhall would have told us. Surely?'

'I wouldn't put anything past those sneaky bastards.'

Porter considered for a moment, shook his head. 'No. Strickland would have told us. I'm sure of it.'

'The Russians, then. Could be a belt and braces thing.'

Which was a more likely scenario, Porter thought. The Russians wouldn't fully trust Lansbury. They would be aware of his slippery reputation and his shifting allegiances. They would want someone else close to him, someone he would regularly confide in. Such a person would report back to the Russians, telling them what Lansbury had said, who he had met with. The Russians would then know whether he was telling them the truth, or if he was saying something completely different behind their backs. The sleeper would be a valuable secondary source of intelligence.

'Either way, we need to dump her,' said Bald. 'Get rid of her before she blows our cover.'

Porter shook his head. 'We need to call it in.'

'What for? She's got to go.'

'Strickland needs to know,' Porter snapped. 'That's not up for discussion. I'll get on the blower. You keep an eye on the assistant. Make sure she doesn't make a racket.'

Porter dug out his handset from his jacket pocket, opened the flashlight app, tapped in the encryption code and pulled up the false screen. Found Strickland's number and dialled. The line rang for seven long beats. Porter caught himself eyeing up the minibar. The voice whispered in his ear again.

Urging him to have a drink.

This was supposed to be a straightforward BG op.

Now we're dealing with a possible Russian sleeper.

Strickland answered and said, 'What's going on? Have you planted the bugs yet?'

'Not yet. We've got a problem.'

Strickland paused. 'What kind of problem?'

'BROKEN RECORD's assistant. We found her in our room when we got back to the hotel.'

Another pause. 'What was she doing there?'

'Going through our luggage. She found the bugs. Knew what they were for, and all. Recognised the equipment.'

'Shit,' Strickland hissed. She took a breath, collected herself. Then she said, 'Tell me exactly what happened.'

Porter gave her a blow-by-blow account. Told her about how Jansen had used the biro technique to break into his holdall. How she had tried to weasel her way out of the situation by accusing them of spying on Lansbury. The way she had hesitated when Bald had offered to put in the call to the principal. Strickland listened mostly in silence, interrupting on a few occasions, asking Porter to repeat exactly what he or Bald or Jansen had said.

'Has she admitted to anything?' Strickland asked.

'Not yet, but her story doesn't add up. And how would she know what the bugs looked like?'

'She might have seen them on TV. Lots of spy thrillers have that stuff nowadays, I guess.'

'Not these bugs. Only someone who's been trained to use them or look for them would know what they were. She's definitely working for someone,' Porter said. 'Unless she's one of ours?'

'Not as far as I'm aware. She could be with Five, but I very much doubt it. Too much of a coincidence. She has to be with the Russians.' A pause. 'Do we know if she's spoken to her handler yet?'

'Not as far as we know. She was still going through our kit when we found her. She wouldn't have had time to make her report.'

'Where is she now?'

'In the bathroom. Tied up.'

'Does she know who you really are?'

'We didn't tell her anything. Said the devices were a routine part of our kit.'

'And she believed you?'

'I'm a Blade, not a fucking mind reader,' Porter growled. 'But she definitely suspects something is up.'

'So if we let her go and pretend as if nothing happened, your cover is at risk of being blown.'

'That's about the size of it.'

Silence. Porter peeled the phone away from his ear and checked to see if the signal had broken or something. It hadn't. 'Ma'am? Are you there?'

Strickland exhaled heavily down the line. 'How long until BROKEN RECORD is due back at the hotel?'

Porter glanced at his watch. Eight minutes past eleven in the morning. 'He's got an interview with a hack at around one o'clock. Two hours, give or take.'

'Then there's still time.'

'For what?'

'You need to get the assistant to talk. Convince her that it's in her best interests to cooperate with us. If we can get her on our side, we might be able to contain the situation.'

'And if we can't?'

'Then you'll need to make her disappear.'

'We're gonna need leverage,' Porter said. 'Whoever she's working for, they must have some serious dirt on her. She's not gonna work with us unless we give her a bloody good reason.'

Strickland was silent for a long beat. 'Give me an hour,' she said. 'Then we'll get back to you.'

TWENTY-TWO

The call ended. Porter listened to the dampened silence on the other end of the line, an invisible band tightening around his chest. He could feel his stress levels building, the minibar calling out to him. Porter clamped his eyes shut and tried to focus on the other voice in his head. The sober voice. *Don't fucking go there*, it warned him. *Not this time. Not after everything the booze has cost you. You can't let yourself down in front of Jock.*

He set down his phone on the desk, pulled Bald to one side and quietly recapped what Strickland had just told him. Bald pulled at his chin as he listened.

'What are we supposed to do until Strickland gets back to us?' he said angrily. 'Sit here twiddling our thumbs and hope that her boss doesn't come knocking on the fucking door?'

'We don't have a choice.'

'Aye, we do. Just get rid of her. Problem solved.'

'Six thinks there might be a cleaner way of fixing it.'

'I don't give a toss what those bullshit merchants think. That Doris came within a whisker of blowing our cover. If we hadn't stumbled upon her, she would have given us up by now.'

Porter shrugged. 'Those are our orders.'

'What now, then?'

'We wait to hear. Then we'll talk to her.'

'Assuming she'll agree to cooperate.'

'We're not dealing with the head of the FSB here. If she is working with the Russians, she's a low-level recruit. She'll crack under the pressure, as long as Strickland comes up with the goods.'

'She will,' Bald said. 'That lass won't let us down. It's the tossers above her we need to fucking worry about.'

He dropped into one of the armchairs and grabbed the remote, settling in for the hour-long wait. Porter checked the time again. Ten minutes past eleven. A little over an hour had passed since Lansbury had met with his Russian contacts. Less than two hours until he was due back at the hotel. And Porter and Bald wouldn't hear back from Vauxhall until midday at the earliest.

We're up against the clock now, he thought. If me and Jock survive this scrape, it'll be by the skin of our teeth.

They passed the time browsing the English-language news channels, constantly checking their phones for any word from Six. Every so often Porter got up to check on Jansen. The PA had stopped crying now. She lay curled on the marble floor in a foetal position, staring vacantly into space.

Which was fine with Porter. They didn't want to be dealing with an emotional wreck. They wanted Jansen afraid but not hysterical. They wanted her to be able to think clearly, to recognise that her best bet was to cooperate with Six.

Fifty minutes passed. Porter checked his phone for the hundredth time. Nothing. The twenty-four-hour news channels were on loop, repeating the same stories about the G7 summit at Loch Lomond. The draconian security measures, the heaving crowds of protestors gathering around Parliament Square, waiting to greet the US president. He was due to arrive the next morning, the report said. Breakfast with the prime minister, tea with the queen. Then on to the big summit. Some of the protestors were planning to raise an inflatable baby balloon over Westminster, according to the report.

At four minutes past twelve, Porter's phone rang. Strickland. He shot out of his chair and answered. 'Ma'am?'

'Okay, we might have something,' Strickland said in her Glaswegian brogue.

'I'm listening.'

'First, the basics. Freya Jansen is a twenty-seven-year-old graduate with a degree in Philosophy from Durham. Father was Conservative MP for St Albans for twelve years, mother a high-ranking civil servant. Freya worked at the Department for International Development for four years after uni, climbed the ranks and left to join BIM as a press officer. She quickly caught Lansbury's eye and was promoted to his team eight months later. Apparently, she had a reputation among the party recruits as a bit of a wild partygoer. Rumours of recreational drug use, a disciplinary warning from the party leadership.'

'How does any of that help us?'

'It might explain how she got roped into working for the Russians. There might be something in her background they're using against her.'

'What else?'

'She has an older sister. Olivia Sopsworth. Eight-year age difference. Junior partner at a prestigious law firm in Holborn. They're very close, we understand. They speak almost daily, according to their phone records.'

'Parents?'

'Father died two years ago, bowel cancer. Mother is still alive but has early onset dementia. Living in a luxury care home in Chelsea. We've sent someone over there to check her out. One of our surveillance officers. He should get there in a few minutes.'

'Does she have a boyfriend?'

'Not as far as we can tell. Profiles on Tinder and Match, both dormant. A couple of brief flings. But then we know that BROKEN RECORD likes the women on his team to be single. Dedicated to the job, available twenty-four seven. That sort of thing.'

Porter clicked his tongue. An intelligent, well-educated young political operator, from a well-to-do family. Jansen probably had her eyes on following her parents into a respectable career in the Westminster bear pit. Getting on Lansbury's team was maybe the first or second rung on what she imagined would be a glorious career ladder.

'How are we supposed to get her to flip?' he asked.

'We'll use the family angle,' Strickland replied. 'She loves her mother and sister, so let's use that against her. Tell Jansen that the safety of her family is under threat unless she agrees to work with us.'

'You reckon that'll work?'

'It's our best bet,' Strickland said.

He got off the phone, told Strickland he'd discuss it with Bald and then call her back once they had the int. Bald listened quietly as Porter talked him through the plan.

'She might think we're bluffing,' Bald argued. 'She'll assume that we're not as nasty as the Russians when it comes to this stuff. Might not take us seriously.'

Porter looked at him. 'Do you have a better idea?'

'I might,' Bald said. 'That surveillance officer Strickland sent over to the care home, to check on the mother. How long until they get there?'

Porter thought back to his conversation with Strickland. 'She said he was on his way. Probably already there now. Why?'

Bald grinned. 'I think we can make Jansen talk. First, we need to get in touch with that surveillance officer. Get them to pay a personal visit to the mother.'

'What for?'

'Listen carefully. Here's what we're going to do . . .'

Eight minutes later, Bald yanked open the bathroom door.

Jansen was still lying on the floor. Her eyes were heavily blood-shot, her cheeks streaked with dark vein-like blotches of mascara. Bald dropped down beside the PA, snipped off her plasticuffs with a pair of scissors he'd taken from his wash bag. He took Jansen by the arm and hauled her upright, her back resting against the bath panel. Looked her hard in the eye.

'Scream for help,' he said, 'pull any shit like that, and we'll drop you like a bad habit. Got it?'

Jansen nodded a reply. She got it.

Bald ripped off the gaffer tape. She gasped as it tore free from her skin, like a drowning person coming up for air. Bald stepped aside, giving Porter space to kneel down beside her. Jansen shifted her weight, rubbing her sore wrists, breathing heavily. Porter unscrewed the cap from a bottle of still water he'd taken from the minibar and offered it to Jansen. She eyed it warily at first. Then she took it and drank thirstily, necking half the bottle. All part of the plan Porter had discussed with Bald. They would go easy on Jansen to begin with. Gentle but firm persuasion would work better than confrontation. Porter had volunteered to take the lead. Bald loomed in the doorway, sinewy arms folded across his chest, ready to step in if Porter needed him.

They had agreed something else with Strickland. Bald had argued that they couldn't trust Jansen. Too volatile, too easily exposed. Not someone they could rely on to keep a secret in the longer term. Which turned out to be a genuine concern at Vauxhall as well. Strickland and Moorcroft had the same fear. She had proposed a second part to the plan. The wheels were already turning on the second part, she had said. But they wouldn't tell Jansen about it just yet. First, they needed her to cooperate.

Porter replaced the cap, set down the water bottle and said, 'Listen to me. We're here to help you. But you're gonna have to work with us. Starting right now.'

'I told you, I don't know anything,' Jansen replied lamely.

'We know you're working for the Russians,' Porter lied. 'We know you've been helping them to spy on your boss.'

She looked away, bit her trembling lower lip. 'That's not true.'

'Whatever it is you've done, it doesn't matter. We can protect you.'

'You're just a pair of bodyguards. You can't do anything.'

'The people we're working for can.'

Jansen snapped her gaze back to Porter. 'What do you mean?'

'We're with British intelligence,' Porter said. 'MI6.'

'You're government spies?' she asked, blinking rapidly. Porter detected a note of scepticism in her voice.

'Not us. We're the hired muscle. But the people we work for are high up in the security services. And we're telling you, working with them is your best chance of getting out of this thing intact.'

She looked away again. 'It's not that easy.'

'You're up to your neck,' said Porter. 'There's no other way out of this that ends well for you. You need to understand that we're the only ones who can help you right now. If you turn your back on us, you'll be putting yourself in danger.'

'Not just yourself,' Bald added. 'Your sister Olivia and your mum Cynthia. They'll be at risk as well.'

Jansen's eyes went wide with shock. She looked up at Bald, glaring openly at him. 'How do you know their names?'

'The people we work for know everything about you,' Porter said matter-of-factly. 'They know about your sister's post-natal depression, your mum's dementia, putting her in a care home. Your history of drug abuse. So you've got a decision to make. If you value your family's safety, you need to tell us what the fuck is going on.'

Jansen wiped the tears from her eyes and searched Porter's face. 'No. You're lying. MI6 wouldn't do anything to hurt them.'

Porter handed the assistant her iPhone. 'Call your mum's care home, if you don't believe us. Ask your mum if she's had any visitors in the past hour.'

Jansen looked at the phone as if suspecting a trap. She took it, tapped the code to unlock and brought up her call history. Pressed the entry for Eleanor Court and put the call on loudspeaker. After several loud rings a frail female voice answered.

'Hello?'

Jansen put on a fake cheery tone. 'Hi, Mum, it's me.'

'Freya, darling.' The voice brightened. 'How are you?'

'I'm fine, Mum. Just wanted to see how you're settling in.'

'Can't complain, dear.' The frail voice paused. 'Is everything okay? You don't sound very well. Is this about that stomach pain you had the other day? I did tell you to call the GP about that—'

'No, everything's fine, Mum. How's your day?'

'Oh, fine. Actually, I just had a visitor drop by.'

Jansen sat bolt upright. 'Oh?'

'Yes, a rather charming young man. James. One of your old friends from university. Dashingly handsome, I must say. Is he the mystery man you've been telling me about?'

'What?' Jansen frowned. 'No, Mum, he's, uh, just a friend.'

'Well, he was *very* striking. He told me he lost your number and has been trying to get in touch with you for weeks. Anyway, I gave it to him. I hope that was all right? He did seem such a sweet young man. You should call him.'

Jansen sat open-mouthed and speechless, colour leaching from her face.

'Dear? Are you still there? Are you *sure* everything is okay?'

Jansen snapped out of her trance, cleared her throat. 'I'm really fine, Mum. Honest. Look, I've got to run. I'll call you tonight.'

'Yes, and do remember to give your friend a call—'

'I will. Bye, Mum.'

'Love you, dear.'

The line clicked off.

'By the way,' Bald said, uncrossing his arms. 'James will be introducing himself to your sister at her house in Berkhamsted tomorrow. Just so you know.'

Jansen stared at the faded-to-black display on her phone, wearing a look of numbed terror. Porter set her iPhone down beside the half-empty bottle of water. She looked up at him, her eyes moist with tears.

'Please. Don't hurt them. They haven't done anything wrong.'

'They'll be fine,' Porter said. 'But you've got to work with us here, love. It's the only way.'

Jansen looked off towards the tiled wall. Porter could see the struggle playing out on her face. She had two options in front of her, neither of them attractive. Either she sold out the people she had been working for and admitted to her role in a criminal conspiracy. Or she stuck to her line, refused to cooperate and put the lives of her loved ones at risk. In the end, she went for the only possible choice.

'I didn't mean any of this to happen,' she said. 'He told me I didn't have a choice. He said if I didn't do it, they'd release the video.'

'Who told you that?'

'I don't know his surname. I just knew him as Boris. I met him at the party conference last November. In Torquay.'

'Who is he?'

'I told you, I don't know. All I know is he had a Russian accent. I met him in a bar in town. First night of the conference. He said he was a journalist from Ukraine, in town to hear what Derek and the other speakers had to say. He was funny, you know. Quirky, not really too macho or anything. He knew how to have a good time.'

'What's on the tape?' asked Bald.

Jansen dropped her eyes to the floor.

'I did some things that night. Things I'm not proud of.'

'Go on,' Porter said.

'We had a few drinks at the bar. Then we went to a club. Boris introduced me to a friend of his. Alexei. He said he was a businessman from Estonia. We went back to his hotel room, did some coke. Some Ecstasy too. Then everything got fuzzy. The next thing I knew, we were in bed. Together.'

She fell silent for a moment. Bald and Porter let it play out. Better to let Jansen finish the story, tell it the way she wanted.

'I left the next morning and tried to forget about it. A few days later, I had a new WhatsApp message from Boris. That's when I saw the video clip. Me, Boris and his friend.' She wiped tears from her eyes, smudging make-up across her pale face. 'They threatened to send it to everyone in my address book unless I did what they said. I didn't have a choice. If I had refused, my career would have been over.'

Porter nodded, understanding. The public-school girl from the well-respected family, the dream job in politics. A video of her getting spit-roasted by a pair of Russian cokeheads would have killed her ambitions. That was for fucking sure.

He said, 'What did they want from you?'

'Just to report back to them regularly, let them know who Derek was meeting, what he was saying behind closed doors, that sort of thing. Nothing else.'

'Why did they want you to search our room?'

'Boris told me his people needed to run a security check on you both. Make sure you were who you said you were. He showed me how to break into your luggage, what to look for. Told me to let him know if I found anything incriminating.'

'Have you called him yet?'

Jansen gave a slow shake of her head. 'I was still searching through everything. Thought I had more time.' She smiled ruefully. 'I was wrong.'

'How did you know we were out?'

'I asked the concierge to call me if you left the hotel. I thought you'd be gone for longer. Figured you had both left to explore the city.'

Porter took a deep breath. 'Listen, whatever you've done is in the past. The people we work for don't care about any of that. But you've got to make this right.'

'Make what right?'

'We're here as part of a major security operation. You nearly blew our cover,' Bald explained.

Jansen frowned. 'I don't understand. Is Derek in some kind of trouble?'

'More than a little,' Porter said. 'But that's nothing for you to worry about. Right now, you've got to help us take care of this problem. If you do, everything will be fine. Can you do that?'

'How?'

'Call your handler. Tell them you didn't find anything. You checked through our luggage but there was nothing suspicious. No listening devices, just clothes and toiletries.'

Jansen shook her head quickly. 'I can't! Boris told me never to lie to them. If I do, he'll release the footage. That's what he said.'

'He's not going to do that, because you're going to play it cool. We'll be here when you make the call. As long as you stay calm, he won't have any reason to doubt you.'

Jansen looked doubtfully at Porter. 'What if he realises I'm lying?'

'We're not asking you to spy on anyone here. You just need to make one call.'

'Think about your family,' Bald put in. 'You need to do the right thing here. For them.'

Jansen looked back and forth between the operators. 'One phone call? That's it? Then we're done?'

'That's it,' Porter said.

'But remember,' Bald added. 'If you try anything funny, if you try to warn your handler or lie to them, the deal is off. We can get to your loved ones anywhere, anytime. Understood?'

Something occurred to Jansen. She looked at Porter hopefully. 'What will happen to me? Once this is over?'

'Do as we say, and this will all be forgotten about. No official records, no criminal investigation. It'll be as if it had never happened. You can go back home, get on with your life.'

'Promise?'

'Aye, we promise,' Bald said. 'Now make the fucking call.'

Porter retrieved the burner phone they had discovered on Jansen earlier. The no-brand Chinese handset. He held it out, gesturing for her to pick it up. Jansen stared at the burner as if it was a bomb. Faced with the biggest decision of her young life. *Am I really going to do this?* She inhaled deeply.

Then she picked up the phone.

TWENTY-THREE

The conversation with her handler took less than a minute. Bald and Porter listened in on the loudspeaker as the guy named Boris answered the call from Jansen's burner. He spoke good, well-pronounced English with only a trace of his Russian accent. Not like the two guys at the Hotel Flamingo across town. The guy named Boris didn't make any small talk. He dived straight in. 'Well? What did you find?'

Jansen gave him the answer she'd rehearsed with Bald and Porter. 'I did as you asked. Searched their luggage, closets, drawers. Everywhere I could think of. All I found was clothes and toiletries.'

Boris No-Last-Name asked a couple of follow-up questions. 'Are you sure? What about their backgrounds? Did you check their credentials with the security company they had worked for?'

Jansen answered confidently and calmly, with the air of someone who had done a thorough job and was certain of her findings. She would have made a fine actress. By the end of it, the handler sounded pleased. Reassured, almost. He thanked her for her work, reminded her to keep an eye on Lansbury and said he would be in touch again soon. Then he hung up.

When it was over, Jansen looked up from the burner screen and said, 'Was that okay?'

'That'll do fine,' Porter replied.

'What happens now?'

They took her out of the bathroom, sat her down on the edge of Porter's bed. Porter glanced at his watch. Exactly half past twelve. Thirty minutes until Lansbury was due back at the hotel. He said, 'Have you got a key card to your boss's room?'

Jansen nodded. 'In my wallet.'

Bald retrieved her Orla Kiely wallet from the side unit, flicked through the card section. He plucked out a key card, identical to the one for their room, and chucked the wallet at her. She pocketed it, wiped her nose with a tissue taken from her other pocket and looked up at Porter.

'So that's it?' she asked. 'We're done?'

Porter's phone buzzed before he could reply. New message. Delivered to the regular phone, not the encrypted mode. From an unknown local number. A message he had been told to expect by Strickland. It said simply, *In car park*. He deleted it, put his phone to sleep. Tucked it away and turned to Bald.

'Let's take her downstairs, Jock. Car's waiting.'

'Roger that, mate.'

Bald grabbed Jansen by the arm, ushered her towards the door. The assistant struggled against his grip, pulling her arm back, panic-stricken eyes flitting from Bald to Porter.

'What car? What the hell are you talking about?'

Porter said, 'There's a wagon waiting in the car park with two guys from the security services in it. They'll transport you across the border to a safe house in Austria. You'll be interrogated and debriefed and taken back to the UK. If you scream or resist in any way, your mum and sister will suffer. Do you want them to suffer?'

Jansen's eyes went even wider. 'No.'

'Then keep your fucking mouth shut and do exactly as we say. Got it?'

'But . . . we had a deal,' she said pleadingly. 'You promised.'

'We lied.'

Bald yanked on her arm. Jansen dug in her heels and stood her ground, shaking her head frantically. 'No, no. Please, no. Don't do this. This is my career!'

'Find another one.'

'I'll work for you! I can be helpful. I can watch Derek for you, like I did for Boris.'

'The people we're working for don't need someone on the inside. They've already got us.'

'But I know things! Please, I'll do whatever you say.'

'Sorry, lass,' Bald said. 'Nothing personal, but we can't have a cokehead knowing our secret. Too much of a fucking liability. You're finished here.'

'Please!'

Porter stared at her with a cold look of indifference.

'At least let me say goodbye to Derek.' Jansen looked desperately from Bald to Porter, searching for a shred of pity in their hardened expressions, and finding none. 'I can't just up and leave. He'll wonder what happened.'

'He'll get over it,' Bald said. 'Come on. The wagon's waiting.'

'Bastards! You can't do this!'

'See this?' Bald indicated his face. 'This is me giving a flying fuck. Now get moving, or your mum is gonna have another visit from James.'

He tugged again on her arm, escorted her out of the room and down the corridor towards the bank of lifts. Porter hurried ahead of them and took the stairs down to the lobby. He waited for the next empty lift, rode it up to the third floor. The doors sucked open to reveal Bald and Jansen waiting in the hallway. Bald shoved Jansen ahead of him into the lift, and the three of them rode it down five floors to the underground car park. Porter stepped out first, checking the coast was clear. Then Bald frogmarched Jansen out of the lift and over to the waiting vehicle. A Volkswagen Jetta, parked up in the shadows. Two forty-something guys Porter didn't recognise were sitting in the front, both dressed in civvies. Two of the assets Strickland had mentioned at the briefing. Local agents, on call whenever Six needed them. They wouldn't know anything about the mission, or Bald or Porter.

The assets had mobilised as soon as Porter had given Strickland the heads-up about the PA. She had told Porter that they would be ready to lift Jansen once she had put in the call to her Russian handler. Better to make her disappear, Strickland had said. They would need to explain her abrupt disappearance to Lansbury, but that was less risky than leaving Jansen in play. The assistant shuffled over to the car, slack-jawed and ghostly pale, eyes frantically glancing left and right, looking to see if there was anyone else in sight. Anyone who might save her. But the car park was empty.

'Please, you don't have to do this,' she said, weeping as they drew nearer to the Volkswagen. 'I won't tell anyone, I swear to God.'

'Shut the fuck up,' Bald snarled under his breath.

'You're ruining my life!'

'Be glad you've got one. Be glad you're fucking alive.'

The two assets remained in the car while Bald and Porter walked Jansen over to the boot and popped it open. The assistant caught sight of the empty boot and went rigid with fear. Bald gave her a shove, forcing Jansen inside. She resisted at first, and then Bald gave her a dig to the ribs and bundled her into the cramped interior. Jansen swore tearfully at Bald, calling him the vilest things her mind could conjure up. Bald simply grinned at her. Women had called him worse. Much worse.

'Her Majesty thanks you for your service,' he said.

He slammed the boot shut, handed over the wallet and passport to the guy in the front passenger seat. Gave a thumbs-up to the driver, signalling for the backup team to depart. They pulled out of the parking space, rolled up the exit ramp and disappeared into the grey afternoon. From the hotel Jansen would be taken to another RV outside the city, close to the Austrian border. The team would transfer her to a haulage truck with a sealed compartment inside an ISO storage container, smuggle her across the border to an MI6 safe house in Vienna. Jansen would be questioned and held there until the operation was finished. If anyone on the Russian side started asking questions, all they would find out is that the PA had unexpectedly absconded from the hotel. They would conclude that she had lost her nerve and run off, perhaps fearful of being exposed by a third party.

Once the Jetta had left, Bald took Jansen's mobile and burner, removed the SIM cards from both, crushed them beneath the heel of his shoe and stamped on the screens. He disposed of the phones in separate bins around the car park, while Porter put in another encrypted call to Strickland and gave her the good news.

'We've got news of our own,' Strickland said. 'Good and bad.'

'Tell us the good news first.'

'We ran the photographs you sent through to us. The two men

pictured with BROKEN RECORD outside the Hotel Flamingo are senior agents with the FSB. We're talking high-ranking officers, closely connected to the Kremlin.'

Porter said, 'How is that good news?'

'We're a step closer to implicating BROKEN RECORD. Whatever he and his friends are up to at the conference, it has to involve the Russian security services.'

'Any clue what they were talking about?'

'Not yet. We have theories, but nothing concrete. Which is why we absolutely need eyes and ears on tonight's conference. It could be crucial to bringing BROKEN RECORD down.'

'What's the bad news?'

'Our surveillance team lost BROKEN RECORD and his friends on their way to the meeting.'

'How?'

'The FSB agents were running counter-surveillance tactics, we think. Our guys followed them to an out-of-town shopping centre. They switched vehicles in the multi-storey car park and gave our guys the slip. We're not sure where they went after that.'

'So we've got no clue who this mystery Russian guest is?'

'No,' Strickland admitted. 'But whoever it is, the FSB clearly think he's important enough to get BROKEN RECORD and his political allies onside. We really need to find out what's going on at this gathering.'

'That won't be easy.'

'Just don't get caught,' Strickland cautioned. 'Otherwise this whole thing is going to blow up in our faces.'

Porter tightened his grip around the handset. He was determined not to fail their mission. He'd fought hard to re-establish his credentials after years of being blackballed by the Regiment head shed. *I fucked up once before*, Porter reminded himself. He cast his mind back to the op in Beirut in 1989. Several lifetimes ago. The teenager whose life he'd spared. A kid who had subsequently killed three good Hereford men. A tragic mistake. One that had cost Porter his reputation, his marriage and his relationship with his daughter. It had taken him thirty years to rebuild his life.

I'm not going to fuck up this time.

'We'll bring the bastard down,' Porter said. 'Don't worry about that.'

He hung up, told Bald the news as they climbed the stairs leading to the lobby.

'One thing's for sure,' said Bald. 'If the FSB are involved, it's going to be a bastard getting eyes and ears on the meeting.'

'We've got the GPS trackers,' Porter reminded him.

'Aye, and what if Lansbury tries to block us, or ditches it again? Then we're really fucked.'

'What about planting another secret mic?'

Bald considered. 'Won't work. That's a one-time trick. After what happened this morning, the FSB will be checking everyone for bugs at this shindig. That's for sure.'

'We'll think of something,' Porter muttered.

'Whatever it is, we'd better come up with it fucking quick.'

Porter tapped his watch. 'We can't worry about that now. We've got to get those bugs planted in Lansbury's room. Now, before he gets back from his meeting.'

Bald nodded. 'Lead the way.'

They vaulted up the stairs.

Twelve forty-five in the afternoon.

Three hours and fifteen minutes until they departed for the conference.

Not long to go now, Porter thought. *Not long at all.*

TWENTY-FOUR

They trotted back across the lobby, took the stairs to the third floor and slipped into their room. Gathered up the surveillance kit spread across their beds and hustled down the corridor to the next room along from Jansen. Lansbury's room. Porter touched the key card he'd snatched from the PA against the door lock and entered a lavish suite the approximate size of a Surrey mansion. There was a main bedroom with a king-size bed, an adjoining lounge with a fifty-inch flat-screen TV, coffee table and a balcony with a commanding view of the Danube. The biggest room in the hotel, probably.

'My kind of gaff,' said Bald admiringly. 'All that's missing is the toot and the Roger Moores.'

'Roger Moores?'

'Whores, mate.'

'Where did you learn that?'

'You move around the circles I do, you pick up the lingo.'

Porter shook his head. 'Me and you lead different lives.'

'Aye. Mine's better.'

Porter ground his teeth. 'Just get on with it. We don't have much time.'

They went to work, following the instructions given to them by Hogan. The Scaley had explained that the listening devices used a lot of energy, which meant they needed to be wired up to a live power source. Porter placed bugs in the power sockets in each room and installed a third device in the back panel of the TV. Meanwhile Bald swapped the charging units for Lansbury's phone and laptop with the modified chargers, so that MI6 could remotely pull passwords, data and files from any devices the target plugged into them. They moved swiftly but carefully, taking care to leave everything exactly as they had found it. Once the devices were up and running they left the suite, closed the door and started back down the corridor. Back in their room, Porter took one of the passport-sized portable drives from his holdall and plugged it in. The bugs in Lansbury's room would automatically transmit their recordings to the passport drive, storing the audio file in a securely encrypted format for Vauxhall to transcribe and analyse at a later date.

Bald stopped abruptly before they checked out of their room again, turned and said, 'Have we got any bugs left?'

'A few. Why?'

'I've got an idea. Don't put them back in your luggage. Hand them over.'

'What for?'

'Just do it.'

Porter gave him the trio of matchbox-sized bugs. Bald tucked them inside his jacket pocket and quickly sketched out his plan as they made their way downstairs.

They hit the lobby at twelve-fifty in the afternoon. Ten minutes ahead of schedule.

The front lobby was bustling with activity. Late checkouts and early check-ins, business types in expensive suits arriving for lunch meetings at the brasserie. Tourists heading out for an afternoon of sightseeing, armed with backpacks and selfie-sticks and bored-looking kids staring dead-eyed at iPad screens.

There was no sign of Lansbury yet so Bald and Porter found a quiet spot to the right of the reception area, planted themselves on a pair of armchairs and waited. For the first time since they had walked in on Jansen in their room, Porter breathed a sigh of relief.

'Bloody hell, that was a close call,' he said. 'Thought that PA was going to blow our cover back there, for sure.'

'Need a drink, mate? Calm your nerves?'

'Piss off, Jock.'

Bald laughed and shook his head. 'Maybe you could do with having a few measures of the demon drink. Get some of your old spark back.'

Porter rounded on his mucker. 'What's that supposed to mean?'

'You've lost your edge,' Bald said. 'That PA was about to scream for help when we walked in on her, and you just fucking stood there. If it wasn't for me, we'd be in handcuffs by now.'

'I was trying to calm her down.'

'Bollocks. You've gone soft. You might be fit and sober these days, but you're a shadow of the hard bastard I used to know in the Regiment. I'm the one having to do all the heavy lifting on this thing.'

'That's a fucking lie.'

'Is it? It was my idea to slap the secret mic on Lansbury. I'm the one who suggested tailing him to the meet. What have you done?'

Porter shook his head slowly. 'I'm just trying to do things the right way. Keep both our noses clean.'

'Aye, and where would that have got us? Nowhere.'

'This isn't like the old days. You can't go around breaking the rules anymore.'

'You forget who we're dealing with,' Bald said. 'Lansbury is a slippery fucker. We're not going to catch him by playing it by the book. We've got to get our hands dirty, whether you like it or not.'

'Vauxhall told us they want a clean operation,' Porter growled.

Bald chuckled and shook his head. 'Christ, listen to you. Six has got you wrapped round their little finger. Face it, mate. You've lost that bit of devilment all of us Blades have got.'

Porter clenched his fist, felt the anger building up inside his chest. He bit back on it and glowered at his mucker. 'You don't understand. It took me ages to sort my life out. Get my head clear. I've got a good thing going on, and I'm not about to piss it away just because you won't play by the fucking rules.'

'Tell yourself that. But there's only one of us trying to put Lansbury behind bars. And it sure as fuck ain't you.'

Sixty seconds later, a Mercedes-Benz S-Class pulled up outside the hotel. Derek Lansbury debussed from the back seat, gave a cursory nod to the chauffeur and another one to the doorman before he swept inside the lobby. He wore a smug grin and moved with an extra spring in his step as he approached the reception. Like a City banker who had just been told the good news about his annual bonus. His grin was so wide you would have needed a ferry to cross it.

Porter and Bald both stood up to greet their boss as he drew near.

'Good meeting, sir?' asked Bald.

'Oh, very good,' replied Lansbury. 'Very productive indeed.'

His eyes were glowing with excitement. There was something about his face that made Bald want to punch it. He faked a smile instead.

'Glad to hear it, sir.'

'As you should be, my good man. A few days from now, you're going to be working for one of the richest men in Britain.'

'Really, sir? How's that?'

'Oh, just a minor business venture I've been working on.' Lansbury tapped the side of his nose. 'I can't say too much about it at the moment, but let's just say that all my hard work is about to pay off. Handsomely.'

Lansbury's grin stretched out even further across his smug face. Bald said, 'Good for you, sir. You're a great man. You deserve it, after everything you've done for the country.'

Christ, thought Porter. Jock's laying it on thick. Not for the first time, he wondered whether Bald was really just following orders. Or was he trying to appeal directly to Lansbury? Win him over somehow? Porter didn't think so, but he couldn't be completely sure. With Bald, you never quite knew where you stood.

'I do have *some* bad news, however,' Lansbury said.

'Sir?'

Lansbury smiled, sheepishly. 'I'm afraid I managed to lose that tracker you fellows gave me.'

Bald's left eyebrow caterpillar-climbed up his brow. 'How did that happen, sir?'

'Honestly, I've no idea. I can only suppose that the damn thing must have fallen off when I nipped out to get some fags. Didn't even realise that I'd lost it until I got out of the car, sadly.'

'No problem, sir. We'll sort you out with a replacement.'

Lansbury scanned the lobby, his eyebrows wrinkled into a deep frown. 'Don't suppose either of you has seen Freya? I've been trying her phone for the past half hour without any luck.'

Porter and Bald glanced at one another. Bald coughed and said, 'Actually, sir, we've some bad news of our own.'

'Oh? What is it?'

'Probably better if we discuss this in private.'

'I see.' Lansbury glanced at his watch. 'Very well. But this had better be quick. I'm due to speak to the *Telegraph* shortly. Give them my side of the mugging story.'

'Don't worry, sir. This won't take long.'

They led Lansbury across the lobby and took the elevator to the third floor. Flanked him as he stalked down the brightly lit corridor and drew to a halt outside his suite. Bald and Porter watched him swipe open the door before they followed him down the short hallway into the lounge area. Lansbury took off his waxed farmer's jacket, laid it over the arm of the three-person sofa. Placed his hands on his hips and cocked his head at his bodyguards.

'Well? What the devil is going on?'

Porter looked towards Bald. The latter dipped a hand into his jacket pocket, extracted the spare bugs and set them down on the coffee table. Lansbury bent down and peered at them. 'What are these?'

'GSM listening devices,' Bald said. 'Advanced surveillance equipment. Otherwise known as bugs. Professional spies plant them in order to listen in on private conversations.'

Lansbury lifted his head, looked closely at Bald. 'Where did you find them?'

'Earlier this morning myself and Porter conducted a routine sweep of your room. We found two devices, hidden in your bedroom and lounge. We presented Miss Jansen with this information. It was our understanding that aside from yourself and the cleaning staff, she is the only one with regular access to your room.'

'That's right.'

'Following our conversation, Miss Jansen reluctantly agreed to a search of her room. After conducting a thorough search, we located an additional device in her hand luggage.'

'Jesus.'

'These are high-grade devices, sir,' Porter added. 'Not available on the commercial market.'

Lansbury's face dropped. 'Freya was bugging my room? *Spying* on me?'

'It appears so, sir.'

'Where is she now? I must talk to her. At once.'

'That's not possible, sir.'

'Why the hell not?'

Bald coughed. 'When we confronted Miss Jansen with this discovery, she denied having anything to do with it, accused us of setting her up and threatened to call security unless we left her room immediately. Having no powers of arrest and mindful of causing a scene, we had no choice but to agree to her request. Miss Jansen said she would remain in her room until you returned so we could clear things up. However, when we last checked on her, we found her room empty and her passport, phone and wallet missing.'

Lansbury looked apoplectic. 'You just let her go?'

'As I said, sir, we had no choice. If we had confined Miss Jansen against her will, we would have risked being detained by local law enforcement on charges of kidnapping and false imprisonment. Porter and myself decided that it would be better to get her to cooperate, rather than bring undue attention to another member of your staff.'

'She's a damn traitor! And after all I've done for that bitch ...' He snorted loudly through his nostrils, rounded on Bald and Porter. 'You should have kept her here.'

'Sorry, sir. We did our best.'

'And we have no idea where she is now?'

'No, sir.'

'Well, that's fucking brilliant.'

Lansbury paced over to the window, stared out across the city, gritting his teeth so hard Bald and Porter could almost hear the enamel crack. He spun back around.

'I don't understand. Gary and Mick, the old bodyguards, swept this room regularly and didn't find anything. How on earth did she do it?'

Bald said, 'It's our belief that Miss Jansen knew in advance of the previous team's sweeps and ensured that the devices were remotely switched off beforehand. That way, the detector wouldn't pick them up.'

'How did she get hold of them? These ... bugs?'

'We don't know,' Porter said. 'But it's unlikely she would have been able to purchase these devices herself. We think someone must have given them to her. A third party.'

Lansbury looked up, his brow heavily furrowed. 'Freya was working for someone?'

'We believe so, sir.'

'Who?'

'We don't know, sir. And it's not our place to speculate. We're just presenting you with the facts.'

For a few seconds Lansbury said nothing. He just stood there, eyeballing the bugs, bristling with rage. His expression darkening, as if a shadow was moving across his face.

'I should have known,' he said after a pause.

'Known what, sir?' asked Bald.

'Someone bugged me. This morning. When I went to meet my ... friend.'

Bald stared at Lansbury, his face not giving anything away.

'I couldn't figure out who might have planted the device on me,' Lansbury went on. 'I was beginning to suspect you two might have been involved. Now it's clear that Jansen was the culprit all along.'

Porter said, 'Who would be snooping on you, sir?'

'I've got enemies,' Lansbury replied darkly. He lifted his eyes to his bodyguards. 'I had a phone call from a contact in the justice department a while ago. He tells me the police have been questioning Gary and Mick about the mugging. My guys are swearing blind that the man who attacked them was an expert in martial arts, not some random thief. They've also got an eyewitness who saw the attacker fleeing the scene. Chap ran like Usain Bolt on steroids, the witness claims. What beggar have you ever seen running like that?'

'Sounds suspicious, sir,' Bald said.

'That's what the authorities think. They're treating it as a planned assault instead of a random mugging. They think my bodyguards were deliberately targeted.'

'By who?' asked Porter.

'I don't know. But the way my life has been for the past few years, nothing would surprise me anymore.' He pointed a long nicotine-stained finger at Bald and Porter. 'You two are going to need eyes in the backs of your heads from now on.'

'That's what we're here for, sir. To keep you safe.'

Lansbury collapsed on to the sofa and picked up one of the bugs from the coffee table. Stared bitterly at it. 'I still can't believe it. Freya. Of all the people.'

'In my experience, sir,' said Bald, 'it's always the ones you think you can trust the most who stab you in the back.'

Lansbury nodded absently as he set down the bug. 'Well, thank God you two rumbled her. Goodness knows what damage she might have done if she'd been allowed to continue. You did well, both of you.'

'Just doing our job, sir.'

'And you're doing a damn better job of it than the last chaps. I'll be sure to put in a good word with my friend Lord McGinn. Tell him about the good work you're doing. How's that?'

A fucking bonus would be better, Bald thought. *Tight bastard.*

'Very kind of you,' he said.

'Any time. And I shall need you two watching my back at this gathering tonight, of course. No doubt some hard-left lunatics will try to infiltrate the event.'

Porter screwed up his face. 'I thought this conference was a secret, sir?'

'It is. But news of these events inevitably leaks out somehow. Our political enemies are always trying to find out what we're up to.'

Bald said, 'We'll need to discuss the security arrangements at this meeting before we leave. The more we know, the better we can protect you.'

Lansbury waved a hand. 'Ask away. What do you need to know?'

'First, where is this thing being held?' asked Porter.

'Koman Castle. A country estate, an hour or so to the south of here. Used to be owned by a Hungarian count, I believe, back in the days of the Austro-Hungarian Empire. There's a stable and helipad, and a thermal spa.'

'You've been there before?'

'A few times, yes. The owner is a personal friend of mine. Fellow by the name of Vitaly Butko. Perhaps you've heard of him?'

Bald and Porter shook their heads simultaneously.

'Who is he, sir?' asked Porter.

'A self-made Russian businessman and art collector. Made his fortune in Siberia in the gold-mining trade. Moved to Budapest and married his Hungarian girlfriend, a former Miss Universe. He's a good friend of President Fodor. He's also one of our key allies in the fight against the hectoring, out-of-touch liberal elites who have corrupted the West.'

Bald said, 'Butko is behind the gathering?'

'He's sponsoring it. Butko has kindly agreed to let us host the conference at his country retreat. He's providing the security, the dinner and entertainment, and he'll sit in on the talks. But that's as far as his involvement goes.'

'What's the security like at this place?'

'Extremely tight. One of the reasons we elected to have the meeting at Butko's castle, actually.'

'Can you give us specifics, sir?'

Lansbury scrunched up his face in thought. 'From memory, there are guards at the gate. Two of them, I believe. Armed, too. Some more chaps patrolling the grounds inside and the rear of the property. Don't ask me how many; I couldn't remember for the life of me. More than a few, at any rate. Plus additional staff inside the house. Oh, and there are dogs too. German shepherds, I believe.'

'Sounds like your friend has got some personal security concerns.'

'He's a man who values his privacy. And he's made a number of enemies over the years.'

'In the gold mine business?'

'He has other interests too. Ones that don't concern you. Two years ago, his eldest son was kidnapped by Chechen criminals and held hostage for three weeks. Butko had to pay an enormous ransom. The kidnappers returned his son, minus three of his fingers and his left ear. After that, Butko vowed never to be a target again. So he invested heavily in his personal security service.'

'Who else is going tonight?'

'I'm afraid that information is strictly confidential. All the guests are sworn to secrecy. No photos, no media briefings, no social media postings. That goes for both of you, I might add.'

'Can you tell us how many people are gonna be there, at least?'

'Forty, including myself. It's a very exclusive guest list.'

'What's the plan once we arrive, sir?' asked Porter.

'We'll get there for five o'clock. There's a drinks reception on arrival, and then the meeting will take place at five-thirty. It will go on for about two hours, followed by a dinner to celebrate our alliance. Should be done by midnight. Going to be quite a lot of sitting around in the car for you two. I suggest you bring a book.'

Porter did a double take. 'We're not going in with you, sir?'

'God, no. Butko's security team would never allow it. The only people allowed inside the meeting are the guests themselves. Not even their aides are permitted to go in with them.'

'What are we supposed to do while you're busy inside?'

'Hang around in the reception. Or pass the time in the car. Whichever you prefer.'

Bald pursed his lips. For an instant he considered arguing the decision with Lansbury. But that tactic hadn't worked before, and he didn't see any reason why it would work this time. If Lansbury didn't want them anywhere near the meeting, their hands were tied. He was the principal, after all. Bald tried a different tack instead. 'Can you at least wear another tracker while you're inside, sir?'

Lansbury shook his head. 'Butko takes his security very seriously. They wouldn't let me within a hundred yards of the place if I wore one of those things.'

'You'll be out of contact, sir,' Bald said. 'We won't have any way of knowing if you're under threat.'

'I doubt that will be an issue,' Lansbury responded confidently. 'There's a detector inside the entrance hallway. One of those walk-through contraptions. The guards have security wands on them as well. I am assured that they're extremely thorough. No one will be getting inside with a weapon, if that's what you're worried about.'

'Every guest has to pass through the gate?'

'Indeed. Even me, and I've been helping to organise the damn thing. So you see, there's really no need to worry about my safety. Once I'm through the cordon, I'll be fine.'

'Yes, sir,' Bald replied through clenched teeth. 'That's good to know.'

They were interrupted by the urgent buzz of a phone ringing. Lansbury reached into his jacket pocket, fished out his mobile. Glanced at the number glowing on the screen. 'That's the *Telegraph*. I'll need to take this. Wait outside. I'll give you a shout when I need you.'

Bald opened his mouth to reply but Lansbury had already shot to his feet and turned away, phone clamped to his left ear as he answered the call. Porter signalled to Bald and they paced out of the room, taking up their stations in the corridor either side of the door.

'Looks like we're in the clear,' Porter said quietly.

'For now,' Bald replied. 'But not for long.'

'You don't think we're safe?'

'The Jansen thing has bought us some time. But the net's closing. Now that those two bodyguards are talking, the police are going to start looking into who staged the attack and why. It won't take a fucking genius for them to work out that someone knocked them on the head so that we could get on the team. When that happens, they're gonna take a long, hard look at us.'

Porter nodded slowly, his mind scrolling through the scenario. 'How long do you think we've got?'

'A few days,' Bald guessed. 'Maybe longer, if Six does something about that investigation.'

'And if they don't?'

'Then we'd better hope that Strickland wasn't bullshitting us about that heli waiting on standby across the border,' said Bald. 'Because we're going to need it soon enough.'

Porter rubbed his jaw and said, 'We've got bigger problems than the bodyguards, Jock.'

'How d'you mean?'

'Getting a bug into that gathering is going to be fucking tricky. Whatever we plant on Lansbury is gonna get picked up by that detector.'

'How the fuck are we supposed to smuggle a device in, then?'

'We're going to need a new plan,' said Porter. His lips widened into a grin. 'And I've got just the idea.'

'You?' Bald chuckled. 'No offence, mate, but you're not exactly the king of crafty plans. That's my bag.'

Porter glared at him. 'You want to hear it, or not?'

'Go on, then,' Bald said, spreading his hands. 'Let's hear it. I could do with a good laugh . . .'

TWENTY-FIVE

The afternoon passed slowly. There was nothing else for Bald and Porter to do except carry out their duties and keep a close eye on Lansbury until they left for the conference. Lansbury spent most of the time in his room, talking on his phone or sending messages. From outside the suite they couldn't hear his conversations, but everything he said was picked up by the bugs they had planted earlier on, transmitted and stored on the portable hard drive in Bald and Porter's room. There was a brief trip to an upmarket restaurant across the street for a late lunch. Which involved Bald calling the manager in advance, letting them know that a VIP was on their way and that his team would need three tables, next to one another, preferably at the back of the restaurant, away from the other diners and close to a fire exit. Bald and Porter ordered in advance, finished their scoff and passed the time with small talk while Lansbury worked his way through a plate of pan-roasted sea bass, potatoes and asparagus, washed down with a glass of Argentinian red wine. Then back to the hotel and another hour waiting outside Lansbury's suite. Bald was reminded of how much he hated close-protection jobs. The long periods sitting on his arse and doing nothing, taking shit from the principal. He bit back on his frustration, focused on the big prize waiting for him at the end of the op.

The steady corporate job. Minimum hassle, six-figure salary. Company benefits. Generous pension. Nigeria or Iceland or Alaska, he didn't give a toss.

He'd spent ten years on the Circuit. Had spent almost as long working for Vauxhall, doing their dirty work. Bald had paid his dues. Now he was ready for Easy Street.

At three-thirty in the afternoon, Lansbury beckoned Bald and

Porter into his suite. 'Call the chauffeur,' he ordered. 'Tell him we're leaving for the conference shortly. Half an hour. He'll know where Koman Castle is.'

'Aye, sir.'

Bald didn't have the number for the chauffeur, so he jogged down to the lobby and got the concierge to call him. Bald gave the driver the address and pickup time and instructed him to bring the S-Class round to the front of the hotel. Then he sent a message to Strickland.

Leaving for meeting at 16.00 hours. Address is Koman Castle. ETA 17.00.

She responded after the usual delay. *Understood. We heard new developments re bodyguard attack.*

Bald wrote, *Orders?*

Continue as planned for now. Will alert you if situation changes.

Bald read the reply, then typed a follow-up message. *Who is Vitaly Butko?*

Which prompted a longer delay from Strickland. He had to wait two whole minutes before she got back to him.

Russian gold-mining magnate and art collector. Very close to the Kremlin and the FSB. Suspected Kremlin agent and Russia's unofficial man in Budapest. Why?

Bald replied, *Butko is hosting the conference, according to BROKEN RECORD.*

Which prompted another reply from Strickland. An empty message with a picture attached to it. Bald opened it. A slender, grey-haired figure dressed in a white dinner jacket and bow tie filled the screen. Vitaly Butko looked to be in his late fifties, with a large forehead and small round eyes, like holes in a block of marble. He had thin lips that curled up at the corners, as if he was smiling to himself at some private joke.

Bald didn't reply to the message. No need. He de-encrypted his iPhone, made his way back upstairs and took up his spot outside Lansbury's suite. Twenty-seven minutes later, Lansbury emerged from his room.

Bald accompanied him downstairs while Porter rushed ahead to bring the Volvo up from the underground car park. They had agreed that Bald would ride up top in the S-Class with Lansbury, with Porter following close behind. If they ran into trouble, they would abandon the lead vehicle and make their escape' in the Volvo. Lansbury seemed impressed by their attention to detail. He made a big deal out of it, praising their efforts and berating the lack of professionalism he felt had been shown by his previous BG team. He told Bald and Porter how wonderful it was to have a pair of ex-SAS heroes watching over him. How he'd thought of joining the Regiment himself once, as a teenager.

Two minutes later, they left the hotel.

Dusk was beginning to gather as the S-Class pulled away from the Royal Duna Hotel. Lansbury spread himself out on the back seat and concentrated on a hefty pile of papers on his lap. Speeches or policy documents, Bald assumed. He crossed out words, rehearsing phrases as he scribbled notes in the margins.

Bald rode up front with the chauffeur. The same bloke who had picked them up from the airport the previous evening. Tibor, the guy with the buzz cut and eyes that were too close together. Porter followed them in the Volvo, sticking to the S-Class like a limpet. Bald kept a close eye on their surroundings. Twenty years of training, hardwired into his brain. Eyes scanning for potential threats, scoping out nearby vehicles. He made sure the driver stayed back from the car in front whenever they hit a red light. Routine stuff. It was unlikely that Lansbury would be targeted without Vauxhall knowing about it first, but Bald didn't want to take any chances. Not when they were so close to nailing him.

The lights along the length of the Chain Bridge glowed like Christmas tree decorations as they headed west across the river. The driver took a circuitous route out of the city, navigating one-way streets and avoiding the big thoroughfares. After three miles they joined the motorway heading south. They bowled past warehouses and car dealerships, fast-food chains and petrol stations. Concrete tower blocks loomed on the horizon, black against the apricot glow of the fast-approaching night. Tibor was a careful driver. He stuck religiously to the national speed limit. The needle never climbed past the seventy mark.

As they continued south Bald kept one eye on the car's built-in navigation system. There was a bright red arrow indicating their current position. A winding blue line showed the route to their final destination, eighty miles south of Budapest. The journey would take them fifty-nine minutes, according to the satnav. Which meant that they would arrive at Koman Castle at around five o'clock in the evening. Half an hour before the big meeting.

He glanced at Lansbury in the rear-view mirror. The guy had stopped scribbling notes. He stared out of the window as the landscape scrolled past, brow wrinkled in thought.

'What's the craic with this meeting, sir?' asked Bald. 'Some big announcement, is it?'

'Just boring policy stuff,' Lansbury replied airily. 'Nothing that concerns you. Not unless you've developed a sudden fascination for the intricacies of right-wing politics. Is that the case?'

'No, sir. Not me. Couldn't be dealing with all that stuff.'

'Then stop asking me questions and focus on your job.'

'Yes, sir.' Bald paused, gauging how far he could push it with Lansbury. 'Just got me thinking, sir. What you said earlier, about the liberal elites wrecking society.'

'What about it?' Lansbury asked distractedly.

'There's a lot of lads in the SAS who feel the same way, sir.'

'Really?' Lansbury looked away from the window, stared curiously at Bald. 'How so?'

'I shouldn't go on, sir. It's not my place to speak my mind.'

'No, no, please continue. I hear stories from the generals often enough, but not from the fellows on the frontline, as it were. I'd like to hear what the men defending our country really think.'

Bald smiled inwardly. He had the principal's full attention now.

'It's the suited-and-booted brigade in Westminster, sir. They're ruining the Regiment. Take Selection,' Bald said. 'The SAS has the toughest recruitment process in the world, right? Everyone has to be held to the same high standard. You either pass or fail, that's it. But now we've got those politically correct types telling us that they're going to let women take Selection. And that's only the start of it. Next they'll be telling us that Selection is too hard and we've got to make it easier for them.'

'Scandalous!' Lansbury exclaimed.

'Then you've got the MoD spending millions on ad campaigns,

promoting diversity and telling people it's okay to be emotional, and meanwhile our lads are having to make do with out-of-date or substandard kit. You've got a defence secretary who spends more time on Twitter than he does making sure that the other nations in NATO are pulling their weight. It's just a load of Establishment bollocks. They claim to support the armed forces, but they don't really give a toss about blokes like me. All they care about is making a name for themselves, sir. In my opinion.'

Lansbury inclined his head at Bald, as if seeing him for the first time. 'I didn't know you felt so strongly about such things.'

Bald didn't. He didn't give a shit about inclusivity or women taking part in Selection. He was an equal opportunities man, when it came to violence and the application of it. The Brecon Beacons didn't care whether you were black, white or purple. All that mattered was whether you had what it took to become a Blade.

'Totally, sir,' Bald lied. 'All this diversity crap is going to run the Regiment into the fucking ground. Pardon my French.'

Lansbury leaned forward, slapped a hand against his thigh. 'You see, that's exactly what I've been saying! You've hit the nail on the head. Couldn't have put it better myself.'

'Just telling you what the lads at Hereford are thinking, sir.'

'What you've just described is precisely what is wrong with our country these days. With everywhere in Europe, in fact.'

'What's that, sir?'

'We've allowed ourselves to be governed by a global metro-politan elite,' Lansbury said, warming to his theme. 'A snobbish Islington set that looks down their noses at ordinary men and women such as yourself, telling you that you're wrong and that they know best, and if you argue otherwise then you're branded as a bigot. If you wave an England flag or say you're proud to be British, then you're an uncivilised racist. I actually think those people secretly hate the country they live in.'

'Bunch of virtue-signalling twats if you ask me,' Bald said. 'We should stick the lot of 'em in a Taliban stronghold. See what they think about inclusivity then.'

'Well put!' Lansbury smiled at Bald in the rear-view mirror. 'It's John, isn't it?'

'Aye, sir. But everyone calls me Jock.'

'Not many Scots in the SAS, I imagine.'

'There's more of us than you'd think, sir. They still raise us hard, north of the border.'

'I'm sure they do.' Lansbury grinned. 'You're an interesting fellow, Jock. It seems I underestimated you.'

'How's that, sir?'

'Most of the chaps on my security detail couldn't express a political opinion if their lives depended on it. They're more interested in steroids and pornography than speaking their minds. I'd simply assumed you were the same.'

'Not your fault, sir. Like you say, I'm just a bodyguard.'

'But you're right. We shouldn't be sabotaging the proud traditions of the SAS. It's supposed to be about being the best of the best, isn't it? Quite frankly if you're not up to scratch then you shouldn't get in. End of.'

'Glad to hear someone's on our side, sir. Just a pity the rest of those arseholes in government don't think the same way.'

'Quite.'

Bald glanced up at the rear-view mirror. Saw Lansbury giving him a big matey smile. His new best friend.

Lansbury eased back into his seat, crossed his legs and turned his attention back to the gloomy landscape. Bald glanced at the clock on the satnav.

Four-thirty.

Half an hour to go.

TWENTY-SIX

They continued south on the motorway. A long, winding stretch of freshly laid blacktop that roughly followed the course of the Danube as it snaked down from Budapest towards the Great Plain. Darkness was beginning to settle like ash across the landscape, blackening the shapes of distant factories and townships. After twenty miles they skirted around the edge of a place called Dunaújváros and crossed a bridge to the eastern side of the river. The landscape became flat and barren. Bald saw ploughed fields and bare trees in every direction, pockmarked by the occasional farm or cottage. Ramshackle homesteads with shuttered windows and tiles missing from the rooftops and rusted Trabants parked outside. But mostly it was an endless sprawl of farmland. Lansbury sat in silence in the back seat, becoming noticeably more anxious as they neared their destination, glancing repeatedly at his watch or checking his phone. Tibor continued to say nothing. Bald was beginning to think that the chauffeur might be mute.

They stuck to the main country road for another twelve miles before they hit a crossroads. Tibor made a left, taking them down a potholed one-lane road, hemmed in on both sides by rows of stark trees and tangled forest. They carried on for three miles, Porter still following close behind in the Volvo. Bald saw no cars or buildings or people. For a while he wondered if the driver had accidentally punched in the wrong destination. Then the road suddenly opened up and Lansbury shot forward in his seat, pointing ahead of them.

'There! That's the place.'

Bald peered through the windscreen, straining his eyes in the encroaching dusk. Two hundred metres ahead of them stood a large country pile, set a hundred metres back from the road and enclosed behind a metre-high solid masonry wall. Lanterns were mounted atop posts along the wall, burning brightly in the fading light. There was an ornate iron gate at the front of the property with a small lodge to the left.

The mansion itself was huge. The size of an imperial palace. It was three storeys tall, with a steeply gabled roof and a medieval turret jutting out of one corner of the main building. Behind the mansion stood a wide parcel of land dotted with patches of dense, gloomy forest.

'Nice pad, sir,' Bald said. 'Your mate's done well for himself.'

Lansbury laughed. 'This isn't Butko's primary residence. More of a private retreat he uses from time to time. Somewhere he can meet with his associates without any prying eyes.'

'Got some good connections, has he?'

Lansbury chuckled. 'That's putting it mildly. Butko is friends with some powerful men.'

The guy was in his element now, bragging openly in front of his bodyguard. Tibor pulled up in front of the gate, stopped and waited while a pair of shaven-headed toughs emerged from the lodge. They were both clad in black trousers and matching dark jackets, like models for a Tall & Mighty catalogue. The new collection, as modelled by steroid-jacked neo-Nazis.

The bigger of the two guys was equipped with a tan-coloured compact rifle. Shorter than a regular assault rifle, with a folded-up buttstock and a Picatinny rail. The guy had it slung across his burly shoulder with a nylon strap. Bald recognised it as a Kalashnikov MA compact rifle. One of the newer Russian weapon systems. Chambered for the 5.45 x 39mm round. Thirty-round magazine. Serious firepower. Not the kind of thing a private security guard would carry, ordinarily.

Bald wondered again about the gathering. He thought about the secrecy. The heavy security presence. The involvement of the Russian FSB.

The mystery guest speaker.

What the fuck is going on here?

The guy with the Kalashnikov hung back while his mate approached the S-Class. He was the smaller of the two toughs, but only just. Compared to Bald, he was still a giant. Six-four, perhaps two hundred and twenty pounds, with hands the size of pork knuckles. His eyes were like bullet holes fired into a paper target. His skin was pale and glistening, chemically mutated from years of steroid abuse. He was clutching an iPad in his right hand, Bald saw. Lansbury buzzed down his window, exchanged a few words with the heavy. The guy with the bullet-hole eyes checked something on his iPad, stepped back and signalled to his buddy. The bigger guy with the Kalashnikov. He stalked back into the gatehouse, pressed a button. A moment later there was a loud whirring sound as the gate yawned open and the S-Class slithered through the entrance, Porter following in the Volvo.

The two vehicles motored down a flagstone driveway lined with soft spotlights. It ran on for a hundred metres to the front of the mansion, where it opened out into a carriage circle. Vehicles were parked up around the edge of the circle, like dials on a clock. Bald saw Range Rovers and Bentleys, Mercedes-Benzes and Chevrolet Suburban SUVs. A couple of Lincoln Town Cars. He counted a total of twenty-one vehicles. Which meant that many of the guests had already arrived. Some would be VIPs, travelling in two-car arrangements like Lansbury. The less high-profile guests would have made their own way there.

The driveway curved round to the left of the castle, towards a four-door garage with a gravel parking area the size of two tennis courts. There was an access road to the right of the castle, leading towards the rear of the property. Several smaller buildings were visible in the middle distance. Bald saw stables and cabins and guest houses, a sauna set beside a small lake.

Directly ahead stood the mansion.

Up close it looked even bigger than from a distance. The windows were each as tall as a person. There were arches and cornices and reliefs, more than he could count. There had to be at least twenty rooms inside, Bald guessed. The facade was painted the colour of honey and illuminated by another bank of spotlights.

Tibor continued down the driveway. He eased off the gas as he steered around the carriage circle before pulling up in front of the entrance, with Porter stopping just behind. A set of stone steps led from the front drive up to the open front door. Two more heavies stood guard either side of the doorway. They were decked out in the same gear as the guys at the gatehouse and brandished the same Kalashnikov MA rifles. Both guys had also shaved their heads. Bald was beginning to detect a theme. Maybe it was a fashion thing, he thought. Like gangster tattoos. Or maybe it was a compulsory part of the uniform. Maybe Butko's security detail operated a shaved-head-only policy.

'Pull up here,' Lansbury ordered.

The chauffeur kept the engine running as Bald hopped out and swung round to the rear passenger side, opening the door for Lansbury. One of the guards stepped forward from his post and addressed Tibor in Hungarian, pointing towards the garage to the left. Telling him where to park, Bald figured. There was a system, presumably. The chauffeur arrowed the S-Class towards the gravel driveway while Bald paced over to the Volvo and gestured for Porter to lower the window.

'Park up next to the Mercedes,' Bald said. 'I'll walk the principal inside, meet you back at the wagon.'

'Roger that, mate.'

Porter buzzed up the window, drove on.

'Come on,' Lansbury said to Bald as he marched towards the entrance. 'Get a bloody move on.'

The last rays of daylight were sinking beneath the horizon and a chill breeze knifed through the air as Bald followed Lansbury up the steps leading into the castle. They passed the expressionless guards and swept into a wide hallway with marble columns and works of art in gold-painted frames and a high-domed ceiling with a mural painted on it. Some kind of religious iconography. A pair of solid oak doors to the left and right, both blocked by guards. Heavyset guys in dark suits were hanging around the room in pairs, eyes darting this way and that. One look at them told Bald that they were close-protection teams for the other guests.

At the far end of the hallway a third door led into an even bigger reception room. A walk-through metal detector had been installed in front of the door, manned by a black-jacketed heavy gripping a security wand. This guy actually had hair. Long on the top, short on the back and sides, with wide apart eyes and a scar above his upper lip. Through the open doorway Bald caught a glimpse of some of the other guests. Mostly men, old and white, dressed in grey or black suits.

There were women too. Lots of them. Young and blonde and curved, wearing tight-fitting dresses that showed off their assets. Bald's eyes almost popped out of his skull at the sight of them. The after-dinner entertainment, he supposed.

A figure strode briskly over to Lansbury from across the hall-way. Short and thin and grey-haired, with an immense slab of a forehead, wearing a white dinner jacket and bowtie. The same guy Bald had seen in the attachment Strickland had sent through to him. Vitaly Butko, the Russian gold mine magnate. The host of the gathering.

'Derek!' Butko said. 'Right on time. Welcome, my friend.'

Butko had a thick Russian accent. He grinned at Lansbury, pumping his hand enthusiastically. He blanked Bald, as if he simply didn't exist.

'Vitaly,' Lansbury said. 'A pleasure, as always.'

'You're well, I hope?'

'Very. And I'm even better now that I'm here.'

The corners of Butko's lips curved upwards in a smile. 'We're all very interested to hear what you have to say tonight. All of the guests are pressing me for information.'

'In good time.' Lansbury peered past Butko's shoulder, craning his neck at the faces in the reception room beyond. 'First, I must speak with our star guest. Is he here yet?'

Butko nodded. 'Our mutual friends are keeping him company upstairs. One of my staff will take you to him.'

'How is he?'

'Okay. Tired, you know? But our friends tell me that he'll be well enough for the meeting.'

'I must have a word with him, before we begin.'

'Do that. Then please, join the other guests. Help yourself to food, drink, whatever you want.'

Before Lansbury could reply Butko had moved off to greet another new arrival. A tall guy, rake-thin, with a clean-shaven head and a diamond stud in his left ear. With his dark suit, black shirt and gold rings on his fingers he looked more like a nightclub owner in a small town than a populist politician. Bald vaguely recognised him as the Italian Minister for European Affairs, Roberto Zanetti.

Fuck me, thought Bald. *Lansbury wasn't lying when he said the guest list for this event was exclusive.*

Butko and the Italian firebrand bear-hugged and joked with one another. Lansbury turned to address Bald.

'I'll be fine from here. Toilets are through there if you need them,' he said, indicating the door to the left of the hallway. 'If you're hungry, use the side entrance to the kitchen. The cooks will fix you something to eat.'

'You sure you don't need us to go in with you, sir?' asked Bald.

'Quite sure. You can message me if there's an emergency. Otherwise I'll see you in a few hours.'

Lansbury had half-turned away when Bald said, 'Sorry, sir. There is one thing. Before I forget.'

Lansbury stopped again, swung round to face Bald. 'Yes?'

'Been meaning to give you this, sir.'

Bald reached into his trouser pocket, pulled out a poker-chip sized coin and offered it to Lansbury. He looked at the coin without taking it. 'What is it?'

'It's an SAS challenge coin, sir. These things are a one-off. Only the guys who've served in the Regiment have one.'

'You wish to give me your own personal SAS coin?'

'Aye, sir.'

Lansbury was momentarily lost for words. Then he said, 'I'm humbled, Jock. Truly. But I couldn't possibly accept it. You worked hard to earn this.'

'Sir, I insist,' Bald replied. 'I want you to have it. My way of saying thanks, for everything you've done for our country. It'd be an honour.'

Lansbury looked genuinely touched. He clasped his hand firmly around the coin and smiled at Bald. 'Thank you. I mean it. I shall keep it by me at all times.'

'No, sir. Thank *you*, for sticking up for blokes like me. About time somebody did it.'

'Good man.'

Lansbury placed a hand on Bald's shoulder, lips spread into the world's smuggest grin. He tucked the challenge coin into his pocket and stood erect. Then he turned on his heels and strode purposefully across the hallway towards the detector. Bald lingered by the entrance, pretending to study the fire escape layout while he watched Lansbury out of the corner of his eye. He strutted through the detector and set off the beeper. The guard with the scarred upper lip held out a plastic tray, gesturing for Lansbury to empty his pockets. He fished out his phone, wallet, keys, a handful of loose change. Challenge coin. The guard flipped disinterestedly through the wallet, placed a sticker over the camera lens on the iPhone, turned his attention to the challenge coin.

Picked it up and examined it.

There was a brief exchange between the guard and Lansbury about the coin. Bald was too far away to hear what was being said, but from Lansbury's haughty tone of voice he had the impression the guy was bragging about it. *That's a genuine SAS coin, young man.* The guard inspected it again. In the periphery of his vision Bald could see the guy puzzling it out. *Is this permitted, or not?* Then he shrugged and handed it back to Lansbury with the rest of his personal effects.

Waved him through.

Bald made his way out of the hallway. He paced down the steps and headed straight for the garage to the left of the carriage circle. The Volvo and the S-Class were parked alongside one another in front of the garage, twenty-five metres away from the front of the castle, their bodyworks illuminated by the security lights mounted atop the garage roof. Further down the main driveway, Bald could see more cars turning up now, headlights burning as they steered towards the entrance. A tall, thin man in a rumpled suit stepped out of a silver Nissan Patrol. Bald recognised him as Henri Marveaux, the leader of the French nationalists. Butko greeted Marveaux warmly as he climbed the steps. The Patrol rolled off and parked up on the other side of the garage driveway from the S-Class and Volvo.

Bald breezed past the S-Class. He gave a nod to the chauffeur and climbed into the front passenger seat of the Volvo wagon. Porter looked a question at him.

'Well? Did he buy it?'

'Aye,' Bald said. 'Prick took the challenge coin right in with him. Guards didn't bother him about it, either.'

Porter grinned. 'See, Jock? I told you it would work.'

'You had one good idea,' Bald said. 'Big deal. I'm the one who had to butter him up on the way down here, telling him what a great fucking bloke he was.'

'You sure you didn't enjoy that? Thought you two would have plenty in common.'

Bald glared at Porter before he took out his phone. 'Just get on the blower to Six. Tell 'em the score.'

'What are you doing?' asked Porter, nodding at Bald as the latter dug out his iPhone.

'Taking photos of the new arrivals. This thing is a fucking who's who of right-wing celebrities.'

'Thinking about a new career with the paparazzi?'

'Piss off and make the call.'

Bald opened the camera app, tilted the phone horizontally and zoomed in on the front steps. From their position to the left of the carriage circle he and Porter had an unobstructed view of the front of the castle and surrounding grounds. On the near side of the castle Bald could see the side door leading into the kitchen, the catering vans parked up outside, waiting staff ducking in and out. He kept his phone trained on the front door, snapping pics as each new car pulled up and disgorged its VIP.

At the same time Porter tapped out an encrypted message to Strickland. *BROKEN RECORD just entered the building. We had to give him the challenge coin. Meeting begins 17.30. All security scans should be complete by then.* He hit the blue send icon and waited.

Sixty seconds later his phone vibrated. *Understood. Hold off broadcasting until 17.30 hours. We'll be on standby.*

Porter de-encrypted the phone again. He picked up the iPad he'd stowed in the glove compartment, unlocked it and opened the rebroadcasting app, ready to begin transmitting the audio back to Strickland and the team at Vauxhall. Porter wouldn't remotely activate the bug inside the challenge coin until the meeting was due to begin at five-thirty. Any earlier was a risk.

The security team might conduct further sweeps before the guests were allowed to enter the conference room. Safer to leave the coin bug switched off until the real action began.

Nine minutes past five in the evening.

Twenty-one minutes until the conference began.

TWENTY-SEVEN

Twenty minutes later, the forty guests filed into the meeting room at Koman Castle.

A massive U-shaped walnut conference table occupied the middle of the room. There were sixteen chairs arranged on either side and another eight chairs along the shorter end section. In front of each chair there was an upturned tumbler, bottles of still and sparkling water, one of each, and a pair of headphones for those few guests who didn't speak English. A small group of translators was sitting in an adjacent room, each one carefully vetted and hand-picked by Butko himself. They would be disposed of by his security team after the event, just in case.

Orders from the man Lansbury was working for.

Don't leave any tracks. No one must know what goes on inside this room.

The house staff showed the guests to their respective seats. Thirty-two of the guests sat on the longer sides of the conference table. The other eight took up their places on the end section. Derek Lansbury sat at an additional table at the other end of the room, facing the conference table. To his right sat Vitaly Butko, his bony hands resting flat on the table. To his left sat the joint organiser, the Hungarian prime minister Márton Fodor, side-fingering his bushy Hussar moustache.

The fourth chair was empty.

A diamond chandelier the approximate dimensions of a UFO hung from the ceiling. The room was adorned with gold: gilded decorative cornices, gold-embroidered curtains, ornate candleholders and framed mirrors. There was so much bling on display the room looked like a rapper's wet dream. To the left of the room there was a discreet side door that remained closed.

Lansbury watched in silence as the last guests took up their places. Around the table sat the leaders of every major populist and fascist movement in Europe. The political heavyweights: Zanetti, Marveaux. Andreas Polster, the silver-haired Austrian Vice-Chancellor. Effenberg, the leader of Germany's far-right group. Edwin de Jong, the dark-haired, pale-eyed Dutchman dressed like a British dandy in a three-piece tweed suit. Then there were the less familiar faces. Munoz, the Spanish aristocrat. Fringe extremists from Finland and Slovakia. Bulgarian and Croatian fascists, the leader of a Georgian vigilante group and Karkamanis, the frontman for the Greek ultra-nationalists. The group was mostly male, with a handful of women.

Some had been elected leaders of their countries. Others were leaders-in-waiting, heads of opposition parties, junior partners in coalition governments. The remainder were smaller but highly influential movements in their respective countries, drawing thousands to political rallies, spreading their message through online news networks, YouTube channels and Twitter accounts.

All of them had a common goal: the destruction of the smug elite order of the West. And they had all received aid from the Kremlin to help them achieve that ambition.

This is like a meeting of Mafia bosses, Lansbury thought to himself. Like something out of a black-and-white gangster film. All the major crime families coming together.

Which was appropriate, he realised. Because they were about to discuss something criminal.

Treasonous, even.

He waited for the hubbub of polite conversation to die down. Then he cleared his throat and projected his voice as he addressed his audience.

'Gentlemen, ladies. Thank you for coming here tonight. It's truly wonderful to be among so many old friends and allies.' He placed both hands flat on the table, looked slowly round the room. 'As you all know, I'm here to represent the interests of our friend in the White House. The president sends his regards, but regrets that prior engagements mean he cannot be here tonight. In other words,' Lansbury smiled icily, 'he's too busy telling the liberal elite where to stick it. He's asked me to stand in for him and oversee proceedings. I assume no one in this room has a problem with that arrangement?'

'That's all very well, Derek,' de Jong, the Dutchman, said in his peculiar high-pitched voice. 'But *why* are we here?'

'I'll come to that shortly,' Lansbury replied. 'But before we begin, I would remind everyone in this room that what is about to be discussed is in the strictest confidence. Anyone caught sharing the details of this meeting – anyone who even acknowledges the *mere fact* of this meeting – will be severely punished. Are we clear, chaps?'

He swept his eyes across the room again. Quick nods. Murmurs of agreement. Although he was addressing several heads of state and junior ministers, no one dared challenge Lansbury's authority. Which was understandable, he thought to himself. *Because I have the most powerful man in the world behind me.*

'Before we get started, we need to discuss something,' Zanetti interrupted. 'We need to talk about this migrant shit. I'm getting killed on this back home, now I've got the fucking gypsies making problems too. We need a joint line on this. Make sure we've got each other's backs, like we agreed before.'

Several voices around the table murmured their agreement. Lansbury raised a placatory hand, calling for silence. After a few moments, the voices died away.

'There will be plenty of time to discuss any concerns you have later on,' Lansbury said. 'Any grievances among us can be aired then. But the main purpose of our meeting tonight is to discuss a matter of vital importance. Not only to ourselves, but to the global political landscape and, indeed, the very future of our nations.'

Lansbury paused, making sure he had everyone's full attention. The guests all sat upright, looking on with interest. Satisfied, he went on.

'I assume you have all heard or read about President Drummond's latest pronouncements regarding NATO. Specifically, the refusal of certain NATO partners to pull their own weight and up their defence budgets, despite repeated demands from the White House.'

'What of it?' asked de Jong.

Lansbury continued, 'The president has made his feelings on the subject quite clear. He has asked me to inform you that he is no longer willing to be taken for granted by so-called allies. The time has come for action. Those are the president's words, not mine.'

Zanetti shrugged. 'So the Germans won't pay their own way while demanding debts from their poor brothers and sisters to the south. You called us fucking here for this?'

Effenberg shot him a cold stare.

Lansbury shook his head. 'The president has reached a decision. He wants to let you know in advance, so you can prepare yourselves accordingly.'

'Prepare for what?' asked de Jong. 'What decision?'

Lansbury took a breath and steeled himself. Then he said, 'Tomorrow afternoon, at the G7 summit in Loch Lomond, President Drummond will inform his peers that the United States intends to withdraw from NATO with immediate effect.'

A hundred metres away, Porter and Bald sat in the front of the Volvo, listening to the speech in stunned silence.

Bald said, 'Did we just fucking hear that right?'

Porter didn't reply. He stared at the iPad, his mind processing the implications of what he had just heard. The signal was jumping between two and three bars. They were out in the sticks. Not an ideal location. But it was close enough to pick up most of what was being said in the conference room.

The sound quality is fine, thought Porter. *We didn't mishear anything.*

The American president wants to pull the plug on NATO.

Jesus.

Jesus fucking Christ.

He thought back to the news items he'd seen on TV. The president giving a speech in the Midwest, railing against America's traditional allies for not contributing more to the NATO coffers. At the time he'd dismissed it as hot air. Empty talk, designed to provoke a reaction and energise the voter base. But now he realised the sinister truth.

The president hadn't been bluffing at all.

Bald said, 'Why would the Yanks quit NATO?'

Porter said, 'I don't know.'

They kept listening.

The silence lasted for what felt like several minutes. Lansbury let it play out, closely gauging the reaction of his peers. There were gasps of shock and looks of astonishment from several faces around the conference table. Some of those listening through headphones pressed them closer to their ears and frowned, as if not believing what they had just heard. One or two reacted with predictable delight to the news: the Bulgarian fascists, the Greeks. Others seemed less pleased: De Jong, the lily-livered Scandinavians. There were no obvious signs of dissent, Lansbury noted. Not yet.

'Who else knows about this?' asked Marveaux.

'Outside of this room? The president, his eldest daughter and his chief strategist. Other than that, no one.'

'Not even his defence secretary?'

Lansbury belted out a laugh. 'Don't be ridiculous. That old fool knows less than the White House janitor.'

'What does the president want from us?' asked de Jong. 'I assume you didn't invite us here as a mere courtesy.'

'You're going to support him,' Lansbury said. 'The president wants full backing from all of you. He's going to come in for a tremendous amount of flak at home and abroad from the Establishment, as you might well imagine. The mainstream media is going to hit the roof. We need each and every one of you to counter that narrative. That means TV interviews, press briefings, tweets, online broadcasts. You'll organise rallies in favour of the withdrawal. You'll be expected to defend his position vigorously at every opportunity.'

'But why is the president doing this?' asked Effenberg. 'For what purpose, Derek?'

Lansbury looked towards the German populist. 'Are you questioning the president's judgement, Lars?'

'Not at all. But this is a momentous decision. One that will affect us all. We're going to need more clarity from you before we agree to anything.'

Heads turned towards the German. With his frayed grey jacket, cashmere sweater and horn-rimmed glasses Effenberg looked more like an academic than a son of a Berlin shopkeeper. A legacy of his years spent studying economics at Oxford, Lansbury understood. Effenberg also drank heavily. From the glazed look in his eyes Lansbury guessed that the German had already downed half a dozen beers that evening.

'I agree with Lars,' Marveaux said. 'As soon as the president pulls out of NATO, the alliance collapses, *non*? The organisation no longer exists. You need to be straight with us, tell us what's going on.'

Lansbury studied his colleagues for a beat, twiddling the challenge coin his bodyguard had given him. He tucked the coin back in his trouser pocket and leaned forward, elbows propped on the table.

'There's going to be a realignment,' he said. 'The president is moving away from the old liberal order, which is decadent and decaying. He wishes to create a new alliance, one based on Christian values ... one that will unite the brotherhoods of Europe. It is transparently obvious that our traditional values are under attack, my friends. We must defend ourselves, before it is too late. Indeed, it is our moral duty to act. The president feels the best way of achieving this is to tear up the old agreement with NATO and seek out friendships with our Christian brothers across the world, wherever they may be.'

Murmurs around the room. Effenberg cleared his throat. 'And the commitment to defend Europe, in the case of an attack?'

'In this new world, our nations will flourish. We will be stronger than ever. NATO has had its day, my friends. Does anyone here truly believe that the organisation is a force for good?'

'But what about our allies in the Baltic States?' Effenberg glanced around the table. 'Who I notice are not with us tonight. If NATO collapses, they will be exposed to attack.'

'They have nothing to fear,' Lansbury replied dismissively. 'They will be given the opportunity to be part of this new alliance, in one way or another.'

De Jong shook his head furiously. 'You're asking us to abandon our brothers to their fate. We can't agree to such a thing. Have they even been consulted?'

Lansbury stared at the Dutchman. 'I find your reaction puzzling, Edwin. You've made several public statements in the past, criticising NATO. Are you saying you have changed your tune?'

'That's different,' de Jong replied defensively. 'I was talking about the reform of NATO. But what your friend in the White House is proposing is nothing less than the destruction of it. Perhaps in America, there is appetite for such a move, but not here. If I go on TV to support the president's decision, we're going to lose all the gains we've made.'

He sat back and folded his arms. Some of the Scandinavians nodded or grunted in support. The godless countries. Lansbury tried again.

'You all stand to benefit personally from this arrangement. Moscow is prepared to make a generous offer. A two per cent stake for each of you, in a Siberian gold mine.'

'Why would the Russians reward us?' de Jong asked.

'As you well know, they have a mutual interest in seeing the break-up of NATO. Since President Drummond cannot pay you directly, his friend in the Kremlin has agreed to pick up the bill.'

De Jong glanced round at the figures seated to the left and right of him, noting the hesitant looks on some of their faces. 'Forgive us. But you can't expect us to sell this to our supporters back home. No Dutch citizen would accept it. You'd turn me into a political outcast.'

'I find myself in the strange position of agreeing with my Dutch colleague,' Effenberg put in. 'We stand to lose too much, Derek. We cannot accept.'

'My boss will be very disappointed to hear that. So will the Russians.'

'That can't be helped,' de Jong responded arrogantly. 'We are, of course, willing to do whatever we can to help out our friend in the White House. But throwing our weight behind this decision is out of the question. Our voters would never buy it.'

'They might,' Lansbury said. 'If you have an effective way of marketing it.'

De Jong's eyebrows came together. 'I'm not sure I follow.'

'The line you're going to use is that NATO is a corrupt and nefarious organisation. It's part of the Deep State, in fact, undermining the will of the people at every opportunity, indulging in lies and fantasy. An alliance that will even go so far as murdering its own citizens and pinning the blame on the Russians. I'm sure your supporters would buy into that.'

'Not without proof,' Effenberg countered. 'We need proof.'

Lansbury smiled. 'What if I told you I can provide someone to do just that? Someone who can offer a first-hand account of the criminal activities committed by a leading member of NATO. Someone who is willing to stand in front of the cameras and publicly refute the heinous lies that a NATO ally has smeared him with.'

Effenberg made an expressive gesture. 'I'd like to know who this person is. Why? Did you have someone in mind?'

'I can go one better than that, Lars.'

Lansbury twisted in his chair and signalled to Butko. The latter called out towards the small door at the side of the room.

The door abruptly swung open. All eyes turned towards it. There was a long pause, and then a white-haired figure stepped through the opening.

'My God,' de Jong said.

There was a collective gasp among the guests. They were looking at a familiar face, ripped straight from the global headlines. An emaciated figure, much skinnier than the one featured on the news, but recognisable all the same.

Lansbury gestured towards the man and then turned to address the room. 'Allow me to introduce our guest of honour . . . Nikolai Volkov.'

TWENTY-EIGHT

A hundred metres away, Porter stared at the iPad. His throat felt as if someone had tightened a garrote around it. *So that's who the mystery Russian is*, he told himself.

Bald said, 'What the fuck is Volkov doing there? I thought he was in a safe house somewhere.'

Porter said, 'Me too.'

He knew the name. Everyone did. The story of the former SVR officer poisoned by Russian assassins in Swindon had hardly been off the front pages for the past two months. No one had seen or heard from Volkov since he had been discharged from the Great Western Hospital and taken into witness protection. Now Porter understood why Lansbury and his FSB handlers had been so cautious at their meeting at the Hotel Flamingo earlier.

Because the guy they were going to meet is one of the most high-profile Russians in the world.

He wondered how Volkov had managed to escape from his safe house. He wondered, too, why a double agent would be appearing at a meeting of far-right leaders organised by the FSB.

In the corner of his eye, he was dimly aware of the chauffeur sitting behind the wheel of the S-Class, parked to the right of the Volvo. His expressionless face illuminated by the green-tinted glow of his phone screen. The guy wasn't taking any notice of Bald and Porter. Hadn't seen the looks of surprise on both their faces when they'd heard Volkov's name.

'Why didn't Strickland tell us about this?' Bald wondered.

Porter shook his head. 'There's no way she would have known about Volkov being at this meeting.'

'Maybe not. But them lot at Six must have known that Volkov

had gone missing. So why didn't they share that intelligence with us?'

'Maybe they have assumed the two operations were separate. Maybe they didn't think there was a link.'

'You need to get hold of Strickland,' Bald said, nodding at the iPhone on the dash. 'Find out if they're listening to this shite. We need to know what the fuck is going on.'

Porter kept the iPad on his lap, rebroadcasting the audio to Vauxhall, while he banged out a message to Strickland. He kept it short. He wrote, *Are you receiving this? Do you realise who is here?*

Strickland came back fifteen seconds later. A fast response. She sent him two messages, not one. The first one simply said, *Yes. Receiving now.* The second message arrived a few seconds later. *Keep phone on. Await further instructions.*

Which could mean only one thing, Porter knew.

Strickland was taking the news up the chain to her boss. Who would take it in turn to his boss. Something as big as this, it would probably go right to the very top of the MI6 food chain. Thirty minutes from now, the most senior spies at Vauxhall were going to be sitting in a plain meeting room somewhere, debating what to do. It would take them at least an hour to reach a decision, probably.

'Well?' Bald asked as Porter set the phone down on the dash.

'We wait,' Porter said.

They kept listening.

The populists looked on in silence as Volkov walked falteringly across the room to the empty chair. He moved with obvious difficulty. The struggle was right there on his face, etched into his grimaced expression as he placed one foot in front of the other. He lowered himself into the chair beside Lansbury and took a long moment to catch his breath. The guy sounded like he was sucking in air through a tube. He looked pale and weak. Exactly how Lansbury assumed someone would look after prolonged exposure to a deadly nerve agent. But there was a gleam in his eye as well. Volkov was enjoying himself, Lansbury realised. Three months ago he had been an unknown exile, living an anonymous existence in Swindon. Now he was back on the big stage.

Lansbury scanned the faces around the table and said, 'I presume our guest needs no further introduction?'

The silence dragged on. Several of the guests stared at Volkov, transfixed. De Jong was the first to speak up. His eyebrows were arched so high they threatened to crawl into his hair.

'This can't be. This is some kind of a joke, right?'

'No joke,' Lansbury replied flatly.

'But . . . how is this possible?' De Jong pointed towards Volkov. 'He's supposed to be hiding in Britain. In a safe house. That's what all the papers have been saying.'

'They were wrong,' Volkov rasped.

Every pair of eyes in the room simultaneously looked towards the Russian as he went on.

'I was in a safe house. That much is true,' he said. Despite his frail physique his voice had a steely strength to it. 'But I was not there of my own free will. I was a prisoner of the British Government. Until a few days ago, when my brothers in Mother Russia rescued me.'

'An incident the British Government was very quick to suppress,' Lansbury added hastily.

'Why would they do that?' Zanetti asked.

'Political embarrassment, I suspect. It's not every day that your star witness for the prosecution is liberated from a top-secret location. The British Government would have been crucified for letting that happen on their own soil. They'd look even more incompetent than they already do. Which, let's face it, would be difficult right now.'

Lansbury grinned, but no one else was laughing. Zanetti looked incredulous. 'Why would the Russians rescue this guy? He's a fucking snitch. He sold out his own people.'

'More to the point, what is he doing here?' Effenberg demanded.

Lansbury looked towards Volkov and waved an arm in a broad sweep of the room. As if to say, *You tell them.* The former SVR agent's hands trembled as he poured himself a glass of water. He took a sip. Licked his lips. Set down the glass.

'I am no rat,' he said. 'The truth is, I have never betrayed my country. I have never worked for MI6. Never! That is a lie, spread by the British Government. One of many they have told, to smear my good name and hide the truth.'

'Why would the British spread lies about you?' de Jong wondered.

Volkov took another sip of water. Placed his shaking hands in his lap. Lifted his gaze to his audience.

'Because they are the ones who poisoned me,' he said.

Porter and Bald listened in stony silence as the Russian told his story. They had to concentrate hard. Volkov's voice was hoarse and heavily accented and hard to pick up above the background noise of the meeting.

'Nine years ago, I came to Britain as defector,' Volkov went on. 'I told MI6 I was willing to betray my country, in return for good life in London. This was a lie. From the beginning, I never abandoned Mother Russia. In reality, I was on a secret operation to spy on the security services for my country. I was, how you say, a triple agent.'

Porter glanced sidelong at Bald. His mucker's expression had tightened into a scowl.

On the audio, Volkov's voice continued.

'For several years, I continued to live as a double agent in the UK. To the British security services and my handler, I was a defected Russian agent, handing them vital intelligence on the Kremlin. In fact, I was passing them false intelligence. Lies, given to me by my SVR comrades. In return, I secretly reported back to the Kremlin with information I gleaned from my contacts in the UK. The British, allegedly great spymasters, never suspected a thing.

'Until three months ago, when they discovered my secret. Which is when they came up with a plan to poison me with chemical agents, developed at their secret weapons facility at Porton Down. They planned to murder me and blame it on Moscow,' Volkov said. 'I know this, because the last man who visited me was my old handler. We had lunch together, in Swindon. At a cheap Chinese restaurant. Shortly after, I became sick.'

Porter glanced at Bald with a cocked eyebrow. 'Can you believe what this wanker is saying?'

Bald shook his head, anger seeping like acid into his guts. He wasn't a fan of the Firm, but the idea of one of the desk jockeys at MI6 taking out a defector using chemical weapons was laughable. If Six wanted Volkov out of the picture, they wouldn't have done it themselves, Bald thought. No fucking chance. They didn't have the skill set or the balls. They would have picked up the phone to Hereford.

Volkov went on for a long while in his monotone voice, pausing only to take sips of water or when he had a coughing fit. He told his audience how MI6 realised he was feeding them false intelligence and plotted against him. How they had framed Moscow for the attack and used bogus witnesses and falsified evidence to back up their case. He told them how he was visited in hospital by MI6 agents who warned him against spilling his guts. How the heartless Brits had ignored his requests to let him speak with his daughter and had instead kept him a virtual prisoner at a safe house. Volkov told them about his relief when he had been rescued. He was sure the Brits would claim he had been kidnapped, he said, but that could not be further from the truth. He had gone willingly with his Russian comrades because he was afraid for his life if he stayed in the UK. The British could not be trusted. They were liars and hypocrites. Volkov wanted to tell the world what had happened, so that everyone would know who was really behind the Swindon attack.

Porter said, 'What do you think?'

'It's bullshit,' Bald said. 'Six would never pull this kind of stunt. He'll be telling them the Moon landings are faked next.'

'Sounds like they're lapping it up, though.'

On the audio, Volkov had finished his speech. Porter and Bald could hear thunderous applause ringing out around the meeting room. Some of the populists were cheering or hollering their support.

Bald grunted. 'That mob will believe anything, if it fits in with their fucked-up world view.'

Porter checked his phone.

No word from Strickland.

'Why would Volkov be peddling this stuff, if it's a load of bollocks?' he wondered aloud.

'Only one reason,' Bald said. 'He's working for the Russians now. They must be paying him a great whack.'

'Or they're threatening to kill him.'

The applause died out. The meeting room fell silent again.

Volkov slumped back in his chair, reached for his glass of water and had a long gulp. He took a handkerchief from his trouser pocket and dabbed his sweat-glossed forehead. Forty-five minutes of public speaking had left him visibly drained. Lansbury gave the Russian a friendly pat on the back before he turned to address the other guests.

'I trust that you are convinced of the plan now, chaps?' he asked.

'I have one question,' de Jong said.

'What's that, Edwin?'

The Dutchman indicated Volkov. 'What is he getting out of this?'

'Nothing.'

'Forgive me, but I find that hard to believe.'

Volkov put away his handkerchief, loosened the collar of his shirt. 'I am doing this for my country. For years the decadent West has spread lies about Russia. Now it is time to make them pay. The people deserve to hear the truth.'

'Any other questions for our guest?' Lansbury asked. 'No?'

No one raised a hand. Lansbury turned to Volkov. 'Thank you, Nikolai. You can leave now. Get some rest, old boy. Long flight ahead.'

He nodded at Butko. *We're done here*. Butko beckoned over a pair of heavies standing just outside the doorway of the side entrance to the room. They marched over to Volkov, helped him to his feet and escorted him out of the room.

After the heavies had closed the door Zanetti looked towards Lansbury and said, 'What happens now?'

'At ten o'clock tomorrow morning, Nikolai will give a press conference to the world's media. We're giving you the heads-up tonight – in the strictest confidence, I might add – because this thing is going to move very quickly once the ball gets rolling. President Drummond will release a short statement immediately after the press conference, denouncing Britain for the attempted murder of a Russian national, the illegal use of chemical weapons and the disgraceful propaganda campaign to implicate Russia in the attack. The president will pledge to bring up this incident with his counterparts at Loch Lomond later the same day.'

'What will he say?'

'Britain is a leading member of NATO. Drummond will argue that the alliance has been utterly discredited by one of its members carrying out such a cowardly and unconscionable attack, laying the groundwork for America's withdrawal from NATO.'

'Will that work?'

'Absolutely,' Lansbury replied. 'No one will question his decision to pull out of an alliance whose member states carry out chemical weapons attacks on their own soil. Particularly when the president himself has taken a hard line on the use of such weapons in Syria.'

Polster, the Austrian Vice-Chancellor, had been silent until that moment. With his wrinkled face and nest of silvery hair and Patek Philippe watch clamped around his wrist he looked like a Wall Street banker on the cusp of retirement.

'I agree,' Polster said. 'This will persuade our people back home. They're already sceptical about funding NATO missions. Once they hear Nikolai's testimony, they'll turn on Britain and the other members.'

One by one, the remaining dissenters fell into line. Effenberg quickly followed. Only de Jong held out, reluctant to commit himself to the plan, but under pressure from his political allies and Lansbury, he eventually acquiesced. There was a formal vote on the matter, with every leader declaring their support for the American plan. Lansbury smiled, pleased with himself.

'Then it's settled. At four o'clock tomorrow afternoon you will issue statements of support for the president's decision, welcoming the end of NATO. And the beginning of a grand new Christian era will be upon us. One that will dominate the world for centuries . . .'

Bald and Porter zoned out of the rest of the chatter. On the audio, Lansbury turned his attention to the next order of

248

business. There was some stuff about what to do about the refu-
gee crisis in Italy. Effenberg wanted support for an anti-gay rally
in Dresden. The Georgians were struggling to gain traction in
the polls and requested campaign appearances from Zanetti and
Lansbury. The guards continued their routine patrols of the
castle grounds. Tibor played games on his phone. Some of the
other chauffeurs and bodyguard teams headed over to the side
entrance to grab a bite to eat from the kitchen. On the microphone, Bald heard laughter and joking, the earlier tension of the
conference giving way to a mood of celebration. Lansbury and
his mates were relaxed now. They sounded as if they were enjoying themselves.

At three minutes to seven, Porter's phone buzzed.

Strickland.

He swiped to answer. Turned on the loudspeaker.

'Yes?'

'Where are you now?' Strickland asked. She spoke loudly, as if
projecting her voice for an audience. In the background, Bald
heard someone cough. He figured she was on a loudspeaker on
her end too. In a meeting room somewhere inside Six. The Chief
of SIS was there, probably. Moorcroft too.

'Outside the castle,' said Porter. 'In front of the garage. Why?'

'Can you get inside?'

'Not unless we slap on a couple of pinstripe suits and start slag-
ging off migrants,' Bald said. 'This place is guarded by a small
army. Heavies all over the fucking shop.'

'There's no way of getting to Volkov? You're sure?'

'Not a chance. What the fuck is going on?'

'I need you to listen to me carefully,' Strickland said. 'The plan
has changed. Orders from the very top. The new priority is Volkov.
I repeat, Volkov is the number-one priority from now on.'

Porter and Bald looked at one another.

Porter said, 'What about BROKEN RECORD?'

'He's finished. We've got him bang to rights. He's on tape
openly conspiring against NATO and the British state in return
for taking Russian bribes, along with every other attendee. The
moment we release that material, Lansbury is done.'

Bald gave the iPhone a cold hard look. As if it could somehow

249

transmit his rage to the voices listening on the other end. 'Why didn't you tell us that Volkov had skipped the country?'

Strickland paused. Bald imagined her looking round the meeting room, searching for approval before replying.

'We didn't consider it relevant,' she said at last. 'At the time, we had no specific information linking BROKEN RECORD to Volkov.'

'Bollocks.'

'It's the truth,' Strickland insisted. 'As far as we were concerned, Volkov had been kidnapped by state actors working on behalf of the Kremlin and relocated to Russia, possibly executed. That's all we knew.'

'You should have fucking told us he'd been lifted.'

'That information wasn't relevant to your specific mission. We told you everything you needed to know, and nothing you didn't. We've been on the level with you from the start on this one.'

'That'd be a first, for you lot.'

Silence.

Porter said, 'What do you want us to do?'

'I assume Volkov is still inside the stronghold?'

'For now.'

'And you are absolutely certain that you cannot extract him from his present location?'

'There are guards at all the entrances and exits. Half a dozen of them, packing heat. Plus whatever guys are watching Volkov. We'd get clobbered before we could get within fifty feet of the bloke.'

'In that case, we're going to need to bring some of our other assets into play. Find another way of springing him free.'

Bald said, 'How long is that going to take?'

'We're not sure. Could be an hour. Could be longer. There are a lot of moving pieces on the board. It's going to take us some time to pull everything together.'

Another voice came on the line. Posh, English, familiar.

'Guys, Moorcroft here. Any idea how long BROKEN RECORD intends to stay at this gathering?'

'Until around midnight,' said Porter. 'That's what he reckoned when he briefed us earlier.'

'And there's no chance of him leaving earlier?'

'Not likely. They're having some big celebratory feast. Jock reckons there's entertainment laid on for the populists too. Women and the like.'

'Good. That means we still have time to organise our other resources and formulate a plan before he returns to Budapest.'

'What are we supposed to do until then?'

'Sit tight and keep a mark-one eyeball on the stronghold. Report any suspicious movement to Strickland. Maintain your cover until you receive orders otherwise.'

Bald said, 'Why do you lot give a toss about Volkov, anyway? No one's going to believe his story about the Swindon attack.'

'He's a political weapon,' Moorcroft explained. 'Right now, we're engaged in a proxy war with the Russians. If the FSB extracts Volkov to Moscow, he'll become a propaganda tool. The Kremlin will wheel him out on state TV to humiliate and undermine us at every opportunity. Our credibility will be left in tatters.'

'You're worried about looking bad, is that it?'

'We're concerned about the optics. Returning Volkov to Russia would be the ultimate coup for their president, and he needs a win as much as anyone. We can't afford to let that happen. Understood?'

'Roger.'

Strickland came back on and said, 'Keep the line free. We'll be in touch soon.'

The call ended.

The iPhone screen faded to black.

Bald stared at it. Rage was brewing inside his chest, burning the back of his throat like vodka. *Six has lied to us again*, he thought. It was the same old crap. They send you into the field with the bare minimum of int, playing their cards close to their chest. And it's guys like me and Porter who have to clear up the mess.

Porter said, 'I still don't get it. Why would the Yanks pull out of NATO?'

'The president has a hard-on for getting out of it,' Bald said. 'All he bangs on about on TV. Probably dreams about it. Now he's got the chance with this Volkov business.'

'But why would the Russians get involved? They're helping

Drummond out, offering up Volkov and paying this mob off with gold mine shares. What are they getting out of it?'

'The Baltics,' Bald said. 'That's their end game.'

Porter looked at him. 'You think the Russians would risk it?'

'Why not? Once they get Drummond and his populist cronies to pull out of NATO, no one can stop them. They can move the tanks in, take them countries back.'

'Should we warn Strickland?'

'Six already knows,' Bald replied. 'And if they don't, they need their heads examined. It's fucking obvious. Anyone can see it. Surprised it took you as long as this to figure it out.'

Porter glared at Bald, then looked out of the window. He thought about the Baltic States. Estonia and Latvia and Riga. The nightmare of Russian tanks rolling through European capitals.

Bald said, 'You think Strickland will come through with those reinforcements?'

Porter said, 'You don't?'

'It's Six. I take everything they say with a big fucking pinch of salt.'

Porter said nothing, checked his watch. Five minutes past seven. *We should be done by midnight*, Lansbury had said. Which could mean potentially having to sit on their arses for another four or five hours. Nothing else they could do except keep an eye on the gathering.

And wait to hear back from Strickland.

On the microphone, the populists were having a debate about the wrongful imprisonment of a British far-right activist. Some of the groups wanted to organise a demonstration in front of the Houses of Parliament, demanding his release. Others were not so keen. The French had worked hard to appeal to moderate voters, Marveaux said. They worried about the effect of showing solidarity with the activist.

At eight o'clock Bald heard the scraping of chairs against the floor, the patter of footsteps and the slamming of doors. Then the pop of champagne corks, the tinkle of glasses being clinked as the attendees moved on to another room. The conference was over, Bald guessed. The celebrations were in full swing. Someone asked when the women were going to arrive. Another said he hoped that they were better looking than the girls at the last gathering. There were hearty chuckles all round. Lansbury listened as one of the attendees told him a racist joke. Something to do with Muslims immigrating to Germany to see their doctor. Lansbury thought it was fucking hilarious. His laughter cackled down the audio line.

'At least someone's having a good time,' Bald growled. 'Any word from Strickland about them assets?'

Porter checked his phone, shook his head. 'Nothing.'

'Fuck's sake. What's taking them so long?'

Two minutes later, they heard a pair of engines gunning from across the front of the castle. Bald peered through the windscreen and saw the headlamps burning on a pair of Lexus 570 SUVs parked on the far side of the carriage circle, forty metres away. The two wagons crawled forward, rounded the circle and pulled up in front of the door.

Five figures emerged from the entrance hallway into the cold black of the night, breath misting in front of their mouths. The first four guys were all huge. The four biggest guys Bald had ever seen. They were shrink-wrapped in black 5.11 trousers and jackets over plain dark polo shirts. Civilian gear. An unofficial uniform, different from the heavies on Butko's team. Each guy carried a shoulder-strapped sub-machine gun, the barrels poking out from below their jackets.

The fifth guy was Volkov.

TWENTY-NINE

It took Bald about a quarter of a second to identify Nikolai Volkov. He had seen the former SVR officer's face plastered over a million websites and news reports. Even in Mexico, it had been impossible to avoid his bulbous-nosed, round-cheeked face. The front page of the Cancun edition of the *Miami Herald*, the top story on CNN each evening down at the expat bars. Volkov was noticeably skinnier than in the photographs. His hair was shorter and thinner, too. He looked like a convict on the day of his release from prison. Volkov limped down the steps, taking them slowly, one at a time, the four heavies fanning out ahead of him.

On the microphone, Lansbury and his mates were still chatting amongst themselves, laughing and swapping crap racist jokes, knocking back the bubbly ahead of their slap-up feast.

Porter said, 'Shit. He's bugging out.'

'Aye. And with half the FSB for company, by the looks of it.'

Four heavies on foot, Bald thought quickly. Plus a driver in each Lexus. A minimum of six guys, each kitted out with a Kalashnikov. Bald guessed they would have at least two clips per rifle, minimum. Sixty rounds per man. Two hundred and forty rounds, plus whatever secondary weapons and body armour they might be packing. Throw in the half-a-dozen guards around the castle, and they were looking at twelve heavily armed enemies protecting Volkov.

And we've got nothing to bring to the party except our fists.

Forty metres away, Volkov hit the bottom step and clambered into the rear of the front Lexus. One of the four guys jumped in alongside him. The other three guys hopped into the second Lexus. The backup car, Bald realised. Extra firepower, if the front team ran into trouble. He turned to Porter.

'Call Strickland,' he said. 'Now.'

Porter grabbed the iPhone. Put it on loudspeaker.

The doors on the rear Lexus thudded shut.

Strickland picked up midway through the second ring.

'John. What's happening?' she asked.

'It's Volkov. He's on the move.'

A pause. 'Can you get to him?'

'Not without getting walloped,' Bald put in. 'He's got six heavies with him. Armed. They're about to leave, but if we go now we can tail them.'

'Stay where you are,' Strickland ordered. 'Don't move. Do not attempt to follow him.'

'But we'll lose him,' Bald protested angrily.

'The other assets aren't in position yet. If you attempt a pursuit, you'll blow the operation and alert the enemy to our involvement. We'll lose any chance we have of extracting Volkov.'

Forty metres away, the two Lexus SUVs steered counter-clockwise round the carriage circle. Heading down the main driveway, towards the wrought-iron gate, a hundred metres to the south.

'Guys?' Strickland asked. 'Did you hear me?'

'He's about to get away,' Porter said. 'Jock's right, ma'am. This might be our best shot at lifting the bastard.'

'Stay put,' Strickland snapped. 'That's an order, both of you. Stand down, or our deal is off.'

Bald thumped a fist against the dashboard in frustration and looked away, rage coursing through his veins. He hated the idea of letting Volkov slip away, but the logical part of his brain told him that Strickland was right. Chasing after the Russians was a fucking bad idea. They were in the middle of the Hungarian countryside, late at night. Bald and Porter hadn't passed a car for miles on the drive down from Budapest. If they followed the two wagons, Volkov and his mates would swiftly know about it.

They'd see our headlights. They'd rumble us in about five seconds flat. Nothing we can do.

To the south, the two Lexus SUVs had reached the front gate. The driver in the front Lexus leaned out of his window and signalled to the two heavies. The guy with the iPad ducked into the guardhouse. The gate yawned open.

The SUVs trundled through the opening, turned left and roared off into the dense blackness of the star-pricked night.

'Have they gone?' asked Strickland.

'They just left,' said Porter.

'This is the plan,' Strickland said. 'You need to isolate BROKEN RECORD.'

'What the fuck for?'

'We're going to have to intercept Volkov and his minders. Our assessment is that a coordinated ambush is our best chance of rescuing him. Which means we need to find out where he's being taken. We think BROKEN RECORD might know where.'

Bald fell silent for a moment, dimly recalling something Lansbury had said in the meeting. Right after Volkov had finished giving his address to the populists.

Get some rest, old boy. Long flight ahead.

Porter said, 'You're sure that BROKEN RECORD knows where Volkov is going?'

'Positive. We've been remotely monitoring his iCloud account, using the password we retrieved from the modified phone charger you planted in his room. He sent a message three minutes ago, to an unknown local number. Telling them that the speech was a success and the package would be delivered soon. We think that's a reference to Volkov.'

'Might not mean anything,' Bald speculated. 'He might not have the details.'

'BROKEN RECORD knows the FSB agents. He knows Volkov will be getting on a plane. He's deeply involved. At the very least, he'll have some idea of Volkov's ultimate destination.'

'What do you need us to do?' asked Porter.

'You need to find a way to get to BROKEN RECORD immediately. Question him. Get him to spill the beans.'

Bald squinted into the darkness, working through scenarios. 'It'll mean blowing our cover.'

Strickland said, 'Either we find out what he knows, or we lose Volkov. Just make sure the Russians don't find out what you're up to. We need to keep them in the dark for as long as possible. If they find out what's going on, they'll change plans. And we'll lose the only chance we have of getting Volkov back.'

'And if the fucker claims he doesn't know anything?'

'We'll run some checks at our end in the meantime, monitor local flight manifests. See if Volkov's name crops up on a list somewhere. Our guys are reaching out to GCHQ as well. Something this big, they might have picked up some chatter from the FSB or the Kremlin. Either way, we'll find out where Volkov is going and when.'

Bald said, 'What do you want us to do with BROKEN RECORD? Once he spills his guts?'

'Whatever you want. He's immaterial now. Volkov is our only concern. But whatever you're planning to do, make it quick. We don't have much time. Is that clear?'

Bald glanced at the dash clock. 20.06 hours.

The speech was a success.

Package will be delivered soon.

'Guys?' Strickland repeated.

'Aye,' Bald said. 'We understand.'

'Good. We'll be in touch.'

She killed the call. The iPhone screen dimmed.

Bald turned to Porter. A trace of mischief on his face. 'Come on. Let's give this twat a hard Brexit.'

Porter frowned. 'How? We can't exactly go strolling into the meeting.'

'We don't need to. We'll get the cunt to come to us.'

Porter's frown deepened as he watched Bald whip out his iPhone. He secretly envied this about Jock. His never-ending ability to cook up crafty schemes. Porter felt he had always been a dependable Blade, reliable. A solid marksman, good team player. But he lacked Bald's ingenuity. The guy had many faults, Porter reflected. He was a bastard and a loose cannon, distrusted by his fellow Blades and despised by the head shed. But there were few lads at Hereford who were as effective in a tight spot as Jock Bald.

He might have faked his death in Russia, thought Porter, *but I still respect Bald as an operator. Say what you like, but Jock has got a proper set of brass balls on him.*

Bald brought up Lansbury's personal number and tapped to dial. Porter dabbed down the volume on the iPad, so he wouldn't hear the echo of his own voice via the challenge coin mic.

The phone rang for several beats before he answered. 'I told you not to disturb me,' Lansbury snapped irritably.

Bald put on his best courteous voice. 'Sir, I'm very sorry but we've got a problem.'

'Can't it wait? I'm right in the middle of something.'

'Not really, sir.'

'What is it?'

'We've got Lord McGinn on the phone,' Bald said. 'He just called Porter on a secure line.'

'Wait, Alan is on the line?' Lansbury sounded puzzled. 'Why is he calling your partner's phone?'

'Our phones are encrypted,' Bald explained. 'For security reasons. Lord McGinn thought it better to call us rather than speak to you directly. He has our numbers from the last job we did for him.'

'What does he want?'

'He didn't go into specifics, sir. He just told us he's been briefed by one of his contacts in the security services. Thinks there might be a threat to your safety.'

'A threat?' The laughter and chatter faded into the background as Lansbury padded away from the celebrations. 'What the hell are you talking about?'

'McGinn has heard rumours about an SAS snatch squad, sir. Coming for you.'

Bald heard Lansbury gulp. 'Jesus.'

'It's better if you speak to Lord McGinn yourself, sir. He's on the phone right now. Unless you want us to come in—'

'No. Absolutely not.'

Lansbury swore under his breath, sighed heavily.

'Fine. Keep Alan on hold. Tell him I'll be out in a minute.'

'Yes, sir.'

Bald hung up, noticed Porter staring at him. 'Wait here. Pretend you're talking on the phone. Soon as I get the principal in the back, we'll jump him.'

He flipped open the passenger side door on the Volvo and jumped down to the loose gravel. Cold, crisp air filled his lungs as Bald hooked around the front end of the wagon and drew up next to the S-Class. Tibor was still sitting behind the wheel, watching videos on his phone. Bald rapped his knuckles on the glass twice. Tibor looked up, buzzed down the window. Some kind of jaunty folk music spilled out of the car radio.

Tibor blinked at him.

Bald said, 'I just got off the phone with the principal. He's going to be at least another two hours. He says you should get yourself a bite to eat from the kitchen.'

Tibor's far-apart eyes narrowed. 'I didn't get call?'

'The principal is busy. He told us to pass the message on.' Bald jerked a thumb at the side entrance to the castle. 'I'd hurry up, if I were you. While there's still some grub left.'

That got Tibor moving. He killed the radio, unfolded himself from behind the wheel and set off at a quick pace towards the door leading into the castle kitchen.

Thirty seconds later, Lansbury stepped outside.

THIRTY

The British populist emerged from the castle into the biting chill of the night. He paused at the top of the stone steps, waxed jacket pulled tight across his front as he surveyed the driveway. Looked to the west, spotted Bald standing in front of the Volvo and the S-Class twenty-five metres away. Started down the steps and marched briskly over to the wagon, hands stuffed in his jacket pockets. As he drew closer Bald sneaked a glance round the drive-way, making sure no one else had eyes on them. Most of the other chauffeurs and BG teams were either holed up in the kitchen or inside their cars. A few were sitting in the cars parked around the carriage circle, but Bald reckoned they were too far away to be a problem. The two heavies guarding the front door paid no atten-tion to Lansbury and stared dead ahead, hands resting on the stocks of their MA compact rifles.

Bald took a step forward and met Lansbury a couple of paces ahead of the Volvo. Lansbury glanced quickly at the S-Class before settling his gaze on Bald. His cheeks were flushed with booze.

'This had better be worth it,' he snapped. 'Give me the phone.'

'Yes, sir. This way.' Bald pointed at the Volvo. 'Porter's got Lord McGinn on hold. He's waiting to speak with you.'

Bald led Lansbury round to the rear door on the driver's side. Took one last look around, popped the door open and gestured for Lansbury to climb inside. Lansbury eased himself into the heated interior of the Volvo, rubbing his hands to warm them up. Porter was sitting up front, phone pressed against his ear, as if he was on hold. Lansbury held out his hand.

'Let me speak with him,' he said.

Porter turned around, leaning into the gap between the two

front seats. He unglued the phone from his ear, passed it to Lansbury and said, 'Here you go, sir.'

Lansbury grabbed the handset and looked down at it. There was no live call in progress. Just a black display. The groove between his eyebrows formed into a long V.

'I don't understand.'

He was still frowning at the dark screen when Bald climbed in and yanked the door shut.

'Hit the safety,' he ordered Porter.

There was a simultaneous clunk as Porter flicked the switch for the child safety locks, sealing Lansbury inside. The latter stared at Bald and Porter, confusion spreading across his tanned face.

'What the hell are you doing?'

'Shut the fuck up,' Bald said, before turning to Porter. 'Get us round to the side of the garage, mate.'

Porter mashed the brake and hit the engine start button, revving the engine. Flicked the headlights off and downshifted into Reverse. The Volvo lurched as Porter spun the wheel hard to the left and backed up, reversing from the gravel parking area to the gloomy shadows to the west of the garage, taking them away from the harsh glare of the security lights.

'What the fuck is going on?' Lansbury demanded. 'Let me out of here!'

Bald ignored him. As soon as Porter had brought the Volvo parallel with the garage he killed the engine again.

They were hidden from view. Concealed in the shadows, out of sight of the guards at the castle entrance and the front gate. With the heavily tinted rear windows, no passers-by would be able to see what was going on inside the wagon.

'Let me out, I said!' Lansbury yelled. 'Now!'

Bald silenced him with a dig to the ribs. Zero back lift, a short, sharp blow that knocked the wind out of Lansbury's lungs. His eyes went wide with shock. He jackknifed, gasping for air, hands pawing at his stomach. Bald shoved Lansbury on to his right side, pinning him horizontally across the middle and rightmost seats while he rifled through the guy's pockets. He found Lansbury's iPhone and billfold in his inside jacket pocket. Fished the challenge coin out of his trouser pocket. Lansbury offered no resistance. He was still reeling from the jab to the midriff. The guy was in terrible shape. Probably the only exercise he'd done in the last twenty years was lifting pints of bitter to his lips.

Bald tossed the phone and Salvatore Ferragamo billfold to Porter. He scooped up Porter's iPhone from the footwell, passed it forward. Grabbed Lansbury by the collar of his jacket and pulled him upright.

'What . . . the hell are you doing?' he croaked between snatches of breath.

'Here's a clue,' Bald said.

He took the challenge coin and held it up to Lansbury's mouth. Lansbury stared at it, uncomprehending.

'There's a bug inside this thing,' Bald explained. 'We've been listening to every word you've said in that conference. You and your fucking populist mates.'

Lansbury gaped at the coin. Clamped his mouth shut. His face hardened. 'No. You're lying. That's not possible.'

'We know about your NATO plot,' Bald pressed on. 'We know about the Christian alliance, the shares in the Siberian gold mine. That bullshit story about Volkov being a triple agent. We heard everything.'

The colour plummeted from Lansbury's face. His skin was white as chalk. He eyeballed the challenge coin. As if he stared at it for long enough, maybe he could make it disappear.

'It was you,' he said, looking up at Bald and Porter. 'This morning. At the meeting. The bug on my collar. Freya didn't place it there . . . you did!'

'Aye. That was us.'

Lansbury's face was ghostly pale for a moment. Then his expression shifted, terror hardening into something closer to outrage.

'Who are you working for?'

'Take a wild guess,' said Porter.

'Thames House?'

'Try again.'

'You're with MI6?'

Bald nodded. 'We've recorded the whole thing. You understand? Every word you lot said, they've got stored on a server in London. They can make as many copies as they want. They click a button, and an audio file will go out to the editor of every media outlet in the country. You won't just be finished. You'll be ripped to pieces.'

Lansbury was silent for a beat. His face went through a whole performance. For an instant it looked as if his resolve might crumble. Then he sneered at Bald.

'MI6 wouldn't dare release that audio. That would mean admitting that they've been spying illegally on a British citizen. My supporters would go mad.'

'Our bosses might hesitate. But we won't. Me and Jock have got everything right here on the iPad.'

'Go ahead. Send it out. You don't have anything. All you've got is a few of us agreeing to back the president's decision to pull out of NATO.'

Bald scowled at the populist. 'We've got you on tape getting paid by the Russians. That's fucking treason.'

'That's a sweetener. Nothing more.'

'It's a fucking bribe. This comes out, your reputation goes down the fucking pan.'

Lansbury glared defiantly at his captors. 'I sincerely doubt it. You're going to be overtaken by the news agenda. Twenty-four hours from now, the president's decision to withdraw from NATO is going to be the major story. The fact that I'm agreeing with Drummond at a minor conference in Hungary is going to be of interest to precisely no one.'

Porter twisted round in his seat to face Lansbury head on, anger pulsing in his guts. He imagined reaching out and clamping a hand around the guy's neck, choking the life out of him.

'You're a traitor,' he said. 'You're stabbing your country in the back for a few shares in some fucking gold mine.'

'Get off your high horse,' Lansbury retorted. 'Everyone knows the old order is dead. NATO is finished. Same as the EU. No one has the appetite to fund these smug liberal institutions anymore, and why should they? All the president is doing is hastening the process.'

'And wankers like you are helping him along.'

'I'm doing my part. So what?'

'You're selling yourself to the Kremlin,' Porter said with a snarl.

'You're gonna let the Russians invade the Baltics just so you can line your own fucking pockets.'

'I can't be held responsible for Russian foreign policy,' Lansbury replied coolly. 'If there's a squabble between President Kolotov and his counterparts in the Baltics, that's between them. Nothing to do with me.'

'There's gonna be fighting. People will die. It'll make the eastern Ukraine look like a playground scrap.'

'A small price to pay for the triumph of Christianity. The domination of the Christian world over all others.'

Lansbury glowered at him. Eyes brightly lit, lips curving up at the corners. The look of a man who was absolutely sure that he was on the right side of history, that the ends justified the means. The prick actually believes this shit, thought Porter. He glanced back at the clock on the dash.

20.14 hours.

Remember our orders.

Volkov is our only concern.

Whatever you're planning to do, make it quick.

He turned back to Lansbury and looked him in the eye.

'Volkov,' he said. 'Where are they taking him?'

Lansbury shrugged. 'How the hell should I know? I'm working for Drummond, not the bloody Russians.'

His eyes shifted away, evading Porter's gaze. Tiny beads of moisture formed on his brow. 'You're lying,' Porter said.

'I'm not! For Chrissakes, do you really think the Russians would share that information with me? Now let me go!'

'Tell us. Last chance.'

'I'm telling you, I don't bloody know!'

Bald twisted round in his seat. Cocked his head at Porter. 'Charge up the cigarette lighter, mate.'

Porter thumb-pressed the cigarette lighter receptacle, activating the heating element. Lansbury went wide-eyed.

'What the hell are you doing?' he demanded.

'Talk,' Bald said. 'Or get burned. Your choice.'

'You can't do that. I've got rights.'

'Not in here, you don't.'

The lighter popped out of the socket. Ready to use.

'Christ, no.' Lansbury looked on in horror as Porter removed the lighter from the socket. 'Please, I've told you everything.'

Bald ignored Lansbury's pleas. He pressed down on the guy with his right arm, pinning him against the rear seats. Lansbury struggled, kicking out wildly in a pathetic attempt to wriggle free. Bald kept him in place while he grabbed hold of the populist's left hand by the wrist and held it out towards Porter. 'Fucking do it, mate.'

Porter didn't need a second invitation. He twisted round in his seat, leaned over and pressed the underside of the cigarette lighter against the palm of Lansbury's left hand. Lansbury howled in agony as the heated metal burned his soft, doughy flesh. He tried to jerk his hand away but in the confines of the wagon there was nowhere to go. Porter held the lighter against his hand for five long seconds before he pulled it away. Lansbury slumped back on the seat, clutching his blistered hand, tears sliding down his cheeks, whimpering softly. The stench of burnt flesh lingering in the air.

'Start talking,' said Bald. 'Or we'll toast your balls.'

'Please,' Lansbury begged. 'No.'

'Tell us where Volkov is going.'

Lansbury hesitated, weeping and sniffing. Porter held the cigarette lighter, ready to give the guy another hit.

'Do it,' Bald growled.

'No!' Lansbury cried. 'Jesus, I'll tell you! But I need some assurances first.'

Bald looked at him. 'What do you mean?'

'The minute I tell you about Volkov, the Russians will realise I'm the one behind the leak. They already have their suspicions, after that bug they found on me this morning. If you want me to talk, you need to get me out of here. Take me back home.'

Bald and Porter swapped a knowing look. Both of them reaching the same conclusion. There was no time to lose. They couldn't afford to sit in the wagon for much longer, torturing Lansbury until he spilled his guts. Soon enough someone at the gathering would start wondering where the guy had gone. And go looking for him.

We need answers. Now.

'Sure,' Porter said after a pause. 'Me and Jock will help you escape.'

'You promise?'

'You have my word. But you need to tell us what you know about Volkov.'

Lansbury swallowed and took a breath. Nodded. His right hand holding the wrist of his fucked-up left hand. 'Look, all I know is, he's being taken to a private airfield.'

'Where?'

'Near a place called Békés. In the east of the country. A hundred miles away. Some old Soviet base. The Russians are sending over a jet to meet him there.'

'The Russians?' Porter repeated.

Lansbury nodded. 'He's being taken back to Moscow ahead of the press conference. The Kremlin is going to parade him in front of the British Embassy at ten o'clock tomorrow morning. All the world's media are going to be there. It's a big event.'

Bald puffed out his cheeks. 'Kolotov ain't shy about rubbing our noses in it. He'll be asking Robbie Williams to perform at this thing next.'

'He wants to make a big deal out of the event. He's going to have Volkov walk out on a stage for maximum impact. This is a major coup for Kolotov,' Lansbury said. 'He's got big plans for Volkov, apparently.'

'Who told you that?'

'Volkov. He was bragging to me at our meeting earlier. Reckons that he's going to be a star in Russia. A returning hero. He kept making demands of the FSB agents, asking them for a bigger jet to fly back in, an apartment in a nicer area of Moscow, that sort of thing. The agents told him that he'd get his reward at the airfield. He seemed excited about that.'

Porter frowned. 'What reward?'

'He didn't say. But Volkov was adamant that he wasn't getting on the plane before he got his reward. He seemed very insistent on that point. That's all I know.'

Porter said, 'What time is that jet coming in?'

'Ten o'clock, I was told.'

'How many guys has he got with him?'

Lansbury thought for a second. 'Six FSB agents. The same ones he arrived with earlier. That's all.'

'Anyone else?'

'Not as far as I'm aware. I've told you everything. I don't know anything else, I swear.'

Bald scratched his stubbly jaw, glanced at the dash clock. Twenty twenty-two hours. Twenty minutes since Volkov had bugged out with his FSB heavies. A hundred-mile drive would take them around two hours, he guessed. They wouldn't be taking it slow, not with a high-value package in the back seat. The Russians would be going flat out all the way to the airfield. Which meant they would arrive at around 22.00 hours. The jet wouldn't take off immediately. There would be a delay before they could get underway again. Logistics. Routine checks and procedures. Maybe fifteen minutes.

If we leave now and floor it, we've still got a slight chance of catching the Russians before they can make good their escape.

Lansbury looked at him expectantly. 'Well? What's the plan?'

'Plan?' Bald repeated.

'For getting me out of here.'

Lansbury waited for them to elaborate.

'About that,' said Bald.

He sprang open the passenger side door, slid out and dragged Lansbury from the Volvo, throwing him to the ground. Lansbury cried weakly as he collapsed to the loose gravel. He struggled to his feet, glowering at Bald.

'What the fuck do you think you're doing?'

'We're leaving. You're staying put. End of.'

'But you gave me your word!' Lansbury hissed.

'Porter did. But he's unreliable. As for me, I couldn't give a fuck. Now piss off back to your big bash.' He jabbed a finger at Lansbury. 'Mention this to your Russian mates, and we'll make sure they know who was behind the recording.'

Lansbury's facial muscles were twitching with fury. 'You can't leave me! We had a fucking deal!'

'Here.' Bald tossed Lansbury the challenge coin. 'Souvenir. Next time we see you, we'll buy you a pint of bitter.'

Bald closed the rear door and slipped into the front passenger seat. Porter stared at him. 'What's going on? We're just leaving the bastard?'

'Just drive,' Bald said.

Porter fired up the engine and pulled away from the garage, leaving Lansbury in the shadows, clutching his SAS coin. He wheeled the Volvo clockwise around the carriage circle and bowled down towards the front gate. The guards let them roll right through, no questions asked. They didn't give a shit about anyone leaving the gathering. They were only worried about people trying to get in.

Porter hooked left on the main road, pointing the Volvo in the same direction the Russians had gone. When they were a hundred metres clear of the castle he said, 'That was a mistake. We should have taken him with us. What if he spills the beans to his mates?'

'He won't,' Bald replied. 'He's got too much to lose.'

'You don't know that, Jock.'

'Yeah, I do.' He tapped the side of his head. 'Think about it. If he fesses up to the Russians, he'll be automatically signing his own death warrant. They've got doubts about Lansbury anyway. That's why they honey-trapped Jansen into spying on him. If he spins them a story about us working for MI6, they're going to assume he was in on it from the beginning.'

'Maybe.'

'It's a fucking certainty, mate. Besides,' Bald added. 'If we had slotted him or lifted him from the party, that would have made the Russians suspicious.'

Porter cracked a half-smile. 'For a moment back there,' he said, 'I thought you were going soft in your old age.'

'Me?' Bald laughed. 'Not a fucking chance.'

Porter kept his foot to the pedal while Bald brought up the encrypted screen on his iPhone. As he pulled up Strickland's number he glanced over at the fuel gauge. The needle was slanted past the half-full mark. They had just enough gas in the tank to reach the airfield before heading on to a second RV. But running out of fuel was the least of their problems, Bald realised. They had only the slightest possibility of reaching the airport before the Russians left with Volkov on the private jet. He put their chances of success at somewhere between five and ten per cent.

Better than nothing.

He dialled Strickland. She answered on the first ring. Bald imagined her in a windowless room in Vauxhall, sitting by the secure phone, waiting anxiously for their call.

'Well?' she asked breathlessly.

'The FSB are taking Volkov to an airfield. Two hours due east of here, some place called Békés. They're flying him back to Moscow.'

Bald told her everything they'd learned from Lansbury. He told her about the planned press conference, and the reward waiting for Volkov once they arrived at Békés.

'Where are you now?' she asked.

'We just left the castle. On our way to the airfield. We're going as fast as we can, but we're gonna need some backup when we get there. Volkov has got six heavies with him, armed with compact rifles.'

Bald sketched out the rough plan he'd formed inside his head. He told Strickland that they would need to RV with the reinforcements somewhere near the airfield, put the drop on the Russians and leg it with Volkov to a friendly environment. It would be a close-run thing, but it was their best hope of foiling the Kremlin's plot.

Strickland listened in silence. Then she said, 'I need you to turn around.'

Bald felt his chest hitch. 'What the fuck for?'

'We need you to head to Kalmár. I'll text you the precise coordinates.'

'Kalmár?' Bald vaguely recognised the name from his study of the area around Budapest, back at the briefing room. A small town, a dot on a map. 'But that's west of here. Towards the river. That's the wrong fucking direction.'

'What's your point?'

'This is a load of bollocks,' Bald said. 'We need to be heading east, not west. This is our only chance of getting to Volkov, and you're sending us back the way we came.'

'You have your orders,' Strickland replied sternly in her

269

Glaswegian accent. 'Hurry there now. Someone will meet you at the RV at 21.00 hours. You'll receive a full briefing then.'

She clicked off the call. Bald was left staring into the black void of the road ahead. Three seconds later his phone vibrated with a new text message, from an unknown number. A link to Google Maps. Bald tapped on it, brought up the maps screen. He switched to the satellite view and pinched out with his thumb and forefinger, zooming in on the location. There was a red pin over the end of a dirt track, approximately two miles east of Kalmár. Nothing there, as far as Bald could tell. Just a wide circular clearing flanked by dense woodland. The pin-drop was twenty-four miles from their present location. A thirty-minute drive away.

He relayed their orders to Porter while he punched the details into the Volvo's built-in satnav.

Porter kept his eyes on the road and said, 'Why would they send us in the opposite direction? That makes no bloody sense.'

Bald said, 'I can think of one reason.'

'What's that?'

'Strickland's lost her nerve. She doesn't want to risk a noisy attack in a friendly country. We're not being sent to an RV, mate. We're being sent to a fucking debrief.' He shook his head in bitter frustration. 'They're sending us home.'

THIRTY-ONE

They turned the Volvo around and drove east in angry silence.

Heading away from Volkov.

Towards the new RV.

Bald kept a cautious eye on the satnav, tracking their progress. The on-board computer estimated their time of arrival at 20.59 hours. A full hour before the Russians would reach the airfield to the east. Bald felt a rage firing inside his guts. Sixty minutes from now, the FSB was going to extract a major target from the country. They would deliver Volkov on a plate to their paymasters at the Kremlin. President Kolotov would hold his press conference and chalk up another PR victory over the West. And Six was going to let them get away with it.

The voice inside his head wondered if there was something else going on. *We've learned all this top-secret stuff about a populist conspiracy with Russia to break up NATO. And we know that Six covered up the story about Volkov being lifted from the safe house.*

Me and Porter are loose ends, the voice said.

Maybe this isn't a debrief.

Maybe Six is planning to knock us on the head.

Bald tried to rationalise it. Told himself that Strickland didn't seem the type to screw them over. He'd believed her when she had promised to watch their backs no matter what. But then again, she wasn't the one calling the shots. Moorcroft was. And Bald trusted him about as far as he could spit a grenade.

His head started to throb. The migraine prodded at the sides of his skull, kneading his temples. He clamped his eyes shut, teeth clenched, riding it out. When he opened his eyes again he saw that they had returned to the crossroads three miles due west of

Koman Castle. Porter pointed the Volvo left at the crossroads, taking them south. Deeper into the Great Plains.

The velvet sky darkened as they continued towards the RV, the land around them faintly visible beneath the wan glow of the crescent moon. They rolled on through the flattest landscape Bald had ever seen. There were acres of farmland and telegraph poles and one-house towns that hadn't changed in a hundred years. They passed hardly any traffic. The occasional delivery truck or rattling old Dacia pickup, hauling farming equipment and supplies. They passed grain silos and remote farms and fenced-off timber yards strewn with rusting machinery and tin-roofed shelters. The people in these parts lived a hardscrabble existence, Bald thought. Long hours of backbreaking work, grinding poverty supplemented by state handouts. The forgotten masses. They were only sixty miles from Budapest, but they might as well have been on another planet.

Porter finally broke the silence. 'Why would Strickland take us off the op?'

'Maybe they think they don't need Volkov after all,' said Bald. 'Maybe they reckon they've got enough with the audio of the conference.'

'But Strickland told us that getting Volkov back was a matter of national security. That can't have changed. So why tell us to turn around?'

'Trying to understand how them lot at Six think is a waste of time. Might as well read the tea leaves.'

'I thought you'd be pleased, Jock.'

Bald shot him a hard look. 'What's that supposed to mean?'

'The sooner we're sent home, the sooner you can piss off and get your cosy corporate gig. Thought you hated working for Six anyway?'

'Professional pride,' said Bald. 'I don't give a shit about the Firm. But I didn't put in the hard yards just so some Russian prick can go home and get a pat on the back from his great leader.'

'You sure there's not more to it than that?'

Bald gazed out of the side window. The migraine was scurrying like ants across his skull. He thought back to Playa del Carmen. The two hitmen sent to put the drop on him.

The president ordered the hit himself.

'Let's just say I've got a vested interest in wiping the smile from Kolotov's face,' he said.

Porter glanced inquisitively at Bald, but the latter said nothing more. Bald hadn't shared the story about the Russian hitmen back in Mexico with his mucker, and he wasn't about to confess now. He didn't want to give Porter the satisfaction. It would just give the guy an excuse to launch into another one of his moralising sermons. *You can't go on like this forever, Jock, sooner or later it's all going to catch up with you.* All that shite. So he kept his mouth shut and turned his mind to thoughts of revenge. Kolotov and his cronies had been prepared to put him six feet under. Bald had been looking forward to returning the favour; lifting Volkov would have gone a long way towards levelling the scores. Now he wouldn't get the opportunity.

They lapsed into silence again. Another mile passed.

20.48 hours. Eleven minutes to the RV.

Porter said, 'Something doesn't make sense. Why would Volkov be working with the Russians? They're the ones who poisoned him. They wanted him dead.'

'Simple,' Bald said. 'They're paying him off, and threatening to kill him if he doesn't cooperate.'

Porter chewed on the thought, shook his head. 'But Volkov has been on Moscow's shit list for years. He's given up hundreds of undercover agents to the Brits, and now he suddenly turns around and cuts a deal with the Kremlin? It doesn't add up.'

'He's a double agent,' Bald reminded him. 'Bastard has got no loyalty. Doesn't know the meaning of the word. He's only in it for himself.'

'Sounds like you, Jock.'

'Fuck off, mate. I'll be the first to admit that I've done some bad shit in my time, but I've never sold out my own mates to the bloody enemy. I'm telling you, this bloke would sell out his own gran if there was a few quid in it for him.'

Porter wasn't convinced. 'Volkov wouldn't go back to Moscow willingly. Too much heat. There has to be something in it for him.'

'Like what?'

'I don't know. But whatever it is, it's got to be something big.'

273

'Doesn't matter,' said Bald. 'We're off the op. A week from now I'll be making the big bucks in my new job, and this will be someone else's problem.'

Porter studied his mucker closely. 'You'll hate it. Working in a cubicle for some big fuck-off multinational. You'll be climbing the walls before long.'

'Rather be doing that than working for Moorcroft and his gang. Anything's better than that. They're a fucking cancer.'

'Strickland isn't so bad.'

'She's a good lass,' Bald agreed. 'But she's one person in a building full of back-stabbing twats. You want my advice, you should get out of there.'

'I can't quit,' Porter said. 'This is all I'm good at. It's all I've got.'

'Bollocks. That's just a lame excuse. You're happy playing it safe, taking bullshit orders, being kept under the thumb. Should engrave that on your gravestone.'

'I've got my daughter to think about,' Porter replied tetchily. 'Sandy's raising a kid by herself. She needs her old man around to help out. I can't just chuck my job and go on some big fucking adventure like you.'

Bald laughed drily. 'Your life is tragic.'

'That's rich, coming from the bloke who lost a million in gold and ended up on his arse in Mexico.'

'Minor setback. Temporary blip. I'll get that big money sooner or later.'

'Keep telling yourself that, mate. But I'm the one with the steady career, the family. All that badness you've done, and what have you got to show for it? Fuck all.'

'Better than being a Vauxhall stooge,' Bald said.

'I'm serving my country.'

Bald laughed again. 'Jesus, you sound like a green army recruitment ad. You'll be telling me it's okay to be emotional next.'

'I'm still an operator, at least. I get to do what I do best.'

'You're an old drunk who does MI6's dirty work. Playing by their rules, doing what they say. That's your game. I've no interest in that. Got my own priorities.'

Porter looked at his mucker with a feeling of concern. Despite their differences he admired Bald as a soldier, but he couldn't understand the guy. The bloke had no ties, no settled routine. His whole life was chaos. Who could live like that? Maybe it's better that the op is being cut short and we're going our separate ways, he thought. Six months of working alongside Bald would probably have driven him back to the drink.

They motored on past black fields, the road snaking through pockets of densely clustered birch and oak trees, grey beneath the darkness above. After another quarter of a mile they neared the turn-off for the dirt road and Porter crunched down through the gears, slowing to twenty miles per hour as they turned off the main road. They travelled north along a muddy, potholed track flanked by corridors of pitch-black forest. Bald squinted at the grainy darkness, keeping his eyes peeled for any signs of unusual movement. He didn't think Six would lure them into a trap.

But with those guys you can never be sure.

They followed the track north for three hundred metres, the wagon juddering and bouncing over the deep craters. The path seemed to go nowhere, taking them deeper into the bleak wilderness. And then it abruptly widened into a flat, rough clearing the size of a football pitch. No buildings or vehicles. Just a wide patch encircled by vast tracts of woodland.

No sign of anyone from Six.

Porter pulled up at the edge of the clearing. He flicked on the parking brake but kept the engine ticking, the headlights running on full beam. He glanced around him, scratched his head.

'You sure this is the right place?' he asked.

Bald consulted the map on his phone. The GPS signal was hovering right over the red pin on the map. 'These are the coordinates Strickland gave us. No question.'

Porter frowned. 'Maybe we're early.'

Bald glanced down at the clock on his phone screen. 20.59 hours.

Bang on time, he thought.

So where the fuck is this person we're supposed to meet?

They both stepped out of the Volvo, dropping down to the frozen ground. The cold air nicked knife-like at Bald as he looked around the clearing, his eyes slowly adjusting to the blackness. For a few seconds, he saw nothing but the dark empty landscape, silent and moonlit.

Then he heard it.

A low steady thrum, somewhere towards the horizon. At first the noise was faint, no more than a distant hum. But Bald recognised it all the same. A sound he'd heard many times before.

The unmistakeable drone of an approaching helicopter.

THIRTY-TWO

Bald lifted his head to the sky, straining his eyes as he searched for any sign of the chopper. So did Porter. The sound was getting louder now. An insistent *whump-whump* that carried sharply across the frigid night air, echoing across the vast plain around them. For a moment, he couldn't see anything. Then Porter thrust out an arm and pointed to the west of the treeline. Bald spun round, chasing his line of sight. Between the gaps in the trees he saw a cluster of lights approaching the clearing. A large searchlight, and several smaller ones, some white, some flashing red, cracking and popping in the darkness. They swelled in size as the chopper glided towards the clearing, the thump of the blades rising to a deafening crescendo. Then Bald saw the chopper itself, emerging ghostlike from the darkness, sleek and dark blue, with a bulbous nose and prominent tailfin. A Dauphin Eurocopter AS365 N3, otherwise known as Blue Thunder. Painted in civilian colours and used by the Regiment's CT Team to respond to terror threats.

This must be the same Dauphin that Strickland told us about, Bald realised. The standby helicopter in Graz, Austria.

The engine noise was impossibly loud now. Porter had to raise his voice to make himself heard, even though he was standing right next to Bald. 'What's the Dauphin doing here?'

'Must have been sent to pick us up,' Bald guessed. 'Get us across the border without going through security.'

He turned his attention back to the Dauphin as it made its final approach. The grass rippling, the branches of the surroundings trees shivering beneath the downwash as the chopper swung round, hovering directly over the middle of the clearing. The Dauphin seemed to hang suspended in the air for a moment before the pilots began their slow descent, touching down thirty metres away from Bald and Porter. Rotor blades spinning, engine droning. Wind blasting across the clearing.

A moment later, the door on the side of the main cabin slid open.

Two figures jumped down from the cabin and hastened over to Bald and Porter. They were both in their late twenties or early thirties. Dressed in dark-blue combats and Gore-tex boots, with bulletproof vests over their long-sleeved plaid shirts.

The guy on the left was six foot, darkly tanned and sporting a straggly beard. The black guy on the right was the bigger of the two. His brawny physique was apparent even beneath his outer layers. The dome of his cleanly shaven head glistened beneath the glare of the chopper lights.

Bald recognised their faces as they drew closer.

Two guys he hadn't expected to see again.

He said, 'I don't fucking believe it.'

Phil Lyden grinned at Bald and thrust out a hand. 'Surprised to see us, Jock?'

Bald left the hand unshaken. 'What the fuck are you doing here?'

'We're the standby team. Six called us in.'

Porter looked questioningly at Bald, brows arched. 'You know these two fellas?'

'Aye.' Bald tipped his head at Rowe. The silent partner. 'Anthony Joshua and his mate did us a favour, back in Mexico.'

'A favour?' Lyden spat out the words. 'We saved your bacon, mate.'

Porter looked at his mucker more closely. Bald didn't offer up an explanation, and there was no time to press for one. He turned back to Lyden and Rowe. No need to introduce himself. Porter had seen the pair of them around Hereford a few times, exchanged words with them, been on a few of the same training exercises. They didn't go out for drinks together, didn't have that level of friendship, but Porter knew they were good operators. They took care of business.

'What's going on, lads?'

Lyden indicated the Dauphin. 'Get in. There's no time to lose. We'll explain everything on the way.'

'Where are we going?'

'Békés. The airfield. Strickland's orders.'

Bald and Porter glanced at each other in surprise.

'The op is still on?' asked Bald.

Lyden nodded and said, 'Six wants us to intercept the Russians. We're the only assets who can reach the airfield in time. They told us to RV with you and brief you on the way.'

Bald and Porter swapped a look, suddenly understanding why Strickland had told them to go in the wrong direction. Not to send them home – but so they could link up with the standby team. The Dauphin was one of the fastest helis in the business, with a maximum speed of a hundred and eighty miles an hour. Which meant it could cover the distance to the airfield in around forty-five minutes. Much faster than going by road.

If we leave now, thought Bald, *there's still enough time for us to get to Békés ahead of the Russians and set an ambush for the fuckers.* With the two younger Blades for company, they stood a much better chance of overwhelming the FSB officers and retrieving Volkov.

We underestimated Strickland.

She knew exactly what she was doing all along.

'Fuck it,' he said. 'Let's get moving.'

Lyden and Rowe started off towards the Dauphin. Bald and Porter rushed back over to the Volvo, switched off the engine and fetched the modified iPad from the back seat, checking that they hadn't left any other sensitive materials behind.

Bald sent a quick message to Strickland, listing the bugs they had hidden in Lansbury's hotel room at the Royal Duna and supplying the code for the safe in their twin room. One of Six's local assets would have to gain access to their hotel room, posing as a member of the cleaning staff. Grab Porter and Bald's holdalls, empty their valuables from the safe, remove the bugging equipment from Lansbury's suite.

They locked up the wagon, hurried over to the Dauphin. Porter climbed in first. Bald followed him into a cramped interior cabin and took up one of the seats facing towards the cockpit. Lyden and Rowe occupied two of the seats opposite. There was a whole bunch of stuff on the seats next to them: a military-grade laptop, four pairs of boom mics and headsets for communicating over the internal comms system, plus a block of rubber with a lens on it that Bald guessed was some sort of specialist digital camera.

Lyden was wearing a transponder, inserted into one of the front pouches on his bulletproof vest. A brick-sized black lump with a six-inch cylindrical antenna and coaxial cable hanging out of it. Bald had used something similar during his time at Hereford. The radio was a personnel locator, data transmitter and comms device rolled into one. You could use it to flag your location, send imagery or videos, or have securely encrypted conversations with the command centre.

Whatever the plan is, thought Bald, these lads have come prepared.

Then he saw the dog crates.

There were two of them on the floor next to Rowe. Heavy-duty metal cages with a pair of bolt latches on each door. Inside the cages were a pair of Belgian Malinoises. Medium-sized dogs, similar to German shepherds, lean and muscular, with short mahogany-coloured coats and wire-basket muzzles over their mouths. Both dogs had tactical assault suits wrapped around their bodies, allowing them to fast-rope or parachute-jump into hostile environments with their trainers. Their collared leads were looped around the iron grilles on the cages.

The Malinoises eyed Bald and Porter intently, their tails wagging.

Porter said, 'What the fuck are they doing here?'

'Strickland told us to expect heavy resistance at the airfield,' Lyden yelled above the drone of the heli.

'Six guys,' Bald cut in. 'Packing Kalashnikov compacts. Could be more waiting for us on the tarmac.'

Lyden nodded at the dogs. 'The K9s will level things up.'

'As long as them fuckers don't turn on us,' Porter growled.

Lyden let out a laugh. 'They won't, mate. Don't worry about that. But they'll rip the throats out of anyone who gets in our way. Didn't have these in your day, I bet.'

Bald grunted and looked back towards the cages. He'd heard stories about the Malinoises from some of the guys doing ops in Syria and Afghanistan. The K9s were increasingly used by the

Regiment and had saved the lives of SAS operators on more than one occasion, tearing enemy combatants to pieces and taking down threats with no concern for their own safety. They were fearless animals, intelligent and ferociously loyal. The perfect military dog.

We're going up against six heavily armed Russian operators.

Maybe more.

We're going to need all the help we can get.

Rowe yanked the door shut, gave the all-clear to the two pilots. Neither of the pilots acknowledged Bald or Porter. They were busy running through their take-off procedures, checking the bank of glowing lights in front of them in the cockpit, communicating in short bursts. The pilots would be from 658 Squadron Army Air Corps, Bald knew. The unit that provided helicopter support to the SAS. They would be shit hot. The best in the business, skilled at extreme low-level flying to avoid radar detection or anti-aircraft fire. Some of the pilots Bald had flown with in the past thought nothing of flying underneath bridges or power lines.

Rowe ducked into the aft cargo hold to the rear of the main cabin bulkhead. He returned a few moments later, handed Bald and Porter a couple of ballistic plate carriers, similar to the ones the two younger operators were wearing. Bulky vests with ceramic plate armour inserts on the front and back. Lighter than steel armour, but heavier than a regular bulletproof vest. Good for stopping a medium-calibre round at close range. But the carriers also weighed the operator down, restricting their movement and making it difficult to manoeuvre freely.

'Here,' Rowe boomed above the whine of the twin turboshaft engine. 'Wear these.'

Bald stared at the plate carrier and made a face. 'I ain't wearing that shit. It's like moving through quicksand with one of them on.'

Rowe stared back at him. Giving him the silent treatment.

'It's not optional,' Lyden shouted. 'Put the fucking thing on.'

Bald cursed through his teeth as he took off his jacket, grabbed the plate carrier and slipped it on over his shirt. He fastened the shoulder straps and waistband until it was snug against his chest.

Once they had strapped on their plate carriers Rowe reached

back into the cargo hold and brought out a pair of longs. Compact rifles, black with tan-coloured buttstocks and grips. He handed one to Porter, the other to Bald.

'This is an L119A2 rifle,' he explained to Bald. 'Upgrade on the old L119A1. Same basic design, with a few modifications. Brought it in a few years back.'

Bald took the rifle, eyebrows narrowed, teeth clenched. 'I know what this fucking tool is. I didn't retire from the Regiment that long ago.'

Rowe gave a *who-gives-a-shit* shrug and disappeared back into the rear compartment while Bald familiarised himself with the long. There wasn't much difference between the L119A2 and the earlier model he'd used in the SAS. Both were modified versions of the Colt C8 carbine. The shoulder weapon of choice for the guys in the Regiment. Bald was holding a compact version of the A2, with a ten-inch barrel, Trijicon ACOG x4 scope and red-dot laser sight mounted on the receiver.

Rowe emerged again from the hold clutching eight clips of ammo. He distributed four to Porter and four to Bald. The mags were joined together in pairs with a polymer magazine coupler, with a small gap between them, so that the operator could more quickly reload a fresh clip after emptying the first one. The L119A2 mags carried a standard thirty rounds of 5.56 x 45mm NATO brass, which gave them each a hundred and twenty rounds to expend. Throw in whatever Lyden and Rowe were carrying, and they were looking at around five hundred rounds total. More than a match for the Kalashnikov MA rifles the six Russian agents would be armed with.

Finally. We're in fucking business.

Bald and Porter both inserted one of the coupler mags, into the feeds located on the underside of the receiver. They tucked the spares into the mag pouches on the front of their plate carriers.

A moment later, the pilots finished their checks.

Lyden handed Porter and Bald each a noise-cancelling headset with a boom mic attached. Easier to communicate with one another over the heli's internal comms rather than shouting above the roar of the engine.

The blades whumped. The engine boomed.

There was a shudder, and Bald felt the cabin lurch as the Dauphin left solid ground. The heli banked slightly to the left before levelling out, and then they gradually climbed into the night sky, rising above the clearing and the surrounding woodland. Once they were far above the treeline the pilots pitched the nose down at an angle and the Dauphin glided forward, and soon they were surging across the darkened plain.

As soon as they were airborne, Bald caught Lyden's attention and said into the mic, 'What's the plan?'

Lyden reached for the military-grade laptop, which was basically a Windows portable computer housed in a rugged aluminium shell. He flipped open the screen and tilted it towards Bald and Porter. The main window showed a hi-resolution satellite view of a small airfield surrounded by a patchwork of green and brown fields.

Békés.

An asphalt runway ran east to west across the airfield. It looked to be about two kilometres long, Bald guessed. The minimum length necessary for a mid-sized private jet. There were painted white numbers at either end of the runway: '09' painted on the western edge, '27' on the eastern. Like points on a compass, but in reverse. The numbers corresponded to the direction the runway was facing, Bald knew. '09' faced east, '27' faced west. Something to do with prevailing winds. Three taxiways led down from the runway, spaced out at intervals across the length of the tarmac.

Bald and Porter leaned in for a closer look as Lyden pointed to the markings.

'Vauxhall is monitoring the weather around Békés. At the moment they're telling us the wind direction is running east to west. Which means the jet will be coming in from the west, here.'

Lyden finger-tapped the side of the runway marked with the white-painted numbers '09'. Then he pointed to the other end of the runway, marked with the west-facing numbers '27'. Another taxiway led down from this end of the runway towards a wide tarmacked stand, three hundred metres to the south. Three roads led away from the tarmac stand. Four hundred metres to the east stood a pair of large hangars. South led towards a control tower and a car park, with a long single road running down to the gate at the entrance to the airport. A third road led west from the stand towards a complex of maintenance buildings, four hundred metres away.

Lyden tapped the tarmac apron.

'This is the only stand at the airfield,' he explained. 'The jet is gonna land and come in here while the pilots wait for the Russians to show up. That's where we'll hit them. We'll get into position before the jet comes in, whack the fuckers before they get aboard.'

Porter studied the map and said, 'How are we going to get close enough without raising any alarms? Even at night, there's going to be security lights all over the fucking place.'

'Porter's right,' said Bald. 'We can't hang around the tarmac waiting for the jet to come in. We'd stand out like tits on a bull.'

'We'll be in disguise,' Lyden said.

He traced his index finger across the laptop screen, pointed to the buildings to the east of the tarmac stand. There were three of them, set side by side, like chips on a circuit board. There was a fire dump to the south of the buildings and what appeared to be an abandoned parking lot behind them. Two of the structures were long and narrow and set apart from the third building. Not aircraft hangars. Maintenance hangars, Bald assumed.

The third building was square-shaped and set sixty metres further to the north of the maintenance hangars.

Lyden pointed to it.

'This is where the fire crew is based,' he said. 'According to the plans, there's a fire tender inside with a three-man crew to operate it. We'll overrun the crew, grab their uniforms and the tender and move it into position here.' Lyden traced his finger over to the eastern edge of the tarmac stand. 'This area is a dead spot. No lights. That should allow us to OP the jet, get eyes on the target and slot the Russians when they rock up.'

Bald walked the plan through in his head. They'd practised something similar on a training exercise at Hereford once. Every airport had to have a crash tender in position whenever a plane came in to land. Something to do with safety regulations. The bigger the airport, the larger the fire-fighting capacity. A small airfield like the one at Békés would have perhaps one or two dedicated fire-fighting units on hand to deal with any emergencies in the event of an accident or crash. The unit would follow standard procedure and sit on the tarmac stand near to the parked jet while the pilots waited for their passengers to arrive. No one would bat an eyelid at the fire crew. The perfect OP.

It was a good plan, Bald had to admit. He almost wished he'd thought of it himself. But he didn't share that thought with Lyden. The guy was already full of himself, walking around like he was God's gift. He wasn't about to massage the kid's fucking ego.

'How many workers are we dealing with at the airfield?' he asked.

'Skeleton staff,' said Lyden. 'Six has sent through the data on all that. The control tower only operates part-time, at the weekends, when you've got the flight training school and all the big jets coming in. Monday to Thursday is pilot discretion. Which means there's no one in the tower, no police or patrols, nothing like that. We're looking at a couple of maintenance guys to operate the runway lights, a guard at the main gate.'

'That int had better be spot-on. Because if it ain't, we'll alert every fucker at the airport as soon as we rush them firemen.'

'It's solid,' Lyden reassured him. 'Trust us. This is going to work.'

'Any other planes due to come in?'

'Six is checking that now. But it's a small-time airfield. Not much activity, especially during the weekdays. Maybe a light Cessna or two coming in, but that's about it.'

Porter said, 'What about police?'

'There's no airport security presence. Just the guard at the front gate.'

'Armed?'

Lyden shook his head. 'He's just there to open and close the gate. If they need help they have to call in to the local station.'

'Response time?'

'Anything between nine and twelve minutes.'

'We won't have much time when this thing gets noisy, then.'

'We'll be taking the Russians by surprise,' Lyden said. 'That should give us the upper hand. The plan is to slot them and bug out before anyone can put a call in to the Hungarian plod.'

'And if it goes south?'

'Then we'll have to blast our way out of there.'

'What's the deal once we've nabbed Volkov?' asked Bald. 'Back on the heli?'

'Can't,' Lyden said. 'We're going in at top speed. Pilots reckon they've burned through a shit-ton of fuel just to get us to the RV. They'll have to go technical and fuck off as soon as they've dropped us off.'

Bald grunted in acknowledgement. The Dauphin had a ferry range of four-hundred-plus nautical miles, he knew. At maximum speed, the heli would be eating through its fuel reserves much faster than at cruising speed. A hundred and fifty miles from Austria to the RV, plus another hundred miles to the airfield. There would be enough juice left in the tank for the pilots to turn around and fly back to Graz. But they wouldn't be able to hang around near the airfield, turning and burning, waiting for the guys to do the job.

'If the heli has to go, how are we supposed to bug out?'

'We've already thought of that.' Lyden grinned wickedly. 'We'll steal the jet. Make the pilot an offer he can't refuse and tell him to fly us to Northolt. Six will have a car waiting there for us. We'll transport Volkov on to London for a debrief.'

'Assuming the plane has got enough fuel to get us back.'

'It will,' Lyden reassured him. 'It's got to have enough to return to Moscow. That's a thousand-mile trip. Northolt is about the same distance. Or we can land in France or the Channel Islands. Take your pick.'

Porter said, 'If this goes Pete Tong, we're gonna be stuck in the middle of nowhere, with no clear route to safety, with half the Hungarian police to deal with.'

'It's the best chance we've got. Either we do this, or we let the Russians sail off into the sunset with Volkov.' Lyden smiled at the two Blades. 'Think you two crusties can handle it?'

Bald stared the kid down. 'We've still got it. Don't worry about that.'

'Is that what you fellas tell yourselves before you take out your false teeth?'

'Do us a favour, mate.'

'What's that?'

'Take your lame jokes and fuck off.'

Lyden grinned. The confidence of youth.

They carried on east.

Towards the airfield.

Towards Volkov, and his Russian minders.

The Dauphin screamed across the blackened landscape. Rowe and Bald were huddled around the laptop, doing visual recces of the airfield and surrounding area from the imagery being sent across from Vauxhall. They were studying the entrance points to the airfield, the outlying buildings and the tarmac stand, looking for the most likely area for the jet to park while they waited for the Russians to show up. On the iPad, Porter studied a PDF file: the operating manual for the model of fire tender in use at the airfield. Lyden was on the encrypted comms link to Vauxhall, getting up-to-the-minute weather reports, using the data to build up as clear a picture of the ground as possible. As soon as they scrambled off the chopper, they were going to be against the clock. They wouldn't have time to familiarise themselves with the environment. They would have to go in hard and fast. Take out the fire crew, nobble the Russians and escape on the jet before the police could show up and surround the airport.

We're flying by the seat of our pants here, thought Bald. *Just like the old days in the Regiment.*

Do or fucking die.

Lyden got off the comms unit and turned to Bald. 'That was the ops room. They've been monitoring air-traffic control in the area. There's only one flight due to land at Békés tonight, a Phenom 300 business jet. En route direct from Moscow Vnukovo airport.'

'That's the one coming in for the Russians. Has to be.'

'Is Volkov on the manifest?' asked Porter.

The manifest listed the names of all passengers and crew on a particular flight. Information that had to be submitted electronically to the aviation authorities, at least sixty minutes prior to departure. If Volkov was getting on that plane, his name would have been added to the list.

Lyden shook his head. 'Vauxhall has already checked. The

manifest is showing seven names, all Hungarian nationals. None of them known to the authorities.'

'Then how do we know it's them?'

'Six checked the passport numbers. They're in sequence. One after another.'

'Which means they're fakes,' Bald said. 'They must be using them to sneak out of the country.'

'That's what Strickland reckons too. She says the Russians used the same passports to smuggle Volkov out of the country a week ago, after they lifted him from the safe house. It's got to be them.'

Porter said, 'When does the jet get in?'

'Twenty-one fifty-five hours. According to the manifest, the crew are expecting a quick turnaround. Plane is due to depart again at 22.20 hours.'

'Bound for?'

'Back the way they came. Moscow Vnukovo.'

Bald glanced down at his G-Shock: 21.29 hours.

Twenty-six minutes until the jet touched down. Maybe another minute or two before the Russians pulled up on the tarmac stand to board the plane.

He said, 'How long until we reach the airfield?'

'We're sixty miles away. Looking at an ETA of twenty minutes.'

Which means we'll get in at 22.49 hours, thought Bald.

Six minutes before the jet was due to land.

'As long as the fire crew don't put up a fight,' Bald said. 'We're only gonna have a couple of minutes to suppress those bastards, nick their uniforms and get the tender in position before the jet flies in.'

'That's what the dogs are for,' Lyden replied confidently. 'They'll take care of business.'

'They'd better. Because if we fuck this one up, Volkov gets to stand in front of the hacks in Moscow and give them the story of the century.'

Lyden said, 'One more thing.'

Bald looked at him for a moment. 'What's that?'

'Strickland told us that there's some sort of transaction going down at the airfield. Before the target gets on the plane.'

Bald nodded. The reward waiting for Volkov at the airfield. The one Lansbury had mentioned. *He seemed excited. He was adamant he wouldn't be getting on that plane before he got his reward.*

'Strickland thinks someone might be meeting Volkov at the airport,' Lyden went on.

'Who?' asked Porter.

'They're not sure. But there's three people listed on the manifest for the outward leg of the flight. Two men and a woman.'

'Who are they?'

'Six has done a background check. There's no records for any of the names.'

'Which means they're flying on fake passports too,' Bald said.

Lyden nodded. 'Strickland wants eyes on them before she'll give the green light to attack. She wants to know who is so important that the Russians are flying them out to meet Volkov.'

'Fine,' Bald said. 'Whatever it takes. But one way or another, those Russian bastards are going down tonight.'

He settled back into his seat and stared out of the window. They raced on at a frightening speed, the pilots sticking close to the ground, the scattered lights of the towns and roads below glowing like fireflies amid the black void of the Hungarian plain.

Almost there.

Not far to go now.

Nineteen minutes later, they reached the airfield.

THIRTY-THREE

The runway slithered out of the dark mass of the horizon, a grey tongue streaked with black and illuminated by a series of bright edge lights. Bald sat facing forward, watching their approach through the cockpit window. From his position he could see the tarmac stand situated to the south of the runway. Security lights beamed down on the stand, like floodlights at a football stadium. Further to the south he spied the control tower and aircraft hangars. To the west, four hundred metres away, he glimpsed three poorly lit shapes: the fire station building and maintenance hangars. A narrow road connected the three buildings to the main tarmac stand.

As the Dauphin drew closer, the guys made their final preparations for the assault. Lyden snatched up the rubberised digital camera and tucked it into the spare pouch on the front of his plate armour vest. Bald and Porter pulled the charging bolts on their L119A2s, chambering the first rounds from their clips. Rowe adjusted the straps on his vest and checked on the dogs.

The Dauphin descended towards a bare patch of grass, situated eighty metres west of the fire department. Bald peered out of the side window, ran his eyes over the station. A six-wheeled fire tender, painted the same bright red as a regular fire truck, was parked up in the garage entrance on the left side of the station building. To the right of the garage Bald could see the staff door, stickered with the usual exclamation-marked signs warning off unauthorised personnel.

'No sign of the crew,' Porter observed.

Bald said, 'They'll be inside, getting the tender ready for the jet.'

Lyden said, 'We'll go in through the door on the right-hand side. Let the dogs get in there first, then we'll follow.'

Rowe said nothing. He just stared ahead and looked rock hard.

The Dauphin's rotor blades beat down relentlessly, whipping up a swirl of grass blades and loose dirt as the landing gears touched down. There was a jarring shudder, and then the voice of one of the pilots squawked over the internal comms system, giving the Blades the signal to debus. Porter was nearest to the exit. He removed his headset, wrenched open the sliding door on the side of the main cabin, grabbed his rifle and jumped down from the chopper. Boots thudding against the ground, his suit flapping madly about him, the downwash stirring his grey-flecked hair.

Bald followed.

Behind him, Lyden and Rowe were crouching down beside the dog crates, sliding open the bolt latches.

They untethered the leashes from the iron frames, removed the muzzles and guided the dogs over to the cabin door. Lyden dropped down with the first Malinois, one hand gripping his rifle, the other holding on to the lead.

Rowe was last out of the Dauphin. The second Malinois scampered ahead of him and leaped down to the bare ground, straining at its leash. Bald eyed the dogs for a beat. Their powerful muscles were tensed, dark brown eyes scanning for threats. Calm, obedient, but ready to pounce as soon as Rowe and Lyden gave the word. Their teeth were so sharp they looked like they could tear through metal.

Rowe wrenched the cabin door shut, secured it and nodded to Lyden. The latter turned to Bald and Porter and said, 'Let's go! Move!'

They broke into a run across the downwash-blasted ground. Eighty metres to the fire station building. The fire crew inside the garage would have heard and seen the Dauphin coming in, Bald knew. They would be wondering why a large civilian heli had made an unscheduled landing at the airfield in the middle of the night. Bald imagined the scene inside the building. Heads being scratched, puzzled looks exchanged, one of the crew wondering whether they should check in with the dispatcher.

We've got to hit these fuckers hard and fast. Before they phone it in.

Forty metres to the fire station.

Behind them, the chopper began to ascend into the night sky.

Bald hurried alongside Porter, his right hand wrapped around the trigger grip on his L119A2 rifle, left clasping the underside of the receiver. Lyden and Rowe were racing a couple of steps ahead of them. The two Malinoises strained at their leashes, their black ears pricked. Bald heard the sound of the helicopter engine roaring behind him, blood rushing in his ears. He glanced quickly around. Runway at his nine o'clock, tarmac stand at his three o'clock, the control tower and car park further to the south. No sign of activity anywhere. No planes on the tarmac stand. The airfield was eerily quiet.

Skeleton staff, Lyden had said. *The control tower only operates at the weekends. Monday to Thursday is pilot discretion.*

At the weekends, the place was probably crawling with VIPs, security guards, control-tower operators, maintenance staff, flight enthusiasts. But at nearly eleven o'clock on a Thursday night, the airport was dead.

Not for much longer.

A quick glance over his shoulder told Bald that the Dauphin was pulling clear of the airfield now. Lights winking, beak pitched forward as the heli shuttled off towards the west, slowly picking up speed.

The maintenance staff and the security guard at the front gate would have seen the Dauphin make a swift departure too. But Bald was confident that the few other guys at the airfield wouldn't be concerned by the sudden appearance of the heli. They wouldn't have access to flight manifests or air-traffic control. No reason for them to think there was anything unusual about a civilian-coloured helicopter coming in. And they would be too far away to get a good look at the Blades, anyway.

He swung his gaze forward again. He reached the station building in another dozen strides, pressed himself against the brick-work to the right of the door, Porter drawing up on the opposite side. Lyden and Rowe stopped half a metre from the entrance, stooped down beside the two Malinoises and unclipped the leashes from their collars. On the other side of the thick door Bald could hear the muffled chatter of the fire crew. Two guys. He didn't understand the language but from the tone of their voices they sounded casual, relaxed. Not expecting any trouble.

Lyden looked at Bald and Porter and Rowe. 'Ready?' he whispered.

Bald nodded. They couldn't risk using their weapons to suppress the fire crew. Sounds carried more clearly at night than during the daytime. A rifle discharge would easily travel across the airport, alerting the maintenance guys and the security guards four hundred metres away. They would call for help as soon as they heard the reports. Maybe even warn off the incoming jet. *We've got a potential security situation on the ground. Turn around.*

Which is where the dogs came in.

The two Malinoises dropped into a crouched position, teeth bared, ready to attack. Lyden looked towards Bald and nodded. *We're ready. Open the door.*

Bald pulled on the handle and stepped back from the opening.

'ATTACK!' Lyden shouted at the dogs, pointing at the door.

The Malinoises sprinted inside.

They were fast. They shot forward with astonishing speed, two snarling brown-black blurs, sweeping into the ground floor of the station and looking to hit anything with a pulse. From inside the building Bald heard shouts of dumb surprise. Then a chorus of manic screams and cries, interspersed with the barks and growls of the Malinoises as they tore into their victims.

'Go, go!' Bald shouted. 'Now!'

In the next instant, the four Blades stormed through the open doorway.

Bald was first into the station. Rifle raised, buttstock flush against his shoulder, index finger tensing on the trigger, eyes peering down the weapon's iron sights. Porter at his six o'clock, Lyden a step behind him, Rowe pulling up the rear as the tail-end Charlie.

The door opened out into a brightly lit garage the size of a school gymnasium. Fluorescent light tubes hung from the high bay ceiling. The concrete floor was coated in some kind of hard-wearing resin and painted in alternate thick bands of red, grey and white. At the rear of the building, thirty metres away, a metal staircase led up to the dispatch room on the first floor.

Bald took the left side of the floor while Porter surged forward, clearing the area ahead, Lyden and Rowe following close behind. The four of them arcing their sights from side to side, searching for targets, moving with controlled aggression. Just the way they had trained during endless exercises at the Regiment Killing House.

Bald spotted the fire tender at his nine o'clock. A smaller second firefighting vehicle was parked up in the space to the right of the tender, a modified pickup truck. Some kind of rapid intervention vehicle. There was a load of firefighting equipment stacked against the wall behind the tender. Bald saw free-standing lockers with spare uniforms and gloves and helmets. He saw coiled hoses and oxygen tanks, bolt cutters and ventilation units.

In the middle of the garage, he saw two figures writhing on the ground.

They were both decked out in dark-blue flame-retardant trousers and matching jackets, with hi-vis bands around the ankles and sleeves, utility belts strapped around their chests. The guy on the left was in his late thirties or early forties, with hair the colour of urine and eyes like lumps of charcoal. The guy on the right was younger and skinnier, with a chinstrap beard. Both of them were thrashing about on their backs as the Malinoises tore into them. One of the dogs had its jaws clamped around the forearm of the guy with the piss-coloured hair. The other Malinois had sunk its teeth into Chinstrap's ankle, wrenching its head this way and that as it tore into his flesh. Chinstrap kicked out wildly as the dog bit into him with renewed vigour, drawing another agonised scream from its victim.

Bald swept further into the room.

He couldn't see the third firefighter.

Then he looked across to the rear of the garage.

The third firefighter was twenty-five metres away. A squat, stocky guy, round-faced, with a jowly jawline and thinning dark hair.

He was reaching for the portable radio clipped to his utility belt.

Shit, thought Bald. *Fucker's going to alert the cops.*

All kinds of implications rattled through his mind.

The local police station is ten miles away.

Response time is anything between nine and twelve minutes.

The firefighter unclipped the radio. Another second or two, and he'd sound the alarm with the local plod.

Bald arced across his rifle, thought about nailing the firefighter. A shot to the head. Realised he couldn't. The sound of the rifle discharge. The other maintenance staff would hear. The guard, too.

Then he saw Porter sprint into view in a burst of movement, charging forward with surprising speed for a guy in his fifties. The months of clean living, paying off. Porter caught up with the firefighter before the latter could depress the Push-to-Talk button, reversing the L119A2 rifle in his grip and thrusting out at him with the buttstock, slamming the stock into the base of the firefighter's spine. The guy made a grunting sound in the back of his throat as he tumbled and fell backwards, the radio skimming across the smooth floor.

Porter jabbed the round-faced guy again in the guts, drawing another howl of pain. He took a knee beside the firefighter, flipped him on to his back. Snatched out a pair of plasticuffs from his rear trouser pocket and cinched the guy's hands tightly behind his back.

Across the garage floor, Chinstrap and the guy with the piss-coloured hair continued to scream.

Porter grabbed the firefighter by the scruff of his collar and hauled the guy to his feet. Looked up. Bald nodded at him. One Blade to another, appreciating their handiwork.

'Stick him in there,' Bald said, cocking a thumb at the office situated at the rear of the garage. 'I'll grab the others.'

'Roger that.'

Porter barked something at the round-faced guy, drag-walked him towards the office. Bald wheeled away and hastened over to Lyden and Rowe. They had wrestled the Malinoises free from the other two firefighters. The dogs stood obediently beside their trainers, panting heavily, tongues hanging out of teeth-bared mouths while the operators plasticuffed Chinstrap and his mate. Lyden rose to his feet and swung round to face Bald, grinning.

'Told you these beauties would get the job done,' he said.

Bald grunted a reply. But he was impressed with the dogs. *These animals are the business*, he thought to himself. The guy with the urine-coloured hair was moaning softly on the floor, blood oozing out of a deep wound to his forearm. He had bite marks on both hands, scratches to his face. The dog had done a real number on him. More efficient than chucking a couple of flash-bangs into the room. That was for fucking sure.

'Stop you this,' the fireman moaned in broken English. 'Stop you, please!'

'Shut the fuck up!' Lyden growled.

Bald glanced down at his G-Shock. 21.51 hours.

Four minutes until the jet landed.

Seconds ticking away.

He nodded at Lyden and said, 'Dump these idiots in the office with the other fat fuck. Lock them inside. And make sure they haven't got access to any comms. Then we're heading out on the tender.'

They moved quickly. Rowe tended to the Malinoises while Porter, Lyden and Bald shoved the three firefighters into the downstairs office, a sparsely furnished room as small as a broom cupboard. They bound the prisoners' ankles together with plastic cable ties and stuffed dirty rags from a workbench into their mouths, gagging them. Snatched their portable radios from their belts, padded them down and took their mobile phones too. Locked the door, tossed the key aside. Hastened across the garage floor, fetched the spare jackets from the free-standing locker set against the far wall and put them on over their shirts and bullet-proof vests. Lyden and Rowe reclipped the leashes to the Malinoises' collars. Then they fetched up their weapons and mounted the steps to the tender.

The inside of the cabin was spacious. There were two seats in the front row, with three seats behind on a raised platform, giving the passengers greater visibility through the shatterproof wind-screen. Lyden and Rowe took up the seats to the rear, with the Malinoises resting their paws on the floor beside them. Porter slid behind the wheel, Bald climbing in after him and taking the front passenger seat. He turned to Porter.

'Get us moving. Let's fucking do this.'

Porter flipped the ignition switch, shifted the transmission into

Neutral and depressed the start button. The engine blatted and spluttered into life. He released the parking brake, flicked on the headlights and upshifted into Drive. The tender was an automatic, like most firefighting vehicles. He applied the gas gently at first, gauging the speed and handling.

Sixty seconds to go until the jet landed.

Porter steered the tender out of the fire station, spun the wheel to the left and drove south towards the maintenance hangars, the engine roaring. He passed the hangars and made a right turn, following the narrow road west towards the tarmac stand. Bald, Lyden and Rowe stayed silent, scanning the runway and surrounding buildings, rifles propped against their legs. The Malinoises panting in the back seat.

After five hundred metres they reached the edge of the tarmac stand and Bald threw up his hand. 'Stop here. This'll do.'

Porter hit the brakes and pulled up on the eastern fringe of the stand. They came to a halt in a darkened area, far beyond the bank of security lights near the control tower to the south. The fire tender facing west across the skid-marked tarmac. Porter applied the parking brake and killed the headlights, switching off the engine.

Further away to the west, six hundred metres away, Bald glimpsed the main aircraft hangars, linked to the tarmac stand by another tyre-streaked road. To the south he could see the single-lane road leading past the control tower and the car park towards the front gate, some four hundred metres away. The runway at their three o'clock, parallel to the stand. Bald looked south, scanned the dense blackness beyond the main gate, but there was no sign of any approaching motors.

No sign of the private jet, either.

He checked the time again: 21.56 hours.

'Where the fuck is this thing?' he said.

Ten seconds later, he saw the lights.

THIRTY-FOUR

The Embraer Phenom 300 came in from the west, just as Lyden had predicted. The aircraft was lit up like a Christmas tree. Bald saw a bunch of lights on the wings and underside of the fuselage, along with several smaller anti-collision lights on the wingtips. The lights grew bigger, pulsing and bursting in the grainy darkness. Then came the turbine roar of the jet engines as the Phenom made its final approach to the runway.

Movement in the back of the cabin. Rummaging noises. Bald twisted round in his seat, saw Lyden removing the digital camera from the pouch on the front of his ballistic vest. He connected the camera to the transponder he was wearing, took the other end of the coaxial cable and inserted it into the socket on the side of the camera.

Bald pointed with his eyes at the camera and said, 'What's that thing for?'

'Strickland wants eyes on whoever the target is meeting with,' Lyden said. 'This gadget will feed back any images we capture to the ops room. They'll see what we can see.'

'How long will that take?'

'Fraction of a second. Signal bounces off a satellite, pings it straight to Vauxhall. Magic.' Lyden saw the sceptical look on Bald's face and smiled. 'This shit is standard now. Everything's real-time these days.'

Bald sighed through his nostrils. 'Remind me never to go for a pint with you fellas.'

'Couldn't keep up with us anyway.'

'I'm from Dundee. Drinking is practically the number-one sport up there. I could drink you two amateurs under the table.'

Lyden half-grinned. 'Is that a challenge?'

'Just stating the facts.' Bald gestured to the jet. 'Let's nobble the Russians first. Then we'll see who's really hard.'

He looked ahead again as the Phenom glided towards the runway. Several seconds later the jet splashed down on the tarmac in a cacophony of screeching rubber and whining engines. The aircraft surged on for half a kilometre, the wind acting as a powerful natural brake against ten thousand pounds of metal hurtling along the ground, until it finally slowed to taxiing speed five hundred metres from the eastern end of the runway. As Bald and the others looked on the jet rumbled further along, the eerie blare of the engines filling the night air before it came gracefully round and rolled down the eastern taxiway down to the tarmac stand. The Phenom swept into the stand and turned again, the cockpit swinging towards the west, away from the fire tender. Away from Bald and Porter and the two younger operators in the back seats.

Seconds passed.

The Phenom eased to a halt.

Engine reduced to a faint mechanical hum.

Bald glanced at the road leading to the main gate, four hundred metres to the south.

Darkness.

Still no sign of the Russians.

Porter turned to the guys in the back seat and said, 'What's the plan once the Russians arrive?'

'We'll get a shot of the person the target is meeting with, soon as they get off the jet,' Lyden said. 'Bang it across to the ops room and wait for a positive ID. Once we get the green light to attack, we'll bust out of the tender and send in the dogs. They'll attack the two nearest targets. That should buy us enough time to put the drop on the rest of the heavies and grab Volkov. Then we'll leg it on to the Phenom.'

'Assuming that meeting happens on the tarmac,' Porter said. 'What if they meet on the plane?'

Bald shook his head. 'Volkov is an ex-spook. He might be working with the Russians, but he'll trust them about as far as he can piss. Goes with the territory, when you're in that line of work. If he's expecting to meet someone, he won't set foot on that jet until he's laid eyes on them.'

'Jock's right,' Porter added. 'Lansbury said something similar. Reckoned Volkov insisted on getting his reward before getting on the jet.'

A wave of tiredness settled like fog behind Bald's sockets. He rubbed his eyes and said, 'Volkov isn't the real problem. It's the Russians. There's gonna be six of them and four of us. At least.'

Rowe, stroking the head of the dog beside him, said, 'We've got the Malinoises. They'll take care of a couple of them. Evens things up.'

Bald grunted. 'Even so, we're going to be exposed,' he said. 'Soon as we unleash them hounds, we'll only have a few seconds to close on the Russians before they realise what's going on. And we'll be crossing open ground with no fucking cover.'

Porter said, 'Nothing we can do about that. We're a hundred metres away. We can't get closer than this without looking suspicious.'

'Then we'll have to move forward in pairs,' Bald said. 'Fire and move. Keep the other lot pinned down.' He turned in his seat, nodded at Lyden and Rowe. 'You two will work as a team. Me and Porter will be the second team. Clobber them from different angles. Soon as the first shots are fired, we'll need to keep putting bursts down on the fuckers. Whatever you do, make sure there's no lulls in the fire. The second we stop shooting, them Russians will fucking plug us.'

'We know what to do,' Lyden said. 'Just focus on your own performance.'

Bald's expression tautened. 'Me and Porter were doing this shit while you two were still watching *Teletubbies*. We'll get the job done.'

He faced forward, looked down at his watch: 21.59 hours.

Almost time.

He caught a sudden glimmer of movement at his twelve o'clock and swung his gaze back to the Phenom, a hundred metres downstream from the fire tender. Bald was looking at the tail end of the aircraft, with the cockpit pointing west towards the main hangars. The Phenom was around fifteen metres long, with a similar wingspan. A small business jet. Cabin space for seven or eight passengers, probably. On the left side of the fuselage the clamshell door had sucked open and a small set of airstairs unfolded from inside the door frame, extending down to the tarmac. Like a drawbridge being lowered over a moat.

No one disembarked.

Twenty seconds later, Porter nudged Bald and pointed to the south. 'Jock! Over there.'

Straining his eyes, Bald gazed in the direction his mucker had indicated. At first, he could see nothing except the deserted road and the blackness of the countryside beyond. Then he focused again and saw them. Two pairs of headlamps, beams sweeping through the front gate as they scudded north on the approach road. At a distance of four hundred metres, the vehicles were too far away to identify. Bald watched them as they bowled on past the car park and the control tower, motoring along at a steady clip, not too fast, not too slow, until they hit the floodlit area at the southern end of the tarmac stand.

'That's them,' Bald said. 'That's fucking them.'

The two Lexus 570 SUVs rolled across the stand, heading towards the Phenom in a line formation. Front SUV leading the way, the backup vehicle four or five metres behind. They were the same colour as the two wagons Bald and Porter had seen racing away from Koman Castle earlier that night. Same licence plates. Bald traced their movement for a few beats before he turned to face the guys in the back seats.

'Get that thing ready,' he said, cocking his head at the digital camera. Lyden had plugged his boom mic and earpiece into another socket on the side of the transponder, allowing him to communicate directly to the ops room in London on a secure channel.

Lyden leaned forward in his seat, raised the camera viewfinder to his eyes and trained the lens on the airstairs. Bald looked ahead again, focused on the two Lexus 570s as they rumbled across the stand. The windows on both SUVs were green tinted. Which told Bald that the vehicles were armour plated. Bullet-resistant glass and bodywork, capable of stopping a spray of 7.62mm rounds or a couple of hand grenades. Whatever we do, thought Bald, we can't let the Russians retreat behind the wagons. Once they're behind cover, they'll be able to put down rounds on us.

'Which car is the target in?' asked Lyden.

Bald thought back to the castle. Three hours earlier. A lifetime ago.

'Lead vehicle,' he said. 'The backup team is in the second wagon. Three guys plus the driver. One guy in the front with the driver and the target in the back seat.'

He felt his muscles automatically tense as the cars neared the jet.

This is it. We're about to get into a firefight with the FSB.

The SUVs slowed to a fast crawl and veered sharply to the left, pulling up parallel with the Phenom cockpit, with the second Lexus stopping a couple of metres further back, a metre or so ahead of the jet's left wingtip. The wagons were both parked at a forty-five-degree angle, their front bumpers pointed towards the nose of the plane.

A moment later, three heavies stepped out of the rear Lexus. Two guys from the back seats and a third from the front passenger side. The same three guys Bald had seen climbing into the wagon back at Koman Castle. Two of them could have been twins. Brick shithouses, decked out in a matching uniform of Tactical 5.11 trousers, shirts and jackets.

The third man was older than the Shithouse Twins. Early fifties, perhaps. Hard to tell from a hundred metres away. He was shorter than the twins, short and stocky, with a prominent widow's peak.

All three heavies had their shoulder-slung sub-machine guns half-concealed beneath their outerwear. They would be carrying secondary weapons as well, Bald figured. Nine-milli pistols, within easy reach in case they suffered a stoppage or ran out of ammo with their longs.

The Shithouse Twins and Widow's Peak spread out in a loose semicircle next to the rear Lexus. Hands resting on the buttstocks of their weapons, eyes casually scanning the tarmac stand. None of them paid much attention to the fire tender a hundred metres to the east. Nothing unusual about a tender waiting on standby. Normal operating procedure at airports around the world.

In the next beat, another figure emerged from the passenger seat of the front Lexus. A six-foot-five man mountain in a puffer jacket, bronze tanned, with hands like boulders and peroxide-blond hair sculpted into a flat-top. He looked like the Soviet villain from some eighties action film.

The drivers didn't get out of either wagon. They stayed behind the wheels and kept the engines running, headlamps pooling light on the tyre-streaked tarmac. Ready to drive out of the airport again once the handover had been completed.

The guy with the flat-top haircut walked round to the rear passenger door on the front Lexus, tugged it open, took a step back.

Two seconds later, Nikolai Volkov climbed stiffly out of the back seat. The Russian ex-spy straightened up and rubbed the base of his spine as he glanced around.

Flat-Top turned to him and waved a hand at the Phenom, as if seeking Volkov's approval. The latter cocked his head at the fuselage and nodded, giving Flat-Top the thumbs-up. *This is more like it.* His body language gave off the impression of a guy in control of the situation, aware of his worth and determined to milk it for every last penny.

Volkov thinks he's going to be a star in Russia. A returning hero.

Flat-Top gave his back to Volkov and turned towards the airstairs, his hands folded in front of him. Volkov looked in the same direction, standing erect.

Waiting for his reward.

Two figures disgorged from the plane.

A man and a woman.

They were standing on the airstairs, the guy in front and the woman a step behind. Bald narrowed his eyes at them. The guy looked to be another heavy. He had the same broad physique as the guys spread out across the tarmac stand, the same civvy clothing. Black trousers, worn sneakers, with a bright-blue bomber jacket zipped up against the stabbing cold. Bald couldn't tell from this far away, but he assumed the heavy was armed as well. Presumably with the same Kalashnikov MA rifle as his mates.

From a hundred metres away, Bald couldn't get a good look at the woman. She was standing a step behind Bomber, just outside the entry door, her features mostly obscured by the mounted jet engine on the left side of the fuselage. He caught a glimpse of shadow-cloaked face and mid-length hair, but he couldn't make out anything else.

'Fuck,' Lyden said from the rear of the cabin. 'Can't get a decent shot of her from here.'

'Wait,' Bald said.

Bomber led the woman down the airstairs towards the group waiting for them on the ground. A third figure stepped out of the cabin and followed them down the treads. Another Russian tough, several inches shorter than Bomber and perhaps a hundred pounds lighter, with jet-black hair and a beard as thick as a human fist. He was dressed in a pair of acid-wash jeans and a grey hoodie.

Bald thought, *Three people listed on the flight manifest.*

Two men and a woman.

Strickland thinks someone might be meeting Volkov at the airport.

Hoodie stopped at the bottom of the airstairs and stood to one side. Bomber nudged the woman ahead of him, gesturing towards Volkov. She stumbled ahead of Bomber, stepped into the bright wash of the light from the wingtips and headlamps.

Then Bald got a clear look at her.

She was young. He guessed, early twenties. She had auburn hair and a long, slender physique. She had a timid manner, hands clasped in front of her, head darting left and right. She wore a dark-grey cable-knit jumper, skinny jeans and a pair of white trainers. Bald had the weird sensation that he had seen her somewhere else, but he couldn't quite place where.

'That face,' Porter said. 'I've seen it before. On the news.'

Bald looked at his mucker. 'Who is it?'

'That's Volkov's daughter,' Porter replied. 'That's her.'

THIRTY-FIVE

For a long moment none of the four Blades said a word. They looked on in tense silence as the red-headed daughter of Nikolai Volkov hurried across the tarmac to her father. The Russian ex-spy stepped forward from the Lexus SUVs and stood with his arms outstretched, waiting to hug her. Father and daughter embraced fiercely, watched over by the six Russian heavies. Bald felt his stomach muscles clench, something like a knife moving through him.

'You sure it's her?' he asked, turning to Porter.

'Definitely. She was on the news the other day. Lives in St Petersburg, I think. There was a story about how she'd gone missing after the Swindon attack.'

'The fuck is she doing here?' Bald asked nobody in particular.

But he already knew the answer.

The reward.

'She must be part of it,' Porter said. 'That's why Volkov is working for the Russians. They're not blackmailing the bastard. They've got his fucking daughter.'

Bald looked at him. 'That's why he's betraying us?'

Porter nodded firmly. 'Has to be. A dad would do anything for his daughter.'

Bald heard a series of electronic beeps behind him. He tore his eyes away from the family reunion and glanced back at Lyden. 'Well? Did the image send?'

'They're looking at it now,' said Lyden, pushing buttons on the digital camera. 'Two seconds.'

'Tell them to get a fucking move on and give us the word. We can't sit around for much longer.'

'Working on it, mate.'

He swung back round. Across the tarmac, Volkov and his daughter were still holding one another. Going in for the world record, apparently. Bald dimly recalled hearing something on the news about how Volkov had been forced to abandon his family when he'd defected to the UK. According to the reports, the ex-SVR man hadn't seen his own flesh and blood in years.

An unnerving thought stabbed at him just then. 'Why would the Russians go to the trouble of flying his daughter out here? Why not leave her back in Moscow?'

Porter considered. 'Maybe Volkov didn't think they'd honour their side of the bargain. Maybe he wanted to see her before he'd agree to anything.'

'Maybe,' said Bald.

A second ticked by. Then another.

Father and daughter finally let go of one another. Volkov took a step back from her, one hand resting on her shoulder, the other touching her cheek. Simply taking her in. Even from a hundred metres away, Bald could sense his overwhelming joy.

Behind him, he could hear the low restless growls of the Malinoises.

Any second now the daughter is going to turn away and lead her old man aboard the private jet, he thought. And we're sitting here waiting for Six to get their arses in gear.

Another second passed.

Then Lyden said, 'They've just confirmed her identity. That's Nadezhda Volkov, all right. Last seen in public two weeks ago.'

Bald whipped round. 'What's the score? Are we good to go?'

Lyden pressed the earphone closer to his ear as he listened to the voice on the other end of the comms link. Strickland? Moorcroft? One of the two, Bald guessed. There was a long pause before Lyden looked up and said, 'Orders are to save the daughter if possible.'

'And if we can't?' asked Porter.

'Nikolai Volkov remains the priority.'

Bald sat forward in his seat again and stared through the wind-screen, anger simmering in his guts. This should have been a simple ambush. Hit the Russians hard and fast. Grab Volkov and get out of here.

Now we've got to worry about the daughter as well.

Ahead of them, Volkov exchanged a few words with his daughter. He was smiling and laughing. The happiest man in the world. All his Christmases coming home at once. He had his daughter. The private jet to fly home in. The swish apartment waiting for him in Moscow; the lucrative new career as a well-paid Kremlin puppet. Both members of the Volkov clan were partially obscured behind the semicircle of FSB heavies.

'No clear shot,' Bald groused. 'We can't take the fuckers out from here.'

Porter said, 'We'll have to get closer.'

'How?' Lyden asked. 'You want us to drive over there?'

Bald shook his head. 'They'll see us coming and brass us up. We're as close as we can get without making them suspicious. It's got to be on foot. Fire and move.'

'What if one of the targets gets hit in the crossfire? Or both?'

Something snapped inside Bald.

'Fuck it,' he said. 'We leave the girl.'

'We can't, Jock. Orders.'

'Stuff the orders. She's collateral. The mission is Volkov. We focus on getting him out. Whatever happens to her, tough.'

'She's an innocent, for Christ's sake. We've got to try.'

Bald shook his head. 'That's just the father in you talking. She's a lost cause, mate. There's not gonna be any time to snatch the Doris. I say we go after Volkov and leave her.'

Porter didn't reply.

A hundred metres away, Bald saw Widow's Peak beckoning over the daughter. A universally understood gesture. *I need a word with you.*

Nadezhda Volkov looked from Widow's Peak to her father and back again. She gave Nikolai a peck on the cheek, turned and walked over to the heavy. Stopped in front of him, bobbed her head, waiting for Widow's Peak to address her. The FSB man said nothing. Instead he nodded at one of the heavies standing beside the wagons. Flat-Top. The guy took three steps forward, slipped a hand under his jacket and withdrew the Kalashnikov MA compact rifle concealed beneath.

Nadezhda had her back to Flat-Top. She was still looking

patiently at Widow's Peak, waiting for a question that never came.

Flat-Top stopped beside Volkov's daughter. He drew the barrel level with the side of her head.

And pulled the trigger.

The gunshot cracked across the airfield.

Through the gauzy sheen of the windshield, Bald saw Nadezhda Volkov's head snap backwards. Her arms went floppy, a spray of warm blood bursting out of the bullet-sized hole in the side of her skull. She dropped senselessly to the ground in front of Flat-Top, bright red fluid gushing out the exit wound, spilling across the tarmac.

In the rear seat of the fire tender cabin, Bald could hear Lyden screaming into the boom mic connected to the transponder. 'They've killed the girl! Repeat, the daughter is down!'

'The fuck did they kill her for?' Porter said. 'They needed her alive, surely . . .?'

'No,' said Bald. 'They don't.'

They just needed her alive long enough to persuade Volkov to work for them, he thought. *The bastards were using the daughter to string the ex-SVR man along. Now they've got him in their pocket, they don't need Nadezhda.*

Which prompted another thought.

What if the press conference in Moscow is a load of bollocks? What if they're planning to kill Nikolai Volkov too?

He knew what they had to do.

We can't wait for Six to give the green light. No time. We've got to act.

Now.

Bald snatched up his L119A2 rifle and flipped open the passenger side door on the right side of the cabin, shouting at the others. 'Move! Go, go! Fucking move it!'

He was the first one out of the fire tender. Over to his left, Porter grabbed his rifle and bolted out of the driver's side door. Lyden and Rowe piled out of the back seats with the Malinoises, the former stashing the digital camera in the front pouch of his bulletproof vest before reaching for his weapon. All four Blades ripped off their hi-vis firefighting jackets as they debussed from the cabin, to make them less visible to the enemy as they advanced. As soon as Lyden and Rowe hit the ground they tossed their jackets aside and unclipped the leashes from the collars of the two Malinoises, arms thrusted at the targets to the west as they shouted orders. The dogs bolted forward, racing across the open ground towards the Russians. At the same time Lyden and Rowe hurried forward of the fire tender, taking up their kneeling firing positions alongside Bald and Porter.

'Take out the two at the airstairs,' Bald said. 'Me and Porter will drop the others. Then we'll move in hard and fast, brass up any fuckers still drawing breath.'

'Roger,' Lyden replied.

Bald focused his sights on the heavies a hundred metres downstream of their position. His right knee flat against the tarmac, his left elbow resting against the thick muscle of his upper leg. Porter at his nine o'clock, Lyden and Rowe two metres away at his three, aiming at their respective targets. Ahead of them the dogs were racing towards the heavies. They would naturally attack the targets closest to their trainers: the Shithouse Twins. The twins were standing a short distance from the rear Lexus, with their backs to the tender, laughing and pointing at the dead daughter, their giant shoulders jouncing up and down. They were feeling good about themselves. They had killed the daughter of a traitor. They had the double agent in their pockets and a comfortable flight back home to look forward to. They weren't expecting any trouble.

The Malinoises were fifty metres from the heavies now. Two or three more seconds until they reached the Shithouse Twins.

A couple of metres away, Bald could see Widow's Peak and Flat-Top standing beside the front Lexus. Flat-Top had lowered his gun arm, his head tilted as he stared at the lifeless corpse at his feet. Admiring his handiwork. Widow's Peak was addressing Volkov, waving a hand at the dead body and jabbing a finger at the ex-spy in a threatening gesture.

This is how it's going to work now.

Volkov didn't appear to be listening. He stared numbly at his daughter, his trembling body wracked with terror and despair.

Bomber and Hoodie stood impassively to one side of the lowered airstairs, arms folded in front of them.

The plan was stupid-simple.

The Malinoises would target the Shithouse Twins, taking them out of the fight. As soon as the dogs attacked, there would be confusion in the enemy ranks. The four other heavies would be stunned, wondering what the fuck was happening.

Giving Bald and Porter and the other lads valuable seconds to open fire.

The first rounds would be precision shots, intended to knock down as many of the Russians as possible before they had a chance to organise a defensive position. Lyden and Rowe would target Bomber and Hoodie. Bald and Porter would aim for Widow's Peak and Flat-Top. Once the first rounds had been discharged, the four operators would advance in pairs, firing and moving, keeping the enemy pinned down until they could draw close enough to the aircraft to mop up any survivors.

With the Russians dropped, Bald and the others would lift Volkov and bug out on the jet.

In the next half-second, the Malinoises sprang out of the darkness.

The Shithouse Twins didn't see the dogs coming. Neither did their mates. The six heavies were standing in an oasis of artificial light. The flashing bulbs on the Phenom wingtips, the bright loom of the headlamps from the wagons, the residual glow of the runway lights. All of it messing with their natural night vision. No way any of them could see the two dog-shapes sprinting towards them.

Not until it was too late.

The first Malinois bore down on Shithouse One, sprang up on its hind legs and leaped through the air, pinning itself to his back and tackling him to the ground in a savage blur of nails and teeth and muscle. The Russian screamed as the dog clamped its jaws around his forearm, head wrenching from side to side, as if it was stripping meat off a bone. Shithouse Two heard his twin brother's agonised cries and spun round. He saw the second dark brown dog-blur charging out of the darkness towards him and raised his right arm to his face. Some ancient instinct. A biological defence mechanism, from the days when humans roamed the African savanna.

Protect the throat and face at all costs.

Big mistake.

The second dog saw the raised arm as a soft target. It leaped forward, sinking its teeth into his flesh, knocking the heavy off-balance. He pinwheeled and toppled backwards, crashing to the tarmac, screaming wildly, arms and legs flailing as the Malinois tore chunks out of his forearm.

Across the stand, Widow's Peak, Flat-Top, Hoodie and Bomber all stood frozen, staring in mute horror at the dogs. Wondering, no doubt, what the fuck was going on.

They were still wondering when Lyden and Rowe loosed off the first shots.

Bald was zeroing in on Widow's Peak when he heard the rifle reports at his nine o'clock. Two of them. Single rounds, well aimed, coordinated. *Ca-rack! Ca-rack!* In the periphery of his vision he glimpsed the paparazzi-flash of the muzzles, the tongues of flame spewing out of the snouts of the two L119A2 longs. He saw Bomber spasming as a round slapped into the wall of his upper chest, ploughing a hole through all of his major plumbing. Heart, lungs, all the big vascular structures.

A quarter of a second later, Hoodie took a bullet to the throat. His head jerked back and his body jolted, as if he'd just run into a clothesline. Blood fountained out of the neck hole in a furious spray, scarlet against the black of the night. He dropped to the ground, collapsing in a heap beside Bomber.

Four heavies down.

Four left, including the drivers.

A hundred metres away, Widow's Peak and Flat-Top whipped round, looking towards their slotted mates at the airstairs. Bald calmly lined up the illuminated red-dot sight on his rifle with Widow's Peak. Aimed for the torso. At his side, Porter was training his rifle sights on Flat-Top. The L119A2 longs they were using had a maximum effective range of six hundred metres. Deadly at fifty metres, accurate at two hundred in the hands of an experienced operator. Bald had fired tens of thousands of rounds from similar models over the years. He knew the weapon like the back of his hand. He sucked in a breath, exhaled, depressed the trigger.

The long barked.

The bullet missed.

Bald saw the orange-flared sparks as the round ricocheted off the front end of the Lexus, ten or twelve inches to the left of the Russian. *A shitty effort. You're still rusty*, the voice in Bald's head told him. *All those months of hard living in Playa del Carmen, catching up.*

Coming back to haunt you.

The missed round snapped the two heavies out of their dumb-trance. Widow's Peak and Flat-Top dropped to their haunches, a split-second before Porter squeezed off a single round from his rifle. The round whipped past Flat-Top and carried off into the hollow blackness. Bald fired a three-round burst at the Russians, trying to nail them before they could scramble for cover. The bullets landed short of their targets, smacked into the tarmac half a metre behind them. In the next moment Widow's Peak and Flat-Top dived behind the far side of the front Lexus, disappearing from view.

Five rounds emptied.

All failed to hit their targets.

The younger lads are showing us how it's done. And all we're doing is brassing up thin fucking air.

Bald shut the voice up.

Time to get moving.

He called out towards Lyden and Rowe, 'Moving forward!'

The operators knew the drill. As soon as the words left Bald's mouth, Lyden and Rowe went into suppressive fire mode, putting down three-round bursts on the front Lexus, keeping Flat-Top and Widow's Peak pinned down.

Bald and Porter broke forward, long-striding across the open ground as bullets thunked against the SUV's armoured plating, the dull repetitive clank of metal hammering against metal. A couple of metres to the right of the front Lexus, Bald could see Volkov lying face down on the tarmac, body jolting with every rifle report. The Malinoises were still tearing into the Shithouse Twins beside the rear Lexus, gnawing at exposed flesh while the heavies screamed for help.

There was no danger of the Russians in either Lexus reversing away and escaping, thought Bald. Not with their prize asset pinned down on the ground. *As long as we keep up the suppressive fire, they won't be able to grab Volkov and make a run for it.*

Bald and Porter advanced ten metres, dropped to a knee, trained their red-dot sights on the wagon. Fired. One burst each. Three rounds. The bullets struck the front end of the Lexus in a symphony of cracks and ricochets and thumps.

Ten metres behind them, Lyden yelled, 'Moving!'

Bald and Porter put another couple of bursts down on the front Lexus. Pinning down Widow's Peak and Flat-Top, giving Lyden and Rowe time to rush forward.

Bald thought, *Nine rounds expended. Plus the four I've already fired. Thirteen rounds in total.*

Seventeen left in the clip.

As soon as Lyden and Rowe had caught up with them, Bald and Porter rushed forward again. At his four o'clock, Bald could hear the rolling-thunder boom of rifle discharges as Lyden and Rowe put down covering fire on the Russians behind the front Lexus. The four operators were working like a well-oiled machine, moving in a coordinated pattern, with one pair unloading bursts at the Russians while the other pair hurried forward in ten-metre increments. Steadily closing the gap on the aircraft.

Between the rapid-fire bursts the two Russians returned fire, loosing off wild shots at the onrushing Blades. Bullets whipped and fizzed past Bald and Porter, striking the tarmac behind them. Bald heard a sharp piercing ring as another pair of rounds glanced off the grille on the front of the fire tender, twenty metres further back.

Keep going. Don't stop.

Bald was acutely conscious of the fact that they were running across exposed ground, with no cover in sight. And their enemies were crouching behind a heavily armoured car. If they allowed a lull in the suppressive fire they were putting down, they were going to be in serious fucking trouble.

He ran forward again with Porter.

Took a knee on the tarmac.

Eighty metres to the aircraft.

Lyden shouted, 'Moving!'

Bald tensed his finger on the trigger as he shaped to put down the next burst on the front wagon. Then he spied a flicker of movement at his eleven o'clock, coming from the rear Lexus. The passenger-side door was swinging open. Bald arced his sights across and saw the driver climbing out, holding a Kalashnikov MA rifle in a two-handed grip. The driver had already raised the weapon to shoulder height, the black mouth of the barrel pointing directly at Bald and Porter.

The muzzle flamed.

A pair of rounds struck low, whip-cracking the tarmac to the right of Porter, missing him by inches.

Bald saw the threat.

His mind instantly worked the angles. He could foresee that the driver would get his next shot off before Porter could adjust his aim and centre his sights on the Russian.

The driver's first shot had struck dangerously close to Porter. The second wouldn't miss.

Bald reacted in a fraction of a second. Faster than the Russian. Decades of Regiment training, beasting himself on the ranges and the hills and the jungle, compensating for his ring-rustiness. He centred the red-dot side on the driver's upper torso and fired off a quick three-round burst, hitting him before the guy could fire. The first two rounds tore a chunk out of the Russian's shoulder, pulverising bone and muscle, knocking the guy off balance. The third was the money shot, smacking the driver on the side of his head. His skull exploded like a watermelon in a stunt video. His cranium disappeared in a carmine mist. Blood and brain matter splattered the side window, painting the luxury interior of the Lexus. The guy fell away, the Kalashnikov clattering to the ground beside his limp frame.

Porter glanced quickly up at Bald. Nodded his thanks. A split-second acknowledgement.

Five heavies down.

Three to go.

Fifteen rounds left in the clip.

Porter and Bald emptied another couple of bursts at the front

Lexus, buying time for Lyden and Rowe to advance. Bullets hammered against the side windows, spider-webbing the reinforced glass. Widow's Peak and Flat-Top shrank from view, ducking behind the front wheelbase. Another three-round burst and the clicker-counter in his head told Bald that he was down to his last six bullets.

'Moving forward!' he shouted.

They broke into a run. Closing the distance to the Russians, metre by grim metre. Gunshots intermittently split the air to the right of Bald and Porter as Lyden and Rowe gave them covering fire. Although he wasn't wearing a jacket and the temperature was in the low single digits, Bald was sweating freely. Beads of it dripped down his back, pasting his shirt to his skin. Alongside him Porter was moving effortlessly, and somewhere in the back of his mind Bald realised that his mucker had kept himself in good nick.

Maybe you're wrong about him, the voice inside his head said. *Maybe Porter isn't the lame old soldier you think he is.*

Or maybe you're not as sharp you thought.

He snapped his attention back to the front Lexus, saw a series of white-hot muzzle flashes erupting from the far side of the wagon. Three of them. Six rounds snapped past Bald and Porter, whipping over their heads and glancing off the tarmac. Three separate shooters. Which meant the driver had debussed from the door on the other side of the wagon, joining his mates behind cover.

Now it's four against three, the voice in Bald's head told him. *And the Russians have got the advantage of cover.*

You've got to close the gap. Get near enough to push left, sweep around the side of the two SUVs and put the drop on the remaining heavies. Before they kill you first.

Fifty metres ahead the Malinoises were still attacking the Shithouse Twins. Jaws ripping apart jacket fabric and exposed flesh, drawing blood, tails wagging with the excitement of born predators. The twins were screaming something. Begging for help from their mates, Bald guessed.

Two metres away from them, Nikolai Volkov was still lying face down on the ground.

Bald and Porter kept firing and moving. Lyden and Rowe were coming up fast behind them. Drawing closer to the heavies.

Forty metres to the aircraft now.

Almost there.

Bald rushed forward, caught up with Porter and dropped to a knee beside his old mucker, loosed off another two bursts and got the dead man's click. *Out of ammo.* Porter kept firing while Bald pressed the mag-release button on the side of the receiver, ejecting the spent coupler clip. He inserted the second clip attached to the side of the emptied mag and tugged on the charging lever. The benefit of coupler magazines. Instant tactical reloading. No need to faff around reaching for a new clip.

Another trio of muzzle flashes sparked up from just above the bonnet and boot of the front Lexus. Two bullets struck the tarmac a few inches to the left of Bald, forcing him to lower his head, shrinking his profile.

'Fuckers are getting closer,' Porter shouted. 'Too close.'

Ten metres behind them, Lyden and Rowe had stopped firing as they hurried forward. Bald looked over at Porter. 'We've got to get forward, fucking now!'

Porter didn't move. Instead he dropped to the ground, taking up a prone shooting position. Bald scowled at him.

'What the fuck are you doing?'

'I've got a better idea, Jock.'

Lying flat on his front, Porter calmly lined up his red-dot sights, aiming for the space below the underside of the Lexus chassis. Then Bald understood. There was a six-inch gap between the chassis and the ground, giving Porter a clear line of sight to the lower legs of the three shooters crouching behind the far side of the vehicle. The L119A2 barrel lit up as Porter emptied four controlled rounds at the Russians, spent brass tinkling on the tarmac. Bald heard an agonised cry coming from behind the Lexus. He couldn't see the impact, but he didn't need to. At close range, a 5.56 x 45mm NATO round could do all kinds of damage to the human body. The Russian caught on the other side of the SUV would be writhing on the ground right about now, his leg riddled with hot metal, his ankle hanging off.

Porter glanced up, grinned at Bald. 'Still fucking got it.'

Bald nodded approvingly.

Six heavies down.

Two to go.

There was another burst of gunfire from behind the Lexus. Coming from the shooter at the bonnet. The bullets missed their target, sparking like firecrackers on the ground a metre to the right of Porter. He traced his weapon across a few inches until the red-dot was lined up with the rear wheelbase on the wagon. Three rounds spat out of the L119A2 snout as he squeezed the trigger. Bald heard a brittle sound like an axe splitting through wood. Then another hideous scream, followed by a dull thud and clatter, man and gun toppling to the ground next to one another. Porter fired again, emptying three rounds into the maimed Russian's torso.

He stopped screaming.

Which left just the one shooter left to deal with. And the screaming Russian with the rag-order leg, Bald thought, but he wasn't going to present much of a threat.

We'll finish them two off, grab Volkov. And then we're going home.

Bald was about to call out to Lyden and Rowe at their four o'clock. Let them know we're moving forward again, so they're on the ball with the suppressive fire.

Then he spied a blur of movement at his one o'clock. Forty metres away.

Widow's Peak.

The Russian had rushed forward from the Lexus while the two Blades were dealing with the shooter near the bonnet. Now the heavy had hauled Volkov to his feet and the two of them were hurrying across the tarmac stand.

Escaping towards the jet.

THIRTY-SIX

Volkov and Widow's Peak were ten metres from the airstairs. The heavy was having to slow his stride, matching the ex-spy's pace as the latter shuffled along, moving as fast as he could in spite of his frail condition. With a sick feeling of dread Bald could see that they would reach the airstairs at the side of the Phenom in a few more seconds.

Fuck.

His first instinct was to drop the heavy. Bald swung his L119A2 across to his one o'clock, training his sights on the fleeing figures. But the two of them were struggling along in a tight formation, side-by-side. Volkov on the right, Widow's Peak on the left. The heavy held his Kalashnikov MA in his left hand, with his right hand firmly gripping the ex-spy's bicep. He was using Volkov as a human shield, putting the ex-spy between himself and the four operators to the east.

No way we can take a pop at him. Not from this angle.

'No clear shot,' Bald said.

'Shit,' Porter hissed. 'Bastards are getting away.'

Bald glanced over his shoulder and called across the tarmac to Lyden and Rowe, pointing to the fleeing Russians. 'Get those fucking dogs over there! NOW!'

Lyden and Rowe darted forward, running towards the mangled bodies of the Shithouse Twins forty metres away. To the right, Porter and Bald kept up their rates of suppressive fire on the front Lexus. Porter shooting below the underside, Bald aiming for the space above the bonnet, in case the wounded Russian popped his head above cover.

Volkov and Widow's Peak reached the foot of the airstairs.

Dread seeped into Bald's guts.

Any second now, the target will get on the plane. The door will shut. And Volkov will be gone.

'Fucking hurry!' he bellowed. 'They're getting away!'

Lyden and Rowe swept into view at Bald's one o'clock, dropping down beside the two Malinoises, grabbing them by their collars and yanking them away from the Shithouse Twins. Lyden bellowed an order at his dog, pointing towards Volkov and Widow's Peak, fifteen metres away. A moment later, the ex-spy and the heavy hit the top of the airstairs and plunged through the open doorway. Bald could hear the crescendo burr of the jet engine as it increased power, the Phenom rolling slowly across the tarmac stand, steering towards another taxiway, a hundred metres further to the west. He looked on helplessly, his guts burning.

No.

We're too late.

They're going to escape.

The first Malinois dashed across the stand, chasing down the Phenom as it crept forward. The second dog hurried after the first, lagging four or five metres behind. Although the plane was slowly gaining momentum the airstairs were still in the lowered position, Bald noticed. From his angle he could half-see Widow's Peak standing in the open doorway, grappling with the operating lever next to the entry door, pulling it up to retract the stairway.

In the next breath the lead Malinois caught up with the jet, vaulted up the treads and launched itself at Widow's Peak. The heavy howled, losing his grip on the lever as the Malinois tugged viciously at his arm, dragging him to the floor. The Russian tumbled and crash-landed in the space between the cabin and the stair treads, blocking the cabin doorway, punching the dog with his spare hand as he tried to prise his arm free. Then the second Malinois pounced on him, sinking its teeth into the side of his neck, pinning him down with its paws. The heavy had no chance of wriggling free from his attackers. Bald could see the dogs' arses and tails hanging out of the open doorway as they ripped and clawed at the Russian.

The jet rolled forward, the cabin entry door gaping open.

Bald heard a series of cracks, flicked his gaze to the left. Saw Lyden and Rowe standing over the bloodied, dog-torn bodies of the Shithouse Twins, emptying rounds into their torsos. The Russians spasming as the bullets slapped into them, as if someone had just placed a couple of defibrillator paddles on their chests and hit the shock button.

Fifty metres until the Phenom reached the taxiway. The road led north for three hundred metres, back to the main runway.

We need to stop that fucking thing from taking off.

'Keep putting rounds down on that wounded fucker,' Bald said, turning to Porter. 'I'll push left. Get that wagon moving.'

Porter looked up at him. 'The fuck are you doing?'

Bald grinned. 'You're not the only one with a good idea.'

He took off, breaking left across the stand as Porter kept up his steady rate of fire on the front Lexus, placing single-shot rounds either side of the rear wheelbase, pinning down the last surviving heavy. Bald hooked around the back of the rear wagon and pushed on, sweat flowing freely down his back now, heart pounding madly, the air thick with the metallic tang of blood. In another three strides he hit the back end of the front Lexus, brought up his L119A2 and swept round to the far side of the wagon. Flat-Top lay on the ground beside the rear tyres, his pale face blood-drained, white hand pawing at his fucked-up ankle. Blood and spent brass all over the fucking place. His weapon was lying across the tarmac, out of easy reach.

The Russian looked up at Bald. He saw the look in the Scot's eyes. The cold, merciless glare of a trained killer. Flat-Top raised his hands in terror. 'I surrender! Shit, please—'

Bald didn't let him finish. He tapped the rifle trigger twice, putting a couple of rounds in the Russian's head. There was a backspray of blood against the tarmac as the rounds smashed through his skull at extreme close range, turning his brains to mush. An easy kill, but it still felt good. It felt like winning. The Russian fell back, still and lifeless, as if he was doing the mannequin challenge.

Bald kicked him aside and prised open the driver's door on the Lexus. Threw himself behind the wheel, dumped the rifle on the passenger seat. The engine was running, key fob next to the gearstick. He shifted into Drive and released the handbrake, mashing the accelerator. The Lexus bulleted forwards, bouncing over outstretched limbs of newly dead Russians. Bald broke clear of the bodies littering the stand and jerked the wheel to the right, chasing down the Phenom. The whirr of the jet engines was louder now. Bald could see the aircraft a hundred metres ahead of him, entry door hanging open, dogs faintly visible in the glow of the cabin, still mauling Widow's Peak. The plane swerved sharply to the right as it veered off the tarmac stand before arrowing down the taxiway.

Heading for the runway, three hundred metres to the north.

Bald crunched through the gears, foot to the floor, pushing the Lexus hard. If the plane reached the runway, it was over. Only a matter of time before one of the pilots managed to get the cabin door closed. Then the jet would be free to take off, Volkov would be flown back to Russia. And President Kolotov would win again.

Bald wasn't going to let that happen.

He was tired of being pissed on.

He didn't give a flying fuck about politics, or the future of NATO, or the populists and their crank conspiracy theories. He wasn't a moralist like Porter. But the Russians had messed with him in Mexico. Kolotov had sent his best men out there to put a hole in the back of his head. Bald had taken that shit personally.

Now he wanted revenge.

He pushed the Lexus hard, hunting down the jet. In the rear-view he glimpsed Porter, Lyden and Rowe standing over the slotted Russians, pointing their rifles at the Phenom. Aiming single rounds at the back end of the jet in an attempt to get the pilots to stop. Rounds clanged off the tail and the wings, throwing up a shower of hot sparks. The pilots didn't slam the brakes. Instead they carried on towards the runway at the northern end of the taxi road.

The maximum taxi speed for a small jet was around twenty knots, Bald knew. At its current speed he figured it would take the Phenom another twenty seconds before it hit the runway and commenced its take-off roll.

He pushed the Lexus harder, upshifting into Fifth. The speedometer needle tickling the seventy-per mark, engine roaring, rapidly gaining ground on the Phenom. The gap was eighty metres. Then forty. Then nothing at all. He was coming up fast on the tail, speeding towards the fourteen-metre wing on the left side of the fuselage.

Bald jerked the wheel hard to the left, steering the Lexus away from the wing at the last possible moment. The wagon juddered violently as it swerved off the road and rumbled across the grassy strip parallel to the taxiway. The wheel shaking in Bald's grip, rear tyres throwing up fists of dirt.

A quick glance across at his three o'clock. Between the constellation of bullet-cracks in the passenger window he could see the jet cabin. One of the co-pilots had exited the cockpit and stood over Widow's Peak, reaching for the airstairs lever. The nearest Malinois turned on the co-pilot, clamping its jaws around his wrist while the other dog tore into Widow's Peak with its razor-sharp teeth.

Bald looked ahead. Nothing but bare ground in front of him for a hundred and fifty metres, and then the horizontal grey bar of the runway, edge lights glittering like candles on top of a birthday cake.

He kept pushing the Lexus.

A second later he nudged ahead of the Phenom.

Ten metres, then twenty. Then fifty. The speedometer needle ticked past a hundred miles per. Bald half-circled the wheel to the right and steered the Lexus back on to the smooth tarmac of the taxiway, rocketing eighty metres ahead of the jet. A hundred metres from the northern end of the taxiway.

Now, Bald told himself.

He released the clutch, stamped hard on the brakes. The Lexus lurched forward, almost throwing Bald out of his seat. He gripped the wheel tightly and felt his guts surge up into his chest, the tyres screeching, rubber burning as the wagon rapidly lost speed. The speedometer needle plunged down past the fifty-per mark. In the next instant Bald threw the wheel hard to the right, skidding to an abrupt halt across the width of the taxiway, twenty metres south of the airstrip.

Blocking the road.

A hundred metres to the south, the private jet rolled on ominously for a few moments. For a cold second, Bald feared the pilot might risk going on to the grass to avoid hitting the Lexus.

But no. The jet would lose all stability the moment it left the tarmac. And the pilot couldn't very well drive through the Lexus. The collision would chew up the nose and cockpit, frazzle the on-board computers, render the jet impotent. No way that thing could take off after a side-on encounter with an SUV.

Eighty metres between the wagon and the jet.

Bald heard the high-pitched squeal of the airbrakes engaging, the machine-whine of the engines dying down.

The Phenom slowed to a gentle halt, the nose stopping forty metres away from the passenger side of the Lexus, airstairs still in the lowered position. From his vantage point Bald couldn't see what was going on inside the cabin. But he could hear intermittent cries of pain from the Malinoises' victims, fading in and out above the drone of the jet engine.

Further to the south, sixty metres away, he spotted Porter, Lyden and Rowe, sprinting forwards across the taxiway.

Bald hit the parking brake switch next to the gearbox, engaging it. He scooped up his L119A2 from the passenger seat, leaped out of the Lexus. Circled around the back of the wagon and rushed across the tarmac, his heart thumping frantically inside his chest. Lyden and Rowe reached the airstairs first, a couple of paces ahead of Porter. Ten metres ahead of Bald. Bald saw the two lads charging up the treads, shouting orders at the Malinoises, wresting them free from the two stricken figures in the open doorway. He heard a foreign-accented voice screaming for mercy, interrupted by the throated bark of a rifle. He saw the rag-doll body of Widow's Peak tumbling down from the top of the airstairs, the wet slap of dead flesh hitting tarmac.

Bald sidestepped the dead Russian and followed Porter up the airstairs. Lyden and Rowe shifted to the right of the open doorway, making room for the other two Blades as they ducked into the main cabin compartment. Volkov sat on the divan opposite the doorway, his back pressed up against the armrest, edging as far away from the Malinoises as possible. The two dogs stood watch beside the divan, black eyes locked on Volkov, low-growling and snarling as Lyden and Rowe held tightly on to their collars. Everyone stooping in the low-ceilinged confines of the cabin.

To the left of the divan was the galley separating the cockpit from the passenger cabin. The co-pilot lay sprawled on the floor beside the drinks cabinet, his left hand wrapped around the wrist of his bite-marked right arm. He was puffy-faced and double-chinned, with bowl-cut brown hair and thin pencil marks for eyes. There were a couple of puncture wounds to his forearm, Bald noticed. Not deep. Not enough to incapacitate the pilot, he hoped. But the guy would need to get it cleaned out and bandaged to stem the blood loss. Drops stained his torn white shirt, spattering the grey-carpeted cabin floor.

The other pilot was up front in the cockpit. Bald spotted him beyond the galley and the curtain divider. He stood with his back to the controls, his shaking hands raised in the air in a pose of surrender. Bald ignored him, lowered his rifle and grabbed hold of the blood-streaked co-pilot by the epaulette on his left shoulder, hauling him upright. The guy was stiff with fear, breathing erratically, narrow eyes flittering between Bald and the two Malinoises standing close behind him.

'You speak English?' Bald demanded.

The pilot didn't meet Bald's gaze. He stared at the two dogs, clutching his injured arm, thin lips quivering. 'Some.'

'Listen carefully. There's been a change of plan. You're heading to England. RAF Northolt. Know it?'

The pilot nodded. 'Yes.'

'Pull any tricks, try and fly us anywhere else, and the lads will set the dogs on you and your mate. They'll tear off your balls, face ... everything. By the time they're done, you'll be chewed to shit. Got it?'

The pilot nodded quickly. Bald searched his pasty face to make sure that he understood. There was no hint of resistance there. The guy wasn't a warrior. He flew planes for a living. He wasn't about to argue with the four heavily armed Brits in front of him.

Bald said, 'You got enough fuel on this thing to get us to England?'

The pilot glanced over his shoulder at the cockpit, made a quick calculation. 'We have enough to get us to Moscow. Thousand miles. How far away, Northolt?'

'About the same,' Lyden cut in. 'One thousand and fifty miles, according to Strickland.'

'We can make it,' the pilot said. 'No problem. When do we leave?'

Three or four minutes since the first rounds had gone off, Bald calculated. The guard at the front gate would have been on the blower to the police by now. Cops were probably on their way at that very moment.

'Now,' Bald said. 'Get us ready.'

'But the car ...' The pilot gestured to the cockpit, the Lexus blocking the taxiway.

'I'll move it,' Bald said. He spun round towards Porter and the others, tipping his head at Volkov. 'Wait here. Keep an eye on him.'

Volkov looked up at Bald, eyes brimming with tears. 'Who ... are you?'

'Us?' Bald pointed to himself and grinned. 'We're the fucking SAS.'

Volkov's tear-stained eyes popped wide. 'You're taking me back? To *them*?'

'Aye,' Bald replied. 'We've got orders to bring you back to Vauxhall. Them lot want a word.'

Volkov shook his head. 'You can't do that. Please.' He looked frantically from Bald to the other three Blades. 'They'll find me and kill me if I go back.'

'Who?' Porter demanded.

'My old comrades,' Volkov said despairingly. His breathing was erratic and shallow. 'They told me they could find me anytime. Anywhere. They said it was easy for them. Told me I would never be safe.'

'Not our problem,' Bald responded tonelessly. 'We're leaving. That's it.'

'Now? But ... my daughter.' Tears welled in Volkov's eyes. His chin wobbled. 'My princess, Nadezhda. Please, we can't leave her body here.'

'Tough shit. We have to get moving. Cops will show up any minute.'

'Please, I beg you. Don't make me leave her. Not like this ...

like dog.' He pressed his hands together pleadingly. 'Let me take her with me. All I ask. I do anything. Anything!'

'We can't. There's no time.'

'She's my daughter! Nadezhda doesn't deserve this!'

Bald shrugged indifferently. 'You should have thought about that before you chucked your lot in with the Russians,' he said.

Volkov slumped back in the seat, mouth slackened, tears dribbling down his gaunt cheeks. He stared vacantly at a spot on the floor, looking nowhere, peering into an abyss of unimaginable grief. The kind of despair only known by a parent who has seen their own child die. Porter felt a pang of sympathy for the guy. But then he remembered how Volkov had betrayed his own country, and then later the country that had offered him protection.

Lyden pulled him away from the divan and guided him over to the main passenger section to the right of the galley. There were six seats in an ocean of luxury wood and leather. Four of the seats faced one another in the middle section, with two separate seats located at the rear of the cabin, next to the belted toilet. Lyden dumped Volkov in the middle seat on the port side of the aircraft, facing forward. He sat down opposite, with the two Malinoises beside his feet, remorseless eyes pinned on Volkov. Porter took up the rear-facing seat on the starboard side, rifle across his lap, while Rowe manspread himself across one of the spacious single seats at the back.

At the forward end of the cabin, the co-pilot was leaning into the cockpit. There was a brief exchange between the Russian and his fellow pilot, terse and mute. Discussing the last-minute change of plan, maybe.

Bald turned away from them and hotfooted it down the airstairs. He broke into a run across the tarmac, making for the Lexus 570 parked sideways across the northern end of the taxiway. He'd left the engine running when debussing from the vehicle. Now Bald jumped behind the wheel, hit the parking brake switch and shunted the transmission into Reverse. Backed up thirty metres from the taxiway, braked, turned the engine off. Hurried back across the grass to the Phenom.

The co-pilot was waiting for him just inside the cabin entryway.

'Get us moving,' Bald said. 'We're getting the fuck out of here.'

The co-pilot swallowed, nodded anxiously. He bent down and drew in the airstairs using the lever handle. The steps and cabin door folded smoothly upwards. Once the stairs had been fully taken in the co-pilot gripped hold of the door handle with his left hand and lowered the internal locking handle with his right, sealing the entry door. He ducked into the cockpit, dropped down into the seat next to his fellow pilot. Panels were checked, buttons pushed, indicators consulted. Bald paced over to the passenger seats, slumped into the spare seat opposite Porter on the starboard side of the Phenom.

The jet rumbled forward. It turned left at the end of the taxiway, pointing west down the runway.

The engines blasted.

The jet rocketed forward. The cabin shuddered.

Two minutes later, they were climbing through the night sky.

Bald eased out a deep breath. As the Phenom banked he peeked out of the cabin window at the ground below. At this height Bald could pick out the ant-sized bodies lying on the tarmac, faintly illuminated by the edge lights. Further away a cluster of red and blue police lights flashed in the blackness as they raced towards the airport. He watched them for several moments, swarming across the tarmac stand.

The plane banked again, climbed higher, levelled out.

Bald looked away from the window.

Porter was smiling at him with relief.

'Christ, that was close,' he said. 'Thought we were done for back there.'

Bald nodded with feeling. 'You and me both.' He shook his head wearily. 'Fuck it. Let's just get this twat home,' he said, cocking a thumb at Volkov. 'Then we can celebrate. After the day I've had, I'm gonna need a drink. A fucking big one.'

THIRTY-SEVEN

The co-pilot with the dog-bitten arm told them the journey to Northolt would take around two and a half hours. Which meant they would be landing at the RAF airbase at a quarter to midnight, UK time. They found a first-aid kit stowed in the aft cabin, cleaned out the co-pilot's wound and dressed it, then handed him a couple of painkillers and promised him proper medical attention once they reached England. Bald went off in search of refreshments, parched after the stress of the firefight. He found a rack of soft drinks and mineral water in the cabinet in the forward galley, but no booze. He overcame his disappointment with heroic restraint, grabbed a couple of cans of full-fat Coke and made his way back down the aisle. Chucked one of the Cokes at Porter, cracked open the second for himself. On the opposite side of the aisle, Lyden was busy on his iPhone, tapping out messages to Vauxhall. In the back of the cabin, Rowe had gone into sleep mode. Eyes veiled, head arched back against the headrest, hands planted on his knees.

Volkov gazed absently out of the port-side window with bloodshot eyes, staring into the abyss of the night, hands resting limply in his lap. The ex-spy was taking it hard. First the execution of his daughter, right in front of him. Then the extraction back to the UK. His whole world had been turned upside down.

'They killed her,' he said as he looked out of the plexiglas. The Russian's voice was thin, scratchy and weak. 'They killed my beautiful Nadezhda.'

Bald took a sip of his sugary Coke, stared down at the ring tab. He didn't know what to say. He wasn't a therapist.

'They killed her right in front of me,' Volkov went on, his lower lip trembling. 'Those bastards. Shot her, like animal. She did nothing wrong. All because of *him*.'

Porter inclined his head. 'Who?'

Volkov turned towards Bald and Porter across the aisle. He looked at them for a moment, blinked tears out of his eyes. 'The president.'

'Kolotov?'

Volkov nodded slowly. 'The men who took me to the airport . . . they told me Kolotov had ordered them to kill Nadezhda.'

Bald thought back to something that had puzzled him earlier. 'Why would the president do that?'

'To punish me. That's what they said. The men from the FSB. They said it was the price I must pay, for being a traitor to the motherland.' Volkov sniffed. 'Those bastards, they used me. They promised me that I would be back with Nadezhda, as long as I did what they said. They lied.'

Porter said, 'That's why you were working for the Russians? To get your daughter back?'

Volkov nodded. 'All I wanted to do was protect her.' He looked down at his dirt-smeared hands. 'They said all I had to do was blame London for the poisoning. Take the heat off the Kremlin and make Britain look bad. If I did this thing, they would let me see my daughter again. If I refused, they said they would find me. Poison me again. They would make sure I suffered badly the second time, and they would kill Nadezhda too. I had no choice.'

'There's always a fucking choice,' Bald muttered. 'Grow a pair. Own the decision.'

Jock Bald, therapist.

Porter shot him a look, turned back to face Volkov. 'Why did the Russians poison you in the first place?'

'It doesn't matter.' Volkov wiped tears from his eyes with the back of his left hand. 'Doesn't concern you. You wouldn't believe me if I told you, anyway.'

'We know about your big meeting,' said Porter. 'That right-wing get-together at Koman Castle tonight. Your man Lansbury was wearing a listening device the whole time. Got it all on tape. Me and Porter heard everything. There's no secrets.'

The ex-spy lifted his head, looked at Porter with an uncertain expression. 'You know about the plan?'

Porter nodded and said, 'We know about President Drummond's plan to withdraw from NATO. We know the part you were playing, with the press conference.'

'Your president,' said Bald. 'He's planning to retake the Baltic States. That's why he's going to all this effort to help the Yanks pull out of NATO, isn't it? So there won't be anyone around to kick up a fuss when he invades the Baltics.'

Volkov smiled weakly. 'Fools. There are things you don't know. Things that weren't said at the meeting. Things that Lansbury and the others were not told.'

Porter knitted his brow, glanced at Lyden and Bald in turn. He looked back at the ex-spy. 'What are you talking about?'

Volkov said, 'The American president knows about the plan to retake the Baltics. He's in on it. In fact, he discussed the details of the arrangement with Kolotov.'

'Bullshit,' said Bald. 'He'd never agree to that.'

'It's the truth,' Volkov insisted. 'I can prove it.'

The tears had stopped flowing. The Russian was regaining some of his old strength, the grief-stricken old spy demonstrating his superior knowledge and influence.

Porter said, 'Why the fuck would Drummond let the Russians invade the Baltics? Even he isn't that thick.'

'Because that's part of the agreement he struck up with Kolotov,' Volkov replied. 'The two presidents are carving up the world between them. To create a new Christian empire.'

Bald and Porter and Lyden listened in silence as Volkov explained. Choking back his grief, Volkov told them how he had heard rumours of a planned invasion of the Baltics from his sources in the wide network of Russian dissidents living in the UK. There had been rumours of secret undercover FSB and GRU units being dispatched to the capitals of Estonia, Lithuania and Latvia, with the aim of fomenting unrest among the ethnic Russian communities in each country. The undercover units would spread propaganda, recruit members and hold mass demonstrations, claiming that the rights of ethnic Russians were being violated by the fascist national governments and demanding that Moscow come to their aid. Volkov suspected that the undercover groups were doing more than just stirring up trouble: he believed they were laying the groundwork for a full-scale invasion. With the protests on the streets, the Kremlin would have a credible motive for rolling Russian tanks through the streets of European capitals.

Volkov decided to investigate further. But he was in poor health, and with limited financial means. Few people wanted to talk with an exiled old spy. His investigation stalled. And then, two months later, an old colleague from the SVR reached out to him. A friend who had recently defected to France. He wanted to arrange an urgent meeting with Volkov. Said he'd heard about Volkov's enquiries and had discovered something big.

Over lunch at The Ivy in London, the colleague told Volkov about a meeting that had taken place between the Russian and American presidents. Six months ago, in Reykjavik, Iceland. The official agenda of the meeting had been to discuss the crisis in Syria and negotiate a further reduction in their respective nuclear stockpiles. But there had been a separate discussion between the two presidents. Away from the cameras, involving the two leaders and a handful of their most trusted aides. The contents of that meeting had never been disclosed, Volkov said. But his colleague in the SVR claimed that he had been briefed by someone who had been in the room at the time.

According to Volkov's colleague, the purpose of the discussion had been to divide Europe up between American and Russian spheres of influence. Drummond had long complained about the billions the US wasted defending wastrel European allies. Privately, Kolotov was frustrated by the vast sums of money he was sinking into conflicts in eastern Ukraine and Syria. So the two men had come to an agreement: they would carve up the continent between them.

But dividing up Europe was only the first part of the plan, Volkov said.

'What was the second part?' asked Porter.

'World domination,' Volkov said.

The two presidents, he explained, intended to put aside their historic differences, bringing their great nations together to create a new Christian empire. One that would be strong enough with their combined military, nuclear and political powers to wage a total war against their common enemies: Islam, and China. Only by uniting could the Christian world triumph over the evil order of the East.

'In the past,' Volkov said, 'the presidents of America and Russia saw each other as enemies. No longer. Kolotov and Drummond do not see themselves as rivals in the world order, but as brothers. Christian brothers, engaged in a global struggle against the non-believers.'

'*White* Christian brothers,' Bald observed. 'They're not just talking about a religious war, are they? This is a fucking race war.'

Volkov merely shrugged.

Porter said, 'What else happened at the meeting?'

The Russian said that the two presidents spent the rest of their time negotiating the fates of various European nations. They agreed that Germany, the Netherlands, France, Italy and the UK should remain in the American sphere. The Baltics, Ukraine, Romania, Belarus and Poland would fall under the influence of Moscow. So too would the Czech Republic, Hungary and Slovakia. Austria and Switzerland would be neutral states – strictly off-limits for military occupation or covert action. For the agreement to work, the US would need to unilaterally withdraw from NATO, triggering its collapse. American forces could then stage a tactical retreat from Europe, allowing Washington and Moscow to concentrate their resources on curbing Chinese and Iranian ambitions.

Both Drummond and Kolotov were satisfied with the arrangement, Volkov said. The Americans would save billions of dollars from their annual NATO budget, money that could be diverted towards funding the great coming war of the twenty-first century: the war between Christianity and the East. As for Kolotov, a swift and bloodless conquest of the Baltics, and later on Eastern Europe, would restore his credibility, which had been damaged by domestic crises back home.

With Europe's fate sealed, the two presidents would be free to plot the ultimate destruction of their true enemies. They talked about the possibility of a land invasion of Iran, the removal of the Ayatollah. They fantasised about the complete destruction of

Hezbollah. They agreed to bolster their military presence in Taiwan. Install a puppet leader in Syria. Overthrow the House of Saud.

Wage economic and cyber warfare against China's Communist Party.

Reduce North Korea to dust.

It would take years, they said. Decades, even. But together, they could ensure that the new white Christian empire would prevail.

But for the first phase of the plan to work, Drummond needed support from the populists. Pulling out of NATO was a risky move, particularly in an election year. He had told Kolotov that the Kremlin-funded fascists and right-wing movements in Europe would need to loudly proclaim their support for his decision. With Moscow's consent, Drummond had drafted in Lansbury to secure the populists' backing. Hence the meeting at Koman Castle.

Volkov's SVR colleague had asked him to share this int with his old handler at Six. There might be some money in it, he'd suggested. Volkov had said he would think about it. The tale seemed outlandish to him. Besides, he hadn't spoken to his handler in months. The guy he'd worked with before had retired. The new one never returned his calls. How was he supposed to reach out to him with a fantastic story of ethno-Christian alliances and presidents carving up Europe?

The colleague had flown out to Amsterdam two days later, for a security conference. He never came back. Took a fall out of his sixth-floor hotel window. A tragic accident, the authorities said. Or suicide. But Volkov had his suspicions. Which got him thinking. He sent a message to the handler, requesting a meeting. What harm could it do?

The day before his meeting, he set off for stroll around Queen's Park in Swindon. To gather his thoughts. The weather was unseasonably warm and pleasant. He remembered leaving the house and opening the door to his Vauxhall Corsa, to fetch his cigarettes from the glove box. He remembered feeling something sticky on the exterior car door handle as he touched it. Didn't think much of it.

An hour later, Volkov felt dizzy and feverish. He recalled

struggling over to the public toilets at the far end of the park, sweating profusely. He collapsed outside the entrance, choking, gasping for breath, bleeding from his nostrils. Then his world went black.

He remembered nothing of the next three weeks. Later, the doctors treating him would explain that he had been in an induced coma while they battled to save his life. His recovery had been painfully slow. But after the fog of the first few days cleared, he realised exactly who had targeted him, and why. The Russian security services, clearing up their tracks. Someone had learned that the colleague had information on the NATO plot and was killing anyone he might have confided in. Volkov knew it was only a matter of time before they came for him again.

But then he had received the phone call.

There had been a problem in the weeks leading up the G7 summit, Volkov had been told. Some of the populists who had agreed to back Drummond's plan had started to get cold feet. They worried about the damage to their own political brands. NATO wasn't as wildly unpopular in the coffeehouses of Vienna or the bars of Montmartre as it was in the American heartlands.

So the FSB had turned to Volkov. Made him an offer.

Work for us, they had told him. Persuade the populists to stick to the agreement and you'll be spared. We'll even give you a job in the Kremlin, reunite you with your daughter.

How could he resist?

'Jesus,' said Porter when Volkov had finished. 'Jesus Christ.'

Volkov shook his head bitterly. 'I thought, if I agreed to their demands, I would be safe,' he said. 'I was wrong. I shouldn't have trusted them. Now my daughter is dead. My fault.'

'Aye,' Bald said. 'I'd fucking say so.'

Volkov looked away, wiping the tears from his face with the back of his hand, and gazed out of the window. An old spy in a crumpled suit, alone and destitute, trying to figure out where it had all gone wrong. Bald grinned, toasted him with his can of Coke.

'Could be worse, pal. You're going back to England, at least. Doesn't get much better than that.'

Volkov snorted, glanced back over at Bald. 'Is that supposed to make me feel better?'

'The big beasts at the Firm will give you a new identity, set you up with a place to live. Somewhere nice and remote. I hear the Shetlands are lovely at this time of the year.'

'You don't understand,' Volkov said, turning to address his vague reflection in the cabin window. 'They'll find me. Doesn't matter where I go, I won't be safe. What I'm going to do then?'

Bald shrugged. 'Life's full of uncertainties.'

The Russian fell silent again, watching the black night sky.

A wave of exhaustion washed over Bald, the adrenaline of the firefight leaving his body. He sipped on his Coke, craved something stronger.

Across the aisle he caught Lyden looking at him with an admiring glow in his eyes. 'Me and Jordan owe you fellas a pint,' he said.

'What for?' asked Bald.

'Digging us out of a hole.' Lyden cocked a thumb at Volkov. 'Thought we were gonna lose this one for sure. If it wasn't for you, we'd be in silver bracelets by now.'

Bald shrugged. 'We got lucky. That's all.'

'Better lucky than dead,' Lyden said. He paused. 'Guess it's true what the older lads at Hereford have been saying about you two.'

'What's that?'

'You *are* the real fucking deal.'

'Just doing the job. That's how we get it done.' He turned to Porter, nodded. 'That was some quick thinking, though. Shooting under the wagon. Never would have thought of that myself. Not bad.'

Porter half-smiled. 'Thanks,' he said quietly. 'Didn't do so bad yourself. You might be out of the Regiment, Jock, but you've still got it. I'll give you that.'

Bald laughed easily. 'Never lost it, mate. I've always been rock hard.' He flicked a grin at his mucker. 'How about we grab that drink once we land and hand over our friend here?'

'As long as you're buying,' said Porter. 'And as long as it's orange juice.'

'Is that all? Thought you'd be gasping for a drop of the hard stuff by now. All the shit we've been through today.'

'That's all,' Porter replied firmly.

'Suit yourself,' said Bald. 'Have a Ribena, you southern poof.'

'Scottish wanker.'

Bald shook his head, puffing out his cheeks. 'Fuck me, mate. Your shooting might be up to scratch these days, but your comebacks are still as shite as ever.'

'Jock ...'

'Aye?'

'Fuck off.'

THIRTY-EIGHT

Chukotka Autonomous Region, North-east Russia
Three days later

As the Let L-410 Turbolet made its final approach, Derek Lansbury caught his first glimpse of the Kolimsky gold mine. Through the port-side window of the twin-engine aircraft, the mine was impossible to miss. A sprawling complex of industrial buildings, storage units and factories, constructed in the middle of a desolate Arctic tundra. Smoke eddied into the sky from several of the factory buildings, a column of grey rising into the cloudless bright-blue sky. Around the gold mine was an endless expanse of flat white nothingness. A featureless landscape, frozen and inhospitable, the snow as fine as powder. *Crikey*, thought Lansbury as the Turbolet began its descent. *Vitaly Butko wasn't joking*. The Kolimsky gold mine really *was* at the edge of the world.

Just getting to the mine had been an ordeal. First there had been the flight to Moscow. Then a connecting Aeroflot flight to Magadan, a minor port town some 3,500 miles east of Moscow, in the easternmost wilds of Siberia. Closer to Anchorage than Red Square. From Magadan they had boarded the Turbolet, a private transport plane belonging to the mining company, for the final two-hour journey north to Kolimsky. The flight had been rough, and Lansbury had asked Butko why they couldn't have simply driven to the mine instead. Butko had laughed and explained that no, that was quite impossible in this part of the world. There was an ice-road that connected the town to the mine, Butko said, but it was only in operation for a few months in the summer, when the temperatures rose above freezing. Every winter, teams of engineers had to clear the road with a fleet of snowploughs and load-bearing trucks. Other than that, the only way of reaching Kolimsky was by air.

Lansbury had initially been sceptical about taking this trip. When Butko had first suggested visiting the mine, he had inwardly recoiled in horror. He recalled reading somewhere that the temperatures in that region plunged to minus twenty at this time of the year. There were more reindeer than people, apparently. A visit to a remote, permafrost gold mine on the fringes of the Russian continent wasn't a thrilling prospect. Lansbury had politely declined, insisting that he had too much work to do. Meetings to attend. Press briefings. His podcasts. At some point in the distant future, it might be nice to go, perhaps. But not now. He simply couldn't. Vitaly understood, surely?

'But Derek, you simply must see it!' Butko had told him. 'You own a five per cent stake in the mine now. Don't you want to see what your hard work has brought you?'

'Besides,' he'd added. 'The president will be disappointed if you turn down the offer. And you really don't want to upset him.'

Butko had eventually won him over. He would be making an absolute fortune from his share of the mine holding company, the Russian had explained. Millions. The mine produced ten tons of gold and silver in *a single year*. At the going exchange rate, one ton of gold was worth about sixty-four million dollars.

'Think about that, Derek!' Butko had said. Even allowing for the exorbitant costs of running a gold mine in such an inhospitable environment, the profits were going to be enormous. 'Your share will make you rich beyond anything you've ever dreamed of.'

So Lansbury had reluctantly agreed to the two-day trip. *Besides*, he thought to himself as the Turbolet cantered across the runway, *Vitaly is right. Kolimsky is* mine *now. Or at least, one-twentieth of it belongs to me. I should really take a look round at the operation, see how it's run.*

His involvement wasn't yet official, of course. There had been a hold-up with the paperwork – Butko had mentioned something about needing to grease the palms of a few regional officials, and his people needed to set up a shell company in the British Virgin Islands so that Lansbury's share would remain a closely guarded

338

secret. For obvious reasons, they didn't want anyone in the British media to find out about his new investment. But the deal would be signed off very soon, Butko had assured him. Business in Russia was never straightforward.

The brilliant sunlight reflected mirror-like off the snow, blinding Lansbury as he stepped off the plane. He followed Butko across the tarmac to a waiting Toyota Tacoma pickup truck, parked up to the right of a windowless single-storey building. The building was the processing facility for new workers, Butko told him. Bags were checked in case anyone tried to smuggle in booze or drugs. Alcohol was forbidden inside the mine, apparently. Health and safety regulations. Lansbury, shivering in his snow boots, Fjallraven winter coat, cashmere jumper and beanie hat, wondered again about the wisdom of accepting this invitation. Two days, in this permafrost wasteland! And yet here he was in the middle of Siberia, the Arctic air burning his lungs, a bracing wind stabbing like a thousand knives at every scrap of exposed flesh.

Had this *really* been such a good idea?

Two company security guards stood waiting beside the Tacoma, stamping their feet to keep themselves warm. They were thoroughly wrapped up in black quilted jackets, walking trousers, Gore-Tex boots and ushanka hats with the ear flaps folded upwards. Semi-automatic pistol grips jutted out of the holsters fastened to their belts. Butko nodded a greeting at the two guards and turned to Lansbury.

'Get in, Derek,' he said, gesturing to the passenger seats in the rear of the Tacoma cabin.

One of the security guards, a heavyset man with pinhole eyes and no eyebrows, took Lansbury's trolley suitcase, wheeled it round to the back of the Tacoma and stowed it in the boot compartment.

Lansbury climbed inside the rear of the cabin, scooted alongside Butko. Thin-Brows rode shotgun while the other guard folded himself behind the steering wheel. Warm air blasted out of the radiator, raising the temperature inside the cabin to somewhere marginally north of freezing.

They drove north for half a kilometre, following the rough track that led towards the front of the complex. Freshly cleared snow was piled waist-high on either side of the roadbed. Directly ahead was the security gate, with a small hutch to the left. Twenty metres beyond the gate was the mining complex. As they drew closer to the entrance, Butko pointed out various features. The gold mine was divided into two main areas, he said. East was the mining factory and processing facilities. North was the open-pit mine. To the west, the accommodation blocks for the workers employed at the mine. An insulated corridor connected the barrack blocks directly to the mine, sparing the operators from being exposed to the elements on their way to and from their shifts.

'Impressive, no?' Butko said. 'This place cost us a fucking fortune to build. You wouldn't believe.'

'Y-yes,' Lansbury replied uncertainly. Wishing again that he'd had the courage – gumption? – to turn down Bukto's invitation to this barren land. Damn the man for putting him on the spot back in Hungary. If only he'd had time to think of an excuse.

Still, he told himself. It was only a couple of days. All he had to do was inspect the factory site, meet one or two of the workers, endure whatever godforsaken cuisine they had on offer at the canteen, and then get back on the plane to Moscow. Three days from now he would be back home in Chelsea.

He turned to Butko, decided to ask the question that had been eating at him since they had flown out of Budapest.

'You're quite sure that the president isn't upset with me?' he asked.

The Russian belted out a laugh. 'Of course not! Why would he be, Derek?'

'I thought, perhaps, that unfortunate business with my bodyguards . . .' He shrugged.

'Nonsense! No one blames you for what happened, my friend. Least of all the president.'

'They tortured me, Vitaly. I resisted for as long as possible, I swear. But those animals threatened me.' He shook his head. 'I would never betray Kolotov, you know that.'

Butko patted him chummily on the back. 'There's no need to explain. Really. The president is very understanding about the whole business. You were under a lot of pressure, cornered by two

340

extremely violent SAS men. Who wouldn't have confessed, under the same circumstances?'

'But the operation,' Lansbury persisted. 'Having to call the whole thing off. Kolotov isn't angry about that?'

'Not angry, no.' Vitaly paused while he searched for the right word. 'He's *disappointed*, Derek. But the president is a very forgiving person. He's willing to give you a second chance.'

Relief flowed through Lansbury's veins. He nodded keenly. 'I won't let him down again.'

'I know you won't.'

They reached the security gate and slowed to a purring halt. A guard emerged from the hut, exchanged a few words with No-Brows, waved the Tacoma through. They continued north on the track, the barracks and ablution blocks at their left, the steel treatment tanks and ISO containers to the east. They passed Caterpillar trucks piled high with rock loads and hydraulic excavators and SUVs buried up to the windscreens in pure white snow.

Lansbury frowned. 'Where are we going, exactly?'

'Your accommodation,' Butko said. His thin lips spread into a smile. 'You didn't think we'd put you up in the barracks with the mineworkers, did you? Relax, Derek. You're going to be staying in somewhere far more suitable for a man of your standing. We've even had some crates of your favourite beer flown in for you. John Smith's, isn't it?'

'Very kind of you,' Lansbury replied, feigning a grateful smile. He hated beer, and particularly despised bitter. That was all just for show, part of his carefully constructed public image as a true Brit, a man of the people. In reality, Lansbury much preferred a glass of French cabernet.

They skirted around the edge of the vast open-pit mine, past dormant machinery and piles of rocks. Butko gestured towards the facilities with a sweep of his arm.

'Look around you, Derek,' he said. 'This is all yours now. You're king of all you survey.'

It was, Lansbury had to admit, rather impressive. The scale of it, certainly. And the money he would be earning . . . incredible. He imagined all the things he planned to do with his wealth. The doors it would open. President Drummond wouldn't treat him like a mere underling anymore, not when Lansbury had several zeroes to his name. Who knows, he might even buy a penthouse in the president's Manhattan tower block. The most expensive one in the building. That would really rub the guy's nose in it.

The driver took a narrow ice-track and headed north, away from the main mining campus. The track took them past huge snow-capped spoil tips, a mountain range of excavated earth and rubble.

'The accommodation is outside the mine?' Lansbury asked uneasily.

'We're going to show you something else, first,' Butko replied. 'This won't take long, Derek. You'll be putting your feet up and drinking beer soon.'

They carried on for another nine or ten kilometres past the dumping ground, towards a series of rocky outcrops to the north, until the mine was just a distant speck on the horizon.

The Tacoma stopped.

Lansbury said, 'What are we doing here?'

'Get out, Derek,' Butko said.

For a moment, Lansbury hesitated. Then he suddenly realised: this must be the planned extension of the gold mine. Hadn't Butko mentioned this before, in passing? Something about additional deposits in the area, new opportunities to expand the mining operations. *This is why Butko insisted on bringing me out here,* Lansbury told himself happily. *The chap wanted to unveil his new business plan.*

He was going to be even richer!

He debussed from the back of the Tacoma cabin. So did Butko. So did No-Brows and the driver.

The two guards stood either side of Butko. Gloved hands resting on the butts of their holstered pistols. Butko extended a hand towards Lansbury and said, 'Take off your jacket.'

Lansbury chuckled nervously. 'You can't be serious. This is your idea of a joke, is it?'

'No joke.'

Lansbury started to worry. 'But ... the temperature. I'll freeze, Vitaly.'

'Just fucking do it.'

The guards shaped as if to deholster their pistols.

Lansbury swallowed, unzipped his Fjallraven coat, handed it to Butko. The wind ice-picked at his torso, finding tiny gaps in his under-layers, cold burning his flesh. He shivered.

'Your hat, too,' Butko said.

Lansbury took off his hat.

'And your gloves,' Butko said.

Lansbury took off his gloves.

The cold numbed his fingers. He couldn't feel his toes, his testicles. His teeth chattered involuntarily. 'I d–don't understand. What's g-g-going on?'

Butko ignored the question. He handed the gloves, hat and coat to No-Brows. Then he pointed to a spot on the horizon. Lansbury squinted at it. He saw nothing but flat, frozen wasteland.

'The nearest town is about two hundred miles that way,' Butko said. 'I suggest you start walking. It's going to be dark soon, and the wind chill gets very bad at night. The dry, cold air will burn your lungs, cause internal bleeding. Although personally I think the hypothermia will kill you first.'

Lansbury stood, mouth agape, trembling with the fear and the flesh-burning cold.

'What the hell are you doing?'

'The president sends his regards. He's sorry things had to end this way. But you betrayed him, and he cannot let your treasonous behaviour go unpunished. However, Kolotov is willing to give you a chance to redeem yourself. If you can make it as far as the nearest town, all will be forgiven.'

Lansbury looked aghast. 'Dressed like this? In these conditions? I'll never make it!'

'In all likelihood, no. There was a gulag here once, in Stalin's time. I hear one prisoner escaped and actually made it thirty miles before he died. But it's better than a bullet to the head, no?'

'You can't do this!' Lansbury screamed. 'We had an arrangement!'

Butko gave an indifferent shrug. 'We did. Not now.' He smiled thinly. 'If I were you, I'd get moving. The bears come out at night. Plenty of them in these parts. I hear they get hungry at this time of the year. Not so many nuts and berries left for them to feast on. And don't even think about coming back to the mine, either.' He nodded back in the direction of the security guards. 'My men have orders to shoot any trespassers on sight. For security reasons, you understand.'

'No! Please, for God's sake!'

The Russian placed a hand on Lansbury's shoulder. He was shaking violently from the cold, ice thickening in his nostrils. 'Good luck, my old friend.'

Butko climbed back into the wagon. No-Brows and the driver followed. The Tacoma reversed, snow crunching beneath the tyres as it pulled away, heading back in the direction of the gold mine.

The cold spread through Lansbury, chilling his insides. His hands and feet and face were completely numb. Every intake of breath stabbed his chest, felt like he was swallowing shards of broken glass.

In the distance, he heard the howl of a Siberian husky.

Lansbury turned away from the mine, and started walking.